MW01610014

Randall.

Cassie Alford

Trigger Warnings

THIS STORY CONTAINS TOPICS OF VIOLENCE AND
MURDER, ASSAULT, DRUGS, AS WELL AS ORGANIZED
CRIME.

LILING'S PREFACE

I want it all.

I've always been ambitious, always wanted more. I want to be somebody important. I want status. I want respect. I want money. The only way to get the things I crave is by working hard and working harder than everyone else.

My work ethic has always been a source of pride. *No one works harder than Liling.* It's how I know, deep in my bones, that I'm bound for success. I live by these rules that have been crafted by my Mama, perfected by myself:

1. If I'm unable to do something, then I'm not working hard enough.

2. Being tired is a sign that I've been working hard.

3. If something hasn't worked the way I wanted it to, then I didn't want it badly enough.

4. Respect needed to be deserved.

Right now, I'm focusing on graduating. Then, I can focus on the wealth, the status, and the money. It's a time where I am in full control of my life. I can sink or swim, and I'm ready to teach myself how.

I'm not in college to find love. It's a distraction. A waste of time. It would take a very special person to show me what the true benefits of having a partner are. I believe I work better on my own, but I understand that two people can achieve more than one.

Maybe, there's someone out there who can help me achieve my goals. Someone who is willing to work hard for me. Someone who wants what I want just as badly as I do. Someone who respects me and forces others to respect me too.

Even if I never find a person who can help with these things, that's alright. I don't *need* anyone else.

Liling Zhu is strong, all on her own.

RANDALL'S PREFACE

I don't really have much direction. I don't even have a strong sense of purpose. I guess you could say I'm still looking for whatever I'm looking for.

When I do find that purpose, I know - with a little bit of persistence- I can do anything I set my mind to. I'm a hard worker, I just need to know what I'm working for.

I'm in college not knowing why I'm here, or why I'm bothering with it at all. Aimless. I feel aimless. Still, I have the feeling that I'm on the cusp of something great. Someone great.

Falling in love seems like it'd be a great adventure. If I could find the right person, I'd do anything for that person. Anything. Maybe that's what I need, someone to follow. Someone else who wants to do great things with me. Someone to do great things for.

That's it. I'm working toward someone; I just don't know who yet.

1.

LILING

I've always believed I'm smarter than most of the people around me. It's made life easier for me. Once I started and was able to be in control of myself, I felt like I could start excelling beyond everything I'd been so far, which was nothing.

Nothing. No one. I'm nothing. I believe going to school will fix that. That's what my parents have told me - that becoming educated was one of the greatest achievements I could hope for. That, and finding a husband and having many children.

My area of study is business. I will be an executive somewhere. I don't know where, and I do not care, as long as I get there. We're in the nineties, and I'm going to be a part of a new generation of women who lead by example, don't apologize, and do whatever they're inclined to do. It's 1993, and I'm ready to leave old gender roles behind and follow the path I've made for myself.

It takes money to rule the world, and I've found a way to make it for myself without working at some filthy minimum-wage fast food restaurant. I write papers. I write a lot of papers, on nearly any subject. I've most likely read or studied whatever someone could ask me to write. If I'm unknowledgeable in the topic one of my peers is asking me for, I'll do enough research to write the paper and present them with an A+ written article. The additional research comes at a surcharge, of course.

I work at the university library, so I have near-constant access to a computer with word processing software and printers with unlimited printing credits. I can hand-write a paper for students whose professors are resistant to the rise of technology, but that takes more time, and it requires more money.

My business is mainly word-of-mouth. I earn one person an A, and they send all their lazy friends to me. I can charge a desperate student nearly anything if I promise them a good score. I understand, more than most, that desperate drive to please parents. I have two sisters, and I want to be better than both of them. Second oldest, most successful. That will be Liling.

I always meet new clients at my dorm; a small room with two beds on opposite sides of the room and drab green carpet. My side of the room is pristine with a tidy desk and a bed that is made in clean white sheets as soon as I wake up each morning. There are less listening ears in my dorm, as my roommate is rarely there. She wastes her time with her boyfriend and neglects her studies. I judge her for it, but I enjoy having a nearly-private college experience.

After work, around seven in the evening, I'm meeting with a new person who was referred by someone I've been writing papers for at least three semesters. I always collect information before I work with anyone. Every new paper is a new risk; a new way to get expelled from not just this university but also get myself barred from all universities.

His name is Randall Persch. He's another business major in his third year with a dismal 2.5 GPA and will need a paper to get him through his junior year. When I answer the door of my dorm, I'm met with a young man who smells like cinnamon bark cologne with red-brown hair, blue eyes, and a boyish charm that would have a less-focused woman flustered by his innate confidence. I may be a devout woman of God, but even I get distracted by his sharp, smooth, jawline that sits under an amazingly attractive smile.

He's loud and friendly; I find that abrasive. His eyes have an energetic spark, as if he's genuinely happy to see me, as if he already knows me. He introduces himself before I'm able to start the conversation myself. "Hi, are you Liling? My name is Randall. My friend, Dan-"

"You can come in," I tell him, stepping aside so I could close the door behind him. Once he walks in, I continue to take in Randall Persch. Randall is tall and is a nice dresser, which I appreciate. He wears a dark blue sweater with a white collar and tan dress slacks. Randall stands confidently but has a casual air about him, walking with his hands in his pockets and leaning against the wall as soon as he's inside.

Formally, I tell him, "I'm Liling, I understand you need a paper?" It's best to get right to the point. I'm very sparing with my use of polite smiling and small talk. I've learned that if you give a man too much attention, they assume you're interested in them. I'm not interested in this man, and he seems like the type who is used to having women fawn over him. He's charming, I can see that, but that is not relevant to anything.

Randall is perhaps slightly put-off by my tight demeanor, but still has a kind smile. "I'm having a hard time in my macro class." He shakes his head, his reddish hair is shined and gelled in little arcs around the top of his head, as if he saw Leonardo DiCaprio's styled mess of gel and thought he could do the same. I'm not sure if I should be impressed with the effort or worried that he seems so eager to let others make his decisions for him.

I nod. "You need this paper to pass your course?"

"This is for my midterm. I'll need to do well on this one so I can have a chance at passing the class. A thousand words."

I wonder what someone like him is even doing in school. I wonder how he hasn't needed my help before. I note that his shoes are beat to shreds and this throws off the rest of his outfit. "Can you afford my services?"

I can see he is fazed by the fact that I'm not wasting time being sweet and I am not going to be impressed by his pretty eyes or his boy-band hair. Randall reaches into his back pocket, taking out a tattered brown leather wallet and retrieving the most miserable looking bills I've ever seen.

I make a point of not even letting our fingers touch as I take and unfold two fifty dollar bills. I raise my eyebrow at him. "This won't get you an A."

He wrings his hand and lets out a breath. "Well... I s'pose that might be suspicious anyway, after the shit I turned in last time."

I narrow my eyes at him, not caring for his choice of words.

"What if I don't need anything spectacular? B minus would bring my grade up. Can that get me a B?"

"No." I hold the cash back out but he doesn't take it. He pulls out another fifty this time. "You're tough, you know that? What about now?"

Now, I'm holding a hundred and fifty, and he's still under my current rates but there's something just so pathetic about it that I'm feeling charitable. I could write a thousand words in an hour. "Will your professor take a printed report?" Printed reports are safer. They are harder to track.

The poor idiot looks at me blankly. "I think so... I didn't ask."

I sigh. His life must have just been made too easy by being a semi-attractive white man. "Fine. Come back tomorrow."

Randall's face lifts in a relieved smile, and I change my mind - he is actually very attractive. "That soon?"

"It's only a thousand words."

When Randall smiles, I notice he has a small gap between his front two teeth. "I appreciate it, I really do-"

"You're paying for a service, you don't need to thank me. Do you thank your waitress for doing their job?"

Only the very edge of his lip curls upward. "I do, yes." Randall tells me blankly. "Don't you?"

"You can come back tomorrow," I remind him.

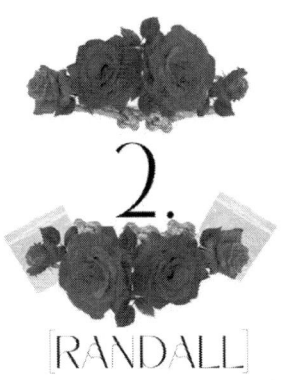

2.

[RANDALL]

Liling is absolutely the most gorgeous woman I've ever seen. I don't even know her last name yet, but it doesn't matter because I took one look at her and knew someday she'd have my last name.

Who knew finding someone to write a paper for me would change the rest of my life? When that door opened and I looked at Liling, I knew I was looking at my future.

I'm not too proud to admit that I'm just not good with academics. I'm going to school so I can at least reach becoming a mid-level manager somewhere, anywhere, and maybe make enough money to someday buy myself a house. Now that I've seen the woman I'll be buying a house for, my motivation has been renewed.

Liling. She's breathtaking. She's different- and I mean that very literally. This campus is full of blondes named Jennifer and Lisa. Liling is a… she's a Liling. I wish I had some way to look up her name and figure out what exactly sort of name that is because maybe that would impress her.

It took her less than five minutes to get me out of her dorm and I know I've got my work cut out for me. I'd like to think I'm fairly attractive, but she looked right through me without even noticing how nice my arms would look around her body.

Liling has these striking, narrow brown eyes that look at me with absolutely no warmth, but I hardly notice because I'm too busy figuring out how I can get her to talk to me like a person. I see two empty beds and know we could put one of them to good use.

Her voice draws me in next. She's got this smooth, low voice. It's the kind of voice I've only heard on VHS tapes that are in the curtained area at the video store. It's a loveless, luring voice that I'd dive straight into the ocean to get to.

Liling has black hair that's blown out in big sweeps around her head, just like all the girls are doing these days. Her bangs rest just above her eyebrows and it makes me focus on that intense stare of hers. She wears dark lipstick, brown or something, and now I'm looking at her mouth in a way, she must've picked up on because she's decided to be even less friendly as we continue to talk. I'd given her a hundred dollars and she acted like I was a sorry excuse for a man for thinking it was enough.

When I've handed her even more money, I'm looking at the way the jeans hang on her thighs and how I wish her purple shirt fit tighter. In the most respectful way possible, Liling is an absolute knockout.

I'd leave her dorm after giving her more money than I should have since I'm dirt poor, but it's an investment in my future. Plus, I've taken on a new side hustle recently, and in another few weeks I'll be set. I'll be making more than enough to impress someone like Liling. I'd see Liling again and I'd be ready to knock her socks off. If I was lucky, maybe even more than her socks.

One look. That's all it took for me to know what I was working toward.

Since I'd given so much of my bill-paying money, I'll be busting my ass at work and putting in some extra hours. I have two jobs. I work at a pizza joint on campus, and I also sell cocaine.

Sometimes I work at the front counter, sometimes I deliver pizza in a ratty old car, sometimes I make enough money to feed myself for a month after selling a few clear bags of white powder. I think having a job is good, because not everyone works in college. I have two jobs.

I think girls like to see a man who works hard. I bet Liling wouldn't be impressed by someone who has no job. I wonder what kind of options she has. She's too pretty to not have a boyfriend. Then again, if she treats all men the way she treated me when we first met, maybe she is alone. I'll find out tomorrow.

When I get to work, I'm eager to tell my best friend about having met my future wife. His name is Gordon, but he goes by Gordy. Gordy and I met at this pizza place, and we've gotten along since the beginning. Gordy doesn't go to school but campus has a lot of jobs and Gordy needs money. I need money. Gordy hasn't sunken as low as I have in terms of employment but I don't think he's completely opposed to it. Gordy already has a record, so he's trying to be more careful.

Gordy is a short guy with brown hair and brown eyes and a pointed nose that's slightly off, as if he got creamed in the face one day and it never got fixed. Gordy isn't exactly the nicest, or the most sophisticated guy, but he's sort of down for anything and I like that about him. Gordy's gruff and I don't always take things seriously and somehow it's made what I hope is a life-long friendship.

I wait for Gordy to hang up the phone, watching him struggle to get the black curled wire from around his ankle as he puts the head back in the receiver on the wall. Gordy knows I've turned to cheating to get through my macroeconomics class. "You get your paper?" Gordy's now struggling to get the pen he's found to write an order on a piece of paper.

13

"Tomorrow," I tell him, looking at the other orders of pizza boxes that are being slid through the kitchen window. "But the girl that writes the papers? Gordy, you should've seen her."

At this, Gordy's looking at me like I'm stupid. "You fall in love any time you see someone with big tits. Idiot." I wish he'd get his red shorts out of his ass and not be so judgmental about this.

"That's-" I pause, because he isn't wrong necessarily but this time it really is different. "I couldn't even tell because her shirt was big but no, Gordy, she's gorgeous. She's the most beautiful creature I've ever seen." I thought of those eyes. "She's smart, I can tell. Real smart."

"Then she won't be interested in your dumb ass." Gordy is sort of mean to me too but I also like that he'd probably punch somebody's lights out if it came to that.

I move to where there's an overflowing trash can and figure I should take it out before our manager comes and starts telling us that we're not working hard enough. I'm aware that working with my best friend is a privilege. "Well, she's not interested, yet. She just hasn't been put under the Randall Persch charm mode."

Gordy took the order he'd written and passed it through the kitchen window to Sol, one of the cooks. "I hope this woman is as hot as you say, so she can humble you when she leaves you in the dust."

I shake my head at him, still holding a tied bag of trash. "I'm telling you Gordy, I'll get her. I'll figure something out."

"You're going to figure rejection out," Gordy says, his shoulders slouching when the phone rings again. It's going to be a busy night of selling pizzas to shit-faced drunken college students getting ready for a football game.

I'm not going to be discouraged by Gordy. Gordy isn't a romantic like I am. Gordy will sleep with anyone that isn't

14

repulsed by him and doesn't think love is real. I know love is real, and I know love at first sight is strong. I spend all night thinking of the woman with the beautiful eyes and big hair and plan for ways to impress her.

Liling Persch. Someday, that'll be her name, and I'll know exactly how to get those eyes to look at me with love.

LILING

I worked the night before at the library, which was quiet since there was a game and not enough students care about their studies on a game day. During this time, I write Randall's paper and start reading for another one I'm working on for someone's English thesis.

There's no reason to feel bad about making my money writing papers for students. It's a need that would exist whether I did or did not write them. If it wasn't me, it'd be someone else. I don't have parents that are putting me through college. I'm expected to go to college, but I'm also expected to work it out for myself. My older sister has done it, and I will not be the failure.

By the time Randall Persch is back at my door, I've almost forgotten I'd told him to come back today at all. Randall smells like grease, wearing a bright red shirt and matching shorts. The shirt reads CAMPUS TOWNE PIZZA. By the smell of him, he must've been working for hours but he seems just as happy as ever to see me.

"Hi, Liling." Randall's hair is poking out from a white cap that has the same name as the shirt in red font. "How are you?"

"Come inside," I tell him. I don't like talking business with the door open. I don't trust anyone with my secrets. For those who buy my papers, their motivation to keep their mouths closed comes from keeping their own academic careers intact.

Randall responds as if I've invited him in for anything other than an academic paper. This time when he comes in, he's looking around my dorm with more interest. "So, you got a boyfriend?"

I'm taken back by not only his boldness but also his poor grammar. "Why would you need to know that?"

Stupidly, I feel my cheeks flushing, so I turn my back to him so I can retrieve his paper from my work desk and get him out of my dorm. I hear the springs of one of the beds coil under his weight and know that he's making himself too comfortable. It's rude.

"You're too pretty to not have one," Randall tells me. I'm aware I'm pretty, and it will take a lot more than some sweet talk to get what he wants. There actually isn't a way for him to get what he wants. I have so many things planned, and Randall Persch is not one of them.

"I don't need a boyfriend," I tell Randall shortly, flipping through a stack of six papers, typed and ready.

"Need, or want?" Randall continues. He's already such a bother. I will not be offering my services to him again.

I've found his paper, and I turn to look at him sitting on my roommate's bed. "It's the same answer for you, either way."

Randall has a charming smile, I'll give him that. The way he seems unafraid to make a fool out of himself is interesting, to say the least. "So, no boyfriend." Randall doesn't sound like he's teasing, but I don't know what he thinks is going to happen.

"No boyfriend." Randall is very close to meeting a different version of myself.

I hear the coils of the bed move again. "What do you do in your free time?"

"I don't have free time." I'm curt in my responses.

"I bet you read," Randall tells me.

I sigh, finally giving him just enough to make him shut up and stop firing random things at me. "I read a lot. I go to church. I visit my parents."

A nicer person would ask him questions about himself, but that's somebody other than myself. I'm entering into the less friendly Liling. The version that doesn't even attempt to be semi-cordial. I hold my hand out, wanting him to take the paper and leave.

Casually, Randall leans forward for the paper but I have to step forward to make up for the distance. Randall takes the paper, and looks it over in a way that I can tell he isn't truly reading it. He'll probably hand it in without even proofing it. "Give me one thing," Randall says, still looking down.

I'm confused, and I don't have time to play his games. "I've given you the paper," I say. "It's all you can afford."

Randall laughs, and I notice that he has small dimples in his otherwise flawless face. "No, give me one thing that'll make you smile next time you see me."

Men. They think of one thing. "I won't be seeing you again."

Randall is still grinning at me. "Come on, one thing," he guides. "One thing and I'll leave."

I will not be playing his games with him. Nice looking men think they can do whatever they want just because they've got good hair and soft eyes but I will be the first to tell them the world was not created to serve their every whim. "You'll leave now," I tell him, putting steel in my voice.

Randall sighs but still wears a grin as he stands. He tucks the paper in the band of his shorts, folding the freshly printed paper. I think he's going to finally leave because I've been rude to him, stepping just to the right of the doorway so he can pass.

Instead, Randall doesn't leave. He stops just before I think he'll go and he's standing too close to me, lifting an arm to rest against the edge of the doorframe so there's too precious amount of space between us.

He's taller than me, not by a lot since I'm not particularly short, but he's able to look down at me with twinkling blue eyes and a smile that brings the dimples back out. "You're really pretty, you know that?"

I'm now focusing on looking as unfriendly as possible. I am not interested in Randall Persch. "Yes. I know that."

He laughs at this, as if I've said a joke. "You're not impressed by me, are you?"

Unwavering, I tell him, "I don't need a boyfriend. Especially one that can't manage a short essay about economic indicators." Surely, he must know he isn't enough for me.

It's as if I haven't even tried to stomp on his stupid little heart. If anything, he cranes his neck even closer and I can't step back without awkwardly hitting the small table that has a bowl for keys by the door. I'm not going to retreat, this is my dorm. I am in control.

"You need to leave," I tell him.

Randall nods, turning his head as if contemplating something thoughtful. "One thing," he says again. "One thing to make you smile."

He is exhausting, he is forward, he is truly not going to leave. I tell him something quickly, something that isn't impossible so that he can't say that I haven't given a real answer but not something I expect can be accomplished in any sort of way. "A thousand words on why you think you have any sort of chance with me." It was meant to be an insult, not a challenge.

Randall has a very boyish laugh, full of genuine joy. "Next time I see you, you'll have a smile for me." He winks at me and says, "It was nice to see you, Liling."

I couldn't get the door shut quickly enough. He's odd, I think. I tell my younger sister about him when we talk on the phone later. I get along the best with my younger sister. My older sister and I are constant competitors. My younger sister is sweet and has missed me since I've been at school. My sister thinks I need a boyfriend, but she's young and thinks the point of going to school is to find an educated man you can get married to, assuming our parents don't pick somebody for us.

That's not why I'm in school. I'm in school for myself. I'm in school because I don't trust a man to determine my future. I'll get my own life sorted out first, and figure out the man that goes into that life later. Whoever that is, I know it isn't someone like Randall Persch.

4.

[RANDALL]

I leave Liling's dorm and know for sure this time that she's the most enticing woman I've ever met. She wants absolutely nothing to do with me and it's driving me crazy. She's all I think about. I think about her the whole drive home, and I think about her when I'm in my own dorm room while my roommate is out.

I tried to read through some of what she'd written for me. She made good points that even sounded like an idiot like me could've maybe written it. If this was a B paper, I wonder what Liling's mind could pull if I gave her a few hundred more dollars.

Macroeconomics is my lowest grade, with statistics a close second. I'm not bad at math, but I'm bad at understanding complex business topics. The kind of career I think I'll have, I really just need to be good with people and have a degree that looks good on paper. I'm good with people. I'll be real good with Liling.

After another day has gone by and I work another shift with Gordy, I am almost, *almost* convinced that maybe he's right and I'm only interested in Liling because she's pretty. This thought occurs to me when a beautiful brunette comes in and I can tell she's really into me. I can tell I'd get her number if I asked. I've written my own number on pizza boxes plenty of times and gotten plenty of nights out of it.

Something about the brunette was too easy. She was easy in a literal sense, and I like the way Liling was intent on making me work. Things are better when they're earned. I let the brunette leave and Gordy tells me what he would've done with a girl like that, which is a bunch of crap because Gordy is too ugly to get girls like that.

I work all weekend, getting stuck with a lot of delivery duty which meant I worked alone. The nice thing about deliveries is that I get better tips. I'm saving up while also trying to make sure my student loans don't get too out of hand. I'm pretty close to accepting that I'll always be in debt and maybe I should just spend the money on things that are important. Flowers. I bet Liling would like flowers. Lilies. It was close to her name, it was clever.

After work, at night, I work the parties and sell little bags of happiness to students who have too much cash on hand. I told myself I'm never going to try what I sell. It's a little hypocritical, sure, but I need to keep a clear head. In this line of work, I've met a lot of interesting people, and I've met a lot of people who definitely need to stop the drugs. That doesn't mean I'll stop selling it to them, though. People will ruin their lives either way, why not have a little fun and make money off of it?

It's good money, what I make now. I've only been at it for a month or so, and in a month, I'm considering quitting the pizza place so I can sell more. I'm starting to be in a little less debt, and pretty soon I'll no longer be able to refer to myself as dirt poor.

This kind of money, I don't know how else I'd come by it. In the last month, I've eaten better than I ever have before, I've started to plan big things, like getting an apartment, and now I could take care of a girlfriend if I had one. I'll have one soon.

It's not a safe profession, by any means. I put myself with dangerous people. Drug addicts who are desperate. Drug dealers who don't tolerate mistakes. I've seen other people who sell fool around, make mistakes. The people who make mistakes seem to disappear.

By Monday, I go into the lecture hall where my macro class is. There's a two-hour seminar on fiscal policy and I can't help but wonder how this is going to help me manage a pizza store of a national chain someday. At the end, I turn in my paper and am maybe a little nervous that somehow the professor will know I've cheated. At the same time, I can already tell that Liling is too smart to get caught.

I want to go see her again but I'm not going to. I'm going to make her smile. One thousand words, she said. One thousand words on why I think I have a chance with Liling. It's funny, because I know she thinks she got me to lay off. I know she won't expect me to do it, but I will. I could write a thousand words about the things I want to do with her in her dorm but I'm going to be a respectful gentleman about this.

One thousand words about Liling. I'd give her a thousand words and more. It'd take time, but I think that's ok because she'll just be surprised when I find a dictionary and put a thousand words on paper. I'm almost lucky that Liling gave me something so easy. She could've asked for my left hand and I would've given it to her… or given her someone's hand, at least.

5.

LILING

I've had a good week, financially. I've made six hundred dollars from writing papers for other people. The word processors in the computer labs have revolutionized paper writing for me. If I'm ever able to get myself a personal computer, I'll be able to do so much more business once I'm not constricted to the operating hours of the library.

The weather has taken a stark turn toward fall in the last week. The weather has cooled considerably, the warmer weather of the early semester having left us for auburn leaves that travel on a chilled wind.

My older sister has announced her engagement, so I'm going to drive home for a dinner in her celebration. Twenty-four. Lhasa has gotten herself engaged at twenty-four after having finished her studies at the end of the previous school year. By the time I'm twenty-four, I'll need to have done the same.

I can handle the academic route with ease. It's finding someone to marry that's challenging. I'll need to be nicer to men. I have two years to learn from my sister and learn how to surpass her. After I meet her new fiancé, I'll have a schematic to work from to know what my parents expect. Without even meeting him, I know he'll be perfect.

Lhasa is always perfect. Lhasa is everything I need to be. She's smarter, she's prettier, and she's probably found a businessman with a healthy net worth who never misses church and always visits his mother.

I've already been critiqued harshly against my sister. She's always outshined me, and I'm tired of it. I'm tired of losing. It's only a matter of time until my younger sister, Lishui, becomes another entrant as my mother's favorite.

I'm walking so fast through campus that I almost miss him. I see him in the distance - walking in a green windbreaker with a Panasonic CD player attached to a thick black cord that bumps against his chest as he walks. Randall Persch. I slow my walk slightly, as if he were some sort of threat.

It's clear he doesn't see me, in his own world as he adjusts the metal wire over his head so the black sponges of the earphones rested more easily over his ears. I look at how his hair pokes around the metal frame, and notice the confidence in how he walks. I wonder what sort of music someone like Randall listens to.

Randall, thankfully, has not plagued my doorway since I'd dodged him by giving him a silly task. He's not someone I would ever date. It's good that he hasn't come back, because there's something about his absurd confidence and unjustly attractive face that has me occasionally thinking about it. I don't need the distraction.

Someone else has flagged Randall down, and I'm content to slow my walk to make sure he has time to finish his distance across the intersecting sidewalk so he doesn't see me. By the time I've driven home, I've expelled all distractions out of my mind.

Walking to the door, I'm repeating my recent accomplishments in my head. I'll need to find a way to work them all into conversation. The semester is still young, so reporting options are limited but I'm sure Lhasa will have something beyond her engagement to bring forward.

My parents are nice people, they're just quiet and strict. As soon as I'm through the door and taking my shoes off, my mother has pointed out I've gained weight and that my hair is too big, my lipstick is too dark, and my sister has been home for twenty minutes, even though she's driven out of state. Lishui, at least, is happy to see me and offers no criticism.

My mother is a very small and frail-looking person. I feel like she's always looked the same age, or that she's never been very youthful in appearance. Her hair has seemingly always been in a short black bob that's now speckled with gray hair; I think she really ought to fix it up. Lines of aging are surfacing despite how much she reminds us to stay out of the sun.

I greet Mother and Lishui at the door but I'm already focused in on the voices carrying from the dining room. I can hear Papa, Lhasa, and a new male voice that must be Lhasa's fiancé. After telling me, "Dinner will be ready in ten minutes," as a greeting when she takes my jacket, Mama rushes back to the kitchen as if she has no more time to welcome me in.

Lishui waits for Mama to leave before saying, "I can't wait to go to college like you." Lishui is seventeen, and has been accepted into the Michigan State University, just as I have. It's a breath of fresh air to know she's at least on the same playing field as myself and isn't going to what's almost an Ivy League school, like Lhasa is.

Lishui is a cute little thing, wearing a purple corduroy romper with a modest white shawl over her shoulders. Her hair is in a ponytail with a pink plastic bead, and it looks like she's experimenting with some blue eye shadow. I wonder how Mama let that happen.

"How perfect is he?" I ask quietly, nodding in the direction of the voices. Lishui has always shared my general annoyance for the perfect Lhasa.

At this, Lishui rolls her eyes as she flips her black hair over her shoulder. "He's working on a graduate degree, has prominent family back in China, and is a devout worshipper of our Lord and Savior Jesus Christ." Lishui still has a little baby of a voice, protruding innocence and youth.

When Lishui tells me this, I steady myself with a breath. Of course, Lhasa has found a Chinese business tycoon who goes to church. She's checked every box she's expected to. "Maybe she's pregnant," I say as either a joke or wishful thinking. I'll never catch up to Lhasa if she doesn't make a mistake at some point.

Lishui laughs at this and takes my arm, telling me, "I miss you so much." Lishui leads me into the dining room, where a circular mahogany table is adorned with red placemats and white china dishes that are ready for dinner. Mama has gotten out the good plates and silverware for our guest.

When I see the man Lhasa has brought home, I know there's no way to ever top her. He's gorgeous, he's tall, he somehow even looks like a good, reserved, Christian man. His English name is Frank, his mandarin is perfect, and he's already bought himself a house that he and Lhasa can make a million perfect, devout Christian babies in.

My father has barely noticed anything I've said to him all night, because he's focused on his new son. His balding head and circular glasses have been bouncing all night as he enthusiastically nods to everything Frank the Genius says. To me, Frank is dull - even by my standards. There's a small, petty, part of me that hopes Lhasa also finds him boring, hoping that this is only a marriage of convenience and that she's not getting *everything* she wants.

It's been hard to work in updates from my own life. My recent test score has rendered me unimpressive, and my class load is something expected of me. There's no reward for doing what I'm told. Another day of living under Lhasa.

The worst thing about Lhasa getting engaged is that it now puts a spotlight on myself. Now, it's *when is Liling going to find a good Christian boy?* I likely don't actually have two years to find someone before Mama starts pulling at her connections. I'd rather find someone for myself, because that feels like a greater accomplishment. Lhasa found someone on her own, so if I need Mother to find my partner, then it's as if I wasn't able to do it myself.

Good, tall, Chinese, smart Christian man. That is who I need to find.

The entire drive home, I'm thinking about where I can find someone like this. I need to find a new church on campus. One with a better pool to draw from. By the time I've made it back to the dorm hallway, I've decided that after I get through this semester, I will most certainly take dating more seriously and find-

"Liling, hey!"

The voice stops me mid-planning. I look up near the end of the hallway, and there is Randall Persch leaning against my doorway as if he's waiting for me. I'm immediately scowling, thinking of how many people must have passed and seen a man waiting for me. They probably think he's my boyfriend, or that he's waiting for me to get back so we can-

"What are you doing here?" I ask him with no friendship in my voice.

Randall grins at me, wearing black dress pants with the same blue sweater I've seen him wear before. Triumphantly, he holds a stack of written papers I already know have my name written all over them.

6.

[RANDALL]

I am just too pleased with myself. I am pleased with myself for writing a paper so fast, and I'm pleased that I can tell Liling genuinely wasn't expecting me back. This means that she *must* be impressed by me.

I've got my essay in hand. At the top of the paper, I have it titled *1,000 Words on Why I Know I'll Be a Great Boyfriend to Liling*. I had to write the title very small to get it to fit at the top of the paper. I have it double spaced, and even counted the words so that it is one thousand words exactly.

As soon as she sees me, she nearly grimaces but I'm focused on the way the black tights are clinging to her calves under a long green dress that's peeking from under her winter coat. "What are you doing here?"

I ignore her tone completely and instead offer her a triumphant smile. I'm just too eager to hand over the essay she had no idea I'd actually write. When she snatches the paper from my hands, I notice her nails are painted orange and I think about those orange nails going through my hair.

Liling looks at the paper with a long face, her dark eyes inspecting the paper under long, black lashes. "You wrote a paper," she says blankly, one hand holding the paper and the other to unlock her door. She huffs at me, and once the door is open, she's practically shoving me inside as if she doesn't want to be seen lingering in the hallway, but I don't care. This just means that I have successfully gotten back into Liling's dorm room, and once again, her roommate isn't here.

"I wasn't being serious about this, Randall," Liling says, shutting the door with exasperated flourish.

"You told me what you wanted, and I delivered," I tell her, spreading my arms. She's just now started to actually read what I wrote down and I'm waiting for her to smile.

Liling holds the paper in front of her, stretching her arm like it makes it easier to read. She recites the line she's working on, "*Randall Persch will make a great boyfriend to Liling because he's not only very attractive, but he has a good job at a pizza place and has a promising lead on a better paying job at a motel.*" Her eyes look up at me from the paper, and I really want to cross the room over to her.

Instead, I tell her, "I think that's a major selling point."

She tilts her head, narrowing her eyes. "A selling point?"

"Sure," I say. "Some people think they need to wait until after college to start working because it's too hard to take classes while having a job, but not me. I'm a hard worker."

Liling sighs, looking back at the paper. "We met because you can't even earn a passing score on your own."

I fire back at her, ready to volley. "We met because you can't even earn money by getting a normal job like everybody else." I'm not the best person to pass judgement on this but it's probably too soon to bring up the cocaine. I see a cross pendent glimmering on her neck and figure she's probably not a junky.

I think I almost went too far when she looks up at me, like she could just throttle me right there. I'd let her try, because it'd get

30

her hands on me. Instead of saying anything, she keeps reading. I watch her eyes move across the paper and she doesn't say anything, she keeps reading until she's flipped through the second page.

As she's almost to the end of the second page, she starts doing something weird with her face. It's like she's stretching her jaw out while also driving her tongue into the bottom of her cheek.

She's trying not to laugh.

She tries to keep a straight face, but I've done it. She stifles a laugh in a heavy breath, and her face finally rises into a smile and I'm reminded that she's the most gorgeous woman I've ever seen. I'm instantly consumed by the way her white teeth emerge from behind her darkly painted lips. "Your paper has references," she says, her fingers playing over her mouth. "You have reference material in a paper about why you should be my boyfriend."

"Of course," I tell her. "You told me what you wanted me to do, so I wanted to do it right."

She's still smiling, pinching her lips in like she wants to hide it when she stops looking at me to look at the paper and flips to the last page, where I have all of my sources listed and then she laughs again.

Randall Persch knows how to impress a woman.

She shakes her head, moving onto the next page. "This is ridiculous."

While she's reading, I'm taking cautious, slow steps toward her so that she doesn't notice I'm preparing to storm the gates. By the time she notices that I'm once again in her personal space. I've again got her somewhere where she can't back up because there's a desk behind her and I'm close enough to smell the sweet scent coming off of her.

She's still amused but has tensed once she notices how close I am to her. "This isn't going to work," she tells me, holding the paper out so one end touches her stomach and the other touches mine, as if the paper will keep us separated.

I step forward and the paper starts to crinkle. "Then, give me another thing."

Liling looks up at me, her brown eyes hiding behind her fluffed bangs. "What?"

"One more thing." More crinkling paper. "One more thing that'll make you smile for next time."

Liling shakes her head like I'm being ridiculous, still clutching onto the paper like it's going to stop me from getting any closer. It's already bent between us. "I didn't think you'd write an entire paper." Her voice is softer. I want to hear more of it.

"I told you I'd do something, and I did it." The paper has now been completely crushed between us, the lined pages crammed between our abdomens. "Whenever I say I'm going to do something, I'll do it. And if you ask for something, I'll make sure you get it." I'm so, so close to her now. Lavender. That's what she's wearing. She smells floral.

I've cornered Liling in close enough that I can feel her breath on my chin as she tries to muster more strength in her voice. "I'm not asking you for anything, Randall."

This makes me chuckle, and there's no closer I can get because we're already toe to toe. I've been told before that sometimes my flirting style can be abrasive. I've only met this woman once, but I don't care; why not try something? Why wait to start forever later than right now?

I've come too far to not at least try to get what I want. I can have Liling, I know it. I've impressed her, and I just need to see if I've impressed her enough.

I kiss her. I give her no further warning, I just cram my mouth against hers until I feel her lipstick smearing all over my mouth and I hungrily take in everything Liling is.

Liling lets me take her in. She takes some of me too.

My heart is pounding as our mouths are colliding and her chest pushes up against mine. I now have my arms spread out so they're clutching the desk behind Liling and she's stuck between my arms and the desk but she's not trying to escape, she's almost folding into my right arm.

I'm obviously excited that I'm getting exactly what I want but I'm not trying to be too enthusiastic because it feels like I could scare her off at any moment.

She makes just the smallest of sounds when her mouth opens for a breath and I take the extra space to push even further into her face. This is also where I go just a little too far with the woman who thought she was too good for me. My hands start moving away from the desk, and one finds her thigh and moves up, and this is where her hand touches mine but is pushing it away.

I pull back immediately, my lips buzzing in a way I hope hers are too. Her face is flushed and she's now separating us with her other hand, the paper resting at our feet. "You - you should leave, Randall."

I give her a soft smile, not too bent up about leaving because I know I'll see her again. Honestly, this night has gone out even better than I'd planned. "If you're asking me to leave, then that's what I'll do. I'll always do what you ask me to."

Flustered, I feel her hands push at my abdomen and she says with her regular steel, "Yes, I'm asking you to leave." Liling's stone face is back.

I sigh, pretending to be disappointed when, in fact, I've never felt more alive. I nod, separating until I can't smell her anymore or feel her heart beat against mine.

I'm not going to leave without hearing her voice one more time. I want her to ask me for more, I'll give her anything. "Give me something else, Liling." I tell her from the doorway. She's still pinned herself against the desk.

She's slowly getting back to her regular fiery self. "I'm not playing games, Randall."

"And neither am I, Liling," I tell her. "I want you to like me." I want her to love me. "I want to pass whatever tests you throw at me because I want you to play along. Give me something else."

Liling huffs, and she slaps her thigh impatiently in the exact spot I'd touched her.

"I'll write you another paper," I offer.

She's stretching her jaw again, and now I've made her smile at least twice. "Bring me something that shows you know *anything* about me. Anything beyond-" She bends over to pick up the tattered paper and reads my words back to me. "Something a little deeper than *'We're both gorgeous people and our kids would rule the planet.'*" She has to practically bite her cheek to hold any sort of seriousness.

I grin at her, the woman I can feel is thawing before me. "Deeper?" I ask. "I can go deeper." I wink at her, leaving just as her eyes widen and before she can forbade me from returning.

LILING

Randall Persch is quite possibly the most annoying, overconfident, slimy man I have ever known. I have told him so, so many times that I am uninterested, and he somehow takes that as a challenge.

I had what was nothing more than a… an outlier in my own behavior. He confused me. Tricked me. If anything, I let Randall kiss me only to prove that I am, in fact, stronger than this man. I'm stronger than his childish dimples or his constant joking.

Still, there's a self-loathing in knowing that I met a man all of two times and let him touch me. What sort of woman does that? My behavior was deplorable. Proving a point isn't worth going to hell for.

I've not given him everything he wanted, but some of the things he wanted. All he wants is my affection, he claims. In all honesty, no one has ever wanted to be my boyfriend. Men have been quick to invite me to their dorm but I've always known none of them are looking for anything long term. I don't need temporary, I need a foundation. Not now, but at some point.

Now, there's a man who claims to be everything I'm looking for. I have no idea how he could think this; he doesn't know me. It's suspicious on his part, for him to be fixated on me at all.

He's even written a thousand words on the topic. After Randall left, I took the paper off the floor and smoothed it out. I gave it another read, chewing at my nail as I did, smiling to myself because it's actually very funny. Randall is charming. He's stupid, but he's charming.

There is something impressive about his tenacity. There is a part of me that wants to believe he has a true interest in me. Surely, a lesser man who is only interested in sex would have given up by now. I excel in running off men. Randall isn't running away, though. If anything, he's keeping up.

Randall leaves me thinking about him long after he's gone. There's a girlish part of me that wants him to figure out the next thing I've asked him for. I think maybe I should even entertain his advances, or at least some of them. Then, I remember Randall is not anyone I could ever bring to my parents. I rethink that maybe it's best to leave Randall alone.

It's as if I can still feel his hands, though.

8.

RANDALL

Liling. She let me touch her. Kiss her. It wasn't much, but it was enough to reaffirm that I have found the love of my life. I know I'm breaking through her armor. I just have to keep going. She gave me another thing to work on; she's playing along.

Liling Persch. That's what I'm working toward.

I tell Gordy about my little victory. About Liling.

"You've been working for this bitch for weeks and you're getting hard over a kiss and a little thigh work?"

I hate when Gordy is like this. "Don't call her that," I tell him. We're in the back of the store, folding pizza boxes ahead of the rush. "And she's just... she's a classy woman. That's why she's waiting."

"She's playing games with you," Gordy tells me.

I'm folding boxes way faster than Gordy is. Gordy's a bigger guy with grubby fingers and he's always a little greasy. "You just need to see her. Then you'll understand."

"I thought you told me this obsession is more than her just being hot," Gordy points out, the stack of boxes next to him leaning to the left.

"It's a lot more than that, Gordy. It's..." I can't explain how Liling has taken over all my thoughts when she hasn't said one nice thing to me. Someday, Gordy will see. I don't even know if Gordy can fall in love, anyway. He's not a lover, he's just a fucker.

I spend most of my shift delivering pizzas. Most of them are going to different frat houses. Fraternities intrigue me but I don't have money for dues or time for initiation. Instead, I can live vicariously through pizza deliveries.

The delivery I'm making is a frat house with big, white columns guarding a green door of a three-story house. The lawn is already trashed with red plastic cups and other litter. Sometimes, tracking down who is paying for the pizza can be hard, but I see somebody I know.

His name is Greg, known colloquially as Stoner Greg, and we had a class together last year. He invites me to parties at his frat house, even though I'm not a member. I'm very likable, I wish Liling would see that. Greg's also the person that got me into the hard and fast world of selling coke.

Greg is on the deck, leaning against one of the white pillars with a blunt in his hand. He's the first to notice me pull up with several boxes of stacked pizza. "Woah, Randall, out here earning a buck, huh?" Greg is a very short guy with a mop of brown hair that hides brown eyes and a face of acne.

"I'm working hard," I confirm for Greg. "You guys are really keeping me busy."

Greg calls over his shoulder "Pizza's here! Who the hell has the money?"

Greg takes three of the boxes from me and leads me inside. The inside of the house is an even bigger mess than the outside. Someone really ought to get things put together. It's disgusting in here.

There's a room to the left of the entryway with a massive wooden table that's scuffed up and also littered with blunts and paper plates and old pizza boxes. Greg decides that whoever was supposed to pay me is taking too long and he takes out his wallet.

"How're your sales going?" Greg asks as he thumbs through the cash.

I know he isn't talking about pizza. "Better than ever."

Greg laughs. "Right? People can't keep their hands off it."

Greg and I run in different circles, so we're not really in competition of each other. It's a big campus. "I'm going to see Toby later today to restock."

"He's been off lately, have you noticed?"

I thought about Toby, who gets the drugs from a boss I've never met, then he gives it to me to sell once I turn in the cash I've already earned. Toby's always been flighty. He's not exactly a kingpin. If anything, he comes across as someone who got into this by accident and is too scared to get out of it. I respond with, "Toby's a weird guy, but he helps me make a lot of money, so I won't complain."

Greg hands me cash with his dirty fingers. "Sure enough. Well, you're all set, but you're welcome to stay, man." Greg sounds faded himself.

I look around the dirty frat house with purple walls and peeling paint, hearing the swelling beat of rap music from multiple rooms of the house, all at war with each other. This isn't where I want to be, or who I want to be with. I've got one more stop to make before I can go visit my favorite new obsession one more time before I'm ready to give her the next thing on her list.

■ ■

Toby lives in an apartment that's deceptively grubby on the outside but is fairly well kept on the inside. It's like he wants to live somewhere inconspicuous. No one realizes how much money the guy is clearly making until they step inside.

From the outside, the apartment is a disaster. It's a seedy apartment complex that looks like a converted motel. The complex would look abandoned if it weren't for the cars parked in the littered parking lot. I step over potholes that are full of brown water and fast food wrappers, past overflowing trash cans and ignoring the stifling smell of marijuana leaking out of someone's window. If this was all selling got me, then it wasn't worth it. This isn't the kind of place I could show off to Liling.

Toby is almost friendly, but there's something off about him. He is a drug dealer, after all. Then again, so am I, and my social skills are great.

Toby is of average height, with green eyes that are always shadowed by dark pits under them, greasy blonde hair that I can't tell whether he's trying to get into some sort of dread loc or if he just doesn't pay attention to it. He's a bigger guy, with a big gut that's rarely fully covered and pants that always need to be higher.

I've never been near him on a day he doesn't smell and I've never been near him when he doesn't find a way to start talking about some sort of weird xenophobic conspiracy theory. I figure he must reel some of his crazy in when the bosses come - when the cartel reps are around. I've seen them get into their car when I was coming by but I haven't talked to any of them.

From what I could see, they were dark skinned - Hispanic or something, maybe. Toby is always sayings crazy, off the wall things to me, but the people I saw didn't look like they'd care to listen. The only thing I really know about them is their name, who we sell for.

The Padillas.

For the time being, I didn't want to know too much about them. They feel like this dangerous cloud that is always over our heads, but as long as we don't poke at it, we won't get rained down on. I would stick with Toby.

Inside Toby's apartment, things are clean, new, but the place doesn't seem lived in. It almost looks like a model room or a hotel. There's no pictures, no artwork, not even a house plant to provide any warmth. I feel like I'm here all the time. I'm always selling, so I'm always coming back for more.

Toby will give me a brown lunch sack that's full of smaller bags I can sell off individually. I bring back cash to Toby, he gives me a cut. It's supposed to be Toby's problem if one of his sellers doesn't have money. I don't know what happens if I'm short, and I'm not going to find out.

After enduring Toby's rant about the president, the price of gasoline, and his ex-girlfriend, I'm beyond ready to leave. Toby's a creep. He's a creep that pays, at least.

I love the feeling of a pocket full of cash and a mind full of Liling.

9.

LILING

I always sit in the front row of classes when seats aren't assigned. I'm able to hear, the professor is able to see how attentive I am, and I'm able to see when Randall Persch is waiting in the hall for my class to get out.

He arrives five minutes before the professor dismisses us, so I am distracted for five minutes exactly. I could break out in a sweat knowing he's in the hallway waiting, watching the side of my face.

We're dismissed after being assigned partners for a project due at the end of the semester. I take my time talking to D'Marius because I know Randall is waiting. When we're done talking and I'm walking out the door, I'm not sure if it's better to ignore Randall completely or remind him that his presence in my life is unwanted.

Randall's grin is too big, too charming when he falls into step next to me. "Hi, Liling." I ignore him. "How was class?" More silence from me, until he puts his arm over my shoulder. "Bad, then?"

I'm not going to throw him off because I've got enough venom in my voice to make any man obey me. "You have three seconds to remove your arm before I make a scene."

Not even embarrassed, he gingerly removes his arm. "If that's what you want, that's what I'll do."

"I want you to stop pestering me."

"I'm still working on your assignment," Randall tells me. Apparently, he doesn't listen to *anything* I ask him to do.

"I don't actually want you to do that."

Randall continues to walk with me, and I worry he's going to follow me all the way back to my dorm. "Then, what do you want? Other than for me not to put my arm around you?"

"Nothing."

"Can I hold your hand?"

"Of course not."

"What can I hold?"

He's obnoxious. Absolutely obnoxious. So much so that I stop walking in the middle of the sidewalk, intent to give him my full attention, if that's what he thinks he can handle. "Randall. I want you to leave me alone. Alright?"

"For how long?" He isn't taking this seriously.

I wipe my hair back, feeling hot with annoyance. "Forever, Randall!"

He stretches his arm out, thinking. "Gee, that's going to make it hard to marry you someday."

I start walking again. "You're ridiculous," I throw over my shoulder.

He, of course, keeps walking with me. "Fine, you think I'm ridiculous," Randall pants. "Just tell me what kind of man you want me to be and I'll work on that."

"An invisible one," I snap.

He grins. "So we could do everything by touch."

I really am going to lose my mind talking to this one. "I'll make you a deal, Randall."

43

He grins victoriously, happy to have pried any sort of conversation out of me. I really think he's happy as long as I'm talking to him in any capacity. "I love deals."

"I'll tell you three things about myself and then you leave me alone."

"For how long? And don't say forever."

I'll buy myself some time, any time, until I can figure out how to handle him. "Three things, three days. You do not talk to me for that time period."

"Hm," Randall frowns. "That will throw off our honeymoon by three days, but go ahead."

I sigh. "I have two sisters. I like musicals. My favorite show is Little House on the Prairie."

He grins wide enough that his dimples have surfaced and I can see the small space between his front teeth. "You know what my favorite episode is?"

"What?" I ask, more in a *what are you talking about* sort of way than it is an inquiry.

"I like the episode where the Ingalls go camping with the Olsons. When the kids are collecting leaves for their school project."

Of course, he already seems to know all about my favorite show.

Randall Persch, what a peculiar man.

10.

|RANDALL|

It's Tuesday and it's been three days since I've seen Liling last. Liling wants to test whether I actually know anything about her. I get that, on some levels. She's just testing whether I'm just a stupid guy after a pretty girl. I am, but my reasons are deeper than she thinks.

I'm starting with my pal in my macro class who told me about Liling in the first place. His name is Daniel but he goes by Dan. Dan is a big, bulky kind of guy. Football team big. He's got this cool hair that's sort of like a controlled Afro cut in a square shape on top of his head. Dan's a cool guy, and he's friendly enough when I start asking if he knows anything about Liling.

Dan has one of those really deep voices, like his body doesn't know he's only in his early twenties. He tells me that Liling is in another one of his business classes and tries to remember what she said during class introductions. "Let's see, her last name is Zhu." He's counting facts on his fingers. "Her hobbies are reading, and I think she said she goes to church or something like that."

I was taking notes. "Do you know how to spell her last name?"

Dan laughs. "Hey, man. You tryna be a player over there or some shit?"

I laugh too. "I don't know if I'd say that. I'm just stepping up my game."

▪▪▪

I really think the stars are trying to align themselves just to get me and Liling together. On the same day I start to learn a little bit more about Liling, I get the paper back that she wrote for me from my professor. A high B, just like she said it would be. Not a single claim of academic dishonesty.

I figured this was as good excuse as any to go see Liling. I have two hours between my class and going back to work. This time, I'm not showing up empty handed. As much as she rolls her eyes, I think Liling secretly likes the lengths I'm going through. She can tell me I'm not what she's looking for but I don't believe her for one second.

After paying my bills, I've got twenty dollars and a friendly attitude, and this is enough to get myself some cheap flowers at the florist shop on the edge of campus. They're not the freshest, hence the stark discount, but they're better than nothing. I got lilies. Lilies for Liling - it really works, doesn't it?

For an added bonus, I used the graded paper I got back and wrapped it around the base of the flowers with a rubber band. Maybe she'll think it's cute.

Since I have work to go to, I show up at Liling's dorm in my red uniform. My timing is perfect because, as I'm arriving, someone else is leaving. It's a girl who's putting a wallet back into her backpack. Liling sure is resourceful. Since someone just left, I let myself in, knowing the door is still unlocked and Liling is inside.

"Hi, Liling."

She knows my voice now. When she flips to look at me, she's maybe slightly displeased but she's not angry which is already progress. The first thing she does is note the flowers in my hands

46

and her shoulders sag a little, as if I'm really that tiring. "What are you doing here, Randall?"

I hold my arm out, the moisture from the flowers are starting to seep through the paper. "I wanted to say thank you for the paper, again. It's going to bring my grade up."

I'm very pleased that she doesn't argue about taking the flowers from me. She's noticed the wrapping and inspects it, taking the papers off and is now reading any notes the professor's written in red pen. I didn't even do that. When she's done, she puts the wet paper down and runs her thumb over the orange flower petals. I got orange and yellow lilies because they matched the color of her nails the last time I'd seen her.

"I told you there's no need to thank me," Liling said, looking at the flowers. Liling's got a great voice. It's really smooth and mature and I want her to say my name again with it.

"If I didn't come to thank you, then I couldn't see your face again."

She's stretching her jaw until the signs of a pinched smile is hiding on her face. She composes herself with a little exasperated breath and *she* takes a step closer to me. My heart starts to get excited by the prospect. "Randall, you're very sweet, but you really need to stop coming around. I'm not interested."

My heart speeds again for different reasons. I really thought I was getting somewhere and I don't like how genuine she sounds when she's telling me things I don't want to hear. "Well... you have to have a reason, don't you?"

Liling shakes her head, and she's holding the flowers lower. "No, I don't. If I tell you I'm not interested then frankly, you don't need to know any more than that. I don't have to explain myself to you. You're no one to me, Randall."

She doesn't know she's holding my heart, so she doesn't know how much it hurts when she clenches her fists. "But I'm trying to be someone to you, Liling."

"And I'm saying you need to stop trying," Liling says sharply. "No, Randall."

I'd like to think I'm an even-tempered person, and I'm generally calm. But like I said, I'm also a little hurt now, so I'm going to volley back some less than kind things. "What, like you've got so many other options with the way you act? I know I'm the only one who-"

"Let me stop you there." Liling has this coldness in her voice that just takes the sound from my mouth and replaces it with sand. Her eyes have gotten so hard and her face is so foreign to me all of the sudden.

Liling even goes as far as to take another step closer to me but it's almost like she just needs to make sure her hits land. "Randall, I need a very specific type of partner, when I decide that I want one. I need someone focused, I need a good Christian man, and I need someone I can bring to my parents without feeling ashamed." Her eyes look me over from my head to toe. "You are none of those things, Randall." She flings her arm back out with the flowers as if they're just the worst things she's ever seen.

My throat feels thick, and I'm looking at the carpet as I take the flowers back. "Gee, I didn't know I was so out of my league, I guess."

Liling sighs, but I still haven't looked back up at her. "I told you many times I'm not interested. We've only just met, and there's no reason for you to act as though you have a claim to me or my time."

I nod, bringing in my top lip. I really do feel like shit now, and I'd rather be at work cleaning cheese from the floors than enduring any more of this. "Ok, I hear you." I clutch the lilies awkwardly in my hands. "It was good seeing you, Liling." I don't sound all that convincing when I tell her this.

When I leave, I show myself out and I hear the door lock as soon as it's shut. By her door, leaning against the wall, I leave the flowers and a little index card I'd had in my pocket where I'd written a few things I learned about Liling Zhu.

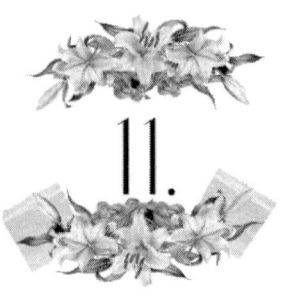

LILING

I'm fully aware that I'm not a nice person. I've never been especially warm. Telling myself this makes it easier to ignore my own feelings when I feel like I might be a bad person. It feels as though I've finally gotten rid of Randall. I crushed him. I'm fine with knowing that; I need to be.

Randall wears his heart on his sleeve, and I'll never forget his look of utter disappointment before he left my dorm for the last time, holding orange flowers he'd wasted his money on.

Randall Persch was not what I needed. I let him get away with more nonsense than I'd usually accept from anybody else simply because of his confidence and because he's easy to look at. Randall Persch clearly is motivated, and I'm sure he'll be a great boyfriend to someone who *wants* to be his girlfriend. There's no logical reason as to why he was ever fixated on me in the first place. The only thing we potentially have in common is a moral compass that doesn't always point in the direction that it should.

On Wednesday, I work in the library again and I pass off two written papers. I also collect another three hundred dollars for papers I'll start writing at some point in my shift. I like working at the library. Beyond the advantages of having computer access, it's quiet. I like the smell of old books and paper. I like to be surrounded by other people who are taking their academics seriously.

When I return from my shift, I ignore the fresh white lilies at my door waiting for me. I don't bring them inside, just in case he comes back.

By Friday, there has still been no resurgence of a red-haired man with dimples trying to convince me to give him my time. There are more flowers though, red roses. By the time the red roses are delivered, I bring all of the flowers inside before my neighbors get too curious as to what's going on.

With the lilies still inside, I now have a vase of white lilies and red roses. They look beautiful, the room smells floral, and now I think of the man I scorned every time I enter my room. I can't help but wonder if he knows what he's doing.

I work for three hours and call my sister around eight to check on her. Lishui is sweet and always eager to hear about college life. I play with the cord of the phone while Lishui tells me about her honors English course, even though I'm a little distracted. I almost want to tell her about Randall, if only the amusing story of his perseverance.

Ultimately, I decide not to divulge anything to suggest I'm not completely focused on school. Lishui will ask too many questions, which I won't really have answers for. Plus, the phones at the end of the dorm hallway aren't very private, there's always someone walking by. I don't need other people to know I have a boy coming in and out of my room on a frequent basis. I wonder how many people have seen him drop off flowers. I wonder who sees the flowers and assume he's a boyfriend asking for forgiveness.

By Sunday, things are back to normal. The only thing that's continued out of its rightful cycle are the flowers. He won't stop. I'm running out of space. Somewhere, there must be a florist running out of flowers. By Sunday morning, I've got four bouquets. If I'm able to catch him in the act, Randall is going to get another scolding.

Besides that, I'm working as normal, I'm writing papers as normal, and I'm going to church as normal. I've found my own church to go to while I'm at school. Once a month, I drive to my parent's church to worship with them but today I'll visit one on campus.

The church is close enough to walk to, and I love this building; it's beautiful. It's a behemoth of stone with Greek-style columns and stained-glass windows. Inside, there's checkered brown and tan marble floors where the windows throw rays of sparkling red, orange, and blue lines of light.

The melody of the organ permeates from the sanctum, leading me into a massive room with pews of seating and more magnificent colored windows. There's a center aisle that's flanked by rows of benches on both sides. I typically sit near the back on the far left.

Near the end of the row, I sit next to an elderly woman whose hands shake as she holds a hymnal. I arrive ten minutes before service starts and do some friendly congregating until the organ signals that it's time to start the service.

We've begun singing the first hymn after the pastor greets everyone and opens in prayer. This has always been one of my favorite hymns. It is called *In the Garden*. Together, the congregation sings, and I appreciatively take in the sound of collective singing, loving the sound of many voices all singing one loving tune.

I come to the garden alone
While the dew is still on the roses
And the voice I hear, falling on my ear
The Son of God discloses

It's always been a peaceful song to me. There's a comforting beauty found in its simplicity. There are songs about crucifixion and death but this one is about having someone who is always with you. This one is about someone who listens. This one is about peace.

And He walks with me
And He talks with me
And He tells me I am His own
And the joy we share as we tarry there
None other has ever known

I am keeping my head down, singing the hymn although I know most of the words by heart. In my peripheral vision, someone has come in late and claims the spot next to me on my left. I mind my own business, not looking at this person as they quickly grab a hymn from the shelf on the back of the pew. He uses the pamphlets that are passed out upon entrance to find the hymnal number and find his place, joining with everyone else. After some frantic flipping, there is one more voice praising with us.

He speaks and the sound of His Voice
Is so sweet the birds hush their singing
And the melody that He gave to me
Within my heart is ringing

The voice next to me is almost too familiar. It's a voice that's annoyingly in my head far too often. It's smooth, it's kind, it's a voice that is a promise in itself. I can't help but take a shy peek to my left, just as the smell of cinnamon bark meets my senses.

Randall Persch is standing next to me singing my favorite church hymn.

And He walks with me
And He talks with me
And He tells me I am His own
And the joy we share as we tarry there
None other has ever known

He's chosen to keep his eyes on the words but I can tell by the way his face lights in a smile that he knows I'm looking at him in stunned silence. If we weren't in a church, I might just go ahead and kill him.

I look down at my hymn so not to gawk too much, but I can't help myself. I have to look at him again. Something about how he looks now is as if I'm only really seeing him at this moment for the first time. In all honesty, he's too pretty.

He's still looking at his hymn, a soft smile as he smoothly sings. The rainbow lights of the stained windows are shining over him, a ray of blue light slicing through his hair. I am literally seeing him in a new light right now. He's wearing the blue sweater again with brown dress pants and a dark blue tie.

I stayed in the garden with Him
Though the night all around me is falling
But He bids me go, through the voice of woe
His voice to me is calling

I look back down at my hymnal and finish the song. It's a beautiful song, I am in a beautiful church, and I'm standing next to... I'm standing next to someone I should be kinder to.

And He walks with me
And He talks with me
And He tells me I am His own
And the joy we share as we tarry there
None other has ever known.

There's more praying after the next song and plates are passed down the pews for offering. I try to studiously ignore Randall because I'm supposed to be focusing on The Lord. To Randall's credit, he is, at least, being respectful. He even put a few crinkled bills in the offering plate as it passes him.

After the offering, another hymn is sung and I can hear Randall's charming rendition of *Bringing in the Sheaves* next to me. Randall continues to participate throughout the service. He sings the songs, he bows his head in prayer, and he sits attentively during the sermon. It is not until an hour and a half later, when service has concluded, that I finally let out a held-in breath of both annoyance and awe when I look him in the eye.

Before I'm even really able to scold him, a couple in front of us catches Randall's eye as they're leaving and they welcome him because they haven't seen him here before. Watching Randall, I know he is so different than myself. Randall is great with people. He's got a natural, friendly charm that it would seem everyone except myself gravitates toward.

When Randall is done talking and the other couple has moved on, he steps out of the row and smiles at me, as if proud of himself. He gestures for me to go ahead of him, and I'm fully ready to stomp out of the church and leave him behind. Just before I pass him, Randall snakes his arm into mine. I will not make a scene in here, so I let him, but my arm tenses from irritation that I hope he doesn't mistake for acceptance.

Randall walks me out of the church but leans in so he can talk into my ear. "I went over the list of things you said you want in a partner." Randall says, keeping his face light and friendly as he's nodding at people who greet us in passing. "I figure I can be at *least* two of the things on your list. Three, in time."

I keep my eyes focused on the sunlight that's coming from the open doors ahead of me. "One church service does not make you a Christian," I murmur, trying to keep this conversation to ourselves.

Randall chuckles. "No, but a lifetime of standing next to you in a church just might."

I can feel a blush surfacing, and if I could stop it by sheer will, I would.

"And I'm already focused," Randall continues. "So how about you tell me something else I can give you and I'll keep working on being someone your parents won't be ashamed of in the background?"

We're outside and I'm leading Randall off the sidewalk so we can stand under a cherry blossom tree that's starting to brown from the fall temperatures. "Randall Persch, you really are something, aren't you?" I ask him.

I haven't said it too kindly but he's still clearly happy just to be having this interaction. "I'm trying to be some*one*."

He's so earnest. His eyes are so kind. I almost want to apologize for how I chased him off last time he came to see me. I talk lightly, trying to keep myself sounding at least a little lady-like. "Perhaps I should have asked for something harder last time, you're clearly not giving up as easily as I'd hoped."

"I'd give you the stars if it'd make you smile when you look at me."

He really is ridiculous. I start walking past him because I can't keep the smile off my face and I'm possibly a little happy that he's chosen to follow me. "That was just too cheesy, Randall," I say over my shoulder because I know he's following me.

Because I didn't shoo him away the last time, he's taken my arm again and tells me, "A good, Christianly gentlemen would walk you back safely."

I decide I'll let him do that. I just won't let him know how much he's amused me or that I am actually very impressed he somehow worked out which church I go to and sat through the entire service. I look at the warm sun reflecting on his face and decide to pull my focus elsewhere. "You wear that sweater a lot," I note. It's a good sweater but there's some frayed threads in various spots.

Randall looks down at his own sweater, smiling at his chest. "It's the only good shirt I have. I just try to change through different pants and hope nobody notices."

"Hm," I say. "The tie is nice."

He looks at his tie too. "Stole it from my dad. He never wears it, anyway."

There are a lot of couples walking through campus, and I wonder if anyone has seen the two of us walking together and assumed we are just like them.

I'm surprised Randall has gone as far as he has without talking. It's only when my dorm building is back in view he slows down and lets go of my arm. His demeanor has changed slightly when he tells me, "And I'm sorry for being rude the other night. I'll admit I have a temper, and when I snap, I really snap. I won't talk to you like that again."

He says it like a promise. I'm looking into those blue eyes and see no deception. Just Randall Persch, exactly as he is.

The moment almost feels too intimate, and I need to lighten it. "What was it you said earlier?" I ask him, watching his face gratefully move from apologetic as he realizes I'm being the tiniest bit playful with him. "You said you'd give me the stars?"

Randall grins and puts his hands on his waist. "I give you the stars, and you give me a smile."

I start to laugh but then I quickly stop, because if that's the deal, then he hasn't earned another smile from me yet. I take a breath to make myself appear more serious. "Fine, Randall. Bring me the stars, and we'll see what we can do."

The light in Randall's eyes told me that stars was exactly what he was going to find for me.

12.

RANDALL

I was pretty sure Liling would be my future wife before, but now I'm sure of it. I'll admit, when she told me I was none of the things she wanted, she almost had me. I almost believed her. I felt pretty cheap there for a minute. But I think I can already read her well enough to know when she really means something. She didn't mean it when she told me I wasn't good enough for her. She *did* mean it when she said she wanted me to give her the stars.

I don't know how I'll do that yet, but I'll figure it out.

The only thing is, it could take some time to find a way to give Liling a galaxy. I don't want to stay away from Liling for as long as it takes me to figure that one out.

Gordy is in a sour mood because he's been dumped by his girlfriend. Gordy isn't good with women. He's too gruff and doesn't want to spend time or money on big gestures. I think Gordy will be single for most of his life, and if he does ever have a wife, it will only be a matter of time before it's prefaced with *ex*.

I work two days with Gordy the Grump. I'm tucking away every penny I earn, and I use my first break to plan my next move. I still don't have the stars mapped out. Gordy and I worked through our Wednesday night shift making very little money but at least we have a good time. I think Gordy and I could have fun doing just about anything together.

It's barely November, but it's already getting way too cold to walk around comfortably. My breath is coming out in clouds of white in front of me as Gordy and I argue about whether Janet Jackson is actually a good singer or if she's just hot. Gordy likes country music, so he's not convinced she's got any real talent.

We're walking toward where my dorm is, past the library. I'm listening to Gordy tell me about why someone named Garth Brooks is the actual definition of musical talent when I see her.

Liling Zhu. Soon to be Liling Persch.

She's not here, outside, she's inside. She's in the library. I can see her through the series of tiny square windows. It's dark outside, so even if she happened to look out the window, she probably wouldn't see us, but I can see her easily. She's stunning.

I grab Gordy's arm and force him to a stop. Gordy almost trips over me when I stop his movement and he's pretty pissed at me. "What the hell are you doing?"

"Gordy." I don't know why I'm whispering, as if she could hear me. I just know she'd hate that I'm getting to see her when she can't control exactly how I see her. I think Liling's got a thing with control.

Gordy is trying to see what I'm looking at because I haven't told him why I stopped us yet. "It's too cold for this," he grumbles.

"There, Gordy." I point because I know she can't see us. "Look in the library. You see her?" Liling has a big red sweater, and I could tell she was wearing dark red lipstick too. God, her hair is something to look at.

Gordy squints. I want him to see what I see. "The Asian girl?" I don't like that he doesn't seem impressed. Everyone should fall in love with Liling when they see her for the first time.

"Liling," I say, like it's a correction. "That's her."

Gordy scratches his chin, his breath forming puffs in front of his mouth. "It's hard to see if she's all that and a bag of chips from here."

"She's so many bags of chips, Gordy." Liling is the whole convenience store.

Gordy sighs, still squinting and watching. Liling is so beautiful, working diligently. She's got a cart of books in front of her and she's moving books onto it. I didn't know she worked at the library. Now that I do, I know where to find her when she's not in her dorm room.

I'm still ogling Liling from afar when Gordy says, "Stay here." And before I can grab his arm again, he's taking confident strides toward the library. Toward Liling.

"Gordy!" I'm whispering again because I think she *will* hear me if I yell.

"Or come, I don't care. I have to see this shit for myself." Gordy's walking away and I'm backing near a tree because I don't like how this is going. Gordy won't like Liling, I know. Liling will hate Gordy, I know that.

I'm not going in there with him. I want to see Liling more than anything but I'm almost afraid of what sort of wrath Gordy is going to pull out of Liling because sometimes he's just so terrible.

Gordy is now inside the library, a building I'm sure he's never been in before. He's at the front counter, and I realize that Gordy, like myself, is still in his fucking work uniform. The uniform Liling's seen me in before. She's going to know we work together and she's going to think I sent him and think I'm obsessed with her. I am obsessed with her, but in a young love sort of way, not a psychotic stalker sort of way.

Damnit, Gordy.

I'm watching Gordy and Liling talk inside. I wonder if Gordy at least pretended he had a reason to be in the library. He isn't even a student. He's not even a fucking student and he's inside the student library talking to Liling.

I can't really see either Liling or Gordy's face from this angle. They talk for what feels like too long. What is Gordy saying? Is he in there fucking everything up for me? Maybe I should go inside and intervene. I had to work very hard to get Liling to be friendly toward me even once. She expected the stars before, and after talking to Gordy, I might owe her the whole solar system.

When Gordy comes out, I turn my back and start walking so that if Liling looks out the window, maybe she won't see me. Maybe she won't see the person with the identical pizza uniform walking under a street light.

Gordy catches up to me, his shoulder bumping into mine as he tucks his hands into his jacket. I'm keeping my head down. "She's hot, I'll give you that," Gordy tells me. "Really fucking hot."

"Gordy," I warn. I want him to appreciate Liling, not covet her. He should be more respectful when he talks about my future wife. "What did you say?" I ask him. The sidewalk is wet from a rain and I worry that it's going to freeze overnight and be a shit show in the morning when I'm trying to walk to class.

Gordy scratches his chin again. "I asked if she had a book. She said it's a library, there are a lot of books. I say it's called The Giving Tree."

I groan. "The Giving Tree? Gordy, it's a university academic library."

Gordy keeps going. "You know what she asks me?"

We're almost back to my dorm, and I don't know if Gordy's earned an invitation to hang out inside. "What?"

He thinks this next part is just too funny. "She asks if Randall sent me."

I'll kill him. I hang my head back and rake my hands through my hair. "Gordy, you're such a dumbass, you know that?"

"I told her no." Gordy's voice is raised in amusement, as if any of this is funny. "Not that she believed me."

"Gordy, I was just starting to get her to not hate me."

"You want my official recommendation?" Gordy asks. We're at my building and he's stopping under the light of the door like he isn't planning on actually coming inside.

I'll humor him, but I'm still very annoyed. "Sure."

Gordy is quick and direct. "Cut her loose. Leave it."

I frown at him. "Gordy."

"Throw a rock, and the first girl it hits will probably be better than her."

"Gordy."

"Go into any lecture hall and yell the name 'Jennifer' and pick the first girl that puts her head up."

I sigh, my own hands are getting too cold to stay out here much longer. "What's wrong with her?"

Gordy puts his arms out as if trying to convey some sense to me. "She's *mean*, Randall. And I know from your own blabbering that she barely gives you the time of day, anyway."

"I'm working on it," I argue.

He rolls his eyes. "Randall, if I looked like you, I would be getting so much ass without even having to work half as hard as you're working right now."

I give him a sarcastic smile. "Gee, you think I'm pretty, Gordy?"

He snuffs a laugh. "Shut up, you know what I mean. I'm saying you shouldn't be working this hard to get your dick-"

"Some things are worth working for, Gordy." I start to open the door, the warm air coming out in blasts to beat out the cold. "Liling is one of those things."

63

13.

[RANDALL]

I made it about twenty minutes before I couldn't stand the thought of Liling wondering what the hell was wrong with me. I needed to do some damage control. As quickly as I can, I take a shower in the disgusting communal showers. When I shower, I think about how someday I'm going to have my own private shower that's clean and not used by hundreds of other people. The only people that will use the shower will be me and Liling. Maybe even at the same time, if I'm lucky.

When I'd gotten in, I had set out my good blue sweater and my jeans and a towel. When I got out, my towel was gone and my goddamn sweater was stolen. There are just some days where I can't have shit. My good sweater is gone - the one Liling said was a good sweater.

So, at this point, I'm wet and I'm shirtless as I walk back to my dorm and pick the second best shirt I have. It's a gray button up with a small coffee stain that can stay tucked under my jeans as long as I don't stretch.

I really liked that sweater. It was the only thing that didn't make me look like the white trash I'm trying not to be.

I'm not in the best mindset when I knock on Liling's door. I'm still mad about the damn sweater. The library is closed now so if

Liling isn't here, I'll have to put my hands up and admit that it isn't my night.

But Liling is here, and she's changed into her night clothes, and it's enough to make me forget the clothes I'm not wearing and think about the clothes that Liling's not wearing.

The lights in her room are off, except for a study lamp at her desk. She's squinting when she opens the door since the hallway lights are probably searing her eyes. She doesn't sound too happy to see me. "Randall, what-"

"My friend's an idiot," I blurt out.

She sighs and steps aside so I can come in. I think Liling is a private person. When the door shuts behind me, we're shrouded in the soft light of Liling's study lamp. There's an open book and a red typewriter on the desk.

Liling stands against the clean bed that must be hers. The other one looks like it hasn't been used in a while. "He asked for a children's book. Does he even go here?" She crosses her arms and holds herself tightly. She wasn't wearing a bra, I realized to my own excitement.

"No," I confess.

"So, you sent him in?"

I spread out my hand, like I was calming a wild horse. "I did not do that," I tell her. "We were walking by the library and... I saw you. I didn't know you worked there."

She narrows her eyes at me. I've never seen her barefaced, without any makeup. She really is stunning. Liling Persch. I just can't wait for it. "And you see me through the windows and what?"

This story is actually starting to embarrass me. "I pointed you out and... I might've mentioned you to Gordy before. He wanted to see you."

Her eyes are so intense. They're cold, but they're looking at me and that's all I need. Instead of ripping my story apart any more, she takes a look at what I'm wearing and I instantly know what she's thinking. "No sweater?" She asks. Her eyes flick to my stomach. "Your shirt is stained."

My whole body sags until I've fallen onto her roommate's bed. "Somebody stole my sweater while I was in the shower." I'm looking at the ceiling and there's a brown water stain.

I hear the springs strain as Liling sits on her own bed. "Somebody *stole* your sweater?" She almost sounds like she thinks it's funny.

I lift my head to look at her. She definitely thinks it's funny, but it's not. It was the only good shirt I had. "Stolen- in broad shower light."

Liling pinches her lips.

"It's not funny." I put my head back down.

Then, I hear one of the most beautiful little sounds. Liling is laughing, a tiny controlled laugh, but it's joy from the garden of Liling.

I feel better already. "You know what's even worse?" I ask.

Liling giggles. *Giggles*, and says, "What?"

I sit up, leaning forward so that I'm resting my hands on my knees. "It wasn't even *that* nice of a sweater. You've seen it."

"Mmhm." Liling seems to be leaning forward too.

"The worst part is that, since it's not even that great of a sweater, I feel like someone took it just to be mean. Just to ruin my day. And you know what? It worked. My day is ruined. My *one* good shirt. Gone."

Liling bursts out laughing. She has a very light, girly laugh that doesn't match her controlled, smooth voice. She's so damn pretty when she's happy.

I'm trying not to laugh because I decided I was in a bad mood, but I want to experience what it's like to be happy at the same time Liling is. "And I think it's your fault," I tell her happily.

She straightens, but is still smiling. "How is it my fault?"

"Because I had to shower to make sure Gordy didn't freak you out and I needed to make sure you don't think I'm anything like him."

"He's just your coworker." Liling's voice is like a purr.

I hang my head. "He's my best friend."

This amuses her too. "But you're not anything like him, hm?"

I don't know what it is, but I could almost swear she's flirting with me. Maybe she isn't, and it's just me that's about to start the flirting but I say, "I'm a little more of a romantic."

She rolls her eyes, but she still seems amused, so I'm now at the edge of the bed opposite hers. "Gordy doesn't have a girlfriend," I continue.

She lifts a brow. "Neither do you."

She's funny, but I'm going to get off this bed now. I'm off the bed and on the floor directly in front of her. This instantly changes the room, changes Liling, and she's not smiling anymore. I'm on my knees in front of her, looking up at her. I bring my arms to rest on her knees, and she's so, so tense. "I'm working on the stars, still."

It's hard to see, but I know her face would be flushing if there was enough light to see it. Mine sure as hell is. Liling is looking down at me, her hair is shrouding her face a little bit with her neck bent down. "Randall." Her voice is a warning, but it's still soft.

Instead of backing off so soon, I'm pushing the edge of her white t-shirt up just a little. Not much, but enough to see just a little more her fantastic legs that are gleaming in the light of the lamp. "Randall," she warns me again.

I have to do it. I have to touch her in some other way. I have a hand on each leg. Without breaking eye contact, I very carefully lean forward, and place the smallest of kisses on her left thigh. She's so still. I kiss the same spot on her right leg. They're smooth.

Liling looks at the door, and I look too. When nothing happens, I move the shirt up further. "Randall." Another kiss on her left leg, higher this time. She lets out a sharp enough breath that I meet her eyes again to see if I went too far.

She's looking at me with those brown eyes and I can't read them. I really want her to say something. I want her to give me permission to keep going.

I straighten myself, still looking at her. I didn't even notice how fast my heart was beating until I try to talk to her. "Are you alright?" I ask her, making my voice as soft and smooth as the honey that coats her own voice.

Her breath is a little uneven when she looks at the wall. She says, "I don't know."

"Do you want me to leave?"

She's still looking at the wall, and I can see her throat bob. "I don't know." She hates that she told me that, I can tell.

Liling likes control. She wants to call the shots, so I'll let her. "Let me make you a deal." I have to hope she calls in my favor. I keep my voice down when I speak to her. "Ten seconds. Give me ten seconds and if you want me to leave, I'll go." I smile at her. "That doesn't mean you won't see me once I pull the stars down for you, but I'll leave you alone for the night, at least."

At this, she looks at me with a soft, placid smile and I'm very aware that I'm practically between her legs. I'm on my knees for her and I think it's the best place for me to be. She's almost too quiet when she says, "Ten seconds."

I won't waste a single second. Ten is not enough time for Liling, but I'm going to make it count. I'm done with her legs, I'm leaning up, still on my knees, but reaching for her lips before she rethinks the ten seconds thing. I was making it up as I went but now improvising has brought me to Liling, and she's everything I've ever wanted.

Ten seconds. Just ten seconds of me kissing her mouth gently while I'm still gripping her thighs. Ten seconds where my thumbs are digging into her legs while I can feel what Liling's tongue is like. Ten seconds, and I'm counting them out, and I'm still counting as we far surpass them.

We're still together, we're still breathlessly colliding our faces into each other, and every move I make feels like it could be my last because I'm worried I'll do something to scare her off. So many seconds go by, it's just me and her. When her legs part a little, I'm worming my way between them, on my knees because it brings me that much closer.

It's when I let one of my hands leave her thigh to move her hair back that her legs clench my waist that she abruptly pulls away. It's like even she's surprised that her body let itself be touched by mine.

We're both staring at each other now, and I'm still between Liling's legs. My hands fall back to her shirt, but I pull the fabric down a little, like I know this moment is over and she's about to revert back to the Liling that's going to pretend she isn't interested in me.

Her breathing steadies. "You should leave, Randall." She doesn't even seem angry.

I look up at her beautiful, soft face. I smile at her, giving her one last kiss to her thigh over the shirt this time. "That was more than ten seconds, Liling."

14.

LILING

Randall Persch. All night, I'm thinking about Randall Persch. I let him touch me. I let him kiss me. I nearly had my legs wrapped around him like we were... Randall Persch is a dangerous distraction.

The terrible thing is I want the distraction. I want Randall to come back. I want Randall to take a lot more than ten seconds or however much time I'd given him. I know Randall will gladly accept all the time I give him.

I probably shouldn't have let last night happen. It was improper. As I think about my shirt riding up, I'm pulling the crucifix out from behind my blouse and holding the necklace between my thumb and my index finger. I need to keep my focus, and I need to not degrade myself. Sex isn't supposed to come before marriage. Last night wasn't that... but I'm sure it's probably applicable to things I'm not to be doing with men that aren't my husband. Men that would never be my husband.

Alright, no more Randall. For now. Instead, there are other pressing mistakes I need to tend to. It's another man, and his name is Santosh. Santosh has purchased several papers from me before. I've made a lot of money from Santosh simply because he's too lazy to try. His parents are paying for his entire educational experience, and he knows he only needs a degree with his name on it in order to earn his parents' fortune.

Santosh speaks as if he owns the world, and I find him grating. I do not like the way he speaks to me. The way he speaks to me… it is very unlike how a certain someone else would ever speak to me.

Something about Santosh is persuasive in an aggressive way. He's clearly someone who knows how to talk himself into what he wants, and what he wanted was a shining paper for his class before he'd fully paid for it. I usually require money up front, before I spend any of my time on it. Then, he says he can pay me in full once I've done it. He points out that he's purchased several papers from me and attempts to remind me how much money he's already given me, as if I should be thankful.

Some of his points almost make sense, so I tell him, "Fine, pay me when you come pick up the paper." It's a long paper. It's a paper I would usually charge three fifty for just because it took me a lot of time to do it. When Santosh shows up, he tells me he deserves just one free paper because he's purchased so many and he'll purchase more. Just one, he says.

Of course, I tell him there's no way it's going to happen. No way. He has the audacity to be angry with me, as if he's owed this. His anger is startling. I'm not someone who scares easily, but when there's an angry man in your room while you're alone, and you're a young woman being yelled at by someone who's bigger than you, meaner than you, stronger than you, it changes how you think you might act.

I don't know if I really agreed to it or if I was just threatened into it. Either way, I feel small after the interaction. I'm angry at myself and angry at Santosh. I know he'll do this again. Now that I've let him get what he wants once, he's going to ask for it again. Men. They're all terrible.

There's no recourse I can take. I can't very well report this sort of behavior without exposing what I've been doing. Part of me likes the idea of taking him down with me out of spite, but Santosh is a person who would likely come out better than I. He has too much money to fail. A nice feeling, that must be.

I've made a mistake. It cost my time, my money, and also the chances of having a good day. I'm angrily putting books back in the library, pushing a cart around in front of me to tow the books throughout the library. It's only ten in the morning, and not many students have come in yet.

Not many students have entered, but of those who have, Randall is one of them.

Of course, Randall has found me first thing in the morning. I don't even smile when I see him approaching, entering the long row of books and I can tell he notices. He was probably expecting the same Liling he'd lured out last night. That's not what he's getting. Give a man the smallest of things and he'll ask for more.

When he's finally come up to me while I'm checking the tag on the book, he says, "Good morning, Liling." His voice indicates he's chosen to ignore that I don't seem pleased to see him.

"I'm working, Randall," I tell him as I stuff the book where it goes and go back to my cart, which Randall is blocking. I shoo him with my hands until he steps aside, his smile slowly leaving his face.

"I just wanted to come say hi," he tells me, falling in line with me as I walk further down the aisle.

I've decided I want him to leave. I'm in no mood to entertain a conversation right now. "Hi," I say through gritted teeth, not looking at him.

But Randall is not in a giving mood, it would seem. He's decided he's taking more and he quickly steps in close to me so he's in front of me and the bookshelf is behind me.

I can feel my cheeks heating as I make sure there's nobody around before I look back at him with the most venom I can possibly give to a man and let him live to survive. "Not. Here."

More amused, if anything, he runs his tongue over his lips. "Then where?"

"Randall." I'm hissing at him now.

Randall sighs, looking at me with displeasure. "What could I have done between last night and this morning? Are you alright? I guess I thought you were ok with-"

I take in a deep breath, so sharp that it stops Randall from talking because not even I have realized that I'm so frustrated that I could almost cry if I were weak enough to do that sort of thing. I only let his blue eyes touch mine for a second before I look up at the corner of the room. "Randall, can we not do this now? It's not about you, but I'm going to continue to be very rude to you if you stay."

Randall's voice is harsh when he speaks again. It has hardened into a shell that I hadn't heard his words fit into before. "If it's not about me, then who's it about?"

I've moved onto frustration because he hasn't left yet. Now, I look at him. He hasn't backed up an inch and we're still way too close to each other. We're still close when his right-hand rests on my hip and the other is gripping the shelf above my head. "What's going on, Liling?"

I want to tell him. I don't know why. It's like sharing this information means I'm not experiencing it alone, even though it's not a problem that anyone can fix. "It's this person that I wrote a paper for." I begin. I tell him all about Santosh, and how I've written him many papers over the last two years. I tell him that Santosh is an insufferable jerk who gets what he wants.

Randall's face is so, so serious. I haven't seen him with this sort of focused anger yet. When he asks, gently, why I let this

73

paper out the door when people have tried this before, I confessed that I had a bad feeling about him. I was a woman alone with an angry man and I acted like one.

Randall is so displeased that it's hard to tell who he's mad at, or why he's even angry in the first place. The whole time I speak, he's hyper focused, and our eyes don't break contact once unless I'm the one who chooses to look away. When I'm done speaking, he drives his tongue into his cheek before checking his watch and saying, "Are you alright?"

It's almost a confusing question. "I'm fine, I'm just mad at myself."

He shakes his head. "Don't be mad at yourself, you didn't do anything wrong. He looks around us again to verify the library is still little more than a ghost town. When our eyes lock onto each other's again, he tells me, "Don't do your business alone in your dorm anymore, Liling. It isn't safe."

At first, I think he's just being dramatic. "Randall,"

"I'm serious, Liling." His voice is so sharp when he's telling me what to do. I'm not sure how I feel about the tone. "No more of that. You do it here, or if you really insist on your dorm, then wait until I can be there. Let me know when you need me, and I'll make it work."

"I am not your responsibility," I snap. He must be out of his mind, making such assumptions.

Clearly frustrated, he shakes his head. "You're my *only* responsibility right now."

I roll my eyes at his dramatics, pushing him away from me so that I can go back to pushing my cart. Randall catches me before I'm able to fully slip around him. "Randall."

"Will you just listen to me for a minute, damnit!" I see his face shrink down when I raise my brows into my hairline as I wordlessly inquire who he thinks he's talking to.

I decide I don't like being told what to do. Not by him. I don't say anything as his blue eyes search mine for context clues. I'm already learning that the cruelest thing I can do to this man is not say anything to him at all. It drives him mad.

I don't say anything, but after another moment of searching, something clicks in Randall. Just like that, he's back, and he's got a stupid grin on his face. Checking his watch, he tells me he'll probably be late for class. "When's your last class over with today?"

How is he- he's so frustrating. I want to be angry, and I want him to recognize that I'm angry at him. We're still standing confusingly, inappropriately close in public and one of his hands is still on my jeans. There's buzzing in my face again. "I have back-to-back classes from noon to four in the afternoon. Then I'll be back here until the library closes."

Randall looks at me with a small, wondrous smile that almost makes me feel more important than it should. "You work really hard, don't you?" He doesn't know it, but I thrive on little compliments like that. When he sees the smallest of pinched grins escape my lips, he takes this as permission to quickly lean down and kiss my forehead.

I'm about to give him a warning snap when he laughs at my widened eyes and I feel the pressure of his fingers close around the belt loop of my jeans and he's using it to pull my body into his. I catch myself against his chest and now both his hands are keeping my waste fastened against his. "See you later, Liling." This time, when he kisses my head, I bow into it and let myself be just a little bit appreciative of Randall Persch.

75

RANDALL

Santosh Subramanian, count your fucking days.

I leave the library, only able to keep myself feeling calm until I walk out the door. I felt myself getting worked up with Liling, so I had to calm myself down because the last thing she needed to deal with was another angry man.

When I leave, I have every intention of going to my World Studies II course for all of about three minutes of walking before I decide I'm not letting this slide. Liling may have been able to let it go because she'd been pressured to, but I'm not. My goal in life, at this point, is making Liling happy, and Santosh is making that goal hard to obtain.

This is where my connections are going to really help me. I knew that, at some point, being generally nice to everyone I meet was going to pay off. I really am a nice guy, if you don't get on my bad side. People who are on my bad side know I have a temper. If anything, that's why Gordy and I get along. We have the same eagerly aggressive disposition waiting just under our fingernails.

I know two things about Santosh: his name, and his major. He's a chemistry major, whatever the hell that is, so my search will start in the sciences building. There's a coffee stand inside with a girl named Molly. She's pleasant, maybe a little boring, but she's always been sweet on me.

I ask Molly if she knows anyone by that name, which she doesn't. She sends me off with an invitation to come to her sorority party and a free cup of coffee. I only accept the coffee and let her know I have a girlfriend, basically.

My next stop is one of the student centers. There's one at the east entrance of the building, where a girl named Kavita works. Kavita is always a bit of a mess, with her dark hair in a frizzy ponytail and conjoined eyebrows and an oily face that's offset by being a genuinely nice person. She's also a little sweet on me, but who isn't? Other than Liling.

Kavita's wearing a faded Bruce Springsteen t-shirt and a name tag; she knows exactly who I'm talking about. It takes very little sweet talk to use one of the computers to find his student information. Kavita squints at a black screen with neon green words as she types in commands that'll launch a query for Santosh.

As she starts writing things on a pad of paper, she asks "What did you need this for, again? I'm not technically supposed to do this."

"I know." I smile at her appreciatively. "But I'm so grateful for your help, Kavita. I'm rushing his frat and I'm supposed to drop something off for him but I lost the address." A weak excuse, but when said with a smile and earnest tone, it's enough to get Kavita to hand me a piece of paper with an address on it.

I smile at her, extending my hand. "Thank you so much, Kavita."

Kavita smiles back, and her fingers touch mine just a little when she hands off the paper, but even before Liling, Kavita is a little too chaotic for me. I make a mental note that I should swing by sometime next week so she doesn't think I've only stopped to talk to her because I need something. If people feel valued, they'll be around to help you out when it counts.

Santosh doesn't live in the dorms. It sounds like he's got money, so I would expect that he moved off campus as soon as he finished his freshman year and was no longer required to stay in the dorms.

I don't have a car because it's expensive and there's not a good place to leave it parked on campus. Santosh lives too far from my normal bus route, so I walk to the pizza shop where Gordy's working. Gordy works as close as he can to full time and still not work enough to earn benefits.

Gordy lets me borrow his car from time to time as long as I bring it back in one piece and I fill up the tank. The pizza shop is slow because it's still early. "Where're you going?" Gordy hands me the keys before he gets a response.

"I'm going to talk to someone."

Gordy is leaning against the back counter and I'm leaning forward against the front counter by the cash register. "Give me more than that," he tells me.

I sigh and say, "He owes Liling money."

Gordy raises an eyebrow. "And you're going to go get it, Mr. Tough Guy?"

I'm a little less sure of myself. "I am."

"How're you going to do that?"

"It's not just that he didn't pay her, Gordy," I tell my friend. "It's… it's about how he made her feel and it's not ok."

Gordy's voice is serious. "He touch her or something?"

"I don't think so."

Gordy quickly fires back. "You need backup? Don't go just to get your ass beat."

Gordy really is my best friend, and I know he'd come with me if I asked. "I think I can handle it."

I think I worried Gordy, but he looks at me with a smug grin. "If he hurts one super-gelled hair on your pretty little head-"

I laugh, pushing myself off the counter. "I bet Santosh isn't used to being told no."

Gordy lifts his head at me, standing as the phone rings. "Go tell the bastard no, then," Gordy says before picking up the phone.

16.

RANDALL

Santosh lives in a pretty nice apartment. I look at it and almost feel inadequate because I don't know if I'll ever get to live somewhere like here. There's fresh, clean brown carpet on the floor of the hallway I'm walking down that's lined with pots of fake plants.

There's an elevator with gold trim and metallic doors I use to get myself to the sixth floor. Santosh's apartment is almost all the way down the hall once I'm upstairs, on the left. When he opens the door, it's clear he doesn't know who I am, but he's about to.

Santosh is a pretty nice-looking guy, with dark brown skin with an orange warmth and pompous black hair that's got even more gel in it than mine. Santosh is taller than me but I'm angrier, and that'll give me strength.

Santosh even answers the door like a jerk, looking at my clothes like I'm something small. Instead of a real greeting like a normal, decent person, he answers with, "I called maintenance yesterday. "

He leaves the door open for me to follow him. If he looks at me and sees *worker,* then fine. It's gotten me into his apartment with the door shut. I look around. It's a big apartment with an open floor plan. In the back corner on the left is a big living space with huge windows that overlooks the city of East Lansing. There's a long white couch over a zebra patterned rug and a pretty sizable tv and entertainment center.

The walls are decorated with abstract art that also feature animal prints and the floors are black marble that lead from the living area to the kitchen where Santosh is trying to lead me. There are towels on the floor in front of his dishwasher. "It started leaking everywhere when I tried to run it yesterday morning." Santosh slaps his leg impatiently. He's got a thin-cut beard like he thinks he runs Apple or something.

I go up to the dishwasher only because it gets me close to him. Once I'm standing next to him, I tell him, "You owe Liling money."

Santosh is immediately alarmed, throwing his brown eyes in my direction. "Wait- what? Who the hell are you?"

I'm not afraid to tell him my name. "Randall. Randall Persch." I extend my hand but he won't take it.

Santosh is forming a thought but all he can make out is, "You need to leave. Tell that bitch-"

I hit him so hard he smacks his head on the cabinets before he falls over.

There's a rage inside me now, filtering out of me and being directed at Santosh. "I'll leave once you give me what you owe Liling," I tell him. I bet Santosh has never even been in a real fight before.

Santosh's nose is already bleeding. He sits himself up, looking at me with wide eyes. "I'll call the police," he tells me.

I don't believe he will. I know what people like Santosh are like. "No, you won't, for two reasons. One, if I get arrested, I say why I'm here, and both you and Liling get expelled from school. I'm assuming that would get you in some real trouble, wouldn't it?" I look around his extravagant place. "And it might impact your career."

Santosh stands and wipes his sleeve. "My lawyers will have you begging for a deal."

I look directly at Santosh. "And when I make bail, I'll have *you* begging for a deal."

I let it sink in, his eyes finally looking at me as someone to reckon with. "You can't be serious. All of this for a paper?"

"All of this for Liling," I correct. "You owe her three hundred." Now that I see where he lives, three hundred is easy money for him. He didn't pay because he thought he could get away with it.

Santosh wants to be tough. He thinks he can leverage the situation how he pleases. "I don't see how-"

I'll help him see things clearly. He's still too close to me, so rushing at him and shoving him against the wall is all too easy. He falls against the gray walls and knocks into a large black frame. I throw the picture out of my way so I can haul him by his shirt and throw him onto his stomach. He gives some sort of weak grunt and isn't able to speak once I've thrown him on the floor again.

His back pocket bulges from a wallet. I have no problem taking it out for him and opening up the black leather wallet while keeping a foot on his back so he stays down. From the floor, Santosh yells, "Ok, man! I got it! This is ridiculous."

He's got one fifty in his wallet. I can't imagine carrying around that much. I had to save for weeks to pay Liling even once. "Where's the rest?" I ask him. "Guy like you definitely has a safe."

"If I give you the rest, will you get the hell out?"

I take my shoe off his back and he immediately jumps up. "Give me the rest and I'll get the hell out," I say with my usual charm.

Santosh isn't impressed by me. There's a bedroom with a large bed and a black rug over white marble floors. What's probably an authentic cheetah print throw is over the bed. Just as I thought, there's a safe in the corner of the room, hidden behind an end table with a snake plant on top.

I stand closely to Santosh as he takes a large stack of money and takes out another one fifty in clean, new bills. I'm thumbing through what he's given me when I say, "Fifty more and I'll leave."

Santosh's eyes are wide when he says, "I only owed her three hundred."

"Interest," I said. "You're late on your payment." I only vaguely know what interest is, but he hands me more money anyway.

He stands and shuts the safe without locking it. He's taller than me, and thinks he can use the height to his advantage when he tries his luck at Baby's First Punch.

Big mistake.

I grew up in the country when getting into fights is seen as part of growing up to be a man. I grew up with an older brother that would hand me my ass on a daily basis if I didn't learn to wrestle and throw someone larger than me to the ground.

I've got Santosh back on the floor so fast that he's dazed and helpless when I start kicking him in the ribs. He stole from Liling. A foot finds his rib cage and he grunts. He made Liling feel small. My shoes sinks into his pelvis. He made Liling feel unsafe. He's apologizing from the floor.

I'm out of breath, so I stop. "Go sit on your bed," I tell him. Santosh practically crawls to the comfort of any space that's away from me. The safe is still unlocked so I take hold of one of the cash rolls. There's thousands in here. There's rings, and watches, and this guy doesn't deserve any of it.

I'm not here to be greedy, I'm here for Liling. I take a single hundred-dollar bill from his stack at put the rest back. He's incurred an additional fee. As soon as I look at Santosh, he puts his hands up. He's going to bruise. "Will you please leave now?"

I think it's funny he's being nicer now. Using his manners. "Stay away from Liling from now on, you got it?"

He nods. "Don't worry about that, man."

"And if you do *anything* to hurt her in any way, I'll be back and I'll bring a friend." If I told Gordy about this guy, Gordy might want to beat him up just for the hell of it.

"I won't say anything," Santosh promises.

Satisfied, I look around the bedroom and see there's a walk-in closet with the door open. I can't help myself, because something's caught my eye. I'm in his closet now. Right by the door, balanced on a wooden hanger, is a dark blue sweater. It still has the tag on, and it's my size.

The fabric is so soft. I pull it off the hanger and pop my head out the door. "I'm taking this too."

He seems more annoyed than scared now. "Fine, you can take it. Just-"

"I'm leaving," I tell Santosh. I smile at him and nod. "Have a good day."

LILING

I've sat through hours of lectures, I've taken pages of notes, and I'm back to working in the evening hours. I'm tired today, but I remind myself that it means I've been working hard. My grades are high, my bills are paid, and I have a sneaking suspicion I'll have a visitor later today.

I went through my entire shift wondering if Randall would come back. I told him my schedule. He should know where to find me. When I've worked my entire shift without seeing anything from the red-haired wonder boy, I'm disappointed. I'm at a point where I'm done pretending I'm not just a little bit, or very, pleased when he comes around. He's charming, even if he's not forever. I can let myself be a little bit happier until I'm ready to move onto what I truly need in a long-term partner.

I'm working my thoughts through an assignment I have in one of my courses when I'm unlocking the door, only to find it wasn't locked in the first place. I don't know why my mind immediately goes to Randall, but he's not on the other side.

To my surprise, my frequently absent roommate is back, and the room is already in disarray. Britney is nice, but she's too bubbly. She's so unserious. When Britney sees me, her face is the picture of joy and she's hugging me as if I gave her any indication that I missed her too.

"Hey, Liling! How are you?" Britney has taken me into her arms and she smells like bubblegum and her boyfriend's cigarettes. Britney is a classic, girl-next-door, American beauty. She has long blonde hair she curls everyday, clear blue eyes, and the sort of body that most would aspire for. Britney Cole was *that* girl. As a bonus, she was almost too nice to really be sour with for her effortless beauty. She's not very smart, but she's kind, at least.

Britney informs me that she's only here to grab her fall wardrobe now that it's colder. She wants to know all about what I've been up to, what classes I'm in, and of course whether I'm still spending my time alone.

I want to tell her I'm not, not really. I want to tell her about Randall because it makes it sound like I'm not some poor anti-social woman who's alone because nobody likes them. I just don't know how to explain Randall. He's *not* my boyfriend, but he also isn't nobody.

The decision is made for me when someone knocks on the door and I flinch in a way that makes Britney's eyes light up and spring to the door before I can hiss at her.

Just as I thought, Randall is waiting, looking just as handsome as ever. He's got what looks like a brand-new sweater on with his normal brown slacks. His hair isn't as boyband as it normally is, but still gelled in curled strands around his face.

I can see Randall wasn't expecting anyone other than me to answer the door, but he's friendly when he smiles and says hi to her.

Britney, I'm sure, is beaming at him, and then I remember Britney and Randall both fit that mold of all-American beauty and I'm thinking about how these two together would make sense to a lot of people. They're both so perfect, clean looking. I dress in darker clothes of deep red and greens, and Britney is all about pink and purple pastels and she's practically the nineties version of a pinup girl with an updated color palette.

"I'm Britney." My roommate is extending a hand with light pink nails and putting her hand into Randall's.

I notice, with a great amount of satisfaction, Randall seems to look past Britney first, the comfort returning to his face when he sees me. It's only after he sees me does he tell her, "I'm Randall, it's nice to meet you." Before Britney responds, he nods in my direction and says, "I'm Liling's…"

We lock eyes, mine more of a warning. I know the word he would use if I'd let him, even though that's far from what we are. We've never been on a proper outing and he really just shows up on occasion to annoy me.

Randall picks up with, "We're friendly." My cheeks blush because it implies more than typical friendship.

Britney grins back at me as she lets Randall in. He crosses the room in confident strides until he's standing next to me. I don't distance myself because Britney is watching and I'd rather her think that Randall *is* friendly with me. I don't know that Randall is mine, but I know I don't want him to be anyone else's.

Britney crosses back to her bed, where a large blue duffel bag is stuffed with clothing. "I will be out of your hair in like thirty seconds."

I was going to say something to make it seem like we're not going to do anything that requires privacy but Randall starts chatting with her as she packs, and in a matter of minutes, they sound like friends. I don't understand how he does it.

By the time Britney is leaving, Randall is sitting on my bed like it's his, and when she catches my eye, she mouths *Oh my God* and fans herself dramatically before the door shuts.

I want to keep Britney away from Randall.

Now, we're alone. He's looking at me, and I'm… going to stand by my desk because if I can smell his cologne then I'm too close to him.

"I had to work," Randall says, as if he knew I'd been expecting him sooner.

I nod at him. "So did I."

Randall turns on the bed, moving my pillow so he can move back on the bed without sitting on it. Then, he pats the bed in front of him with what I can only describe as a goofy Randall Persch smile.

I eye the bed but sit on it across from him. Now, we're both sitting on the bed, legs crossed.

"How was your day?" He asks me.

"It was fine," I say, sounding colder than I'd wanted.

Randall starts to shift his weight and takes out an envelope that's been folded ungraciously in his pocket. "Here's what's going to happen," he prefaces with, making me narrow my eyes at him. "We're going to have a proper date. A date where we both agree ahead of time that it's a date: you're there, I'm there, and I get at least an hour with you. When you agree to go on a date with me, then I'll give you my present."

"Maybe I don't want your present."

His face falls in a way that's funny to me because he seems like he wasn't expecting me to argue. "Don't you want to know what it is?"

I shrug. "I want to know whether it's worth an hour with you."

His grin is back. "Oh, we'll need more than an hour."

I give him a sour look of mock-disappointment.

He stares at me. "Fine." He awkwardly bends his leg so that he can take a half-crawl, half-hop until he's sitting next to me and our arms are touching. He hands me the envelope just as I remember what I let him do the last time he was in my room.

88

When I take the envelope, it's hard to read his face. It's like he doesn't know what to make of the situation, even though he initially labeled this as a present. I run my fingers along the flap of the envelope to open it. I look inside the bent envelope and blanch. There's three hundred dollars in cash and I instantly know what this is. He went and somehow got Santosh to pay me. He found a complete stranger and got what I wanted, what I'd earned. I had a problem, and Randall fixed it without being asked.

"How did you get this?" My voice is low, my eyes on the bills.

"I asked him nicely."

My eyes dart to his because somehow I know that isn't what happened. "How did you find him?"

Randall smirks. "I have friends."

I stare at him. "Tell me what you did."

Now, his blue eyes are hesitant. "Liling-"

When he shifts his weight, my gaze travels down his arms, down to his wrist, and onto his hand where there is the smallest of purple bruises on the tip of his knuckles. "Tell me what you did."

He sighs; he really does not just want to say what he's done. "Liling-"

"Get out," I tell him. His lips start to form a protest but I say to him, "Tell me or get out."

Randall nearly blurts it out, as if compelled by something other than his own will. "I hit him."

I study him and I can tell he hates it. "Did he hit you back?"

He flinches, confused. Cautiously, he says, "He didn't get the chance."

"Are you alright?"

"I'm… I'm fine, Liling."

His blue eyes. They're honest, even when they're scared. Randall does not lie to me, ever.

He's waiting for me to pass my judgement. He's waiting for me to either give him permission to stay or tell him to get out again. If I wanted him to, I know he'd leave.

"Why did you do it?" I ask him. "Why would you do this for me?"

His look is between something incredulous and something amused. "Honestly, Liling. I did it for you so that you'd start to like me a little more. You know that."

A heavy silence follows. Vents in the wall click and rattle as they start to churn warmth into the room. "Hm," I say, looking at my white comforter. "Start?"

Randall contemplates this for all of half a second before something in his brain snaps and he thinks he's been given some sort of cue. He leans forward so fast, and again, he's kissing me. Again, I'm letting him.

I love the smell of this man. That's one of the things I'm thinking about: cinnamon bark and Irish Spring soap. Randall smells clean. He smells differently when he comes right after work, but it's a spring smell that's fresh and calming and now the smell is mixing with my own.

I let my hand steady his face against mine so gently that I'm barely touching him. This is some other sort of cue to Randall and he's leveraging the awkward lean he's already taking until he's leaning in closer. He uses his position to start pushing and I'm on my back. I'm on my back, on my bed, and there's a man balanced over me. His leg is between mine.

I don't think our lips have come apart for at least a solid minute and I'm not even sure when I've found time to breathe between Randall shoving his tongue down my throat and behind my teeth. His hand is grazing the very top my sternum as if he's nervous to go lower.

And I'm letting him do all of this.

I'm engaging with it.

I'm using my hands to finally run through his hair and feeling his new sweater, which is incredibly soft. It's only when I realize my hand has been on its own adventure for far too long that I retract it and push against Randall's chests, my fingers sinking into the blue fabric.

Randall stops, but he's still hovering over me and we're breathing in each other's air. "Are you ok?"

I nodded with a stiff breath, but I say, "We should stop."

Randall uses his arms to raise himself so his face is a little further from mine, but he doesn't seem like he's too content to stop. Trying to keep his eyes on mine, he slowly lowers again, his lips hover over my neck until they pluck at my skin, a sensitive prick shooting through my neck when the pluck is more of a bite. "Good or bad?" He asks into my neck.

I'm so overwhelmed by it all. We're not supposed to be doing this. This is not what good, respectful girls do.

Impatiently, Randall is nipping my neck again. "Good or bad, Liling?" He bites again and my ankles are curling into his.

I don't know what it is. "Good." My voice is a breathy whisper, likely the voice of sin. My nails play over his back, smoothing down his shirt.

Randall's lips drag down my neck until it's replaced with his tongue. "Good or bad?"

Licking is too much. My neck is wet and I don't like the idea that I'm letting Randall Persch lick sweat off of my neck. "Bad."

His chuckle vibrates over my skin. He doesn't lick my neck again. Instead, he bends his neck, and his nose finds a way into the top of my shirt, and somehow without unbuttoning my shirt, he's found a way for his lips to meet the very top of my chest, just before the most intimate parts of me begin. "Good or bad." His lips brush my skin, his voice muffled.

91

As soon as I feel a hand at the top button of my shirt, I'm shutting this down. "We really need to stop, Randall," I say it with more conviction than I had last time.

He's disappointed. He's sitting up, but he's not off of me yet. He's sitting over my hips now, and I'd say I'm more pinned. His face is red at the mouth from my lipstick but he's looking down at me with a cat-like hunger. "We should stop so we can save it for our real date." He swipes at his lips with his wrist.

He's too funny, sometimes. I catch my breath, the heat leaving my face. "You think you're getting a date?"

Randall feigns outrage. "I'm demanding one." He squeezes his legs so his knees press into my pelvis.

I lift my brow at him. He's too pretty, even when looking down at me like he is.

"I'll beg for one," he corrects. He launches himself downward until my neck is wet from his kisses and it's made me unbearably ticklish and I'm gasping for air between laughs as he mercilessly pelts me with his lips and says "Liling, please." A small kiss. "Please go out with me." Another kiss. "I know I'm a loser, but please spend some more time with me."

He tries to switch sides but I catch his chin with my hands. "You're not a loser, Randall Persch."

RANDALL

Liling really feels like my girlfriend now. Sure, we haven't gone on an official date but I think she's mine now. As much as I want to stay at her dorm, Liling will shoo me out by the end of the night. I think she'd be mortified if her roommate came back and we were snuggling together. I tried to promise Liling I would be on my best, most non-sexual behavior but she said I'd compromised enough of her values for the night. I couldn't have upheld that promise, anyway.

Still, I'd gotten Liling to agree to an actual date with me.

I figure that, once I've completed a real date with her, *then* I can call her my girlfriend. She might not agree to the title, but she somehow feels like my girlfriend already. The date will solidify that.

I've got a plan for the stars slowly coming into play, but it'll take another week to get it ready, so I can work out all the parts. Of course, I'll make sure I see Liling before then so she doesn't think I lost interest in her. I'll never lose interest in her.

Before the stars, I'm going to make sure Liling has reason to think about me at least once a day. I last saw Liling on a Thursday, and after briefly having her pinned to the bed, I knew I'd made my mark for the night.

On Friday, I waited for her to be on her way to classes and walked with her. Liling corrected me and said I was walking next to her, since she can't control whether I do that or not. This is where I learned that fall is Liling's favorite season. It's also where I learned Liling has had enough with the flowers. I personally did not realize how many flowers I'd conned the florist out of until I'd seen them all in Liling's room.

Saturday, I'm spending in the library, sitting at a desk for two hours between a class and going to work. Liling is walking around, putting books on shelves, checking books behind a desk, and doing her best to ignore me when I try to make eye contact as she passes.

I spend the first hour of my library time at a solitary cedar desk and an incredibly uncomfortable blue plastic chair. I write three paragraphs that have been assigned from my World Studies course. During the second hour, I flag Liling down as she passes and threaten to make just enough of a scene that she stops to see what I want.

Through a breath meant to give her the strength to deal with me, Liling tells me, "I'm working." She's standing at the corner of the worktable, across from where I'm sitting. Liling is wearing a red sweater and jeans with a thick black belt. Her hair still reaches down her back in a big puff of midnight black locks.

There's not a lot of people in the library so I think I can get away with distracting Liling without getting her in any sort of trouble. "I'm a student that needs help."

"I think you're a stalker who needs to be escorted out of the building."

I grin at her, smirking at the way the jeans hold her waist. "Are you going to be the one to push me out?"

"Randall."

"Proofread this for me, then tell me one more thing about you and I'll leave you alone." Part of Liling's protests of when I show up and try to be intimate with her or insist that she put up with me at all is that I don't know her. She reminds me I'm some random man that imprinted on her like a lost duckling. Sure, I can see how it might appear like that, which is why I'm here now, adding one experience with her so she can't keep claiming we're random strangers.

Liling and I bicker for another minute or so and I love every minute of it. Love every time she says my name in the way she does, slightly exasperated. After two minutes of arguing, she finally sits across from me, nearly snatching my paper so she can read it. There's nothing special about it, it really is just a paper based on an economic event in Great Britain, but it gets Liling sitting across from me, leaning her head on her hands as she reads my words.

I don't even care if she thinks I'm an idiot, or how many times she uses a pencil to erase a word and tells me to respell it. It's me and Liling, and we're getting to know each other. I imagine a gauge, a meter of how much interaction we have to have before she stops pretending that I'm truly just someone that pesters her and she admits that we *do* have some sort of spark when we're together.

After she passes the paper back to me, I know she's likely brought my grade up just from keeping me from missing points from spelling errors and information that was just plain wrong.

Before she gets up, I quickly tell her, "Now wait a minute, I didn't get my Liling fun-fact."

Liling looks around, checking that there's no one at the desk waiting for her. "You're really a bother, you know that?"

"You can tell me now or you can tell me tonight when we go to the football game." I had wanted to show up and surprise her but this might be a better option. Maybe she won't shoot me down if she has time to wrap her head around it.

"We're not going to a football game," she tells me.

"Yes we are," I tell her. "You, me, and my friends."

She lifts an eyebrow. "All of this?" She gestures at me with a flip of her hand. "Just to get me to a football game?" Unimpressed, but amused.

"Don't get it confused," I start, packing away my pencils into a tattered backpack. "This isn't our date. It won't count."

Her eyebrows push up her hairline. "So you want to bring a stranger to sit with your friends at a football game?" Her tone is amusedly passing judgement.

I stand, black backpack slung over my left shoulder, paper stuffed into a thin red folder inside of it. "I'm just warning you that I'll be around later tonight, so we can walk down together. It'll be chilly, so be ready for that."

"And if I don't want to go?"

"That's fine," I tell her. "I figure we could either go to the game or, if you want, we can stay at your dorm and pick up where we left off." I give Liling the grin of a devil so she knows exactly what is on my mind. I don't think she's as much of a prude as she wants to pretend to be. I'll exploit the situation either way. "As always, it's completely your choice."

Liling stands now too, her eyes falling on someone that is making their way to the counter. "I'm not making any promises," she says in passing.

From Liling, that was acceptance. I watched her leave with a satisfied grin, knowing victory wasn't far. She's coming around to the Randall Persch charm mode. While neither of us will call it one, and there will be hundreds of other people present, Liling and I are going to have our first date tonight.

LILING

He really is impossible. Where do men get this confidence that they can do whatever they want? Perhaps it is from women like me, who are too eager to let them get away with what they want when it involves sweet words and a charming, dimpled, smile.

I have no doubts Randall would do as he said, and come to my dorm expecting me to accompany him to a football game. I have already learned that Randall generally will do as he says. He's clearly eager to prove that he's dependable. It's not that he hasn't shown that he is, it's just that I'm not sure if Randall is who I want to be depending on.

I'm not sure if I should, but I think I'm starting to want to.

I don't even put up much of an argument with him this time. It's as if there's a part of me that is worried he'd actually listen for once and drop the idea completely. This will not be a date. This will be… a prospective venture to see if dating Randall is actually viable. This is actually a good way for me to assess this possibility- it'll be public. It'll keep Randall and his hands where they ought to be, which is not on me.

Since the start of my college academia, I've only gone to one football game as a freshman and didn't care for it. It's loud, it's dirty, and I look at it as watching a bunch of young men wrestle themselves into a future of concussions and brain damage. Still, I find myself walking quickly to my dorm after work to give myself time to prepare.

I decide to change what I'm wearing, even though my outfit will likely be hidden under a coat. I change into a warm white turtleneck but keep the jeans and the black belt. I almost change my bra to match what I'm wearing under my jeans but stop myself. There's no reason to do that. *Absolutely no reason to do that, Liling.*

I freshen my makeup with another layer of foundation, more dark lipstick that's between a brown and a red, and expel flyaway hairs back to where they belong. I look at myself in the mirror selfishly, and thank God for being pretty.

When I answer the knock at my door and Randall sees me, the first thing he says is, "God, you're going to kill me looking like that." I notice that Randall is carrying two jackets he's not wearing.

"What are those?" I ask, instead of validating his original comment.

Randall, as usual, is pleased with himself. He slips past me to lay the jackets on the beds. There's two jackets, identical to each other. They're matching MSU Spartans jackets that are green and fuzzy with white leather sleeves. On the back is the Sparty logo and the year 1992 in large font.

He holds out the smaller of the two and hands it to me. "I've got a friend who works at the school store," he says as I inspect the jacket and appreciate the smell of new leather. These coats are clearly brand new, despite the printed year being one behind.

By the time I look up from the jacket, Randall had already put the other jacket on. "They found this box in the storeroom but

I guess they can't sell them anymore because it's whoever owns the Sparty logo only approved it to be sold last year. They're supposed to be destroyed but," he zips up the jacket. "They're good coats!"

I run my fingers down the fuzzed jacket, stopping where white stitches hold the sleeves to the bodice. It's a nice gift. Accepting it would mean something to him. It'd mean something to both of us.

"Come on, Liling," Randall's voice is a lover's taunt. "We'll be so cute." He grins at me. "Don't you want to match your boyfriend?"

I tilt my head, knowing there's a smile that I can't hide because his ridiculous antics are wearing down the parts of me that always kept me guarded against the world is starting to break away. "Don't you think it'd be odd to call you my boyfriend when I hardly know you?"

Randall crosses his arms, looking like an advertisement for Spartan Outfitters when he says, "Yes, Liling it is *very* odd that I've only seen my girlfriend a handful of times. It's embarrassing, almost." He looks at the jacket he'd handed me expectantly.

Slowly, knowing the ways his eyes follow me and linger, I put the jacket over my shoulder, and weave my arms into the leather sleeves. "Don't get too excited," I tell him, enjoying the way the sleeves go past my wrist so only the tips of my fingers peek out. "This doesn't mean anything." It also doesn't mean anything that I'm hoping Randall might *not* be on his best behavior tonight.

Randall's face is charm and mischief when he takes four steps across the small room until he's standing in front of me, and his fingers trace up my torso as he zips the jacket for me. His eyes are lowered onto his work. "It means everything."

100

I let Randall take my arm as he led me out of the dorms and we started our walk toward the stadium. The only reason I wouldn't let him call this a date is because that meant he'd need to take me out again.

LILING

I walk arm in arm with Randall until we reach the football stadium. It's just as I remember it: an arena of drunk college students cheering and fornicating and drinking even more. It's almost too much, but Randall's arm seems to pinch my own even more as he weaves us through the crowds.

Randall looks content as we walk together, as if he thinks he's winning, or that he's exactly where he wants to be. I've known this person for a few weeks. He's been endlessly persistent and patient.

He's eager to chat while the stroll is still quiet, before we've reached the stadium and we're just walking on a paved path through arching trees of red and gold leaves. "You might like the fall, but I already miss summer," Randall tells me.

It's not that I thought Randall had the mind of a second grader, but I note how he remembered something I'd told him in passing. "What's so great about stifling heat and insects?"

"When we get back to the summertime, I'll show you," Randall says, his cheeks raised as his over confidence continues to astound me. "I'll take you up to Holland, and we'll go to the beach."

I thought about that little future - myself and Randall sitting in the sand as waves wash over our feet. I thought about how, if Randall seemed to be as fixated as he is on me now, he may absolutely adore me by the time summer came around.

I look at someone like Randall and have this silly, girlish feeling that I could make him part of my future if I wanted to. I almost shake the thought out of my head as soon as it's landed there. No, I have plans. There are predetermined things I want. I take a peek at Randall, looking at his hair that's not as gelled as it usually is so the red-brown tufts look softer.

Maybe I could change some of the things I'd determined about what my future looked like. Just as Randall told me, he was willing to try to be all the things I'd told him I wanted in a future partner. Perhaps I wasn't making Randall my future, but I was making Randall just a part of it. Not all of it.

I had this thought in the back of my head as we walked. Randall did most of the talking, telling me things that popped into his head and feeding off the small bits of information I'd given him as we strolled.

"So we're sitting with some of my friends," Randall begins explaining to me as the stadium came into view.

I'm hesitant in asking, "Do they know you've kidnapped me and are bringing me to watch a football game?"

His grin is positively devilish when he looks down at me. "Oh, they know about you." The crowds have gotten fuller, people walking toward the blaring party music of the stadium in droves.

Now, I have to raise my voice over the volume. "And who do they think you're bringing?"

"My new girlfriend."

Randall's antics could perhaps be amusing on their own but were less so when he was actively telling other people that we

103

are together. "I'm going to make sure everyone knows you're a liar."

Randall's laugh huffs in a white cloud in front of his face. "They know you're playing hard to get," Randall tells me as he eyes our interlocked arms. "But I'm not sure your claim will be believable when we show up holding onto each other in matching coats."

I, of course, try to pull my arm free because he was right about this but Randall's arm stubbornly locks over mine. "Randall," I warn.

"Keep saying my name," he says with encouraging tone. "I love to hear it."

"I think you need to focus on listening."

He responds by creating an even more snug grip on me. "I'll listen to anything you say." He lets my arm drop and I note how cold it actually is out here.
■■■

Randall's hand finds itself on my back as he leads us to our seats and introduces me to his friends. I've never been overly fond of introductions, but they're important to me. It's a moment of judgement, where people are deciding whether they like me, if they think I'm smart, pretty, clean, important. I hesitate to think of what Randall's already said about me, and if there's high expectations to rise to.

Today, I'll meet just a handful of Randall's friends, although he seems like the type of person who has a lot of friends in a lot of different circles. First is someone I'd already met days ago. His name is Gordon and I'd quickly decided I did not care for him. Gordon uses poor language, looks generally soiled, and smells like cigarettes. He also seems to be Randall's best friend. Gordy is a short man with a hooked nose, his brown hair kept in a buzz-cut close to his scalp.

The other two people that have come are women. The first seems friendly enough, although she is definitely attached at the hip to the other woman, and I know I'm not likely to find a close friendship in them. The first woman's name is Ginger and she has light skin with brown hair that's folded into two short braids that rest under her ears. She's wearing a light green windbreaker that won't do much to protect her from the wind that keeps ripping through the stadium.

The second woman I instantly do not like. I don't like how her smile seems fake, her words misleading, and how her eyes never seem to leave Randall. Her name is Natalia.

Natalia has olive skin and dark hair. Instead of blowing her hair out like most women are doing these days, hers is kept sleek and straight. Her eyes are painted in purple and her lips are natural, as if she knows that she needs little makeup to catch anyone's attention. She wears a red vest with white sleeves coming from under it and oversized jeans.

During the game, I sit between Randall and Natalia, with Gordon on the end on Randall's other side and Ginger on the opposite end by Natalia. Randall is an absolute animal during the game. He seems to understand the sport. He's cheering, he's clapping, he's jumping, and I decide there's no reason that football should be the phenomenon it is.

As much as I have a distaste for my surroundings, I make a decision. I decide I am being judged by these new people and I want to keep my options open. Something about the woman next to me is driving me to be the best version of myself. I'll shine tonight. I'll be friendly. I'll talk to anyone who talks to me. I know that, when I want to be, I can make just about anyone think I find them special. By the end of the night, even Natalia will think we could be friends.

At half time, Randall and Gordon leave to get hotdogs for the group and Randall, feeling confident by the show I've been putting on and the people around that are keeping me on friendlier behavior, leaves with an unpermissioned kiss on my forehead. I give him a look of feigned exasperation but let him leave without a scolding.

The three of us women take our seats, and I'm keeping my hands under my arms to keep them warm. My thin white gloves aren't barring enough of the cold. Natalia's cheeks are red from the cold, but she still seems nearly perfect. I can tell she's getting ready to speak to me from the playful little smile that never leaves her lips and grows any time she talks to Randall.

"So, I hear you're giving Randall a hard time." Natalia has a higher voice, a little nasally and brassy. "Good job."

I smile back at her because I am being Liling the Jewel right now. I remind myself I'm who she wants to be. I'm pretty, I'm smart, I hold the eyes of the person who holds her own. "I wouldn't want to make things too easy for him."

Ginger bends forward so she can see around Natalia. "Randall's a great guy, he really is." Ginger has a very young sounding voice with a heavy midwestern accent.

After some more time, I think Ginger is fine. She seems harmless enough, even when attached to the other one. "He's been trying his hardest to convince me of that."

Natalia speaks as though she's joking, but something about how she says it doesn't quite land with me. "He's gorgeous, he's funny, he's nice, why would anyone *not* be interested in him?"

If I were not in Liling the Jewel mode, I might be bold enough to ask whether she's ever been interested in Randall, or if she maybe still is. "You really can't say that around him. Give any man too much confidence and they become dangerous."

Natalia and Ginger laugh at this, with Ginger agreeing, "I think I like you."

Natalia's comment seems much less genuine. "I think we'll all become good friends, if you and Randall work out, that is."

I smile at her but I'd decided definitively that I dislike her and am glad to be what sits in the way of her view of Randall. When Randall and Gordy come back with the food, I'm even more friendly with Randall and I can tell by his silly little face that he's all too happy with me.

Admittedly, I end up enjoying my time spent next to Randall and feeling the warmth of his breath on my ears as he talks with me throughout the game. I let him keep his arm over my shoulder, and I let myself lean into it.

By the end of the game, I have a piece of paper with Natalia's phone number written on it and have been invited to go shopping with her and Ginger. I haven't decided if I'll go with them or not. I miss my little sister, maybe I should just do some shopping with her.

Randall walks me back to my dorm, arm in arm again. I can feel eyes on my back, wondering what Randall's friends will say about me now that I'm out of earshot.

"Did you have fun?" Randall asks me, jarring me from my inner thoughts.

I'm too tired to do too much playing with Randall, and give him an honest answer. "I did, but I'm freezing."

"We can warm up at your dorm."

I could easily let that face lead me astray. "I've got a blanket."

Randall laughs at this and says, "You could put a blanket on top of you or you could put me on top-"

"Definitely not," I cut him off with a stern tone.

He pretends to be serious, though he rarely wears a genuine frown. "Alright, fine. But you're going to miss me tonight." When Randall did leave, dropping me off at my door with little more than a peck on the forehead and suggestive look, I *almost* missed him.

LILING

      Randall showed up to church again. I like having someone to sit next to. I like the sound of Randall's voice when he sings, and I like the feeling of his arm resting against mine.

22.

RANDALL

I'm going to give her the stars tonight.

I've got it all planned out. I don't know what I was thinking when I was being Romeo, talking about the stars, but it made me get creative. When I say creative, I mean I had to come up with something stupid and hope Liling thinks I'm charming enough not to consider it lazy or stupid.

I really think she's coming around to me. She doesn't scowl when I show up, she doesn't put up as much of a fight when I try to get her to go anywhere with me, and she only corrects me 60% of the time when I call her my girlfriend.

It's taken four months to be ready to give her the stars. There's not really a good reason for that, especially since when what I've got planned is pretty lame. But, within those four months, we've done a lot of other things.

In October, I got her to go to a Halloween party. I'd tricked her into telling me her costume ahead of time so I could coordinate. She was Daphne and I was Fred. I ended up getting wasted and I woke up on the floor of Liling's dorm. I got an earful about how she had to walk me inebriated through the hall so she could make sure I didn't choke on my own vomit. Still, I remember her making out with me against a wall and I had the lipstick stains to prove it.

In November, we (but mostly me) challenged ourselves at finding a movie to go to every weekend. Our favorite of the November options was *Mrs. Doubtfire.* Liling doesn't know this, but I rented out an entire theater every week we went. Liling is a little more friendly in a private setting.

In December, we saw a Christmas parade, spent hours in the mall doing our Christmas shopping, and I was able to drag her to another party with my friends. I've got her *almost* speaking to Gordy with minimal respect.

Between all these little things we've done together, I find even smaller moments with Liling, and each one feels better than the last. I see her almost every day. I'm at the library, she's picking up a pizza, I'm stopping by her dorm. I show up each and every week to church with her and it's almost hypocritical the kind of mood it puts her in when I sit next to her for an hour in a chapel. It's honestly a joke that she refuses to admit we're dating. I think she just gets amusement out of it, if anything.

When I told her I was ready to give her the stars, I told her she'd have to meet me at my dorm tonight at nine. She raised her brow at me. She claims I'm at my worst behavior when I'm at my own dorm. She refers to it as 'The Pit' and has a problem with the cleanliness of said pit. I'll have it cleaned by tonight.

Liling has begrudgingly agreed to meet me at my dorm later tonight. I've made the necessary preparations to make sure my own dorm will be roommate-free for the night and I'll make sure I have everything in order by the time she gets there.

The other notable movement in my life is my side hustle, which has quickly turned into my main hustle. I'm selling coke like it's… well, like it's crack. Toby is getting sick of seeing my face so often. No one hustles like I do. I'm hitting the streets every day, and I'm putting away money like nobody's business. It's my business, I guess.

After selling everything I had in stock, I'm at Toby's apartment. He's got another ten pounds for me to sell, but not before he complains about every little problem in his life. Toby's current ailment is some woman he met during speed dating who hasn't called him back. I've watched him check to make sure his voicemail box is working three different times.

I do get some useful information, eventually. Toby's in charge of six other sellers, and I outsell them all. That's something to be proud of. Sure, it's coke, but no one moves coke like Randall Persch.

Sometimes, I even do a few extra things for Toby, and he'll slide me some extra cash. I'll deliver to other sellers, getting to know them in the process. It seems like no one actually likes Toby, he's just a vehicle to make some decent money.

On this day, I'm ready to get in and out, but I think Toby thinks of me as a good friend (because I'm so gosh darn friendly) and he's got me having a beer with him while he drawls about how, so far, 1994 is not off to a good start.

"Luis is coming tomorrow, so I have to make sure everything is in order."

Luis Padilla. That's Toby's boss. My boss. Luis *is* the cartel. I hear he rarely travels without an entourage and that he scares the shit out of Toby. Toby is a coward, so I'm not sure what that really means.

"Has anything ever not been in order when he shows up?" I ask Toby. I finished my drink half an hour ago and I'm ready to get going.

Toby's eyes are glassy, and he runs his hand through his greasy blonde mullet. "I messed up once. Got the shit beat out of me." He shows me his hand, with a long scar across the palm. "So I won't forget."

I flinch, looking at the old gorge in his hand. "Luis did that?"

"Luis? No. He watches his goons do it," Toby grumbles. "Always travels with his attack dogs that do whatever he says."

I want to ask what Toby did but I don't want to be here any longer and I don't care to know anymore. Whatever it was, Toby probably did something stupid.

It probably should make me feel bad, or feel a lurch of fear to think about, but it doesn't. There's different worlds, and Toby and I are in one where there's different rules. He knows the risks, and so do I. Toby is trying to get by. I'm trying to find a way on top of it all. Someday, I want to be Toby. Someday, I want to be Luis.

23.

RANDALL

I made it back to my dorm around seven in the evening. This was enough time to set up, just barely. Most of the time was spent speed cleaning and deodorizing. My definition of giving her the stars is taking a lot of liberties and relies heavily on her thinking I'm cute.

The lights will stay off the entire night. I'll call it ambience. I move everything against the walls, trying to give us as much floor space as possible. In the center of the room, I spread out a new blanket. It's red with white checkers and soft enough to get… comfortable. I'm trying not to get too excited thinking about the possibilities this blanket will bring me.

Some days, Liling will let me be all over her. Some days, she remembers she's a good Christian woman that's waiting for marriage and swats me away with one hand while holding the crucifix that hangs around her neck with the other. I haven't gotten Liling to go all the way, but we've definitely taken some pit stops.

The actual stars takes a while. I found these little plastic white stars that glow a pale green in the dark. They're meant for children's rooms but tonight it's meant for *love*. I also bought a red lava lamp simply because it looks cool and I'm trying to bring enough light that we can see some things without seeing the bad things, like everything I've stuffed under the beds.

Now that I'm no longer having money problems, I'm planning on treating the two of us to an assortment of food and snacks. It's a night under the stars, and we're going to have a picnic in January. I have a picnic basket packed with sandwiches from one of our favorite places on campus: chips, drinks, a pre-packaged strawberry cheesecake, and a giant cookie that's the size of my head.

I was able to stash some pine air fresheners around the dorm just before I needed to walk Liling down. I instructed her to wait at the end of the hallway so I could walk her down and we could enter the starry dorm room together.

When I meet Liling at the end of the hall, the sight of her makes me weak in the knees. Liling Persch. That's what I'm working toward. If this vision in a tan dress is my future, then I've got a great life ahead of me.

She's wearing this light brown dress that stretches so thinly over her body it's got me inspecting everything there is to see about Liling. The dress goes down to her ankles, keeping them close together as she walks toward me. Her hair is smoothly feathered over her shoulders and down her back. She's wearing dark lipstick as usual, and I hope to be wearing it later tonight too.

Liling Zhu is the most extraordinary woman out there.

"Hey there," I tell her, trying to pull her close but she's starting out with her Good Christian Woman schtick. Liling is hyper-obsessed with appearances, and getting her to do anything beyond modest hand-holding while in public is a hard sell for her.

"Don't even think about it," she says by way of greeting when her hips dodge my hands. I'll get a hold of them later.

"Are we starting off tonight with you pretending you don't like me?" I ask her.

115

We've fallen in line next to each other; I've at least got a grip on her hand as I lead her down to my dorm. "We're starting off with *you* acting like a gentleman for once."

I laugh at this, having no plans to keep up with this behavior. I stop her just in front of the door, pressing my back into it. "I think you should close your eyes." I don't want the lights of the dorm hallway to ruin the effect I have setup inside.

Liling's great at looking unimpressed when I suggest stupid things. "What're you going to do if I close my eyes?"

I grin at her. Too easy. "Trust me for once, will you?"

She's in a good mood, and I'll capitalize on that later. Once she closes her eyes, I take her by the hand and push my back to get the door open so I can lead her in. I wait until the door is fully shut behind her and she's standing on the blanket before I tell her she can open her eyes. "Ok, go ahead."

I know it's stupid, but I'm desperately hoping she at least thinks it's cute. I don't know why, but I really feel like I'm banking on these stupid plastic stars to change something with us. I made this silly promise months ago, and I'm trying my best to deliver.

When Liling opens her eyes and takes in the dark room, I can just barely make out her pinched grin, a little laugh coming out of her as she dips her head back to look at the ceiling. "Randall, what is this?"

I look up too. "The stars I promised." I've still got her soft hand in mine.

She's still looking up. "How did you get them up there?"

"I'll never tell." Jumping from the bed and slapping the ceiling several times over.

It's a little too dark in here, but I got a small red camping lantern from the store. I bend over to get it on so I can at least see

116

the wonder in her face a little bit. She's looking at the blanket with new interest. "Is this a picnic?"

"It is," I say happily, leading her down onto the floor. It's not the most comfortable, but it's dark and quiet and it's time alone with Liling.

When Liling is sitting, she makes a little grunt as she lifts her leg, pulling something out from under her. She holds a tiny piece of square candy in front of her face, squinting. "What is this?"

"Starburst," I explain. "You think I'd only get you one type of star?"

"Ridiculous," she gripes happily, unwrapping it.

We get the basket opened and eat our sandwiches and work on the snacks over the course of a few hours. We talk about our jobs, and our classes and everything in between. By the end of the night, we're laying side by side, hand in hand, looking up at little stars with the little green lights. A few have fallen over time, but I'm calling them shooting stars.

When it gets too quiet, and I'm getting too nervous that I haven't given her enough, I tell her, "Give me another thing."

She turns her head. We turned the lantern back off, so it's not easy to see her anymore. "I thought we were past that." Her voice is slow and sweet, like molasses.

Sometimes being bold with Liling is best. She has no trouble saying what's on her mind. Sometimes it's good she doesn't always try to spare my feelings. I, at least, know what she's thinking. "I thought you'd stop pretending you weren't my girlfriend by now. I figure there must be something I haven't done yet."

It's not so dark that I can't see the wicked smile play across her face. "I'm surprised you haven't lost interest in me yet."

117

A frown threatens to surface. I'm not sure if this was meant to be self-depreciating or if it was meant to be a joke at my own expense. "Have you lost interest in me yet?"

She studies me so seriously, I might just explode like the bad guys did in Indiana Jones when they saw the Ark of the Covenant. "Randall, I'm here, aren't I?"

I sigh. "I guess. But I want you to be here and be happy. I want you to be here and be my girlfriend."

"You really want the label, don't you?"

"Yes, Liling." I'm calm but there's an edge of frustration in my voice. I lift myself onto one arm, so now I'm looking down at her while she's laying flat on her back.

It's mostly quiet, except for the sound of the fabric of my pants sliding over the blanket. I would try to be light with it, but lately I had been worried that maybe Liling really wasn't going to ever let me be anything official to her. "If you want me to do something, Liling, I'll do it. Just let me know and I'll make it happen."

She turns on her side, propping her head up to face me. Her free hand has found the collar of my shirt. "It's nothing that you haven't done."

"Then, what is it?"

Her eyes are focused on my shirt, her lashes obscuring her gaze. "I really do like you, Randall. It's just…"

I already know what kind of things are important to Liling. What kind of things worries her, the things that keep her up at night. I lightheartedly say, "You don't want a boyfriend your parents will be ashamed of. "Her lashes lift so I could see her eyes. I continue, "Let's not think about them for a second. Think about me. Think about yourself."

Beautiful. She's so beautiful. "Alright. I'm thinking about you."

I take her hand from my shirt and lift it to my lips. "Do I make you happy?"

Liling doesn't struggle with being direct. She struggles with prioritizing herself over her own expectations. "Yes."

"You make me *very* happy. Since the day I first saw you."

"I still don't know what snapped in your little brain when I opened that door," she says with loving amusement. "Relentless."

I chuckle at that. "So, you're already keeping your schoolwork up, you're working, you're going to church, you're doing all of that for your parents."

"Some of them are for me." Her voice isn't that convincing.

I move her hand to my cheek, because I love the feeling of it. "Do something for yourself. If I make you happy, then let me make you happy. I promise we can figure out how I fit into your life, just tell me I can be in it."

It's rare that Liling initiates any of our physical encounters, but she shifts herself down to kiss me. She touches my face with her hand and says, "You're pretty when you're worried."

She's playing with me. I flop back down again and say, "You're pretty when you're cruel." She's got the laugh to match. "You're beautiful right now." Maybe I'd better drop the topic for now. The stars weren't enough, but Liling is in a lovely, cruel mood, and I'm going to see if I can get her to do lovely, cruel things.

It's like she knows how to read my eyes, even in the dark. "Randall Persch," she drawls in her voice of midnight honey.

I've shifted my weight toward her, and I'm kissing her as she's getting ready to use my name as a warning once more. When she doesn't warn me again, and her tongue is meeting mine, I sit myself up to lean over her fully. I don't have a plan for where I'm going with this, but think I do best when I'm improvising.

Another swift movement and I'm over her, and she's not even going to pretend not to be into me. She's raking her claws through my hair, she's scratching my back. I've got my hand though the arm hole of her dress and feeling everything there is to get my hands on. Maybe this is all she'll give me. Maybe I won't get a title, or all of Liling, but I think I can make do with these parts.

Liling is what I want.

I've slid my hand back out so that I can worm her dress up while she's wiggling around beneath me. The dress is up to her hips before she notices. Hearing my own name vibrate in my mouth is one of my favorite things. *Randall,* keep saying it.

She hasn't stopped me yet, and one hand has left my back and it's feeling my chest and stroking it in circular, affectionate motions. The dress is at her naval, and she isn't wearing tights.

I'm going to take advantage of that.

One of my hands drags to her waist, my fingers snap the very edge of her cotton underwear and she nearly jumps up but she can't quite manage it with me on top of her.

"Randall," she hisses.

I laugh, snapping the elastic again. "Liling," I shoot back at her. I've squirmed a few inches down her body. My mouth finds the peak of Mt. Liling, her hands find my head. This works with Liling often, distract her with small, more innocent actions to work towards the bigger ones.

I'm inching my way downward, kissing her sternum over the dress, hands scraping up her thighs. Her knees are on either side of me. She's starting to catch onto me when my lips are playing with the space just above her panties.

Liling lifts her head. "What are you doing down there?"

120

I don't say anything, but look at her in the dark, my fingers finding their way under the cotton. This is where I'm expecting her to remind me of the vows she's made to Jesus. I love the guy but I'm having a hard time convincing Liling it won't count as sinning if she ultimately marries me.

Before my fingers make any progress, she starts trying to right herself. I catch her legs with my hands, so that her bottom doesn't leave the carpet. "I'll make you a deal, Liling."

"You're *not* being a gentleman," she huffs. She's at least sat up so she's leaning back on her elbows, probably glaring at me.

I laugh over her panty line. "Ten seconds," I tell her. We play this game all the time.

"You're not getting those off," she promises me.

I kiss her over the material again. I can work my way around them, hands free. "Deal." If she was going to argue, she doesn't do it fast enough. My head is close enough to where it needs to be. Just as I told her, I keep her underwear on, but I dive between her legs, headfirst.

I honestly think Liling is so innocent with these things that she genuinely didn't have a clear idea of where my tongue was going to go, or what I was going to do with it. Some men won't do these sort of things, but some men don't understand how to take care of a woman. This is about her, and I don't think she's noticed I've only got one hand on her.

She squeals in surprise as we pass ten seconds and my tongue has fully worked its way around her underwear and is covering new grounds. Up and down, left and right, I'm learning all about my favorite woman.

"Randall." I come up for air for half a second and she's not looking at me, she's hanging her head back, slowly working herself back onto the blanket that's getting twisted under us.

121

I keep going. She's going to love me someday. I'm going to keep showing her love now. Up and down. Left to right. Right to left. In and out. She's breathing so hard, she's making so many noises, her legs are keeping my head right where I want it to be.

"Randall."

I hope she can feel my smile against her. I wish I could see the smile I know is playing on hers.

"Randall."

I'm going to spell my name with my tongue.

"Randall."

I'll spell her name too. Her hands are gripping tightly to my hair, and it's driving me wild. I'm showing her that, and I'm doing a good job with myself too so I have nothing but enthusiasm to offer her.

We're there now. I've got her. I've got myself. In and out. Right to left. Bottom to top, over and over. I draw her artwork of circles and triangles and whatever a trapezoid is. She's got it all, down here.

She only gets to the first letter of my name before she's half-hissing, half-purring, and it's sending me over onto the blanket but I'm going to keep going just a moment longer to make sure Liling gets every moment of ecstasy she deserves.

It's only when a final, long breath pants out of her and her legs relax on the floor that I pull myself out, resting my head on top of the underwear I guaranteed her would stay on.

She's breathing heavy still, her hands stroking my head like I'm her dog. She wraps her legs over my back, and I made sure to get myself back into my clothes so later she can tell herself she's still a good girl. Anything for Liling.

My eyes are dragging as my head rises and lowers with her breathing. "Did you like the stars?"

One hand continues to play with my hair, the other making lines behind my ear. "I think the stars are beautiful, Randall."

LILING

I woke up on the floor of a dorm, lying next to a sleeping man. My mother would be so ashamed of me. When I wake up to the low light filtering in through the window of Randall's room, I'm trying to figure out if I really did all of those things last night. Who was that woman?

The crucifix around my neck sits heavily on my chest. I pinch my eyes shut. Last night, Randall sat heavily on my chest. I need to believe it doesn't count. *No, it does not count. Our clothes were on. That couldn't get me pregnant. I'm still clean.* I'm looking at the stars again, looking like nothing more than cheap white plastic cutouts stuck to the ceiling in the morning light.

When I stretch my legs, feeling the stiffness that comes with sleeping on the floor, I swear I can still feel what he did to me. What I let him to do me. The other thing that troubles me is that I don't feel bad about it in the way I know I should.

I feel bad because I've been told that I'm supposed to. I should feel bad because it was sinful, and slutty. Randall isn't my husband, and that would not even have brought us good Christian babies. It was pure lust. It was desire. I should feel bad about acting that way. It was temptation luring my soul.

I don't feel bad, however, because I don't regret the act in itself. I don't regret letting Randall be close to me or sharing something like that together. I don't regret that Randall is sleeping next to me now.

Over the course of the night, he's moved himself up to lay next to me. At some point, he had an arm draped over me and at some point I had a leg draped over him. Now, when I look at him sleeping soundly next to me, I think about how nice it is to wake up next to Randall Persch.

His hair is peacefully tussled, losing some of its order from how many times my hands kneaded it and even more so from sleep. His brownish hair looks the most red when it meets the sun. Very gently, I stroke some of the hair off his brow. I could make this my hair if I wanted.

I look at him, he twitches once in his sleep so I gently start running my fingers along the downward incline of his nose bridge, and where it stopped at a rounded point. That could be mine, too. His dimples, his hands, his arms, all of them could be the body parts of Liling's boyfriend. All they needed was permission.

He's so handsome. He's so sweet. He's a hard worker. Now, it seems like I'm trying to convince myself that Randall *could* be my boyfriend, and why not? Randall's got a job, he's taking classes, and I do think after a few years in church with me, he could be a good, respectable man. With Randall, I'd never have the Chinese business tycoon or doctor my parents want, but maybe it's alright. I can get Randall most of the way there, in time.

I think about the loving words Randall tried to fill me with last night. I think about Randall telling me to think about myself. To be selfish. I look at his angelic sleeping face and know he's right.

I want to do something for myself. Maybe I'll never be like Lhasa, doing exactly everything right. Maybe I'll be my own person, and end up better for it. Maybe I need to start being the Liling that Randall wants me to be, because it's who I think I want to be.

It only takes another few moments of petting his hair until he wakes gently, his blue eyes knowing exactly where my own eyes are. His smile is all too sweet. "Morning."

"Good morning," I say softly.

Randall stretches, his arm pulls behind his head, his legs going straight out. "I've got to say, waking up next to you is the best way to wake up."

I'll drive just one kiss into his neck before asking, "Randall?"

I pull myself back because if I give him more than that then our chances of talking are over. Randall needs little encouragement to act like a man. "Yes, Gumdrop?"

"I-" He has caught me off guard. "Don't call me that."

"I love pet names." Playful, he's too playful.

"I don't."

He lay across from me just as I was, using his arm to support the weight of his head. "It's like I've got this cute name for you that only I can call you."

I'm looking at Randall in a way that I know conveys the same lust I'd felt for him last night. "Girlfriend," I tell him. "You can call me girlfriend and no one else can."

The grin on Randall's face breaks my heart and mends it all in one beat.

His smile is wide, exposing the small space between his front teeth, his blue eyes being pressed upon by his cheeks. "Yeah?"

I'll kiss the nose that's mine now. "Yes."

He's kissing celebrations into my neck, his hands on the most ticklish part of my midsection. "Girlfriend," he says into my neck.

"Mmhm," I say lovingly, patiently.

"Tonight, I'm taking my girlfriend out to dinner."

"Tonight, your girlfriend has to go home," I correct.

"Then, I'll see my girlfriend after that." He's trying to be sneaky in how he shifts his weight, as if I don't know he's preparing to climb.

I lift my arm over Randall's head so I can look at the small golden watch that sits on my wrist. I don't have much time to get back to my dorm to grab clothes and a shower. "I'm not going to start being late to things just because I have a boyfriend." I'm only being cute, because Randall's been something of a boyfriend long before today.

His red head pops up. "Gee, Liling. If I had known all it would take to call you my girlfriend was to eat you-"

"Randall," I hiss at him, dragging his head away with a palm on his forehead. I don't care for Randall's mouth, sometimes.

A rich laughter reverberates within him. "What do I get if I do it again?" He's too fast and I'm laughing too hard to do any good in throwing him off of me as my dress is riding up and he's trying best to work his way into my legs, which I've tightly closed.

"Randall, I need to leave!" There is no way he would be listening to me when my voice is a lover's giggle, a melody that Randall was intent on bringing out with his fingers and his tongue.

Then, the handle of the door starts jiggling and someone is walking in while Randall is busy trying to pry his legs between my knees. I let out the most frightened, mortified sound I've ever made as Randall snaps his head up and looks at the door.

A young man with his curled hair in short black twists and a tie-dye t-shirt walks in but immediately stops when he sees us on the floor. His face is lit in shocked amusement as he exclaims "Shoot, Randall, my bad. I didn't think you were still at it." He never fully entered the room, he's out in a millisecond but I'm already beyond mortified.

Randall is laughing, and I'm going to kill him.

"I'm leaving." I will never be more embarrassed than I am now. This is why I shouldn't be acting like this. I'm going to give myself a reputation. All my years of hard work could be undone in an instant and it'd be Randall holding the scissors.

Randall is squirming out of my way as I angrily pull myself off the floor and fix my dress. "Liling, it's ok."

"It's not ok, Randall," I snap, looking for my shoes. One of them had been pushed under Randall's bed.

Randall's looking too, but I don't want his help right now. "To be fair, I only told him I needed the room clear last night. Even I didn't think you-"

I gave him a murderous look and he stops talking. "It's bad enough I have to do a walk of shame without someone catching the pre-show. I'm going to get labeled as a slut."

"For what? This?" Randall asks. "Completely normal behavior. You're my girlfriend," Randall says in a lacy tone.

I'd found my other shoe and had it on in a heartbeat. "I wouldn't be too liberal with that word."

He laughs like I'm joking. "Ok, I'm sorry. Let me walk you back to your dorm."

"No."

"It won't look like a walk of shame if we're walking together." This is the only reason I let him accompany me back to my dorm. Randall lent me some athletic pants to pull over my dress so that it looked like I was wearing a body suit under them.

128

This made it a lot less apparent that I'm in last night's outfit, especially with the jacket Randall had gifted me in the fall.

Thanks to my bad behavior, I only have twenty minutes to shower and dress before I need to get my day started. Randall is waiting outside the bathroom for me to be finished like the creep he is. He takes one look at my scowl when I see him and says, "It's ok, Liling."

"Don't tell me what's ok." I'm carrying my old clothes in a neatly folded pile under my arms.

Randall's walking beside me with his hand in his pockets, moving closer to the wall to let someone pass. He gives them a nod, as he does, because Randall is always trying to make friends. When he sees I'm intent on not talking to him while I cool off, Randall tells me "If you're mad, just think about it-"

I look at him without turning my head. He has the look he gave me when he was about to say something either stupid or charming. "Think about what?"

"Someday, we're going to get married and I'm going to build you a big house. And we can have sex in every room of the house and nobody will walk in because I'm going to build it somewhere private." Randall wisely keeps his voice low as we walk down the hallway. We're nearing my door. "How does that sound?"

I sigh, knowing it takes too much energy to stay mad at Randall for long. Being mad at him is like being mad at a puppy that's chewed up your shoes. "As long as you build a house bigger than my sister's."

Randall grins at me, opening the door like he's a prince escorting a princess into his chamber. "Deal."

25.

RANDALL

I've done it. At long last, I got her. I got Liling. I'm not even ashamed to phrase it as wearing her down. It doesn't matter how many names she called me at first, now she calls me *boyfriend.* It's the best two syllables ever.

The term was off to a rocky start when my roommate walked in on me attempting to go down on Liling again, but she's over it now. She's forgiven me and forgiven my mouth. Liling the Girlfriend is a lot different than just Liling. Liling the Girlfriend is a lot more… loving. She trusts me, and that trust makes me horny as hell. On that note, Liling the Girlfriend is a lot less sparing of her physical affirmations of love. I can get her to do just about everything, just not all of it. She's weird like that, but she'll never hear me complain. Every inch of Liling is a blessed ray of light I'll happily bathe in.

The weirdly slow trajectory of our relationship is going to make it hard to pinpoint anniversaries. Is January really the first month when I was taking her out in September and feeling her up in August? I'm going to have to interrogate Liling on this.

Liling is every thought that goes into my head. She's driving all of the things I do, good and bad. The whole time we've been dating, I've been keeping this big secret from her. The drugs. Liling isn't an angel, but she's got this rigid sense of right and wrong. While I don't think her bible explicitly says anything about selling drugs, I think the stigma alone would scare her off. That, and it is very illegal. She'd drop me so fast if I got arrested.

Even though it's dangerous, the money is good. I almost got robbed the other night but I'm scrappier than I look, and I held my own in a fight. I haven't been putting a ton of hours at the pizza place. When I am there, the shift goes by slowly. It feels boring now. Sometimes, I'm sifting my hands though mozzarella cheese, and sometimes I'm thumbing through bags of cocaine and stacks of cash.

It's February first, and I'm already focused on what's happening thirteen days from now. I'm going to pull out all the stops for Liling. I had been bankrolling my cash beforehand, on the off-chance Liling hadn't let me use the b word yet. Now, I've got so much saved that I figure I might as well treat her nice.

At the same time, I'm saving for Valentine's Day, I'm also really close to being ready for an apartment. I make enough now for a monthly rent but I want enough to furnish the place. I need a place Liling will stay in. I think about how much friendlier she'll be when we have a little more privacy.

I really will get that woman a house someday. I'll fill it with all of her favorite things, and pray that I'm one of them.

▪▪

My plans to build Liling a big house someday are going to be ruined if Toby doesn't answer his damn door. I'm waiting outside the door of a seedy apartment complex, a big wad of cash stashed under my arm. Toby's been acting weird lately. The last couple times I went to go do some exchanges with him, he was even more bizarre than usual.

When Toby doesn't answer his door, I left and try to call him on the landline that's by the office. No answer. I know the property manager here; her name is Diana and she's sweet as a peach. She says I remind her of her son. Diana says she hasn't seen Toby in a while. This is weird to me, Toby's practically agoraphobic. He never leaves, with the exception of exactly one trip a week to buy groceries. That's it. He doesn't have friends, he doesn't have hobbies; he's just a drug-peddling shut-in.

By the time I give up, I'm pretty annoyed that it'll take me longer to see my next influx of cash. I can't touch what I've got in my pocket until it's paid back to me. It's sort of like the first rule- it's the Padilla's cash first. It's always theirs.

I'm going to bring Liling a pizza. Pretty soon, she'll probably get sick of pizza but until then, I'm going to keep my woman fed. Pizza in hand, I'm wearing the blue sweater I stole from Santosh and a new pair of black pants.

The only reason I knock on the door is that Liling always keeps it locked and I'm tired of looking dumb when I try it. Liling answers the door looking like a goddess, and she's going to get me on my knees for her before I'm even inside the room.

I'm preparing my dirtiest line just to get some color out of her cheeks when I notice the look of genuine fear on her face when she sees me at the door. The smile quickly fades as Liling holds up her pointer finger to her chest, keeping it close to her body. Her face is every warning she's ever tried to give me, pulled into one harrowing stare.

There's a woman's voice on the other side of the door. An older woman. "Liling, who is it?"

I instantly know there's only one woman who could strike so much fear in Liling. It's almost scary, seeing the change in Liling. She's like a supercomputer booting up, a rocket getting ready to launch.

132

Liling looks dazzling, like she always does. She's got on a long-sleeved orange sweater and white jeans. She's not wearing any lipstick, so her naturally pink lips would be taunting me if they weren't pinched into a practiced smile.

The look of terror has melted off her face by the time she's turned to speak to the woman sitting stiffly at Liling's study chair, opening the door as she does. "Oh, Mama, I forgot, I was supposed to work on my project today."

I'm staying glued to the hallway, not coming in without permission. Liling will annihilate me if I mess this up. I know she'll let me call myself her boyfriend but I'm not stupid enough to think it applies around Liling's family.

Liling is picture perfect, putting on her best performance. I bet anyone that's seen this smile before has fallen in love with her at first sight. "Mama, this is Randall. We're working on a school assignment together."

Liling might have to put herself into presentation mode, but I'm always on. If I'm confident in one thing, it's my ability to be liked. I take a small, respectful, step into the dorm and realize there's several people in here.

Liling is standing a respectful distance away from me. Her hands are folded in front of her and she's standing straight as an arrow. "Randall, this is my mother, Mary. Mama, this is Randall."

I nod respectfully, thankful I wore good clothes today and know that Liling is thanking God too. "It's nice to meet you, ma'am."

Mary Zhu is a short, severe looking woman, despite a polite little smile that dons her face. She has a harder face with a small nose, paper thin lips, and short black hair that doesn't go past her ears. She's a woman that looks quiet. Her voice is calm, polite, mannered. "Hello, Randall. It's nice to meet you." She's wearing a stiff-looking black dress with boxy sleeves and black

133

tights beneath it. She could either be going to a funeral or a stuffy church service.

The pizza feels really heavy in my hands suddenly, the warmth of the pizza is seeping through the box and making my palms clammy. There's still three more people in this room, and I'm going to make a good first impression on them all.

Somebody my parents won't be ashamed of.

Liling introduces her father next. His name is John and he has a small flat nose like Liling does. I can see his eyes in hers too. John seems a little more open, but still quiet. This is a quiet family. He also looks the most inquisitive.

Next is Lishui. She's younger than Liling and dresses like it. Wearing a lilac purple shirt with jeans, Lishui's hair has these little purple butterfly clips in her black hair and silver hoop earrings on each side of her face. Lishui's eyes are slightly wider than the rest of her family's, giving her a doe-eyed look of innocence. From what I've heard from Liling, this will be the most laid-back person in the family.

"Randall," Liling continues. I could hear the warmth in her voice when she says my name, even under pressure. "This is Lishui, my younger sister."

Again, I nod and tell her, "Hi, Lishui." I'm glad I've heard the name before so I can pronounce it correctly.

Lishui has a bright, genuine smile. She seems bubbly. "Hi, it's nice to meet you." She's the first one to say something beyond a stiff greeting so far. "Sorry you're stuck with my sister for an entire semester."

I catch the start of a scowl in Liling's eye but she's too focused on staying in her presentation mode. I smile with good nature and pleasantly respond with, "I'm guaranteed a good grade, working with her."

Lishui looks like she's going to say something but Liling is moving on to the last person in the room who I have not really looked at. The person that can only be the oldest of the girls, Lhasa.

"Lastly, this is my older sister, Lhasa," Liling tells me. From what Liling tells me, Lhasa is this impenetrable wall of perfection. She's everything their parents want, she's everything Liling can't be. This rigid, sterile, woman in front of me is part of the reason Liling is so hard on herself.

Looking at her, I don't get what's so special.

Lhasa speaks first. "Hello." She sounds like Liling, or how Liling used to sound when she spoke to me. Controlled, calculated. Lhasa is taller than Liling, slimmer without any notable curves to her and small shoulders. Lhasa's also gorgeous. Absolutely gorgeous. She looks so much like Liling but there's something about the placid, still way she looks at the world that gives her this wolf-like beauty.

"Hi, I'm Randall." I'm making my last introduction, but Lhasa seems the least friendly of all. Her lips barely pull upward.

Lhasa has her hair pulled up in a bun of sorts, out of her face. I notice she's got a pretty big engagement ring on her finger. I'm glad I've seen it, so someday I can give Liling a bigger one. "It's too bad my sister forgot we were coming. It's certainly unfortunate for you, since you seem so well prepared."

I didn't need to be standing any closer to Liling to know that would make her bristle. I'm still grinning when I tell her, "It's my fault, we originally had a different time planned, but I switched my work schedule around."

Lhasa's generic smile remains small when she asks me, "Where do you work?"

"At a pizza place on campus."

135

"Hm." Was all Lhasa said, and I knew exactly what she meant by it. Stuck-up bitch.

Mr. Zhu adds to the conversation for the first time. "Good work ethic starts early, and it can start anywhere."

Liling has a smile that I recognize as her pre-demolition grin. "Didn't you wait until your last semester of school to finally pick an internship?" The pointed question is directed at her oldest sister.

"I took a lot of classes," Lhasa says with fake sweetness.

"Hm," Liling says with the same judgement Lhasa used with me just a minute ago.

I'm going to move this along because I want to get out of here. I'm going to forget about good impressions for now and abandon ideas of getting her parents to like me so that they're happy when we announce our future engagement. I need to get out of here.

It's like Lhasa could feel me start to unravel, and she eyes the box in my hand and says "Do you always bring dinner when you work on projects together? And you do this in Liling's room instead of the library where she works?"

Liling might be starting to lose her cool but if Lhasa wants to test my patience, fine. I can keep a smile on my face and look absolutely unfazed. "Food isn't allowed in the library, and we have a lot to get done."

"What's the project on?"

"Mock business startup. We have to write a full-scale proposal."

"What's the business?"

"Hotel."

Liling cuts in. "Did you want your name on the project too, Lhasa?"

Lhasa's smile is sweet as she drags her eyes from me to Liling. She knows something is off but she doesn't have enough information. She's like Liling. She wants to know everything before she strikes.

LILING

The general consensus is that my project partner is a very polite young man. Dad thinks he can see that Randall has good work ethic. Lishui (telling only me this) thinks he is very handsome. Lhasa hasn't said anything because she's plotting. If Randall wasn't as good on his feet as he is, or if he would have said something lewd as soon as he saw me, like he normally does, it would've been too obvious that Randall is *not* a project partner.

That being said, I am impressed with Randall. Being friendly is a talent I don't believe I possess. I'm so impressed that I show Randall appreciation in my own way. I've written him something that'll give him a soaring grade for his midterm assignment. It'll bring up his GPA and save him hours.

When I hand him the paper and he realizes what I've done, he doesn't argue with it. Instead, his lips curve to the side and he asks "I know last time I paid you in money, but maybe this time we could work something else out."

He's been too devious since I started letting him call himself my boyfriend.

I've been too insatiable since I started thinking of myself as Randall's girlfriend.

**

I hate to think of myself as some lovesick woman, but I think I miss Randall. He's taken on extra hours at his job, and it means he has less time to visit with me. He still comes by, just later and more tired.

It's been two weeks of Randall working tirelessly, going straight from class to work on most days. Not today though, it's February fourteenth. I'm trying not to be too girlish, but Randall has made so many promises about this day that I'm a little curious to see what he's got in mind.

I've, of course, got a small gift for him as well, and I'm excited to see him open it. It's wrapped in shined red paper with red tinsel and a small card. I'm placing the gift neatly on my table when Randall knocks on the door. It's still early, I haven't even gone to the cafeteria for breakfast yet.

I find myself smiling on my way to the door, because I know it's Randall and I know he's planning something goofy and charming. On the other side of the door, Randall is dressed in a long-sleeved white button up and dress pants. His hair is neatly gelled to the left, face hopeful. "Happy Valentine's Day." He's holding a bouquet of lilies and roses; I can smell them even before I've taken them from his hands.

I know I'm grinning like a dumb, lovesick girl, but it might be how I'm genuinely feeling. As soon as I've enveloped the flowers in my arms, I notice that Randall is towing several bags in his other arms.

"Randall," my voice is an amused scold as I let him into the room. I am sure all of the neighboring dorms are used to seeing Randall frequent these halls.

"You don't get to see any of this until later," Randall tells me, setting the bags on Britney's bed. "So don't even try it."

"Fine," I say. "Then, you have to wait for yours, too." Seeing all that he's brought, I wish I had given him more. I should have anticipated Randall would try to go above and beyond.

When Randall notices he also has a present waiting for him, he comes over to pull me in and I let him. Lately, I've felt very possessive of this man, and I can't help it. I love to think of him as mine. This is my boyfriend, my Randall.

When I pull my face away from his after some unladylike behavior, I ask him "Have you had breakfast yet? We could go down to the-"

"Oh, Liling." Randall has chosen dramatics. "Don't even suggest the cafeteria. Not today. We will have three meals together today and not one of them will be at that cafeteria." He's trying to sound disgusted but Randall is rarely serious enough to pull off such a tone. "I've got a whole day planned for us."

Indeed, he did. As Randall leads me by the hand through our day, I'm trying to figure out how he's done everything. What he's accomplished not only takes time, but it takes money and friends.

Everything we do is private. We eat breakfast at a modern little restaurant with no other diners. We sit inside a little café with one table in the center of the floor that's littered with flower petals.

For lunch, we picnic inside a greenhouse with fogged windows and bright lights. The room is full of big leaved plants and flowers. I recognize the blanket that we sat on from just a few weeks ago.

"I want a green room in the house I build you," Randall tells me as he's buttering a biscuit with strawberry jam.

"You talk about our future home as if it's really happening," I joke with him. Lately, every time I correct this fantasy of his, it feels like a hollow, empty threat. I feel the skitter of my heart when I look at him and tell myself that I'm moving too fast. I'm getting too drawn in. I look at Randall and I see the same fantasy he's seeing.

Randall is never too bothered when I try to shatter his dream with my words because he's always had an impenetrable shield of confidence about him. "You talk about our future home as if it's not happening."

I stretch my jaw to hide my smile. Too charming. Simply too charming.

We've already eaten so much food today that I'm unsure how Randall still has one more meal planned for later tonight. He's also been teasing that there's something he wants to show me afterward. With Randall, it doesn't make sense to guess. It's more fun to let myself be swept away by Randall Persch.

We relax at my dorm between lunch and dinner. Randall is unusually tame, considering the day and the fact he knows he has so much time at his disposal. It's not until an hour before dinner that Randall starts shoving presents into my lap.

I pull the first from a large black bag. I feel the limp feeling of something that promises to be clothing. Before my fingers have torn at the soft tissue paper, Randall tells me, "I want you to wear this for me tonight." I keep color out of my cheeks from sheer will, thinking he's bought something that will embarrass me but it isn't lingerie, it's a dress. A stunning, shimmering, green dress. It has thin gold straps, looks to be lower cut than what I usually wear and I'm guessing it will fit me tightly. It's beautiful. It's expensive. Even with a removed tag, I can tell this was not purchased from the clothing section of a superstore.

"Randall,"

"New rule," Randall interjects. "No refusing *any* of the things I give you today."

I narrow my eyes because of how he said it. "How much more is there?"

"Obviously, there are matching shoes." I giggle at him.

"Then I want to at least open your present next," I offer, getting caught up in the joy of seeing Randall's joy.

I already feel that I'm a bit underprepared. I've purchased him a sweater in a color I haven't seen him in. As lackluster as it is, Randall looks nothing less than ecstatic for the sweater when it's revealed to him. "Are you going to let me properly thank you for this?"

I drop my face. "Not however you're thinking."

He has a devilish grin as he starts to lean forward but I stop him in his tracks by holding my finger up. "We still have places to go today and I forbid you from messing up my hair."

"I won't touch your hair."

"Randall."

He laughs, backing off to grab the next present he's got ready for me. Next, Randall pulls out a smaller bag, and inside is a small, flat box. It's a box almost any woman would recognize: jewelry. It's in a bright blue box, fuzzy and petite.

Randall wants more inclusion when I open this one. He moves to sit next to me, our legs pancaked against each other. Randall pushes the box over my lap, looking at me joyfully in the eyes before he flips it open.

My mouth drops when I see what he's gotten me. It's too much. I don't know how he's done it, but he's done too much. It's a necklace. It's a gold chain that has a series of small emeralds in a string of jewels. Each emerald is encrusted with gold meant to match the chain. I've seen enough of my mother's jewelry to know real gold and emeralds when I see them.

"Randall." My voice is a whisper. It's so beautiful.

He's capitalizing on this, he's burying his head in my neck as I gawk at the jewels in front of me. "Say my name again, just like that."

And I do, because I'm trying to figure out how someone who works at a pizza place part time is able to afford this. There's a reason why there's not a lot of women my age sporting jewels like this, even small ones. Who has this sort of money at this age?

I fold my arm over his head, only kneading his hair for a moment before I finally ask. "How did you do this?"

I can't see his eyes because he's still in my neck. "Just hard work. You're worth it."

He's hiding something.

"Randall." This time, I'm not saying his name the way he likes me to.

Now, he leans back into his own space. "It matches the dress," he says simply.

I'm almost at a loss for words. "This is too much."

"But you like them?"

This is not the point. "Yes, but-"

"Then you're keeping them," Randall says matter-of-factly. "Remember the rules?"

"I didn't think the rules applied to precious jewels." I'm looking at the necklace again. I want it, I really do want it. I'm not ashamed to admit I want luxury. I want pretty jewels and gold and I dream of someday having massive rocks on my fingers and diamonds hanging from my neck.

When Randall thinks I'm looking at the necklace, I catch his confidence falter for just a second, as if he thinks I really might reject this. This is a big gift. Like the matching coat, taking this means something. I smooth my hair to one side of my shoulder. "Help me put this on."

27.

RANDALL

Everything is going perfectly. Perfectly. Right now, I've got Liling in a dress I bought her, glistening with jewels that I gave her. We're eating in a private dining room at the kind of restaurant where it's over a hundred dollars a person. I'm glad I've been saving for months, so I could do this. With Toby being MIA, I'm going to be bled dry after this, but I don't care. Liling is smiling at me.

I watch her talk. I'm listening, but I'm also trying to make sure I remember every moment of this - of realizing I'm actually in love with her now. Yeah, it's early, but it's real. Sure, I've been fascinated by her from the first moment, but this, this is something. This is Liling.

She's glistening. She's a jewel, she's precious.

I have shrimp and steak, Liling has lamb. I order a chocolate cake and Liling has a strawberry cheesecake but we sample each other's desserts. The restaurant is dimly lit, with dark carpet and dark walls. There's a candle on every table and a small string ensemble on an upper level so that the music is soft but it's real.

We're having an amazing night but I still have one more thing to show her. It's something I'm proud of. I did it for Liling, but also for myself. I think I'm going to be like Liling - someone who craves luxury. I work hard, so I should have nice things. Not everyone would do the sort of things that I'm doing to make a living, but that's why a lot of people will never live the way I'm going to live.

∎∎

I have an apartment now. I signed the papers weeks ago and started moving in furniture last week. New furniture. I'm so lucky, I know that. Actually, it isn't luck, it's hard work.

Gordy's been helping me over the last week. He's helping me remember things I need, but also being the friend I need. Sometimes, I remember I won't be working at the pizza place forever, and I wonder where that will leave Gordy.

I've got the entire place furnished and cleaned, and it's ready to entertain. Liling immediately notices I'm not driving her back to campus. I'm borrowing Gordy's car again. I paid him by having the mess cleaned up. Otherwise, there would have been no getting Liling into this thing. Maybe a car will be the next thing I get myself, if I can ever get a hold of Toby to start selling again.

"Where are you taking me now?" Liling's looking around at signs that we pass and buildings that indicate any sort of destination.

"One more surprise," I tell her, smiling when I notice she's stroking her necklace again. I won't say I can't believe we made it this far, because I knew we would. I'm proud that we made it this far.

I wanted to have Liling close her eyes but there wasn't a realistic way to get her up there so I just had to let her see where we were. Liling was puzzled as we pulled into a modest apartment complex that mainly targets college students with parents to pay rent for them so they can live close to campus.

145

I live on the third floor, second door down from the stairs on the left. The building has that smell that nearly every apartment complex seems to have. When I'm jamming a key into the lock, I ask Liling, "Ready?"

Liling is so pretty when she looks me in the eyes. "I'm ready."

There's nothing too special about my apartment, other than the fact that it's mine. I lead Liling in, her red nails wrapped around my fingers. Once I have the light on, I look around with her. The furnishing of the living room is minimal. It's a black couch, a TV on an entertainment center.

Liling is taking it all in. "What is this?"

I'm purposeful in my words. "It's ours."

Her eyes dart to mine. "Randall."

I laugh. "Fine, it's mine, but I want you here with me as often as possible."

At first, it wasn't the reaction I was expecting. She isn't in shock, she isn't in a state of joy. She's calculating. I follow Liling as she inspects absolutely everything: the fridge, the walls, the bathroom.

When we make it to my bedroom, she stops at the doorway. There's a full-sized bed with a navy blue comforter. I'm really proud of the bed. My whole life has been slept on a twin bed with no room for anything but sleeping.

Liling isn't looking at the bed, she's looking at the left side of the room, where two mismatched desks are pushed against the wall, sitting next to each other.

"One for me, one for you."

Liling isn't always good with expressing herself, or talking about emotions, but I can tell this is meaningful to her. Sometimes I think all Liling wants is to make decisions for herself and not have someone tell her what she's going to do.

146

It's been too long since Liling's said anything. This is a big moment, and I'm waiting for her to acknowledge that. "What do you think?"

Instead of answering, she ventures to the desks, tracing her nails down the wood of the desk, flipping on the desk lamp on the second one. She's folded her arms into her chest as she looks out the window. She suddenly asks, "How did you do all of this?"

I give her a small grin. "Hard work."

She doesn't smile back. "Randall."

"What?"

She purses her lips, looking at the ceiling. "You know, Randall, I'm not bad at math and I'm not stupid."

"I never said you were."

Her brown eyes drill into me. "Tell me or I'm leaving."

I decided to take a chance and play with her. "How will you get back to campus?"

"Randall." Liling is stubborn. She'll walk herself back before she falls through on making a point.

I sigh. "I have a job, Liling."

She's quick to shoot me down. "You have a part time job at a pizza place. That doesn't afford you an apartment, a whole day of private dining, furniture, this necklace, all of it. Randall, where are you getting all of this?"

I just stare back at her because I don't know what to tell her. She's too smart. She'll pull apart lies, and I don't want to tell them to her. I didn't think this far ahead. I didn't think about the possibility of Liling leaving me, because that's what she'll do if she finds out. I'm hopeful, but I know there's no future where Liling dates a drug dealer.

"Randall."

I'm so fucking scared right now. "If I tell you, will you prom-"

Liling doesn't make deals. She's so fast, she's a whirlwind. She's opening the desk drawers, she's looking for something I haven't told her.

Because I'm an idiot, she's going to find it.

She's going to find my records. She's going to find the nondescript receipts that Toby gives me. While they don't explicitly say 'Gave Randall crack,' they're enough. They show tallies, they show dollar amounts. Everything she needs to destroy me in one unlocked desk drawer. I watch her face fall as she reads my own incriminating evidence. I watch her heart break as she realizes I'm not who I said I was, and if anything, I'm just as worthless as she knew I was from the start.

"Liling." I'm taking soft, careful steps toward her.

Without looking up, she snaps her hand up, daring me to come closer. One hand clutches the paper, the other is digging red nails into her arm. Her eyes are swimming over my papers. She's got receipts from Toby, bank statements, everything she needs to know that I'm not worthy of her.

I have no idea what she's doing. She's not yelling, she's not crying, she's not leaving. Instead, she sits at one of the chairs, flipping through papers, one hand clasped around the side of her neck. "What're you actually selling?" When I hesitate, she says, "Lie to me, and I leave."

It's only because she's still inspecting the papers rather than looking at me that I have the courage to respond. "I sell drugs on campus."

"What do you sell?" She asks again. Now, she looks at me. She looks serious. She looks furious. She looks disappointed.

"I sell cocaine on campus." I've never been ashamed of what I do until now. Until it cost me Liling.

She's blinking rapidly, her waterline getting heavy when she looks away. I see her shake her head, like she's telling herself to focus. "For how long?"

"Liling, it's not like-"

"How. Long." Liling's words compel me like electricity compels someone seated in the electric chair. No matter what I say, I can't be saved.

"A few months before we met," I mutter, feeling defeated.

Liling's pressing down on her nails, chewing her lip and not looking at me. "Alright." She stands, straightening her shirt.

"Alright?"

I already know Liling's callous look before she starts speaking. "I'm leaving." She starts to remove herself from my bedroom so fast, and I'm left following her in a nervous stream of words.

"Hey, Liling, wait. Please, just hang on a second."

She doesn't even turn while she speaks. "I'm not doing this, Randall."

"Can't we talk about this?" I plead, watching her put her shoes on.

At this, she stops and whips her head at me. "Fine, discuss what?"

"Wh-" Maybe there isn't much of an explanation I can provide here. "I just... don't want you to leave me," I mutter sheepishly. "I'm still the same person, I just-"

"You sell drugs." Liling's brow is raised, waiting for me to lie to her. "Liling Zhu is dating a drug dealer. Say that out loud and tell me it doesn't sound ridiculous." When I don't have an answer, she finishes putting her shoes on, snatching her purse from the countertop.

"Liling." I feel more desperate once she's unlocking the door. "We're twenty minutes from campus, I'm not letting you walk home." Chivalry, Liling likes chivalry.

She also likes doing whatever she wants, and she likes men who aren't selling coke. "Randall, you will never *let* me do anything. You will never presume to tell me what I can and can't do." As soon as I start trying to apologize, she whips her hand up in a very *talk to the hand* sort of way and she's slamming the door in my face in the next minute.

Of course, I'm going to follow her out, chattering apologizes all the way out to the phone where she's angrily putting quarters into the booth until she's able to make a call and get a cab.

The entire time we wait for the cab, I'm throwing just about every excuse and apology I can think of. None of it registers. She doesn't say a word to me. There's nothing I can do but watch her get in the cab, because I know if there's one way to burn a bridge with Liling, it's trying to control her in any way. She'll destroy her own foundation before she lets somebody else bring her down.

Watching Liling leave is like watching my future drive off a cliff. There's no point to *any* of this without Liling. Liling Persch. That's what I've been working toward. Now, I have nothing.

LILING

Men really are terrible. The worst. I'm glad I've been telling myself I don't need one for all of these years.

**

I can lie to others, but I'm not great at lying to myself.

29.

[RANDALL]

It's been four days since I've had any contact with Liling. The separation is killing me. I've showed up at her dorm, at the library. I can't find her. I've tried calling her dorm hallway, I've tried her classes, she's being elusive.

Four nights in this stupid shitty apartment alone. I've been getting terrible sleep. It's a new place still, it sounds different, it smells different, and the person I thought would be here to adjust with me isn't here.

I'm watching morning cartoons with a bowl of cereal, not hungry but eating because I feel like I should. The cereal has been in the milk long enough to be soggy.

I'm alone, I'm miserable, and I'm broke again. I'm putting my bowl away when I hear a quiet, tentative knock at the door. I practically run to open it because I'm so whipped that I know *who* knocks like that.

Liling.

I'm an idiot that doesn't know what to say, since apologies didn't work last time. "God, you're going to kill me looking like that."

152

Dressed in a long black coat with dark lips, hair in a puffed ponytail, Liling looks anything but amused. "Is that really the first thing you're going to say to me?"

I step aside, pleading with my eyes for her to come inside. "Tell me what you want me to say and I'll say it."

With a pouty face, she pushes past me and lets herself inside. This is good. She's back in my space, and the proximity is charging my spirit like a battery. Without saying anything else, she marches herself back to my bedroom and I hear her start filing through my things again. What's mine is hers, I guess.

When I catch up to her, I ask, "What're you looking for?"

"Where are you putting all of this money?" She holds up one paper; I can tell it's got Toby's handwriting.

I take the paper from her because it gets me just a few steps closer. "I have a bank account. I keep some cash."

She shakes her head, leaning on the desk with a hand in her hair. "You can't do this, Randall." She sounds so disappointed, and my brain is reeling, trying to think of what I can say to beg with her before she leaves again, even though something feels off.

"It's good money, Liling."

She shakes her head again. "You can't just put all of this money in your bank account without having a legitimate source of income to have earned it." I don't respond because I don't know what the hell she's talking about. "And you can't keep receipts this obvious out. You have to keep this locked up, Randall."

"Liling, I'm really confused. Just tell me what you want and I'll do it. I'll stop, I promise." I'm at her side, I'm on my knees, looking up and trying to get her to look back at me. "Tell me what you want," I repeat.

153

She sighs, looking down at me. "You're going to get arrested if you don't act smarter."

"I-" That's probably true. "I'm just trying my best to be something."

I feel like I am kneeling before a goddess as she reaches down, her nails delicately scratching my chin. I'm here, basking in her divinity, praising the very essence of her. "What are you trying to be?"

I grin up at her. I can't lose what's mine. "Yours. I'm trying to be yours."

30

LILING

I should have known better. I should have known that there are no men that look like Randall and act like Randall without there being some sort of dirty little secret. He's a drug dealer. Of course he is.

The worst part of it all is that I'm not sure that I care.

I think I'm angriest about the lying. I don't want to be in the dark. I don't want my boyfriend arrested for selling illicit substances because he's making stupid mistakes.

Randall's so scared of me - of what I'll do. He's only ever wanted to be perfect in my eyes. I spend the whole day making him tell me absolutely everything. He tells me about how he got started, about how and where he sells, and how much he makes.

He makes a lot.

I understand why he does it.

I'm not leaving. I'm not running. I'm taking over.

31.

RANDALL

I don't know what I was expecting, but it wasn't what I got. It wasn't Liling telling me I'm not discrete enough when I sell cocaine. It wasn't Liling going through my records and telling me what I'm doing wrong, and what I need to start doing.

I wasn't expecting Liling to want to stay the night with me. I wasn't expecting Liling to watch the new TV I bought with me on the couch while we ate stovetop popcorn.

This was the first night where she slept next to me where it was predetermined that we'd be doing that. It wasn't an accident of someone falling asleep. Liling is laying next to me, knowing what she knows.

This whole time, I thought I was the one making things happen, but maybe it's Liling. Maybe it's just the universe, or God, or something I'll never understand. I'll never understand how I found someone even more ambitious than I am. I think I found someone who understands what kind of work it takes to get ahead in this world. The fastest way to living like the people who were born rich.

It feels like I've been given permission. I can keep doing what I'm doing. She made it clear that I'm not afforded any more secrets from her. I tell her everything. I tell her where

I'm going, what I'm doing, what I'm selling. Liling told me that, for now, I need to stop putting my cash in the bank and keep it in the safe until I have some way to show legitimate earnings, whatever that means.

I've got everything I need now. I've got a partner, a job, a place to live, a future. Over time, all these things are going to improve for me. I'm going to make Liling my wife. I'm going to keep selling until I can get myself and my family whatever we want. Someday, we'll be our own bosses, and we'll live in our own world.

The world of Persch.

32.

RANDALL

I've recovered. Liling isn't being pissy with me anymore. It was a little tense after Valentine's Day. I think I lost some of her trust, but I'm working on gaining it back.

That was a few weeks ago, and life is different now. I have my own place. It takes longer to get to both work and campus with the buses, but Liling and Gordy have cars, so sometimes I'm able to a catch a ride. Liling stays over with me often, but she's still got that thing about being a good girl, and apparently, there are still some things she's waiting for. Honestly, I'd give her a ring now if she wouldn't laugh in my face. I've already thought about it. The day we graduate, next year.

Until then, I need money. I had a lot saved, but I also bought a lot to pull off Valentine's Day. Toby's been missing for weeks, meaning my only source of income has been the pizza place. It's not enough.

I'm back at Toby's door again today, knocking on the door. I need to get in contact with him. I need to sell. Diana says she hasn't seen him, and his rent is past due. This time, when I'm at the door, I'm not really expecting an answer, but I am expecting to get in.

I've picked locks before. At a shitty apartment like this, it's not that difficult. My plan is to get in and have a look around, make sure Toby isn't dead on the floor or anything.

I use a narrow file to put into the lock and start jimmying it around, working the lock until I'm able to turn it from the inside. I'm able to open the door and come inside Toby's apartment.

The first thing that hits me is the smell. It's the smell of rotting food and garbage. The place looks mostly the same, but it feels emptier. I can't imagine anyone is living with this smell. I know I'm not going to find Toby, but I'm going to look around anyway.

The living room looks like it's been disturbed. The black cushions of the couch are partially or completely removed, like someone was desperately looking for something between them. There's a square cherry wood table that sitting crookedly across from the couch. There's white powder scattered over it, like Toby did a quick line and left.

Toby's bedroom is uninteresting. It's just as messy as the rest of the place, just as void of signs of life. The bed is unmade, with the sheets curled off of the mattress. There's an unsightly number of tissues on the table next to the bed.

I'm going to act like I don't know what's going on there and head to the bathroom. That's where Toby stashes things. Next to a stained toilet, there's cabinets under the sink. If one were to rummage behind the roll of toilet paper, the mostly full boxes of tampons, and the cleaning supplies, they'd normally find some coke.

But there's not any. It's all gone. There's some dust from something that wasn't fully closed at some point, but no bags of cocaine. No lockbox of cash, nothing. This isn't what I wanted to find. Everything's gone, and it's definitely intentional. If Toby isn't here, then I don't have a way to make real money.

Even though I don't think there's anyone else to care, I put back all the boxes into place. Putting the boxes back into place is a little bit of a loud process, since the cabinets were stuffed full in order to create a hiding spot. I'm knocking boxes and bottles of cleaner and trying to restack them. I'm so involved in it that I don't even notice that someone's come into the bathroom and they're pointing the barrel of a pistol at my head.

"Stand up."

My eyes focus on the polished silver of the open end of the gun. My eyes travel from tattooed knuckles, up a tanned, toned arm until I find who's preparing to blow my brains out on this disgusting bathroom floor.

"Stand up," he says again. It's a big, meaty Hispanic-looking guy. Huge. Colossal. He's got brown eyes, black hair that's shined with a perfect part on the side of his head, and a black soul patch under his bottom lip. This man's a tank with a scowl. He's wearing a white pocketed shirt over his wide body that has little cream color designs on it.

It's when I'm standing slowly that I notice there's another man behind him. Darker skin tone, slimmer with thicker hair in a frizzy ponytail, but still larger than I am. He's also got a gun, but it's still attached to his hip.

Alright, so somehow I might have messed up by coming in here, but I'm Randall. I make friends, and I don't get my head busted open.

Before I can start figuring out what's going on, there's another voice from the direction of the living room. It's a rough, dry, authoritative voice with an accent attached to it. "What's going on in there, boys?"

The big guy in front of me smiles a little bit, keeping his eyes on mine. "We found something, boss."

"Come show me, then."

The second man that's behind the one pointing a gun at me backs out of the bathroom to make room. The muscled one in front of me keeps his aim, telling me, "You walk out of here with your hands up and don't do nothing stupid." He's got an accent, too, but his voice is deeper and smoother than whoever's in the living room.

"Is that really necessary?" I ask. "I promise I'll behave."

He laughs. That's a start. "If you behave, you live a little longer."

I'm moving now, and my hands are up. "Oh," I say. "Is that my best-case scenario?"

The second man, who's wearing an open leather jacket over a wifebeater, laughs. "Damn, you talkative, huh?" He stays in front of me while the big guy is behind me, letting his gun push into my back as we're going back to the living room. I'm trying to figure out if I'm about to be kidnapped or if I'm even going to leave this apartment alive. Scratch that, I'll be fine. This is a misunderstanding.

In the kitchen-living room space, there's three more Hispanic men. I'm starting to think I've somehow gotten myself mixed in with the cartel drug-lords Toby answered to.

There's one man by the door, standing in a closed jacket that's oddly big on his short, narrow body. He is, without a doubt, the most terrifying man I've ever seen. He's covered in ink; his face, his neck, every finger, almost every surface of him. Even his shaved head has inked symbols and designs that hide whoever this man really is. The tattoo on the side of his face of a large moth is what catches my attention first before noticing that among symbols and flowers, a lot of the tattoos are bugs;

161

caterpillars, beetles, spiders. He's the bogeyman. He waits with his arms folded in front of him. The darkest man that lead me in here takes a position by the couch, eyeing me as I enter, acting like he's standing guard to the man sitting on the couch, the cushions have been put back.

Right away, I can see the man sitting on the couch is the one running the show. He sits with his legs spread wide, arms stretched over the back of the couch. He looks me up and down, asking, "Found a little mouse in the cupboards did we?" It's that dry, crackling, snake-like voice I'd heard before.

"He was going through shit in the bathroom," the big man behind me says.

They have me standing in front of the table while this man inspects me and I inspect him back. I feel like speaking first is going to give me some control, and I can insert myself as anything other than an adversary here. "Hi," I start. "I'm Randall." I was going to step forward and extend a hand but I'm yanked back so fast that the muscles in my shoulders are painfully jarred.

The person in front of me still hasn't broken a smile, even with me attempting to be friendly. He's like Liling: calculating. Calculating whether I'm a threat. I don't think this person responds well to threats. "Who are you, Randall?"

It feels like a trick question. Admitting I sell cocaine is usually not in my best interest. I can make some assumptions on who these people are, but I don't really know for sure. I'm going to be bold and stupid instead. "Are you... are you the Padillas?"

This is the first real emotion that registers. His brow raises with cruel amusement when he tells me, "If you don't answer my fucking question, then I'm going to get bored with you. You don't want me to get bored when I'm talking to you."

Ok, I'll work on making friends later. I don't need to be explicit. "I work for Toby, or I did."

"Did?"

I wet my lips, looking in the direction of the bathroom. "I haven't seen him in a while." I wonder if these men have anything to do with that.

The man in front of me stands now, and I'm able to take him in. He's as thin as a cigarette, with rich brown skin and hair that's closely shaved to his head. He has sunken in cheeks that are cut over harsh cheekbones under void brown eyes. "You work for Toby?" He repeats. There's a long tattoo that at first looks like it's just a line but I think it's actually thinly printed cursive font that runs from behind his ear, down his neck and plunges under his shirt. He also has a sleeve of tattoos going up only his left arm. I see flowers and crosses, skulls, a pistol, as well as a woman's name inked in intricate calligraphy over his wrist.

I nod. "Yes, sir." This guy looks hardly any older than myself, but I know when to shut my mouth and follow orders.

He laughs. "Ok, so you're smart, huh?" His accent gets heavier when he speaks faster. "If you work for Toby, then you work for me."

The Padillas.

He is the definition of control. And he's tall. Too tall, too skinny. "What were you looking for in the bathroom?"

Ok, this might not sound good out of context. The last thing I need is for the cartel to think I was here to steal from them. "I came looking for Toby. When he wasn't here, I started to see what he left behind."

"Hm." He looked down at me without bending his head. "And what did you find?"

"Nothing."

163

"Nothing?"

I shake my head.

"Hm." He starts to walk toward the bathroom, calling over his shoulder without turning, "Show me where nothing would be, if it were here."

Sure, let's follow the drug lord into the bathroom. I'm going to start walking before I can be pushed. This is a time to be compliant.

Before we get to the bathroom, the bear behind me growls, "I don't need to warn you to behave, do I?"

I stop at the bathroom door and try my best to look friendly. "I behave better when I know who I'm talking to."

He cocks his head. "You don't need to worry about me, you need to worry about *him*." He points with his head toward the bathroom. "And the minute he tells me he's done with you, then you worry about me."

"And when I want to make friendship bracelets, what can I put on it?"

"You talk too much," the thin man in the bathroom calls. "That's Rogelio, now get your ass in here."

I grin at the big man in front of me. "Hi, Rogelio," I say quietly, stepping into the bathroom before I get myself shot. I think the big guy is at least slightly amused with me.

The leader, and maybe least amused one of all, is waiting for me in the bathroom, his hands on his hips as he glares at the doorway. There's a massive golden watch that's blitzed with diamonds on his wrist. It matches the three or so big, golden rings he's got on his fingers. Alright, he's got money, I get it.

"What were you looking for in here?" He asks me impatiently.

I point with my head to under the sink. "He used to keep a stash in there, and some money." At this point, I know who I'm talking to, mostly. I know that everything Toby has is only because of this man... or maybe someone above this man, I don't actually know how far up the chain I'm dealing with.

I squat down, opening the drawers, and the man does too. He smells like cigarettes and something else that vaguely reminds me of a bonfire. "I already checked," I continue. "Nothing." I don't know if I'm telling him something he already knows or not. For all I know, Toby's gone because this person put a bullet between his eyes.

The man roughly knocks over the things inside the cabinet, undoing my work in leaving it how I'd found it. He does something between a sigh and a growl. "Didn't think he had the balls to leave with my shit."

Now, I'm crouching next to a presumed drug lord in a bathroom, looking at toilet paper and sanitary napkins. I really want to ask questions, but he seems like he's really not into any attempts for me to be friendly.

The man stands. "When's the last time you saw that fucker?"

I'm still squatting, looking up at him. "Three weeks ago or so? I picked up product a few days before and came to exchange." As I say this, I'm realizing that means I might technically owe someone money... maybe. I usually give money to Toby and he gives me a cut of it. I don't know if Toby is on a similar schedule or-

"So he gets a new fucking shipment and then skips town?" He's directing it to Rogelio, behind me. He points a finger at nobody, making a vow. "He's dead when we find him." I'm going to stay quiet here, or I was, but he's looking at me now. "You know where he is?"

165

I'm quickly shaking my head. "No idea. I'm only here because I got curious. He just up and left."

He stares at me, deciding whether I'm lying or not. Through a closed mouth, he runs his lip over his teeth. "What's your name again?"

"Randall."

"Randall What?"

"Persch."

"Spell that."

"P-e-r-s-c-h."

"Randall Persch," he repeats, looking down at me, his sunken cheeks set in a scowl. "You know who you're talking to, Randall Persch?"

"I tried to figure that out, but I got in trouble for asking," I answer, taking a risk with my usual foolishness.

There's a silence in the pause as everyone realizes how stupid I might just be. Rogelio snickers behind me, as does the other person whose name I don't know yet. Finally, the smallest of smiles is on his face. See, I can make friends. "What the hell is wrong with you?"

I have on my good-natured smile. "We can try again," I offer, hoping it doesn't get me yanked again. "I'm Randall." Again, I extend my hand, and the man is just amused enough to take it.

"You look like a fucking boy scout, you know that?" The man asks.

I shrug. "I've been told I'm pretty."

He levels his face a little. "Fine, then, Boy Scout," he says, shaking my hand. The rings are cold against my finger. "Luis. Luis Padilla."

So, I was right.

166

We release each other's hands as more amusement reaches Luis' face. "Does that name mean anything to you?"

"It makes a lot of sense that you're looking for Toby, too," I reply.

Luis is less amused. "Jesus, do you ever answer the question you're asked?"

"Sure," I say.

Behind me, Rogelio says something in Spanish that I don't understand and the others laugh.

Luis walks past me, speaking to his men in Spanish again. Just like that, it seems like they're leaving already. After the last thing that Luis says, the one with the leather jacket that was behind Rogelio hands me a slip of paper with a phone number on it.

Luis says, "If you get in contact with that fucker again, call me first."

I look at the paper, knowing that, if Toby is found, he's only going to be found once. At this point, he's as good as dead, wherever he is. I don't know much, but I know that stealing from the cartel isn't going to do him any favors.

"Hey," Luis snaps. "You understand me?" He's standing in a formation with his other four men by the door.

"I understand," I say quickly. I fold the paper and put it in my pocket.

Luis nods, ready to leave. "Stay quiet about this, Randall Persch, and count your lucky stars. Not a lot of people get to walk away from this world so easily once they're in it."

All of them leave, taking all the malice from the room with them. I don't remember registering my heart rate increasing, but it's slowing down now. I just met a drug lord. I met a man who's presumably rich beyond his means because he's figured this world out. He's found a way to swim by making himself the shark. He could've eaten me alive, if he wanted to.

I want to be like that. Shit, I don't have to be the shark, but could I at least be the barracuda that swims besides the shark?

Not a lot of people get to walk away from this world so easily once they're in it. This could be a new start for me. I could get my life on a cleaner path. I could get a job as the assistant manager at a hotel or something, make an honest living.

An honest living wouldn't let me live like a king. It wouldn't put jewels on Liling's neck or buy her the house she deserves.

Not a lot of people can leave the world I've briefly been a part of, just like Luis said. But I don't want to leave that world, I want to run it.

I start running toward the door.

33.

RANDALL

I take off running down the hallway, trying to find Luis and his crew before he leaves. I see the tip of someone's black hair going down the stairs, so I'm quick to follow. When I get to the bottom of the steps, there's only one direction to go so I go down it quickly and fly around the corner.

Another gun in my face.

Instantly stopping, I realize that maybe chasing after a drug lord is not the smartest thing I've done.

Rogelio has the gun again, and the rest of the men looked alarmed and have hands on their wastes. "What the fuck is wrong with you?" Rogelio asks incredulously.

Luis is behind the mob. He doesn't seem too happy to see me already. "You forget something, Boy Scout?" Smoke trails from his mouth.

I'm out of breath and trying to ignore the gun that's still pointed at me. "What're you going to do about Toby?" I pant.

Luis looks bored, and he's warned me about that. "If I find him, I'll kill him."

I shake my head. "Obviously." He lifts a brow as I continue. "I mean- who's taking his place?"

Luis laughs. "I'll have to put a wanted ad out." A couple of the men laugh too.

"Don't," I say, "Let me do it."

Luis inspects me, stepping forward. Somehow his men know to step out of his way, even with their backs turned. When he's standing in front of me and I smell the cigarettes again, he asks, "That's a pretty big job, Boy Scout," he says quietly. "I don't think you know what you're asking to do."

I smile like it's nothing. "I'm Toby's best seller. Your best seller." I start making my case, counting my attributes on my fingers in front of him. "I know all the other people he's got selling for him, I work hard, I'll do what needs to be done, and most importantly, I never forget who's in charge."

I've brought an amused smile of wonder to Luis' face. He balances the cigarette on the edge of his lips, letting it hang from his mouth. "Hm," he says, before puffing smoke out of the side of his mouth. "Alright," He announces loudly, causing his men to stand up straighter. "Everyone back inside."

▪▪

We went back up to Toby's abandoned apartment and I make a case for myself. This is an opportunity. I won't get anywhere by letting life happen to me. So, I sell some cocaine, big deal. I've also been making a lot of money while doing it. Now, I can make even more.

Luis and his men follow me back in inside the stink-ridden apartment while I convince Luis that I can be the new Toby. I even go as far as to say that I can be better than Toby was. There's no way that Luis is going to stop trying to sell in this area because Toby's gone. He can take his time looking for someone new or he can go with me.

I tell him I already know all Toby's other sellers. I can get back in contact with them, tell them we're back in business, and hit the streets. Luis is skeptical of me, which is understandable.

170

Not as many people are as enthusiastic as I am with being promoted in the world of cocaine sales.

"It's more than just getting people their product," Luis tells me, leaning against the corner of the kitchen counter while I stand flanked by Rogelio. "You have to be able to keep your people in line, too. Because if you don't, I do, and I don't have time to do your job for you."

Keep people in line.

I have a vague idea of what that means. Keeping people in line- I've done that before. Santosh trying to stiff Liling on the money he owed her- I kept him in line. People make mistakes, and I correct them.

"I can do it."

Luis looks at me, passing judgement. "I don't know, Boy Scout. I just don't know you." He takes a step closer. "I don't know shit about you. How do I know you're not going to get me in trouble? How do I know you're not going to steal from me, like that other bastard?"

I shrug. "I want to make money, and I don't want to die."

At that, Luis laughs, his men laughing too once Luis does. "You're funny, I'll give you that."

"I'm determined," I tell him as if I'm correcting him. Not being taken seriously is one of my ticks. I'm a hard worker, and I don't really care for having that work ethic called into question.

Luis checks his watch, says something I can't understand that causes his group to start walking toward the door. "I'll think about your offer, Boy Scout." He throws the cigarette he'd been inhaling onto a dirty plate that had been left on the counter. "But to be honest, you're a risk. I got my own guys, and I'd rather take the time to get one of them then taking a chance on you."

This isn't how I want things to go. I need this money. I just took on a lot of financial commitments with the understanding

171

I'd be making the kind of money I make when I'm selling. The pizza place isn't going to get me by and I don't know if I can wait to graduate. Even if I graduate, *this* is where the money's at. "I'm just trying to-"

"I don't give a shit," Luis says, cutting me off. He stands by the door, looking at me like I'm nothing. "I don't give a shit about what you got going on. I care about the people in my world, and you're not in it."

LILING

It's been a few weeks since I decided to ignore the fact that my boyfriend is a drug dealer. I'm telling myself that he works hard, and he's got something to show for it. I shouldn't be impressed with how much he's gotten for himself through illegal means, but I find hard work attractive.

I know Randall isn't going anywhere. I need to stop kidding myself. Randall is mine. He wasn't what I was expecting out of a college boyfriend, but he's here, and he's staying. I'm so delusional that I wear the emerald necklace he's given me everyday, with my silver cross pendant peeking from under it, hidden beneath my shirt.

It really is a special necklace. Randall had to work hard to get this for me. He's given me gold and jewels. Out of all the jewels he could have given me, he knows green is my favorite color. Randall's been a bit sullen lately, but seeing me wear this necklace makes him happy. It makes me happy too.

To feed into the delusion that there might be a chance Randall is going to be mine forever, I wear the necklace to dinner with my family. Sunday morning was lovely. Randall, as he's been doing for months, sat next to me for church service. We sang our hymns and said our prayers, and I thought about how Randall really is a good man. He's just selective in his goodness.

Randall and I eat lunch together; greasy fast food with a boxes of fries and a sandwich. Randall still eats chicken nuggets but he informs me that there is no age limit on good taste.

As I drive home, I'm rethinking the necklace. Someone will notice the necklace, ask about it, and then I'll have to explain Randall. I'm not ashamed of Randall, but I know this announcement is going to be met with resistance. They'll say I'm not focusing on my school, they'll say I need someone more like myself, which will be code for another Chinese person.

In one turn, I decide I'm going to take the necklace off, and by the turn after that, I've decided it doesn't make sense to hide Randall. Hiding him would imply there's something wrong with him, which there isn't. As I pull up the driveway of our small ranch home with white siding on the upper portion of the house and a brick base, I think it's better they know about Randall. The sooner they know, the sooner they can come around to the idea that I've found someone on my own, even though he isn't handpicked by Mama.

I'm still wearing my church clothes. I have on a yellow dress that reaches into a petal shaped skirt at my knees and flat white shoes. The emerald necklace sits in what I think to be a fashionable contrast of color over my neck, with a charm bracelet from Lishui around my wrist.

Inside the house, the warm smell of Mama's cooking is the first to greet me. I miss Mama's cooking, and the familiar food that's always here. If Randall wants to continue to be my boyfriend, he's going to have to be introduced to some new foods. Randall claims he loves to cook, but so far I've only seen him make boxed macaroni and unseasoned hamburger meat at his new apartment. He's very close to losing his meal-preparing privileges if he presents me with another plain chicken breast.

Mama, as usual, is first to notice my entrance, and she seems to be in a good mood. It takes a full minute of being inside to receive my first criticism. I look tired.

Papa greets me warmly and says, "Because she's working hard!"

Lhasa sits on a bar stool at the countertop near the stove, where Mama has a round dish full of steamed food nearly ready to serve. Lhasa has brought her fiancé, and as I look at him, I'm having trouble remembering his name. "Are you excited to almost be done this year? Are you taking summer classes?"

This is her greeting, and we hug each other while we prepare to try to be our parent's brightest star for the night. "I am taking summer classes. I'll be starting a teaching assistant role with Professor Brackett, so I'll really only have a week off."

"It will all be worth it when you've got your degree," Papa comments. Yes, that's supposed to be the only thing I'm focusing on. School. Marriage. Babies. In that order, always.

When dinner starts, Lhasa is controlling the entire conversation, talking about wedding planning and I still cannot remember what this man's name is. I have the name Robert circulating in my head.

After listening to Robert and Papa hold their own conversation, I lean in my chair, closer to Lishui, who turns her head towards me. "What is his name again?"

Lishui, her hair in two low ponytails over her neck, whispers, "Frank."

"Not Robert?"

She pauses, chewing her food in thought. "Now I'm not sure. Dare me to ask Lhasa?" She whispers playfully.

I pinch a smile and nod, knowing Lishui will do it.

175

Lishui leans in the opposite direction, toward Lhasa who's next to the fiancé who's next to Papa who's next to Mama. Lhasa has her hair in some sort of hive, little pearl earrings bobbling as she leans to see what Lishui wants. I watch her face contort in annoyance, hissing something at our younger sister.

She leans back to me, and I can see that Lhasa is annoyed that we're collaborating. "It's Frank. We should know this by now, apparently."

I nod, trying to be more serious when Mama notices our giggling. Most everyone has finished their food by the time I realize I really haven't had much to say this entire night. Sometimes being unrecognized is best. At the very least, it means I haven't caught anyone's attention in disappointment.

But whenever there's a moment to feel good about myself, there's my mother.

"Liling." Mama is taking the conversation over.

I neatly lower my napkin from my mouth to my lap. "Yes, Mama?"

"Tell me about school, still doing well, yes?"

I nod, eager to talk in this aspect as I'm doing everything I'm expected to. I report back that I have high marks in my classes and I've applied for senior year internships already.

It's sweet little Lishui that notices the necklace first. I should have taken it off. Her fingers reach out to lift the golden chain off of my neck, holding it over her hand. "This is pretty," she dotes. With Lishui, I know her affection is genuine, and she's not trying to expose anything in front of the rest of the family.

Mama nods, and Lhasa has zeroed in on it. "It looks real," Lhasa says, and I love the smallest hint of jealousy in her voice. If ~~Robert~~ Frank had bought her jewels other than her engagement ring, she'd be wearing them.

176

"It was a gift," I say with sweet assuredness. My stomach is churning slightly, knowing Randall won't be my secret anymore. The only remaining thing I'll have to keep to myself is the status of my half-virginity: that will be a confession I take to my grave.

It seems Lishui understands instantly. Her face lights up in excitement but she isn't going to say anything. It is Mama that asks, "Someone gave you that?"

"*Who* and why would someone give you that?" Lhasa asks me, tapping her ring finger absent-mindedly on the table.

This doesn't need to be a big deal, but it will be. "My boyfriend gave it to me on Valentine's Day." There it is, and there are my parents preparing to strike down this talk of foolishness.

"Boyfriend?" Mama screeches, putting her fork down. "What do you mean, boyfriend?" She looks at Papa, whose face has taken a steely disposition. "We did not give you a boyfriend."

"I met him at school," I say calmly.

Mama's brow is pushing down on her eyes, very unhappy with me. "Liling, how can you have a boyfriend we haven't met?"

"You're supposed to be studying," Papa reminds me. The worst to come with him will be later. Mama scolds, Papa screams.

"My grades are still just as good as they were before," I remind him. I made it clear with Randall that he cannot become a distraction. He hasn't listened, but I've managed to keep my scores up.

Lishui is going to try to learn information with easy questions. "What's his name?"

My smile is genuine when I think of my silly boyfriend. "His name is Randall, he's very nice."

It's as if everyone knows this name but are collectively trying to recollect where they know this name from. Of course, it's Lhasa who remembers first. Her question is a triumphant

177

drawl dripping with judgement. "Randall?" She asks. "Randall, the pizza boy Randall?"

I meet her in the eye, daring her to be just a little more transparent of how unimpressed she is. "Yes, that Randall."

Lhasa doesn't need to respond because Mama is all over it. She's vigorously shaking her head. "No, this does not work." She's waving her hands in a cut off sort of motion. "You have to stop."

I'm going to stay calm, quiet. "Randall is a very good man, Mama. He works hard, he studies with me, and we go to church together."

It's as if she considers this before she looks at Papa. Papa says, "You can worry about dating after school. We'll find someone for you."

"I appreciate it, Papa, but right now I don't need you to find anyone." I look at my plate, wishing I had more food to distract myself.

"Your mother and I know what you should be looking for in a partner. Someone who can spiritually guide you, someone who will be a proper head of household," Papa says, with Mama nodding enthusiastically.

I bite back the response that I don't need to be led spiritually and to remind him it's not the 1950s.

Before either of us can argue this more, Lishui adds, "He seemed nice!" Lishui could benefit from my bravery as well. She would much rather meet someone herself rather than picking someone off our parents' short list.

I nod, happy to look at Lishui's kind eyes because Mama's are making me melt. "He's a bit goofy, but yes, he's very nice." Thinking of the way his cheeks dimple when he smiles makes me smile too.

Mama will continue to argue with me while Papa decides to wait until after dinner. After dinner, Papa takes me outside and berates me for my poor choices and my wavering sense of responsibility. I can feel Mama, Lhasa, and Lishui listening at the window, my cheeks heating with their gazes.

Liling messed up.

But I won't let them have this. Randall, that is. Everything else I'm expected to do, I've done it. This, Randall, is one thing that I'm doing for myself. I've made Papa so mad that I'm essentially told to leave, with Mama suggesting I get ready for classes tomorrow morning.

I feel like the worst of it is over. Everyone knows. Some of them are disappointed in me, one person is happy I've fallen, and one person is excited for me. Now, all I can do is convince them of Randall's worth. It'll happen in time. They'll see it when months have gone by and he's still around. They'll see it when we graduate together, and when we go on to move up in our careers, and when we continue to be successful together.

Randall can see I'm tired when I show up at his apartment. He understands how taxing the combination of Mama and Lhasa are after just one meeting with them.

The two of us will be spending the night watching a movie. I'll lean against Randall while he lets me vent and I start to think that it would be nice if this is how things stayed. Randall and myself, in our quiet world.

LILING

I let Randall know my parents are aware I'm in a relationship, but I did not tell him what I endured afterward. Randall doesn't like when people don't like him. I don't have that problem.

Already, we find ourselves in the month of May. Spring classes are ending with little time left before my summer classes begin. Randall isn't taking summer courses, and he's intent on whatever he means when he says he's 'making money moves.'

I've been doing research for Randall. He needs someplace safe to keep his money, even though there's been some sort of a hitch in whatever operation he had going on before. Regardless, he needs someone to help him keep his head on straight.

For the time being, Randall is focused on what's to double as an apartment-warming party and end of semester celebration. When I point out that it's going to leave his apartment in a wreck, he claims there will only be a handful of people. I am doubtful because Randall seems to know everyone.

In the end, we welcome more than a handful, but less than I feared. Three hours into the party, I'm letting Randall make his rounds while I stand next to Ginger and watch him mingle. He floats around with so much confidence, knowing he is well acquainted with everyone in this room. Everyone loves Randall.

I also am in my people-pleasing mode tonight. I don't have the energy to keep it on all the time, but for the night, for Randall, I can shine just as brightly as him. Liling the Jewel makes an appearance. I have welcomed everyone in, made sure they know where the food and drinks are, and where the bathroom can be found.

There's loud music playing from a large stereo Gordy brought, making it somewhat difficult to hear. Ginger is next to me, drink in hand, talking about her failed English Theory course. I bite my tongue in asking how she failed it in the first place. It wouldn't be very jewel-like of me.

Ginger and I get along fairly well. She's a bit meek, and her personality changes depending on who she's talking to. It's like she needs the leader at all times. Sometimes, it's me, and she'll agree with most things I say and adopt a quieter personality. When Natalia is around, she's cattier, sluttier, and turns into a little minion.

When Natalia does walk in, I know my time having a girlfriend is over. It's time for fake niceties and sidelong glances. Natalia, I don't like her, and Randall knows it at this point.

I had felt good about my outfit, but it's clear Natalia has chosen a very different direction to go in tonight. I'm wearing my hair in a big perm, with dark red lips and smokey eyes. I've got a light acid-wash jean jacket over a white tank top that's a bit lower than I'd normally wear. I match this with jeans that sit high on my waste over black boots. I thought I looked nice, as did Randall, but then Natalia walks in wearing a skin tight dress and I wish I'd dressed nicer.

The she-devil walks in a deep red dress with a plunging neckline that dives between two shoulder pads. She's wearing black tights that are somehow more suggestive than if she didn't wear anything under the dress at all. Her dark hair smoothly flies behind her as she confidently picks out Randall from the crowd, as if to welcome herself to the party.

I watch their interaction like a hawk, and make a decision. Formal-wear is always better. It commands attention. The easiest way to beat Natalia is to mimic her and then do it better.

Next time, I'll be ready for her.

■■■

Overall, I think I actually enjoy hosting. Amongst other people our age, it appears Randall and I have our lives together. We're playing house, and I enjoy having it on display. I want people to see me with Randall and think it makes sense. Randall is a gem himself, and I want to shine with him.

I've replenished bowls of chips and now I'm going to Randall's bedroom to powder my face. I'm enjoying the quiet of the bedroom, taking a deep breath and turning myself off for just a minute. The door is cracked open, but I'm partially concealed behind the open drawer of Randall's dresser that houses a mirror on the inside.

In the hallway, I hear voices filter through, as if coming from the bathroom but stopping before they'd reached the party.

I instantly feel myself shrivel into Mean Liling when I hear Natalia's nasally, slanderous, voice. "You can tell a man decorated this apartment."

Ginger is, of course, the voice that responds. I'm powdering my face much softer now, even the sound of the brush hitting my face is getting in the way of a conversation I very much want to listen to. "I'm surprised Liling hasn't put her little touch on it." Ginger is skating the lines between us, but I know she'll defect over to Natalia in a few more moments.

"Maybe she doesn't come over a lot."

"Maybe."

182

There's a pause, as if the very mention of my name seems to just kill off their party mood. I can feel the music vibrating through the walls, and wonder how no neighbors have complained yet.

Natalia is ready to keep talking, as she always is. "But God, doesn't Randall look good tonight?"

There's giggling now, and my face is flushing because I hate that other people talk about *my* Randall like this. "Shh, I haven't seen *her* in a while, she could be anywhere."

"Maybe she left." Natalia has the blissful tone of inebriation in her voice. "Because God, if she hadn't shown up when she did, I would have cornered him by now and let him put it *all* the way back."

Ginger gasps. "Oh my gosh, shhh!"

"All the way down. Until it hits that hangy thing."

Ginger is hissing and shushing. "Seriously, stop!"

"You can tell she's stiff, I bet she couldn't beat me in bed."

"You're slutty when you're drunk," Ginger laughs. "But he seems to be head over heels for her, so I don't think you and your big mouth are going to cut it."

"I've got tricks," argues Natalia.

Ginger laughs again. "No more drinks." They're both laughing, but it stops suddenly, as if the very sight of me appearing in the doorway took the sound from their throats. I watch their faces, instantly blank and then flushed as they realize I've heard their entire slutty discourse.

I keep my voice low and sweet, because I know there's force in my composure. First, I look at Ginger and shake my head. "Ginger, sweetie, it's a wonder you don't have back problems from being everyone's doormat. Do you ever get tired of trying to

183

be everyone's lap dog?" Her mouth drops and I know I've lost any relationship we might've had.

"And you." I focus on Natalia, who looks at me starkly. "For as good as you claim to be, odd how you're still wholly unimpressive to Randall, isn't it?" I smile at her, petting the emeralds around my neck.

Natalia is preparing to chew me out but I am not done. She starts with, "Listen-"

"I'm not done speaking," I inform her. "You two can stay, if you can behave yourselves and sober up." In all honesty, I'd rather them stay and watch to see what it looks like when I'm winning. I look between them both now, I am strong. I am respected, and those who do not see this in me can leave. "If you're not going to play nice, then I'll ask Randall to have you leave. And when I ask Randall to do something, he does it."

Natalia lifts her brow, putting all her weight on one hip. "You want to bet? We've been friends since our freshman year."

"Yes," I tell her, looking at her shoes and she does too. I would love to have her watch how fast Randall will throw away a long friendship for me. I want her to see I have that power. I meet her eyes again. "If you can behave yourself once you're sober, maybe I'll let you continue to run in *our* circle after this." As long as they remember who to exult. I smile at her, leaving her and Ginger with open jaws as I go back to the party and make a beeline for what is mine.

**

Randall is positioned by the counter, looking like he's going to get himself a plate but abandons the idea when he sees me coming. He is under the influence of alcohol and all too happy when I drape myself over him. In these situations, Randall needs

184

little encouragement to let his hands wander, although I'll keep him in line since we are in a room full of people.

He loves when I play with his hair, and his head is bowed below my chin. I tussle, he kisses. I make sure I'm looking directly at the hallway, so by the time Natalia and Ginger slink out they can see where Randall and I stand. Natalia locks eyes with me, and I stare back at her, Randall obliviously kissing my neck as my arm hovers over his head.

Ginger is first to start pulling Natalia toward the safety of the far corner, where Greg sits by the balcony door cracked open so he can smoke what is definitely *not* a cigarette. At my neck, Randall pulls his lips to my ear. "What is this, you marking your territory?" He is not quite as oblivious as I thought him to be.

A cruel smile plays at my lips when I turn my head to meet his ears. "What if I am?"

Randall grins at me, and gives me a wet kiss on the nose. "As long as it means I'm yours." I only wish Natalia had been in earshot.

I kiss his nose, feeling that lustful pull within my body. "You're mine."

Randall laughs, and I can smell the beer on his breath. "But does *everybody* know I'm yours?"

I straighten my face into a warning, hearing the scheming in his voice. "Randall."

"What?" He asks innocently, starting to revolve me so that my back is against the counter. He happily kisses me, a little wetter than normal with his lack of sobriety, breathing me in like oxygen.

My cheeks flush with heat, kissing back partially because I'm slowly becoming obsessed with Randall and his happiness, and partially because I know people *are* watching. I try to stop him before he gets *too* excited. "Randall." The words are lost in

185

his mouth. I turn my head and he continues into my neck. "Randall."

I feel his laughter echoing in my skin. "Liling."

"I think everyone knows we belong to each other," I say lightly.

Without warning, Randall laces his fingers behind me and latches them together at the top of my thighs. He lifts me, hauling me up against the wall so that my face is more at level with his own. Pinned between the crook of the counter and the wall, hands on my rear, Randall is really putting on a show now.

"Tell me again and I'll put you down," Randall taunts happily, aggressively pressing his mouth to mine before I can even ask what he's drawling about now.

From across the room, Gordy calls, "You two are disgusting!" There's a mixture of laughing and cheering.

I briefly glare at Gordon, my arms around Randall's neck. "Tell you what?" I whisper, starting to be uncomfortable with just how much everyone knows we're together now.

He grins into my cheek, bowing his head so that his hair is tickling my face. "Tell me I'm yours again."

"Randall," I laugh, turning it into a scold.

"I can hold you here all day."

He'll try it, I know he will. Across the room, Natalia and Ginger look like they've had enough. My point has been made. Randall still has me pinned into the wall, hoisted above his body. Randall is still wearing a mischievous grin as Natalia and Ginger approach. Natalia's smile is tight and false.

She's going to completely ignore me so that she can say her goodbyes to Randall. "We're going to get going," Natalia says over the music. Randall smiles back at her, my hand is over his shoulder, fingers twirling a curl between my pointer and my thumb. "I don't think this party is our scene." She thinks she's clever, throwing this idea at Randall.

Randall may be silly at times, but he sees and hears more than he takes credit for. "Well, have a good night then."

Natalia's face drops so fast it almost hits the floor.

"Don't forget your jacket," I tell Ginger. She sucks her lip into a fake smile and we watch them leave.

"Why don't you like her?" Randall asks once they've gone, looking up at me.

I look down at Randall, moving my hand to stroke his hair, weaving it between my nails. "Because you're mine."

36.

[RANDALL]

Liling practically lives with me now, but she won't admit to it because she's desperately trying to convince herself she's the perfect, virtuous woman she was raised to be. We've been together for a few months now, officially. It's also been months since I've sold anything, or made any decent money.

I'm going to fix that problem today.

As far as I know, Toby was never replaced. None of his sellers have been able to move product. It also means that everyone who was selling for Toby has money they never paid up the line. That's where I come in.

Someone has to get everyone back in line, go collect money, and get everyone ready to start selling again. There's risk in this. Luis may not be paying attention now but he'll pay attention when I collect his money.

I'll either get myself killed, or I'll make a lot of money.

Until then, there's Liling.

We're moving so fast. We both feel it, we don't care. Love is weird. It's like I know Liling isn't perfect, but I don't care. It's like my idea of perfection is whatever Liling is.

Liling is in love with me too, but I don't think she'll admit it until our wedding day. I'm fine with that. She's better at showing her love than she is at vocalizing it. But I've got her now.

I'm fully aware Liling told herself I'm just a college boyfriend. For a while, I didn't care, because getting to boyfriend status was an achievement in itself. I see her changing, slowly. I'm not temporary. I'm not a college boyfriend. I'm *the* boyfriend. First and only.

The two of us are laying on the couch. I'm laying with my back pressed against the sofa, Liling is in front of me, sticking closely to me so we don't fall off together. The movie we're watching is wholly uninteresting, so my hands are going to slowly start exploring. Liling's a big fan of my handiwork.

Liling's voice drawls in sleep. "What do you think you're doing?"

I've got one hand maneuvering around a bra and the other around her pajama bottoms. "Appreciating you." Her ankles curl. I know she's a show-er, but sometimes I wanted her to be a teller. "Do you like being appreciated?" I ask in her ear, through her dark hair that smells like tea tree shampoo.

Liling's dark chuckle is going to test my commitment to staying semi-decent. "Don't be dirty."

I press harder. "Tell me or I'll stop."

"You say that like it's a threat," Liling chides, her ankles still grinding into mine.

"I haven't heard you complain before." My right hand has made it through all the layers it needs to. I'm going to be persistent. "Tell me."

She won't do it. Instead, she's going to take my left hand and put my fingers in her mouth. It's going to be so easy to kill me. Ten fingers and not one of them is dry. When she's taken my fingers back out of her mouth she puts it back over her blouse. "Now you tell me or *I'll* stop."

I'm burying my head into her hair even more. "I'll tell you whatever you want to hear." I need more room than this couch has to offer. "We should move to the bedroom."

Liling's cruel, beautiful, laugh fills my ears as she carefully dislodges my hands so she can turn to me. Our faces are so close together that I have to use my arms to keep her up on the couch. Our foreheads touch. "And why do you think we need to move to the bedroom, Randall Persch? What do you think is going to happen in there?"

I smile wide at her, my wrists are pressing into her backside as I keep her up on the couch with me. "A little more than what's happening now."

She tries to distract me with kisses, her arm is folded up against my chest.

Little by little, we go further and further, but not as far as I wish we'd go. "Is there a reason you like this but won't-"

"Randall." She has her warning tone that is very good at getting compliance from me. "I can't, you know that."

"We can pray for forgiveness afterward" I try. "You know I'm good on my knees."

"*Randall*," she says in an amused scold, her warm breath huffing in a laugh over my face. "You're impossible."

Fine, I'll kiss her neck until we can get back to where we were. "So, if I marry you then can-"

"Men really only think of one thing," Liling chides, turning back on her other side.

I put my hands back where she likes them. "I only think of you."

"Mhmm," she says contemplatively. Her hand reaches back for me, and I pinch her in closer, making her laugh.

I'm back in her hair, writhing next to her. "Liling Persch. Someday, that's who you'll be."

She laughs again. "Liling Persch," she echoes. I have a new fetish now, and it's hearing those two words next to each other. "How are you going to work that one out?"

I've shown her once, I'll show her again. "Tell me what your name will be and I'll show you."

Her voice is love. Her voice is a promise. Her voice is a prophecy. "Liling Persch."

37.

[RANDALL]

I'm in a happy buzz in the morning. I love falling asleep next to Liling. I love hearing her float around the apartment in the morning before I've woken up for myself. Every morning, I wake to the smell of coffee and the thick, watery humidity that pours out of the bathroom when she's finishing her shower.

Today, Liling will be gone for most of the day, spending time with her sisters and mother as they go dress shopping for Lhasa. I want to get all of my work done so I'm back before Liling is done with her family. I know spending the day with everyone doting over Lhasa is going to put her in a mood.

Toby has, or had, seven sellers, including myself. I'm going to try to get in contact with all of them. I already went back to Toby's apartment and found where he keeps his contacts written down on a notebook of paper.

My plan is to call everyone up, let them know I'm coming to collect money and see if they want to keep selling. If they do, I don't have a plan other than hope Luis lets me fill this position and doesn't shoot me between my eyes.

I start with Stoner Greg, making a house call because it's hard to get an actual call through to him. He's an easy pickup.

Even when mostly stoned, he had the forethought to keep Toby's money ready.

"You get promoted, Randall?" Greg asks with amusement when he's handing me the entire stack of his earnings. He's wearing a green t-shirt, which I think paints too clear a picture of him as Shaggy from the Mystery Gang.

Confidence. This *is* what I'm doing. "Toby's gone," I explain, doing exactly what I've seen Toby do a thousand times. I know the rates, I know what to take, and what to give. "So I'll be taking over, if you want to keep dealing."

Greg's an easy sell. "Hell yeah, I've been shit-broke since he went AWOL."

"I'll talk to Luis later and give you a call when I think we'll have some product," I say, as if I'm already used to the ins and outs of distributing cocaine and this is no big deal.

"Shit," Greg says, a smile showing his crooked teeth. "Running with the big dogs now, are you?"

I laugh. "I'm trying to keep up."

"Don't forget about me when you're at the top, ok?" Greg asks, tucking cash back into his pocket.

I have a small notebook where I'm keeping track of what I've been given, making sure it matches how much Greg should've sold. Liling tells me I need to be better about my records, but I need to be discreet about it.

Back at my apartment, I make four more calls, and end up with four appointments to go collect money. They know me, they like me, they accept my transition into this role easily. Life is easy when you make friends as effortlessly as breathing air.

By the time I make my fifth pickup, I start to feel an unease with the amount of money I have in my car. Thousands. Thousands of dollars that belong to the cartel. Just because Luis hasn't collected it yet, doesn't mean he won't come for it the moment he realizes it's moved.

The last two sellers are when I start to run into trouble. It had been going too easy, anyway. The first problem is Yogesh, who was under the impression that because Toby vanished into thin air, all the money he'd collected from his sales was his to keep.

"You should have known better than that," I say tiredly, over the phone. I feel like I've been gripping this beige colored phone all day, the coiled cord pulling at my hair every time I lifted the receiver to my head.

Yogesh doesn't sound like he's too worried, and he should be. If he's short, I'm short. I'm not taking a bullet for him. "I don't have it, so now what?"

"Now what?" I ask incredulously. "Now you owe the cartel money, what do you think happens next?"

Yogesh makes a frustrated 'Gahhh,' sound before saying "I don't know what to tell you, it's gone and it's not coming back."

I feel my temper rising. How does he think this will fly? "Maybe, you sell more and forgo all of your prof-"

"I'm not selling any more," Yogesh says directly. I hear him shuffle with his own phone. "I'm done with it. I'm graduating, so I can't be doing it anymore."

"But you owe money, now," I argue.

"Well, I'm done."

"You, you can't just 'be done' when you feel like it. Maybe, if you had your money ready-"

"If Toby wants his money, *he* can come get it."

My voice is hard as stone. I was his friend, but I'm going to strike that title really fast if he puts me in the position to. "Toby's gone. I'm here. It's not my money, it's not Toby's money, and it sure as hell isn't your money."

194

"Have a good one, Randall." He hung up on me. The idiot really hung up on me.

That's going to be a problem. I don't know how I'm fixing it yet, but I'll figure out the last resolution after I make the last call.

The last seller's name is Craig. He has questions but agrees to meet me in the back parking lot of a K-Mart superstore. Craig's always bugged me. He *looks* like a brown-noser.

Craig meets me wearing a striped blue and pink polo with khaki shorts. He has fluffed blonde hair and green eyes that sit over freckles. "How did *you* get Toby's job?" Craig asks, handing me his stack.

"Hard work," I reply, ignoring his tone while I flip through the bills.

"It's just that I haven't heard anything in weeks." Craig has a whiny, pretentious voice. I don't think he even really needs money, I think selling coke just makes him feel cool, or tough. He is neither, and I wish it was him slipping up so I'd have a reason to hit him.

"You're hearing from me now," I say, counting. He's got the amount he's supposed to have, so I pass him back what's his. "And if you keep selling, it'll be me you keep hearing from."

I see Craig consider this, his beady eyes looking between me and the cash I'm offering him. "Padilla chose *you?*" He asks at last.

"Do you have a problem with me?" I ask Craig instead, looking at him in challenge.

"I've met Luis before," Craig says, like it's an achievement. "I'm just having a hard time believing he put *you* in charge. Mr. Popular is going to be doing all of the Padilla's dirty work?"

"What, did you want the job?" I ask him, doing a scan of the parking lot as I speak.

"It would make more sense if it were me than you."

I give him a look of exasperation. "Alright, if I remember, I'll let Luis know that if I mysteriously disappear, you're ready to go."

Craig rolls his eyes. "Call me when you have something for me to sell."

"Mm." Prick. Out of spite, Craig will be the last person I call. I don't trust that little weasel any further than I can throw him.

Back in my car, I realize I'm going to need a better way to carry all this cash in the future. I have thousands of dollars in several tote bags and plastic grocery bags sitting on the floor of the passenger seat. Maybe I need to not do everyone's pickup in one day. Or make them come to me. That's what I should do. I'm the boss now, or I'm going to be. Yeah, they can come to me.

There's just one person to sort out. Yogesh. I don't know what to do about him yet, but for now I'll move the cash to my bedroom and maybe call him in a few days. If he still isn't willing to cooperate then, I'll have to get creative. Maybe it'll be better with Luis to call him having *most* of his cash, as opposed to making it look like I'm hanging onto what I've collected.

When I'm back in my car, there's a feeling of uneasiness. I look at all the money I have sitting on my floor. I've either done something bold that's going to change my life, or I've done something stupid that's going to end it.

LILING

It's Randall's birthday. June 2nd. Randall wants to spend the day going to the beach. I told him the water would still be cold this early in the summer, but he doesn't care.

"This will be our first trip together," Randall told me. "The second one will be our honeymoon."

I roll my eyes at him and push a present onto his lap. We are both dressed for the beach and will leave once he's opened his presents.

Randall grins at the present that I neatly wrapped in yellow paper. He feels the softness of the package, knowing it must be some sort of clothing. "I hope it's lingerie."

"*Randall*." My cheeks heat. Impossible, he is.

Randall rips open the present in the messiest way possible, and I try to ball up the discarded pieces as he goes. Ever since I got Randall that sweater on Valentine's Day, I see him cycle through the same two sweaters whenever he wants to look nice. Now, it's warm, so I've gotten him three collared polos. One in red, one in blue, and one in green.

Grinning at the shirts, he picks up the green one first. "These are exactly what I needed." He beams at me. "Thank you."

"I thought maybe-" I stop as Randall throws off the white cutoff shirt he'd been wearing so he can put on the blue polo. It's a rich, soft, material that catches the light and hugs his biceps.

Randall stands so he can stretch the shirt down his midriff.

"Randall," I laugh. "I haven't washed it yet."

He blanks. "You wash your new clothes before you wear them?"

"Of course!"

He shakes his head. "I'm wearing this today."

"I don't know that-"

"Let's get going, it'll take a couple hours to drive up there." There really is no stopping him once he sets his mind to something. So we leave, Randall dressed in a lovely blue polo and white swim trunks.

Randall is hefting our beach bags down the stairs of the apartment complex because the elevator is out. I have our cozy red and white checkered picnic blanket folded over my arms, petting the soft material as I trot behind Randall.

In the parking lot, I look around for the dilapidated vehicle that Gordy and Randall practically share. When we get outside, there's another car that stands apart from the rest, and it's the one Randall is walking to.

"I rented this for our trip," Randall says over his shoulder, walking toward a beautiful, freshly polished 1955 pink Cadillac.

My mouth parts in the wonder that is Randall Persch. Of course, Randall would think that we need a pink Cadillac for a road trip. Of course, Randall would find a way to turn what he wants into a reality.

Randall has rented a bubble-gum pink Cadillac, the convertible top is down to show white leather seats. A silver line runs along the side of the car from tire to tire. The tires are white

198

with black rims and the car is so immaculately clean that I couldn't help but run my hand over the top of the door.

When Randall gets to the back of the open-topped car, he stops to look at me, looking all too happy with himself. He puts the bags in the back seat then spreads his arms. "Look at this car!"

I laugh. He's all too handsome when he's this happy. His dimples have a permanent spot on his face when he looks at the car, but he seems even happier when he looks at me.

We have a two-hour trip to Holland, where Randall says his favorite beach spot is. We're going down the highway with the top down, the wind is whipping hair out of my ponytail, deflecting off my sunglasses. It's sunny and warm, and I have two hours of Randall being in an absolutely cartoonish, lovesick sort of joy. I think he's pulling me into the same headspace.

Randall drives with one hand on the white leather steering wheel and the other on my thigh. The radio is playing loudly, and Randall turns it up even higher when he hears the chimes of a song that brings a smile to his face.

As the bass comes in, Randall shouts, "I'll be Aretha, you be George."

I laugh, "Why woul-"

I wasn't prepared for Randall's Aretha Franklin impersonation, or at the ridiculous pitch his voice reaches. *"Like a warrior that fights, and wins the battle,"* He doesn't stop when I almost lose myself in laughter. He goes on to take both the parts of Aretha and George Michael.

By the end of the song, Randall is fully invested into the song, putting all his energy into the big finish, trying to keep up with Aretha's riffs as the music blares down the freeway. "Randall!" I laugh, as he's getting too into his big performance.

"I didn't falt-ERRRRRR," he screeches alongside Aretha.

I'm too happy. Too happy right now. I take in this moment and try to remember everything about this day. Driving down the freeway in the morning heat, top down, sun shining on Randall's ecstatic, beautiful face. Randall is driving with a hand on my thigh, wind whipping through his red-brown hair. He's wearing a blue polo that's too nice for a beach day and cheap, black, dollar store sunglasses. The sound of Randall's crooning brings us to hysterics.

This is it. I am sure this is what love feels like. This summer breeze mixed with the smell of cinnamon bark, music speeding, dimpled-Randall feeling is what I'm going to associate love with.

Randall Persch. That's what I associate love with.

39.

RANDALL

I've had a good week. I spent my birthday with Liling, I made good tips while delivering pizzas, and I have plans to make so that maybe I don't have to deliver pizzas anymore.

I have one loose end. Yogesh. I tried calling him again, but he must have one of those good phones that has caller ID because he doesn't answer anymore. I still don't know what to do about Yogesh. Maybe I could try to scare him into cooperating or something or-

My door rattles when someone knocks on it like the building is on fire. I know it isn't Liling because I've already given her a spare key, and if she does choose to knock, she's so light that it's hard to hear unless I'm already in the kitchen.

From my bedroom, I walk along the carpet until it turns into linoleum. By the time I'm in the kitchen, someone is rapping on the door again. "Hang on!" I call, wondering if Gordy has shown up to hang out and is fucking with me.

Expecting to see my friend, I whip the door open, ready to chew him out for being so loud. As soon as the door opens, there's a painful impact directly at my jaw and I'm being sent back on my ass as my head is filled with the stars I thought I gave to Liling.

I would normally describe myself as a fighter, but everything is happening too fast. I'm barely making a full landing on the floor before I'm pulled up and punched down. I'm not alone in my apartment now, as a group of guys are pushing their way in.

From the floor, I recognize the one that holds a gun to my head. I look up, panting. "Hi, Rogelio," Rogelio glowers at me, pulling dread from my stomach. Rogelio is a man that there's no winning against if it's going to come down to a fight. Maybe he's the scariest of the lot.

Someone steps toward me, brown leather shoes just inches from my nose. I follow the dark jeans up to see that brown, sunken face. "Hi, Luis." My door shuts and locks.

Stay calm, don't be combative, I think. *I understand why they're here, and it's just a misunderstanding.*

I place my hands under me so that I can carefully stand up. "Alright, who hit me? I usually like to-"

Luis grabs me by the collar of the red polo that Liling gave me, pulling me close enough that I can smell the cigarettes on him. He's so skinny that I feel like I could take him on if it wasn't for the group he traveled with. "What the hell do you think you're doing?" He growls at me.

Calm. I'm going to be calm. "I'm guessing you're here for your money."

Luis isn't amused, or patient. "You've got two seconds-"

If he wants to be rude, fine. I'll interrupt him right back. "I told you I could take Toby's job," I argue, and continue when it seems like Luis is going to let me speak. "I told you I know the sellers and can get them ready to go. So I did. I have it, ready to go, locked in my room." Honesty is the best policy here, I think. Maybe. I've been hit several times, so I'm not sure.

I put my hands up complacently. "I can go get it."

Luis studies me, his brown eyes firing into me. "I'll make it so fucking slow if you're lying to me right now." He releases his hands, leaving my collar crumpled.

Luis mumbles something in Spanish to Rogelio who points at me with his weapon. "Show me," Rogelio says with quiet authority.

I nod, carefully putting my hands at my side. I lead Rogelio into my bedroom, where a new safe is tucked under my desk. "You're really fucking stupid, you know that?" Rogelio says quietly, his accent curling his words together.

"I like to use the word ambitious," I say over my shoulder, dropping to my knees to start clicking the dial around until I have it open. My nerves are shot, but I'm going to keep breathing and will this to work in my favor. I'll be fine. I took a risk, and this is the conclusion of the risk I took: the payoff.

I've got almost thirty thousand dollars in the safe. Thirty thousand dollars, and it's not even all that I should have, had Yogesh paid what he was supposed to. Someday, I'll have a safe full of money that's mine to keep.

I start unloading it all, putting stacks on the desk above me. Liling helped me organize the money and put it in presentable stacks, and I'm really glad for that now.

I turn toward Rogelio, who is watching me like a hawk. "You gonna help carry some of this?"

He raises a brow but sighs, tucking his gun away. "I could kill you without it," he warns, stepping beside me to grab some of the stacks.

His forearms are like tree trunks. "I'm sure you could, big guy," I say soothingly, piling the paper of the records I kept on top of the bills. The two of us carry the stacks back into the living room. We put out all of the cash in a pile on the table that sits in front of the couch.

Luis had been looking out the window, dropping his neck to see the view that's nothing but the balcony of the building across from mine and some patchy grass. He walks over to the cash, picking up a pile and handing it to one of his men.

Two of the men started counting while Luis watches, hands in his pocket. "Toby had six sellers," I start, coolly. "I got a hold of everyone, and they're ready to sell again."

Luis tilts his head. He's wearing something similar to what he'd worn before: a vintage style green bowler shirt, with a small floral insignia on the left side of his chest. He's paired it with long cream-colored pants that have extra space as they hang over his thin body. "So you go to all these sellers and tell them what, Boy Scout?"

"I told them I'll be coming by to collect their money and let them know I'll be taking over for Toby."

His eyes are so blank, lifeless, as he stares at me. "Just like that, huh?"

"Just like that."

Luis' stoic face is starting to make my skin crawl. "Toby had seven sellers. Are you lying to me, or have you already lost someone?" Besides Luis, Rogelio shifts slightly, like he's sharing the discontent aggression that's pouring out of the drug-lord.

Freezing, I watch two of his men continue to count, thinking it's better to explain the discrepancy before they say anything. "There's a problem with one of the sellers."

Luis' face barely moves, but I see the change in his mood. It's deadly. The counters stall for half a second, one of them smirking. "What's." Luis is articulating every word with malice. "The. Problem."

"I've been calling one of the sellers, his name is Yogesh," I explain, speaking casually. I'm not nervous. I don't need to be.

I'm going to convince myself. "He doesn't have what he's made from selling. Says he's done."

I wait for Luis to say something as he stands with his hands in his pocket. "Yogesh," He repeats. I nod. "So, you want to be in charge of the sellers but you can't get what's owed on your first run through?"

"I-"

"It doesn't look great for you, does it?" He directs this to Rogelio.

"Doesn't look great, boss," Rogelio parrots.

"You go and take my money, but then tell me you don't have all of it." Luis looks at the counters, one of which is the man with the thicker fro'd hair that is starting to fall into locs. I remember he was standing behind Rogelio in the bathroom when I met everyone. He's flipping through wads of cash at lightning speed.

I'm starting to see why Toby's such a nervous guy, especially if this is the kind of pressure he's under. So far, Luis seems immune to the Randall Persch Charm. My brain is trying to churn out some words that will appease Mr. Padilla. Before I even fully form my first word, Luis cuts me off again.

He puts his hand up, thinking. "You know where he lives?"

I already know where this is heading. "Yes."

Luis takes out a stick of gum from his pocket. "You want this job?"

It's me or Yogesh, at this point. "I do."

Luis says something in Spanish that makes the person who was waiting at the door, leaning against the wall, to fully stand. "Diego will take you. Come back with Yogesh. We'll talk." I take in Diego again, the one covered head to toe in tattoos. He's wearing the same oversized black leather jacket, hanging stiffly off of his body.

"You going, Boy Scout?" Luis asks, interrupting my thoughts. When I look at him, he says, "We'll hold down the fort."

There's really not a lot of wiggle room here. "Sure, he lives nearby. Really close." Offhand, I don't love the idea of leaving the cartel at my apartment. However, I'm not in a position to tell any of these men what to do.

"Good." Luis sounds bored. "Then, I guess you'll be back soon."

I nod, taking a look at my escort: man of ink. Luis is saying something to Diego before I get to the door. Diego takes keys out of his pocket.

As I put my shoes on, getting ready to willingly go on a trip with a cartel member, I ask, "Hey, Luis?" Luis had turned towards the table, but now seems surprised that I have the gall to speak to him directly. "Was it Craig?"

His face reveals nothing. "Why?"

"Wouldn't you want to know?"

For some reason, Luis finds this funny. "Keep an eye on that one, Boy Scout." That was confirmation enough, so I put my shoes on and follow Diego out of the apartment. When all this is over, I'm going to go visit Craig. He took his own risk, but he's not going to have the same luck I did. Or at least the luck I think I'm having.

I follow Diego outside to the parking lot where the two massive SUVs are parked next to each other. I still haven't heard a word from this man. "So, Diego, was it? My name is Randall." Diego looks over his shoulder, a small gold hoop bobbles on his earlobe, but doesn't say anything. "How long have you been with Luis?" I try. Still, he doesn't say anything so I drop it for a while.

Diego unlocks his car, unlocking the door for me as well. It's a brand-new car, clean, except for some loose powder that is all too recognizable for me. I have a thing for nice cars, and this one is lighting up my brain. It has a car phone! Someday, I'll buy myself a car that has a car phone, a sunroof, and all the bells and whistles. That, or a muscle car. Whatever catches my eye.

Once we're both in the car, there's some awkward silence as I buckle my seatbelt and Diego stares at me. It takes a minute to realize what he wants. He's waiting for directions. "Oh," I say bashfully. "Take a left on Saginaw." He starts driving, and I pray Yogesh is at his apartment.

We drive in silence, no words exchanged except for the directions I give Diego. Once we turn right at a traffic light, I tell Diego that the apartment complex is 5 minutes down the road on the left. "Did you know Toby?" I ask. Nothing. "You know, Diego, I'm very persistent. Give me a couple months and we'll be best friends."

Finally, I hear Diego say his first word and it's not even in English. I don't speak Spanish, I'm pretty sure he just called me stupid. I laugh, amused by how little I got from him. "It's not the first time I've been called that, and it won't be the last. I'm sure I'll hear it again before the day's even over." Diego suppresses a smile, ink moving along his face as the muscles struggle to hold their place, but still does not say anything.

I point to the right, because we've reached the apartment complex Yogesh lives at. Diego parks the massive SUV in the free spot by building four. Yogesh lives in building five so I'll have to walk down.

I'm unsure if Diego was planning on coming with me or not until he finally says, "Better to walk." Now, having said three words, I can hear that Diego has an extremely thick accent, and I have to focus to make sure I catch everything. "If he won't walk."

207

Diego shrugs, pulling his lip down. "I drag." Diego is smaller in stature than the rest of his group, but there's nothing about Diego that appears weak.

"Got it," I say quickly. "Well, let me try and hopefully I come back with him." Diego is out of words for the moment, so I let myself out of the car and try to find the apartment.

This is a standard college apartment that's rundown, smells like weed, and there are bags of trash in the hallway from people who are too lazy to take it to the dumpster. Yogesh lives on the first floor, and I find his apartment with ease.

When I knock on the door, Yogesh answers within a minute. He's met me before, so he knows to be displeased when he sees it's me. "Listen," he says. "I already told you I'm done."

"And I already told you that you can't just be done when you owe money." I keep my voice low. Before he can argue, I say, "Listen, I have a scary.... I don't know... I think he sounds Colombian, let's go with that." Diego has a different accent from Luis and the others. "Colombian, waiting outside. He's given you two options: you can walk out or you can be dragged out. Pick one."

Yogesh blanks. Yogesh doesn't look dressed for the day; still in pajama bottoms and an old red T-shirt. His rich black hair is a mess and there's still sleep in his eyes. "Are you being serious?"

"There's not a whole lot of good jokes about cartels," I say dryly. "Walk or be dragged," I remind him.

I'm coming out with Yogesh within five minutes. Diego is waiting outside of the car, leaning against the hood. When he sees us, he unlocks his car and opens the back door. He doesn't speak to Yogesh, but gestures to the backseat. Yogesh looks at me, and I can see it sinking in that he knows he's in some trouble. I don't know what Luis has planned, but I nod as if it's ok to get in.

Diego and I exchange looks as we get in the car and I think maybe I do know what Luis has planned.

We make even better time on our way back. Nobody talks. I don't know what to say to Yogesh, and I know Diego probably won't answer anyway. When we arrive back at my apartment, Diego turns toward the backseat. "Stay," is all he says. This is a relief to me. Whatever is going to happen, it's not happening in my apartment.

It's a relief, at least, until I see Liling's car parked a few spaces down.

40.

RANDALL

Ditching my babysitter, I'm abandoning the car and running through the parking lot, and up the stairs. I think I even caught Diego off guard. That, or he knows he can catch up and kill me later. If he tries to stop me before I get back to my apartment, I'll fight him. Liling unknowingly walked into my apartment and was probably met by a bunch of cartel members counting money in the living room.

In the minute and a half it takes me to run up four flights of stairs, my imagination has gotten the best of me and I'm in a cold sweat when I barrel through the door.

Inside, it's… confusing. There was talking, and laughter and smiles that instantly disappear when I burst into the room. They're all staring at me like *I'm* the crazy one.

The first thing I do is scan the room for Liling, who's sitting on the couch next to Luis. She's looking at me with surprise, but she looks normal. She's got her hair up in a ponytail and is wearing a lavender spaghetti strap blouse with a white skirt.

Panting, I ask her, "Are you ok?"

I watch her face slowly, cruelly form a smile. "I'm fine, Randall." She hesitates, pushing her bangs back. "Are *you* alright?" I'm at a loss for words. Not only is she fine, it looks like she's entertaining, like we're just having guests over and she's keeping everyone happy while I run to the store for brats.

Even Luis is different. He seems to be functioning more like a normal person. He's more relaxed, he's got this goofy sideways grin that smooths out when he nods towards the door. "Where the hell is Diego?"

I almost feel embarrassed about running through the parking lot. "I, uh, lost him."

As I say this, Diego comes in briskly, also panting. He gives me a look like he's just hoping Luis gives him permission to throttle me. I don't know what he says to Luis, but it sounds like cursing. Whatever he says, he conveys the sentiment in less than five words but it makes Luis laugh again.

"Shit, Boy Scout, you need to relax a little bit." He looks at Liling with a smirk I don't like. He's got a wedding band on, but that doesn't mean I trust him. "I'm a gentleman, always."

Liling pulls her lip in the way she does when she's trying to keep her smile in check before meeting my worried glance. "Do you need a glass of water?" She chides.

"Um, no. I'm fine." I fight the urge to double check that she's really fine, not buying that she somehow managed to get everyone in the room in such high spirits. She really shines, when she wants to.

Rogelio is sitting on the dark red recliner next to the couch that has its back facing the window. He speaks to Diego. "*Se comportaron todos?*"

Diego nods but gestures at me. "*Hablador.*" And all of the Spanish-speaking people in the room laugh. Whatever Diego says, he's apparently funny when he chooses to talk.

I want to get this moved along, and I wish Liling would come stand by me. "So," I say awkwardly, knowing that Liling knows the kind of things that I do, but so far the things I do have not included duressed transport that could be considered kidnapping. "Yogesh is in the car."

Luis nods, getting more serious, like I'm ruining the mood. "I guess we should get going." I must have looked confused, so Luis adds, "Unless you want us all to braid each other's hair and stay longer."

"We can go," I say quickly.

Luis says something to his men and Rogelio, Diego, and the third man who I haven't learned his name yet stand up. Liling stands too, and she warmly says, "It was good to meet you, Luis." She's so warm and genuine, and I know just about anyone could fall in love with Liling if she looks at them like that often enough.

Luis smiles at her, taking her hand and says, "You know what, *Diamante*, keep your boyfriend in line and I'll see you both at the end of the year. I like to bring my people together once a year."

She's beaming, flawless, magnificent, poised, and perfect. "That sounds wonderful." She crosses the room, taking my arm and tells him, "I think you'll find Randall is one of the best people to have in your corner," she says, kissing my cheek when she's finished. I'm too flustered to really take in what she's saying.

Luis chuckles. "If you say so, *Diamante.*" I need to learn Spanish. Luis' eyes fall on me next. "We'll be waiting, Boy Scout. Hurry up."

I nod at him. "Ok, I'm coming," I tell him. The men all leave, and I'm spinning Liling around by the shoulders to inspect her fully. "Are you ok?"

I hate that she seems amused. "I'm fine, Randall." She takes hold of my chin. "I was definitely surprised to find your apartment full of strange men, to say the least."

"They just showed up and-"

212

Liling's hand runs over a tender spot on my cheek. It felt like a bruise waiting to form. "You're strong, Randall." Liling says seriously. "You can do this. We can do this."

I'm lost in her. "We can do this," I parrot.

"It's going to be hard, but I'm going to be right here waiting, when you get back." Her voice is a warm embrace, and it's meant only for me. "I talked you up," she adds, lovingly before she starts to scold. "I don't think he has the same sense of humor as you."

"I'm beginning to see that."

This world I'm going into- it's treacherous. When I first started, I wasn't responsible for anyone else. I have a family, technically. I have a brother and a dad, but Liling is different. Liling is mine. I feel a responsibility for her and her safety. I think she feels the same way about me. It's the two of us, going into this together.

That's why I know I'll be successful.

Liling's voice interrupts my inner monologue. "Go do what needs to be done." She's firm, but she's sweet, she's right.

I'd kill for this woman. Starting now.

I'm not an idiot, I know what's going to happen. I know what happens when someone steals from the cartel. I have no doubt this is Luis' elaborate way of making an example out of Yogesh. Maybe it's a warning for me, but I don't need to be told how to keep my hands clean, so to speak.

"I'll be back," I tell Liling, forcing my regular demeanor back into my voice. "And when I am, let's pick up on where we left off last night."

She narrows her eyes at me. "We need to rest for church tomorrow."

I laugh. "I'll make sure we get good sleep."

"Go." Liling gives me a quick kiss before she's pushing me out the door. "Be yourself, and everything will be fine."

■■■

Ten minutes later, I'm in a car with Luis Padilla. The group took two cars. I'm sitting in the passenger with Luis driving and the last of the men I haven't finessed yet. His name is Oscar.

Oscar looks different than Luis and his other men, looking more Afro-Latino with skin that's even darker. His black hair is thicker, but he starts pulling at the front, smoothing it back until it's pulled into a bun on top of his head while we drive.

The car that trails us is being driven by Diego, with Rogelio and Yogesh in the car as well.

"You got yourself a good woman," Luis says in his dry voice. His knuckles clutch the steering wheel, his fingers glistening with the gold of thick rings. If he had been the one to punch me when I opened my door, my face would have been split open.

I decide to test if he's a romantic like I am. "I knew that the minute I saw her."

Luis laughs. "Love at first sight, eh Boy Scout?"

"Something like that, depending on who you ask. You're married?"

Luis holds up his left hand, the wedding band being the most understated of the jewelry he wore. "Four years." Luis is maybe in his upper-twenties, older than me, but only slightly. "We've got our first kid coming."

"Congratulations," I say easily.

"So, as you can imagine, I have to be extra careful about who I let work for me. It takes one weak pillar to bring down the house."

I'm going to keep things light. "So, you're saying I got the job?" I ask, as if the job in question isn't moving and distributing illegal substances.

214

Luis chuckles. "You're persistent, aren't you?"

"I'll make you a lot of money," I promise.

"Diego says you talk too much," Luis says. "But Rogelio likes you." Luis looks in his rear-view mirror, making contact with the person in the back. "Oscar?"

I turn and look at Oscar. Oscar looks at me. "I think anyone who has the guts to do what you did has what it takes to roll with us."

Luis nods introspectively, glancing at me before returning to the road. "Or, he's just stupid."

Oscar laughs with a nod. "Yeah, boss. Could be that, too."

"Ambitious," I argue.

Luis smirks, scratching his chin. "Ambitious, fine. But don't try any shit like that again, you got it? You don't take risks. You don't play with my money, and I don't play with your life."

I'm nodding vigorously. "Understood. You don't have to worry about me."

"Because I got other people to keep track of. Different areas. I can't do a personal trip every time someone does something stupid."

"I can handle myself," I promise.

Luis' eyes flick to the mirror again. "Yeah, well, we'll see about that one, huh Boy Scout?"

■■■

We end up driving further than I thought. Luis owns a storage container lot near Flint. I'm sure someone like him gets a lot of use from it. There's a lot of places to keep things - people. There's places to keep trucks and boats and just about anything that needs to be hidden could find a home here. That, and it's loud. Between the nearby train tracks, the highway, and the large commercial vehicles that are being moved around, sounds are garbled together and lost.

Luis pulls his SUV to the very back of the lot, where there's two oversized storage units that are separated from the rest. There's an additional gate to get past, with an armed guard who raises the bar when he sees us coming.

"Is this a warning for Yogesh or-"

"This is a test," Luis says. I know who the test is for.

By the time I see Yogesh again, his brown skin is glistening with sweat, and his hands are tied. Rogelio and Diego look bored. It's business as usual.

Luis inspects Yogesh as he gets out of the car. "You the one who sold *my* product and then took *my* money?"

Yogesh starts blubbering incoherently. "No, I wasn't-"

"I don't like liars," Luis says. "But I'll give you the same deal I'll give Toby, when I find him," Luis says.

That can't be a good deal.

Luis continues. "And Randall," My eyes snap from Yogesh to Luis at the mention of my name. "Is going to make sure all his sellers know exactly what kind of deal you got." He looks at me. "Right, Boy Scout?"

His sellers. I nod. This is a part of my job now. "I'll make sure."

Luis takes out a cigarette, and Diego lights it for him. Luis puffs into Yogesh's face. "Anything you want to say, thief?"

It's hitting him. Yogesh knows it. I know it. He's not leaving this place alive. "Please, I'll do anything. Just tell me and-"

"At this point, the example you'll make is worth more to me," Luis says. He speaks louder, as if talking to his men, and maybe me, now. "And we're not going to be putting up with it anymore, huh?"

"No more," Rogelio echoes. Diego nods. I think Rogelio is essentially second-in-command here. I'm trying to learn everything I can, and understand the hierarchies.

Luis takes a step back. "No more." He nods at Rogelio, who pistol whips Yogesh so fast and so hard that he's on the ground immediately. The other three men descend like wolves. They work as a team, beating their enemy. They ignore the pleading, the bleeding, the crying, the pissing.

This is the world I'm in now. If I'm not here, standing and watching, then I'm there, on the ground bleeding. *This* is how Luis lives the way he does.

I'm watching Yogesh have his life beaten out of him and I'm not feeling the way I'm supposed to be feeling. I'm thinking about myself, about Liling. About the life I'm going to build for us. It's us or them.

Luis lets it go on for a while, stopping his men before Yogesh loses consciousness. "Enough," he says something to Diego and Oscar, who respond by dragging Yogesh by his shoulders up against the wall of the storage unit. They sit him up, but his head slumps to the side. A low moan escapes from Yogesh's mouth. There's several teeth littered on the spot where Yogesh was beaten before he was dragged.

"Here, Persch," Luis calls over his shoulder. He's standing in front of Yogesh, with all his men standing to his left.

I swallow and move to stand next to Luis on his right. Luis looks over at me, and I already know what my test is going to be before he's even handed me a pistol with a silencer on it. "Can you do what needs to be done?"

I take the gun, holding one for the first time in my life. "I can do it." I only know what I'm doing because I've seen it on TV before. There's something to pull back with my thumb and then I pull the trigger- easy, right?

217

It really was.

I'm glad Yogesh is out of it. It makes it easier. He's not looking at me, he's not pleading, he's barely here. He won't even know. This will probably be the easiest kill I ever make. After this, it'll be harder. It'll be more dangerous.

I lift the gun, and I shoot. It was that easy.

When I do, Rogelio snickers, saying, "Shit aim, man."

I've hit Yogesh square in the throat. It nearly blasts his windpipe open but he's somehow still alive. He's gurgling as blood pours out of the hole in his neck.

Luis almost looks disappointed. He holds his hand out so I pass the gun back to him. "Welcome to the family, Persch," Luis says without any warmth in his voice. "Just remember." He looks me directly in the eye, and puts his hand out, pointing the gun at Yogesh again. He fires the weapon, lodging a bullet straight into the forehead. "Family is forever."

LILING

One more month. One more month of Randall's nonsense; his library visits, his flowers, his bounding confidence in himself, his touches. He's been nothing but joy lately; he smiles, he sings, he's a man that feels he has life under his thumb.

It's July now, and I'm thinking about how I'll enter my final school year with a boyfriend who I have a feeling will be leaving my final school year with me.

Randall and I have developed this habit, as part of my denial that I'm living with him in any capacity. I never spend Saturday nights with Randall; I always return to my dorm room. Then, in the morning, I go to church as I always do on Sundays, and Randall will show up minutes after me in the pews, as he always does.

This Sunday morning, I'm wearing a sleeveless, collared floral dress with a white base that's peppered with red and yellow and green flowers. The dress goes to my ankles and dances above red heels that are strapped around my ankles. After applying some red lipstick and combing my hair so it cascades over my shoulders, I'm ready to go.

I'm in a happy daze because I love the relief of a slow Sunday morning. Tomorrow is my birthday, and it's brought a goofy mood into Randall as he teases whatever he has planned.

It's when I'm locking my door that I hear it, I hear them. Unannounced, uninvited, there's a band of well-dressed Chinese-Americans coming down the hallway, happy with the smiles of people who have planned a surprise visit. Lishui, Mama, and Papa have all caught me off my guard.

Lishui is wearing a red maxi-dress as she's speeding down the hallway, Mama scolding behind her. "Happy early birthday!" Lishui chants as she envelops me in a hug.

I hug her back, knowing my easy Sunday Morning is now a little harder. "What are you all doing here?" I ask through Lishui's hair.

My parents have now caught up to me. "We thought we'd celebrate your birthday early, since it is on a weekday," Papa says, also hugging me in greeting.

Mama will not hug, but she tells me, "We will go to your church today and then we can go to lunch." She speaks like she's giving instructions, adding, "Lhasa could not make the drive today."

"Hm," I say, trying to feign disappointment. "I wouldn't want her to overwork herself on my account." Only Lishui recognizes my sarcasm.

Papa, dressed in a suit, checks his watch. "We should get going, when does your service start?"

I think about how Randall is going to arrive before I do, and how he will not be prepared for who I arrive with. "Ten. It'll take ten minutes to walk there." I also think about how, since I have told my parents that I'm dating, Papa isn't scolding me for it, Mama is pretending it isn't happening. I'm sure she's still trying to find someone for me.

220

As we walk, no one has asked about Randall, so I'll wait until we get to church for them to realize this relationship is still happening. They've only met him one time, but maybe seeing Randall as a new man of Christ will improve his appearance in their eyes. I think it will take little convincing for Lishui.

The weather is warm enough that Papa has started to sweat by the time we arrive, but he has a brown handkerchief to dab his forehead with. I can already see Randall from here, waiting outside by the doors. When I get here first, I go inside and sit. If Randall gets here first and sees I haven't arrived, he'll come back out to wait. I suppress a smile at the sight of Randall standing in a green polo and dress slacks, his fiery brown hair gelled neatly to the left.

Lishui sees him first, remembering the charming pizza boy that arrived at my dorm months ago. Her brown eyes grow, looking at me. "Get ready," I mutter, straightening my spine.

Randall sees me now, and he sees who I'm traveling with. I see the little bit of surprise register away from his usual golden-retriever demeanor. He stands up straight, he takes his hands out of his pocket, and he plasters on a polite, ready-to-please smile. I send Randall an apologetic but amused look, only as calm as I am now because I know my parents won't make a scene in the Lord's presence.

Mama sees Randall now. Names, she's bad with, but a face, she never forgets. Her little face drops, her bob bouncing on her shoulder when she whips her head at me. "You bring the boy to church?"

"We go to church together every week," I tell her. She is silent, because it's hard for her to argue that this is bad.

Papa is doubtful, his face contorting in annoyance. We've reached Randall, who is gearing up to be just as charming as ever.

Normally, Randall puts his arm around me as soon as I'm within reach, but I can see he's waiting to follow my lead. Good boy.

I'm going to rip the bandaid off first, and take a few steps ahead of my family to greet Randall first. I'm going to keep my hands to myself, going to stand just in front of him, slightly to his right. "Sorry," I whisper first. Then, I put on my big, fake, family-friendly smile as the rest of my family has caught up to us.

Randall is in the same set of mind I am: it's parent pleasing time. He's extending a hand to my father as soon as Papa has begrudgingly approached. "Morning," Randall says smoothly. "It's good to see you again."

Papa is cautious, but polite. "Good to see you." His voice does not match his words.

Mama is a little better at hiding her distaste when she greets Randall too. The only reason she is anything other than a fan of Randall is because I've attached the word *boyfriend* to his name.

Sweet Lishui is the bubbly, open energy Randall needs. "Hi!" She's ecstatic at the idea of boyfriends, and is glad I'm the one taking this burden because if I pull it off, maybe she can try the same. I like the idea of Lishui and I picking our own partners when Lhasa used family connection.

There's a bit of a pause, but Randall fills it with small talk. "Beautiful morning,"

Papa nods. "Yes," is all he says.

"Let's go sit down," Lishui cuts in with cheer.

"I'll show you where we like to sit," I say graciously. I want to take Randall by the arm but I'm unnerved by how poorly my parents are already reacting, so I skip this.

All in a row, we file into my regular pew. Randall sits on the end, with me next to him and Lishui next to me on my other side. My parents are on the opposite end but I know they are watching him with their peripheral vision with much curiosity. I suppress a smile, thinking of the first time Randall appeared by my side in church.

We all take out our hymnals, ready for the first song, as the organ is ushering in the entrance of worshippers. Randall and I share a hymn, the sound of Randall's tune now a comforting addition to my Sunday mornings.

Lishui is sneaking looks from beside me. Randall sings loud and confidently. Our worship leader has already tried to poach him to join the praise team but Randall is not so confident that he'd want to stray from my side to sing songs he's only just learning.

I catch Mama's eye and I see it. She's thinking. She's hearing, she's seeing. It can be hard to win Mama over, but someone who presents as a Good Christian Man, she won't argue with that. I will make sure she never knows what Randall really does, or how I support it. How I enable it. I will never stop working to be perfect in my parents' eyes.

> *Why should I feel discouraged,*
> *Why should the shadows come,*
> *Why should my heart be lonely*
> *And Long for Heav'n and home*

Papa is studiously reading from his hymn, as if he hasn't been singing this song for years. I look at Randall, whose dimples are ever present as he's choosing to also keep his eyes on the text. I feel it again, and I have to look at the back of the head in front of me to focus. That pull, that whisper, that warmth that makes me think only about Randall and the closeness I want from him. With him.

Love. Love. Love. I haven't said it, because I don't think I should be feeling it. Not yet. It's far too soon. Far too soon. But when Randall is so obviously feeling it, I feel like I'm dragging my feet.

When Jesus is my portion
My constant friend is He
His eye is on the sparrow
And I know he watches me

Randall isn't a college boyfriend. He's not temporary. He's mine. I'll push away anyone Mama tries to bring to me. I'll shove away anyone who tries to come between us. Randall will too.

Someday, I'll laugh at myself for being so resistant. I could have made things easier on myself. I shouldn't have worried so much about whether I was doing the right thing. I need to start worrying about whether I'm happy because right now, I am very happy. I have love, I have a future, I have assurance.

I have everything I need, but I know that I'll have so much more. More of Randall, more of life, more of everything. To me, Randall is as beautiful as the hymns he sings by my side. He is happiness, he is freedom, he is a protector.

I sing because I'm happy
I sing because I'm free
For His eye is on the sparrow
And I know He watches me

42.

RANDALL

It's all coming together. Everything. I spent Liling's birthday getting on her parents' good side. We went to church, we had lunch, and by the end of the day, Liling informed me that she'd been given permission to date me until the end of our senior year. She's taking the victory, and isn't arguing it for now. My takeaway is that Liling sees herself arguing it after our senior year. I've got her hooked on the Randall Persch Charm.

In the last month, I've been making more money than ever. There's a saying- 'sells like crack.' There's a reason for that, and I'm benefitting from it. Honestly, what I do now is almost easier than what I did before. I personally don't sell anymore, I keep track of people who are. I'm down to six, with Yogesh having disappeared. Luis took care of the body. It was clearly something he and his men do with ease.

I've got Gordy working with me now. He doesn't sell or anything, but he's muscle when I need it. Sometimes I solve problems for my sellers, sometimes my sellers are the problem. The shit with Yogesh can't happen again. If one of my sellers is short, I have to come up with the difference because it's got to get to Luis one way or another. That means I need to motivate my

225

sellers not to put me in that position. I'm a little less friendly than before.

The first time I used Gordy's help was paying Craig a visit. I worked a shift with Gordy and asked, "Would you want to make some stupid money doing some stupid things?"

Gordy responded with a shrug and, "How stupid are we talking?"

I talked, Gordy beat. He's got a lot of pent-up anger, Gordy does. All I had to say was that there was a score to settle with Craig. Craig tried to go over my head and get me in trouble. I needed Craig to know he answers to me now. Craig hasn't stepped out of line since I watched Gordy break a rib.

I quit the pizza place. Between finishing my classes, which feel pointless now, and my role managing sellers, I don't feel like I have time for a real job. Liling reminded me I need to have a legitimate source of income. I'm glad she told me, because I wouldn't have known otherwise until it fucks me over when I need to pay taxes or buy a house. Now, I have a part time job as an assistant manager at a small family-owned motel. I work mornings, take classes in the afternoons, and grab spare moments with Liling whenever I can.

I don't know how yet, but I think the motel is going to be better for operations, somehow. I just haven't worked it out yet. Until then, I'm enjoying the quieter work. I don't have to clean or cook or drive, I just manage people and apologize to customers for things that are out of my control.

No more Randall the pizza boy, now it's Randall the assistant manager of a modest motel. That's moving up. I have a pager now, too. Its sole purpose is providing a way for Luis to let me know I need to run to a phone and call him. He doesn't check in often, but when he does, he doesn't like waiting.

Liling's made financial improvements too. She still writes papers, but she'll write on credit now, for an additional fee. A lot of people take her up on it, now that it's offered. If someone doesn't understand the repayment terms, well, she's got me and Gordy for that. I can't prove it, but I think having me take care of things my way turns her on. She's always so happy when I get back.

Anything for Liling.
All of it for Liling.

43.

RANDALL

I'm learning the ropes quickly in my new position. It's honestly not so hard. I've got all of my sellers, including Craig, in line, and I'm making Luis and myself a lot of money.

For now, Luis is keeping a close eye on me. He or Rogelio calls often, and Luis shows up personally when it's time to collect money. Luis always travels with a group, and they're always armed.

For now, I'm focusing on learning who each person is, who does what, and how I become one of them. So far, I feel like I'm on trial, and they're all waiting for me to screw up.

Luis is in charge of it all. He *is* the Padilla cartel. Luis is stiff around me, but has more patience and almost has a sense of humor when he's talking to one of his men. Luis is tall, and has a habit of standing eerily still, but his eyes follow everything that happens in every room.

Rogelio, a great bear of a man, seems to be Luis' number two. Rogelio seems the most well-rounded. He's serious when he needs to be, but doesn't come off like he's waiting for a reason to kill somebody. Rogelio clearly has his role as Luis' favorite and he takes this seriously.

On the other side of the spectrum is Oscar. Oscar seems to be the group's least favorite. At times, he's a bit of a class clown, seeming less acquainted with everyone else. Oscar, as far as I know, has lived his entire life in the U.S., and he doesn't have an accent like the others do. Oscar doesn't seem to have a defined role, he just does whatever Luis or Rogelio tells him to do.

Then, there's Diego. Diego scares me. Diego is a shorter, boxier guy. He's more ink than skin, and he hardly ever talks. Diego is Columbian, and I don't know much about what he does because of his lack of talking. I'm not well enough acquainted with the group to start asking questions. Diego tends to stand by the door, like he's waiting for something to happen. Even with his lack of talking, I'm still trying my best to get everyone in Luis' group to like me.

"He don't want to talk to you, Big Head," Rogelio chuffs from my couch, rapidly counting the money he and Luis came to collect. It's all there. Liling helped me count.

Across Rogelio, Oscar is also counting. "He won't talk to me either," Oscar says with a grin. Rogelio seems annoyed by the comment but doesn't add anything.

I start to migrate back toward the couches, noting that Luis has opted to show himself around my apartment and I think is in my bedroom right now. "What can I say? I'm a friendly person." I'm positive these guys will come around eventually. Luis seems like the hardest sell so far. Even though Diego won't talk, he doesn't seem like he's radiating any sort of feral, killer energy.

After another few minutes of counting and checking with Oscar, Rogelio announces, "It's all here, Boss." He starts loading up Luis' cash, separating what's mine to keep. I used to make hundreds at a time, now I'm making thousands. At this rate, I'll do just about anything Luis tells me to do, even if he's mean when he asks for it.

"Good," Luis drawls, wandering back into the living room and cracking open the balcony door so he can smoke while leaning on the wall. It takes me a second to realize he's talking to me. "If you don't screw up, we'll work out an easier exchange. I don't have time to deal with all my reps individually."

I get it, I'm still in probationary status right now. Luis will expect some sort of payment biweekly, and I'll have it, all of it, every time. Every time they visit, I'm going to worm my way into their group just a little bit more. I'll learn what makes Luis happy. I'll learn what Oscar takes seriously. I'll learn what it takes to get Diego to talk. I'll learn what it takes Rogelio to trust.

Over time, Luis will meet Gordy, when Gordy happens to visit while Luis is over collecting. Gordy already knows what I'm into, and Luis has already made sure Gordy understands his place.

What is odd, but not surprising, is that Luis, as well as his cartel, seem to all find Liling very agreeable. Liling goes into presentation mode anytime she finds herself in the company of The Padillas. It's like Liling has made the art of being charming a job, and she's ready to excel in it.

"You got yourself a good woman," Luis tells me. "I've got one of those too. It's good to have someone to work for, at the end of the day." When Luis says this, I think that he gets me. We're the same. "I find my people who have someone to keep them accountable work the hardest. Is she that person for you?"

Liling. Of course she is. "Liling is everything to me."

LILING

August has come and gone. Randall and I have remained busy. We're like well-oiled machines, operating succinctly. I have two summer classes, both of which are coming to an end this week.

I enjoy summer classes. They're smaller, more personal, and quieter. I've been taking courses in management, and less than one week away from completing Business Management III as required for my degree. I'm ahead of schedule with my classes, and will have almost all of the credits I need by the end of the fall semester. For the spring semester, I'll be able to take an easy two credit course and can claim my degree.

It's odd to think that my real life is so close to starting.

In addition to working at the library and writing papers, I have a teaching assistant role for this semester. It's easy, and it will look great on a resume. I grade papers, I help compile lesson plans and I make sure slides are ready to be put over the projector screen for classes.

The classes are led by Professor Brackett. He's an older white man in his sixties or so, balding in the front with gray hair near the back of his head. He wears big, yellowing glasses that look like he hasn't replaced them since the nineteen seventies and the suits he wears always fit him loosely. He's bigger in stature, with a broad build and he's almost always sweating. I've always found him to be peculiar in a *don't get too close* sort of way.

Regardless, I've sunken forty five minutes in the front row of the lecture hall reviewing assignments. Professor Brackett sits behind a large mahogany desk reviewing text and comparing it against an article he has in hand.

The backlights of the classroom are off, leaving ten rows of seating in the dark, and only the front two or so in a yellow glow. The room is completely quiet except for the rustling of papers and the occasional sigh from the professor.

After another half hour of grading, I have my pile complete, and it concludes my work for the night. Combining my stack of papers, I neatly arrange them all and stand, tugging down the pencil skirt of the blue dress I'm wearing over black tights.

Professor Brackett smiles warmly as I approach, standing at the edge of his desk. "These have all been graded," I tell him with a pleasant tone.

"Ah," Professor Brackett chortles, extending his hand. "How did everyone do?"

"Better than the last assignment, definitely," I supply, pushing my hair over my shoulder.

Professor Brackett's eyes don't leave the papers as he continues speaking. "We have what, one week left?"

I don't mind being social on occasion, but I'm typically ready to leave as soon as I've finished my work. "Yes, sir."

He nods, deftly rolling his chair closer to where I'm standing, eyes taking one last review of the stack before setting them on his desk and looking up at me. "One week left," he echoes again. I note his tone, his recent shift closer, and in the pit of my stomach, I know this professor is about to disappoint me. "Have you given thought to where you're going once you graduate?"

Perhaps I'm too quick to assume the worst in people. I hope I haven't let my face drop before I pick my polite, patient smile back up. "I'm going to look for internships in the fall, and go from there." Frankly, I don't care where I go, as long as it pays a lot of money. I'll work my way up, I'll work long, I'll work well, I'll work better than everyone else.

"I can see you're a hard worker." Professor Brackett compliments. "It's not hard to imagine you working in some corporate headquarters." I'm going to respond, but he continues to talk just as I get the first syllable out of my mouth. "I love your work ethic, and I'd be happy to make sure you get a good recommendation, for wherever you go. I'm on the advisory board for the businesses that the university collaborates with to place college students in internships."

Nothing in this world is free. "I hope that you find I did well this semester," I say evenly.

He smiles, still looking at me when he reaches his warm, damp hand, grazing mine and latching his finger just as I try to retract my own hand behind my leg. I instantly freeze, and I know the smile has left my face when he tells me, "But I like to make sure I really know someone before I recommend them."

There's enough resistance in my hand that he can't play coy with pretending he doesn't realize it. I lower my eyes at my hand and say, "I think you may have misunderstood my enthusiasm for this class." I'd like to think I'm too strong to let myself be taken advantage of. He can try this as much as he pleases, but this is not how I gain advantages.

He doesn't even flinch. "I think you may not understand what it takes for a woman to get to where you're trying to go." He's clutching my finger enough to be sore. "I can see your ambition, and sweetheart, that's going to be a long and tough road for you, frankly."

With one tug, I snatch my hand back and tuck it under my armpits. "I can get there on my own."

He laughs. "No, you can't. Not without help, and not with anything less than a glowing review from your past professors and employers to get you started. I'm both to you, Ms. Zhu."

I tilt my head. "This is starting to sound like blackmail, Professor."

He laughs again, his eyes falling to my legs that are showing through my thin black tights; I fight the urge to flinch. I'm going to maintain control. I'm going to shut this down. Liling Zhu will never be a victim. I won't let her be.

"Oh, I don't like that word." He waves a dismissive hand, talking casually. He's all too comfortable behaving like this. "I just want to make sure you understand how long this road is without a friend. Especially for a woman, let alone a woman *such as yourself.*"

I don't know why when he says this I feel not only a heat in my cheeks but also a wet warmth under my eye lids. I'm frustrated, if anything. "Define *friend,*" I command icily.

He stretches his legs out until they're wide open and he leans forward. "As I said, I like to get to know anyone I recommend before I do it. I should think we could go to my loft and- you're twenty one, aren't you?" He winks. "We'll discuss your career goals over wine, and if all goes well, I'll make sure you land exactly where you want to be."

"If all goes well," I echo, after taking time to put the words in any sort of order that makes sense. I feel like I'm taking such shallow breaths that barely register, because one deep breath feels like it's going to let the warmth behind my eyelids out from their hiding place.

Professor Brackett clarifies, as if I needed further explanation to all he implies. "If you behave yourself." The smile of a snake. "And are a lot nicer than you're being now."

My mouth is open, at a loss for words. I'm trying to calculate but I'm either too angry or startled to process.

In this breach of words, the professor adds "See, sweetheart? You get it."

I blink hard and I hate that the threat in my eyes is likely covered by the heavy waterline that's forming. I steady myself with a breath that's not meant to stop potential crying, but to focus my rage. *I'm stronger than him. I'm not a victim. I won't be a victim.* "If you think that you can take advantage of me, you're sorely mistaken." My voice isn't as strong as I want it to be. "And I'll make sure-"

"I'll stop you there," he drawls. "If you think anyone is going to listen to any sort of sob story you come up with, think again. You think you're the first girl to go crying that the professor was handsy when she doesn't get a recommendation?" His green eyes break my barriers and a tear slips from my eyes and I hate myself for it. It's gone before it hits my cheek.

"If you think I can't take you down, you're wrong," I growl at him. I'm strength, I'm resilience, I'm right.

He laughs, noting that I'm about to take a step back, so his arm lunges out again but I'm almost out of reach. His fingers graze my tights, his fingers hook them until they're ripped but he has enough of a grasp to pull me into him. The only thing to steady myself against is the material of his shirt, the cushion of his chest. "Don't be difficult, Liling" he purrs. I can smell his soured breath.

"Let go of me, *now.*" I don't know why my voice doesn't match the anger I feel. My voice is quiet and submissive, and it's scared more than anything else.

235

"How are you going to take me down, Liling?" The professor asks with cruel amusement. "Right now, what can you do? This is where you need to stop being so hard-headed and be thankful for what you're given."

When I start to pull back, there's the alarming sound of more ripping fabric as my tights are still in his fingers, looming too high up on my thighs, I can feel the warmth of his fingers at a height where only Randall's have been. I immediately stop pulling in fear that my tights are going to keep ripping until they're shredded further up my thighs.

"Hang on, there," he coos, as if trying to calm me down. "I'm really not a scary guy, if you just relax, I can show you." His other arm grabs my wrist, and to combat the way I try to throw my body away from him, he squeezes and pulls so hard that my hand is screaming from the tension. He locks his knees into my waist, letting out a breath from the struggle.

I let out a staggered breath as I look at his hand on my wrist, feeling the way his knees dig into my hips. When I see the exposed skin of my thigh, more tears have slipped through. My look is pure murder but it's being sullied by my stupid, weak tears that veil my eyes. "You have five seconds to let me go before I make a scene."

He laughs. He laughs at my anger, at my threat, only releasing his left hand that holds my thigh. He unhooks his hand from my tights so he can move that hand to my side, just below the ribs, making it easier to hold me steady.

The only thing I can think to do is slap him hard across the face and he does something of a hiss. He takes the hand that was on my wrist and grabs the front of my dress so that his face is only an inch from mine. I hear a few seams of my dress pop from the tension. "I love your fight, sweetheart. Love it. That being said, you need time to come to your senses," he tells me. Still

236

clutching my throbbing wrist, he leans closer to his desk, taking a business card and flipping it over. I try to pull away again.

"Hang on," he says warily, taking a black pen and writing on it. When he's done writing, he holds it out to my free arm. "Take it." When I make no move to do so, his grip tightens until my wrist feels like it could shatter. "Take it." It's not a request.

I feel lost when I slowly take the card. I'm realizing that I can be as mean as I want, and try to act as strong as I think I am, but I can't make myself bigger. I can't make myself stronger. I can't make myself a physical threat. There are no words that are going to make me powerful enough to pry his hands away or push his body off of mine.

"Good girl," he says once I've taken the card. He loosens his grip but has not released me. "I'm going to finish up my office hours in the next half hour. Why don't you take some time to collect yourself, fix your face, and meet me at my loft, hm?" He finally lets go of my arm, and I've drawn it back into myself in an instant. My chest is rising and falling so fast but it still doesn't feel like my lungs are working properly. "The choice is yours, Ms. Zhu. You can ruin your life, if you want, or come and be friendly with me. I know you're smart enough to make the right decision."

I feel like a victim.

LILING

Even though it seems that I don't have a single coherent thought left in me, subconsciously I've led myself to Randall's apartment. I don't know what to do, I don't know what to say, I don't even know what happened.

Randall is in his living room, sitting on the floor with Gordy. They're playing the Nintendo, sitting on the carpet to make up for the distance that the controller cords will allow between the television.

As usual, he's in a balmy mood, smiling when he turns his head from the screen. "Hey, Lil-" I must look worse than I thought I did, less composed than I want to be. In one second, the smile is gone. In the next second, he's on his feet. A second after that, he sees my tights and the misshapen collar of my dress and he's at my side. In the following moment, I'm an unrecognizable woman of sobs and tears and misery.

"Liling." Randall's embrace is holding me tightly, and I cry into his shoulder. He starts stroking my head and I lose it again, gripping his shirt in frustration.

"Liling," he says again, prying his arms to create enough space so that he can look at me. "What happened? Tell me what happened." It's no wonder he's so alarmed. I spend so much of my energy trying to be this impenetrable wall, and now he's in a panic himself when the bricks are starting to fall.

Gordy is up from the floor as I'm still drawing ragged breaths out of my body and into Randall's shirt. "Shit," Gordy whispers when sees me, eyes on my legs and then my arm. "What happened there?"

Randall hadn't seen my arm before. He's now seen the red, angry irritation on my pale skin from being held too tightly for too long. I can tell his blue eyes aren't really processing what they're seeing. In a blink, they move from my wrist to my eyes. "Liling." It's almost a threat.

"I'm fine." I sound like I'm trying to argue even though I can hardly breathe. I shake my head. "I'm just being dramatic."

"Tell me what you're being dramatic about, then." he says in a tone of voice I haven't heard him use with me before.

I open my mouth to drag out the first word but my breath hitches on the first syllable, and I'm sobbing again. Randall pulls me in again, resting his chin on the top of my head. He lets me continue to dampen his shirt with my fussing until his voice is a new, pleading sort of tone. "Liling, please just tell me what happened." When he separates himself again, he puts a hand under my chin, his voice as dangerous as a curse. "Who did this to you?"

I briefly bite my lip hard enough to bruise it, feeling both his and Gordy's wary, expectant gazes. When I retell the story of Professor Brackett's proposition, I'm not able to find a spin on it. There's no disguising what the professor wanted, and no way to shape the story in any way that makes me sound like anything other than a victim. I was grabbed, I was caressed, I was threatened. I was victimized.

As I retell the story, I know I did nothing wrong.

I didn't invite that interaction. I didn't ask for anything.

239

Some men are just disgusting.

Randall's face is so unlike any way I'd seen it before. He's so quiet when I speak, and he doesn't interrupt me once. I'm still close enough to Randall that he slowly strokes the small of my back as I talk, working through all of the events. As I finish huffing and crying out about everything that happened from the tights to the invitation to the professor's home, I reach into my small brown purse where I'd discarded the business card. I take it out and look at the printed name and the handwritten address.

Gently, Randall takes this from my hand, even though I wasn't offering it to him. Randall looks at the card, face hard as stone when he says "Gordy, I need you to come with me." My stomach feels like it's been electrified when I hear his tone.

Gordon's grumbled response is instant. "I'm ready when you are." Gordy's always been indifferent toward me, which is partially because of my indifference toward him. Whether Gordy understands that a line has been crossed or if he's simply very loyal to Randall and his problems, I'm glad Gordy is here.

Head still bowed toward the card, Randall's eyes dart to me. "I'll be back."

I'm still sputtering as he starts walking past me, and I know Randall, and I know what he wants to go do. I catch his shoulder before he can fully step around me, Gordy stops abruptly behind Randall. "Randall,"

"Liling," Randall snaps back. "I'm going. I promise I'll be back as soon as I can. I promise." he shrugs my hand off of his shoulder, making a quick exit towards the door.

"Randall!" I call again.

He sends back an apologetic look before he opens the door.

He nearly runs into Luis and his cartel.

Randall halts to a stop, even Luis looks surprised as he hadn't even knocked on the door. "*Hola*, Randall," Luis says, looking Randall up and down. Behind Luis stands Diego and Oscar. "I was thinking-"

"Not right now," Randall says, brushing past Luis and his group.

Luis, Oscar, and Diego look baffled that Randall would do this so boldly, leaving them standing awkwardly in the open doorway. Gordy follows Randall, and I scurry myself to the doorway to look at Randall making a quick exit.

Randall is down the hall in an instant, getting ready to move around Rogelio, who is just entering the top of the stairwell. Diego looks at Luis, waiting for an order but Luis has noticed me standing in the open doorway, ready to chase after Randall. I know exactly how terrible I look. My clothes are torn and ruffled, my eyes are red and swollen, my cheeks already raw from wiping them, and my arm is bruised.

"Oh, *Diamante*," Luis coos in a tense whisper, looking at my legs. He quickly whips his head down the hallway, where Randall has almost made it a few steps past Rogelio who's looking confused as to why Randall is sidestepping without his usual greeting. "Hey, Persch!" Luis fires down the hall in a tone that is nothing short of a commandment. "Get the hell back here!"

Rogelio's face jumps from Luis' tone, and he catches Randall by the back of his shoulder before he can leave. Rogelio uses his free arm to grab the railing to keep them both from falling down the stairs.

"Oh, fuck off!" Randall barks, unsuccessful in throwing the mountain that is Rogelio.

Luis holds a hand out as he speaks, cooing like he's speaking to a child. "Oh, What did he do, *Diamante*? Did he put his hands on you?"

There is so much happening. My professor touched me, my boyfriend wants to kill him, the cartel is here. "Wh- no." I look down the hall at Randall being half-pushed back toward us. Gordy looks unsure of what he should be doing, knowing exactly who Luis Padilla is. "No," I say placing my hands out.

"Then, what's going on?" Luis gestures at my tights, and then my face which is likely red and puffy from too much crying.

Randall looks at me to see if I want to say anything. Rogelio cautiously lets go of Randall while I lower my head, not wanting to explain this story to all of these men. Randall jumps in simply saying, "I'm going to visit the person who sent her back like this."

The hallway is impossibly quiet as Luis takes this in. Finally, he nods and says, "Ok, men." Rogelio, Diego, and Oscar stand straighter. "New plan tonight, let's go get this fucker!" Randall's face matches mine, a look of stupor. Luis smirks for half a second before getting serious. "What? This?" He gestures at my haphazard clothing with a frown. "We don't do *this*."

"We fix it," Rogelio growls behind Randall.

A cartel with a heart, and very selective violence.

Luis nods, saying, *"Vamos!"* and starts shuffling to the door. Now Randall has an army, and he's not going to bother arguing with them, he's leaving with them.

"Randall," I say again, and he mumbles something to Luis who waits at the end of the hallway.

"Liling," he says softly, approaching me again. Gordy is hovering behind Randall, looking impatient and nervous. Maybe Gordy already knows why Luis has the reputation that he does. If he doesn't, he's about to. "Liling," Randall says again. "I need to handle this. My way."

"I know." I'm tired, I feel small, but my fire has not been extinguished. "I'm coming with you."

Randall pauses, his eyes searching mine to see what I'm talking about. "I don't know if that's a good idea." He reasons with me.

I feel it, that drive, that urge, that need to get what is owed to me. Respect and power; it drives me. Someone took those from me and now I'm going to collect. I look at Randall, feeling the tears being replaced with flames. "I know what you're going to do," I say calmly. "I want to watch."

There's a shared beat of silence as Randall's face changes to something that lands between awe, pride, and perhaps fear. Gordy, from behind Randall starts taking a few steps back to where Luis and the others wait and says "I'm going to wait in the car while you two have whatever weird erotic moment this is."

Randall watches Gordy leave before he finds my eyes again. "Are you sure?" He asks me.

I gently hold his face in my hands. This is my face. This is my boyfriend. This is my man. When I kiss him, I let him know all of these things. "Give me three minutes to change. *Don't* you dare leave me here."

Frowning, Randall says, "Fine, you can come."

I narrow my eyes at him, challenging his choice of words. "Randall Persch, I will never ask you for permission to do anything."

This gets a laugh from him, and for just a moment, Prince Charming is back. He grabs my waist and pulls until our toes touch. "Liling Zhu, I want you to do whatever the hell makes you happy."

RANDALL

Professor Johnathan Brackett, count your fucking days.

I don't think I can really describe the rage I felt when Liling walked through the door, crying and angry and hurt. All I need to do is think about her ripped tights and I'm ready to kill somebody.

I have no idea why Luis showed up, but it's a problem for later. Whatever he wants, he's not here because I'm in any sort of trouble, and he seems excited to watch how I handle the situation.

When Liling came out of the bedroom, she only took three minutes, just as she said. She was a different woman entirely. I've always known Liling had this thing with power and perceptions. There was a blip in how she controls those things, and now she's mad.

Liling comes out with such a cruel, fierce, intensity that it gives me a shiver. It isn't Liling Zhu, but it's Liling Persch that comes out with a clean, tear-free face and darkened brown lips. She's wearing a white blouse with ruffles down the buttoned bottom of the shirt, tucked under dark green dress slacks and a thick brown belt. She's wearing a patterned blazer of different color squares of brown, black and tan. The jacket is almost a plaid pattern but is something I've only seen on Liling.

She's stunning, and she really could kill me looking like that. She looks like she could kill somebody else. I pity anybody that stands in the way of this woman. That person will never be me; I'll always be standing beside her, if not just a step behind, taking her lead.

We travel in three cars. Gordy is driving me and Liling in a beat-up red Chevy. Luis and his crew seem to always travel in at least two cars, so there's two massive SUVs being driven by scary-looking Latinos behind me.

I'm helping Gordy navigate the best I can with a map based off the address that's written on the business card given to Liling. Being a professor, Brackett lives close to campus, so there's not too much struggle when it comes to finding a quiet cape cod style home with blue siding and white columns on a porch decorated with flower pots of begonias.

Gordy's slow enough pulling in that he's gotten the attention of someone inside the home, lights of Gordy's car pulling through the windows as he goes up the driveway. Inside the home, an older man with a wine glass in hand pulls back a curtain. From here, I see the change of his face. I see a man who was expecting a nervous, demeaned woman who had been put into place.

Instead, he was seeing the wrath of a strong, confident, vengeful woman. Instead, he's seeing what sort of army Liling could rally in her honor. The professor's face is blank as three cars are parked in front of his house, and there's six men and a scorned woman coming for his door. The curtains shut quickly. I'd be scared too, if I were him.

I instantly take Liling's hand when we're out of the cars, waiting for everyone else to get out. All of this for her, and she deserves even more. When Luis gets out of the car, he looks at the house, taking in the cozy feel of this small home that we're about to turn upside down. "Boy Scout, I can't wait to see you in action."

There's no sign of anyone at the window. "I don't know what I'm going to do yet," I say.

Rogelio lifts his head in a quick nod. "Fuck him up."

Well said. I look at Gordy, now. "Ready?"

Gordy flicks a cigarette onto the driveway, catching Liling's eye. "Lead the way."

I do. Still holding Liling, we climb onto the porch, with Gordy and all the others behind me. There's a glass storm door that I open so that I can knock on a navy blue wooden door. Nothing. The professor is literally hiding from us. We're an ultra-conservative man's worst nightmare; Me and Gordy- young people who don't listen to authority, three armed Mexicans, a terrifying Colombian, and a woman who knows her place is on top of it all.

I knock again, checking the handle afterward, but it's locked.

Behind me, Luis drawls, "Rogelio, *puerta.*"

Rogelio pushes past me, telling me and Liling, "Stand back." Gordy and I give him some room, watching Rogelio prepare himself with a breath. If it hasn't been explained before, know that Rogelio is a big guy. He's tall, burly, with large hands that look like they're made for breaking things and a build meant to withstand. It only takes a single, powerful kick to splinter the wooden door in on itself.

Rogelio lets himself in first, quickly evaluating the home like he's used to doing this sort of combover, already drawing his gun out. It's an outdated home with yellow shag carpet and aged tan patterned wallpaper on the upper half of the room with wooden paneling on the lower half.

"What the hell do you think you're doing?" In the corner of the room, by a small round table of dark, scuffed wood, is who must be Professor Brackett. He stands between the window and one of the table's chairs, looking as if he was trying to peek out of the window. He's a balding man with retreating white hair and a baggy suit. This is the man that put his hands on Liling.

Seeing all of us file into his home, the professor's eyes dart to the far wall of the living room that's frozen in the seventies. There's a green phone plated into the wall, but Rogelio is able to track his eye movement as well. The professor instantly halts his sudden step when Rogelio glides across the room, grabbing the green phone at the base and ripping it from the wall like it's not even attached. The plastic phone loudly clatters to the carpet, and the door is shut and locked behind me.

The professor is now standing in the middle of the room, looking more angry than he is scared. That'll change. I hope his heart starts to race, I hope he starts to panic, he starts to sweat.

Brackett has the nerve to pick out the one person he recognizes. "Sweetheart, I can see you over react-"

I release Liling's hand and storm toward Brackett. Clenching my fist, I funnel all of my rage into this vile man's face. I only hit him once, because my goal is only to shut him up. "Don't talk to her," I growl as the man stumbles back, holding his jaw where my fist met his cheek.

Now, he's looking at me. Now, he sees that I am a threat. I'm running the room. "I don't know who you are but-"

I smile at him, moving my hair back from where it flew when I threw my arm. "You're about to know who I am," I promise. I hold my hand out in a handshake this time. "Randall Persch." I smile expectantly, and the professor is so stunned and confused that he takes it and shakes my hand cautiously.

"I think there's been some confusion," the professor tells me, his eyes falling to those who flank the walls behind me. An army of men, that's what lies behind me.

I nod. "Sure, sure. Let's see if we can clear this up, then, shall we?" Gordy is slowly bordering the room, taking small steps until he's standing behind Brackett. I point a finger at Liling, tilting my body slightly as I do. "Did you put your hands on Liling?"

Brackett's thin lips start forming a word as he looks between me and Liling. He's trying to decide if it's better to lie to me or to rationalize his behavior. In truth, it almost doesn't matter what he says. There's something that's owed, and I've come to collect. "I think that-"

I start clicking my tongue, interrupting him as many times as I feel like. "It's a yes or no question." My words are drawn out, every syllable weighted as soon as it leaves my mouth. "Did. You. Put. Your. Hands. On. Liling?" I repeat.

His green eyes falter, and Brackett runs a tongue over his dry lips. "Well, yes. Just to-"

This time I stop his words with my fist, but one hit isn't enough. One, two, he's on the ground, hitting the red carpet with a force that rattles the floorboards. Behind, there's whispers in Spanish, with Liling staying silent. I peek at her while Gordy pulls the professor onto his feet. Liling's face is stony, but it's strong. Her eyes peel from Brackett and are given to me now. One small nod.

That's all I need to keep going.

I let the professor stand himself up, and I even watch him start to back up, as does Gordy. I let him get as far as the wall before I look at Gordy, who goes to grab the professor by his collar and throws him against the wall. Generations of pictures jump from the wall as Brackett crashes into him, raining glass down before he lands on it. "Get up," I tell him.

Gordy helps with this too, grunting as he pulls Brackett back to his feet. The professor is older, and three hits from me already has him clinging for consciousness. "Wait-" He's so weak to already be this disoriented.

"Do you need to rest?" I offer, sounding sincere. Gordy, my best friend, we're almost on the same wavelength. Gordy is vicious on a good day. I nod at him, and Gordy, who already had the professor gripped by the shoulder, bluntly shoves the older man forward, and I have to step out of the way to avoid being run into.

The professor lands with another rattling thud, only inches away from Luis' boot. This is probably the happiest I've seen Luis, a wicked grin on his face when he looks at the bug in front of him. Luis' black eyes look up at me in question. "May I?" Luis Padilla is ready to get in on the action.

"If you can keep him awake." Is all I say.

Luis nods at me before he looks at his feet again. "Oh, it just isn't your day, huh, Professor?" Luis kicks the old man so sharply that the resulting wheeze hurts even me. "You want to play with our little diamond, eh?" Another kick.

Brackett gasps, curling himself into the fetal position. I walk up, kicking at his exposed backside now. He's still trying to lie to me. "A misunderstanding!"

Luis uses his boot to hitch under Brackett's shoulder, rolling Bracket to his back. I'm standing over him, observing his red, bruised face. *It's not enough.* "Did you rip her clothes?" Foot to the ribs, I'm progressively getting louder with each question. "Did you bruise her arm?" He'll limp from the force that my foot has brought down on his muscle. I splay my arms out, looking down at him. "What's the confusion here, Brackett?"

249

I'm panting, resting my foot on his arm and stepping until I feel his muscles shifting into the floor. Brackett is fading, but I'm still angry. I want to add to my questioning: *Did you make Liling feel small?* It's too personal to put out into the room.

"I guess I didn't think ahead to how far I wanted to take this," I say to no one in particular. I've killed someone before for less than this.

"There's a lot of in-between space for life and death," Luis supplies, like he knows what I'm thinking. Luis' thin frame uses Brackett, who's near hyperventilation in a sweaty, beaten mass on the floor to rest his own foot on.

I blink. "Yeah?" I ask. "You know more than I do."

Luis smirks, turning to Diego with a nod. Diego, is dressed as he always seems to be: jeans under an oversized leather jacket that's zipped shut in all weather. Now, Diego opens his jacket for the first time.

A machete.

That's what he keeps under the jacket.

Diego's coat has to be custom made for him. In addition to the sheathed machete, it has several inside pockets that bulge from what I have to assume are other things meant to bring someone to their knees in one way or another.

I didn't even know machetes came with sheaths, but this one was tucked in his belt in a red leather pouch. Slowly, Diego draws out a long, silver blade that curves downward at the end. It has a custom handle that shines like gold, encrusted with blue sapphires and red rubies.

The tattooed man carefully holds the blade out to me, presenting the handle. "*Esta es mi princesa.*" I have no idea what he just said, but when my fingers curl around the glimmering surface of the jewels encroached by gold, Diego adds, "*Y la princesa es mortal.*"

No one translates these words, but I consider it to be a curse over the weapon. The weight of the blade catches me off guard. Definitely real gold. *Space between life and death.* Do I want to let this man occupy that space? Have I done enough?

I look down at Brackett. "Well?" I ask the man on the floor, panting, and sweating, and wheezing.

Brackett, between a wet chortle, looks at me with green eyes and says "There's no way… she's worth all of this." His vision must be going fuzzy. "Just leave, you can have her."

That was the wrong thing to say.

No one gets to *have* Liling.

For that matter, Liling is worth everything.

"Get him to the table."

Gordy knows I'm speaking to him, and my friend grabs the professor by the body part closest to him: the legs. Gordy starts dragging the professor back toward the table, with Rogelio crossing over to help. Once Rogelio has joined in, getting Brackett back up and seated at the table is easy work.

Before I go back to Brackett, I check in with Liling, who's been quiet during all of this. I'll stop if she tells me to, but I'll also keep going if that's what she wants. Luis and Oscar are discussing something quietly, while Rogelio and Gordy are keeping Brackett upright in a chair that doesn't look up for the job.

"Hey," I say softly, approaching Liling. I'm still holding a machete as if it's normal, the top of the blade piercing the carpet. "Are you alright?" I feel like I've asked her that a thousand times.

Anyone else would be scared right now. Anyone else would've left me for the monster I know I am. But not Liling. Liling is strong, fierce, and she's happy with me. "I'm better now," she whispers, giving this conversation only to me.

I kiss her, just a little desperately, but not for too long. We've got an audience, and I've got one final crime against

251

humanity to carry out. "Once he shows you some respect, then we can leave," I vow quietly.

Beaming, she's beaming at me. She's so damn beautiful. Black hair, dark lips, brown eyes that only look at me. Her petite hands with orange-painted fingernails cup my face. "This is exactly why I came," she whispers. "I wanted to see *you.*"

My heart is doing somersaults, my stomach is jittery. Liling Persch. Liling Persch. Liling Persch.

In the background, Oscar's voice murmurs, *"Los Amantes."* And I feel it has something to do with this quiet, intimate moment we're trying to have.

I stop and grin at Oscar, feeling my mood rising. "What's that mean?"

Oscar laughs, bringing his voice up as he croons, "The lovers."

I don't have to look at Liling to know she's blushing. I laugh, making my way back to the table. Brackett's senses are coming back to him, and his breathing quickens as I approach. I don't think he's registered what I'm holding until now.

Before he can speak, I hold my free hand up to silence him. "You know what they do in some countries when you touch something that wasn't yours to touch?" I ask, relishing the widening eyes from Brackett.

"No- you sick-" He's sputtering. Gordy tenses, knowing what's coming now too. "You can't be serious."

"I think sometimes I'm too nice," I reply. "So, I think people tend to not take me seriously." I think of Luis and his group, who also thought I was just some dumb student at first. I think I'm one of them now.

Gordy and I meet eyes, but it's Rogelio who knows what to do next. He's clearly seen this weapon be put to work before. Rogelio's thick, muscle-clad arms snap out to grab Bracket's left

252

hand, forcing it out on the table. Rogelio gives me an amused look of warning, as if to say, *You better not cut off my hand.*

I have no idea how to use this thing, but I'm not going to risk swinging it. I'll take it in slow, controlled movements. Bracket is screaming now, he's in a full panic, rocking for a split second before Gordy and Rogelio get him back under control.

Carefully, I hold the machete horizontally, one hand on the gemmed handle, the other carefully placed on the tip. I start to get the machete positioned over Brackett's hand, stopping when the edge of the blade barely touches the top of his fingers. Brackett lashes his arm around, slicing his own fingers under the incredibly sharp blade.

Letting out an anguish scream, Brackett yells, "You don't have to do this!"

So much crying, and I haven't even really hurt him yet. "Sure," I agree. "I don't have to do this, but I want to. I think it's only fitting, after all."

He whimpers, and there's a sick part of me that likes it. I want him to pay, I want him to feel pain, and I want to be the one that fixes this. This is my way of doing things now. Lowering my voice and leaning some of my weight onto the knife amidst more pained yelling, I say, "I hope touching Liling was worth it, because she's the last thing you'll ever touch."

It's so easy. Putting my weight down onto my hands that hold the sword. One quick push, teaming up with gravity, I push down the machete and remove the tips of three fingers with ease. In one movement, I slice through three fingers with the same ease of raw carrots.

I've never heard screaming like this. It's animalistic, earsplitting. Oscar comes over quickly, kitchen towel in hand. He's using it not to stop the blood flow of Brackett's hand which is pumping out blood as freely as a faucet pumps water, but he's stuffing it over Brackett's mouth to stifle the screaming.

Standing, I take a step back, inspecting the blood that glistens on the edge of the blade. Brackett is still screaming into the towel while Oscar holds it roughly to his face. Bracket's clutching his mangled and torn hand into his chest, his shirt absorbing the blood that continues to pour.

Oscar leans into Brackett's ear. Oscar doesn't have any accent at all, and his voice is the highest of everyone's. "If you shut up, I'll let you use this towel for your hand. You can cry, but you can't scream." When Brackett continues to wail, Oscar added, "Or we can do a science experiment, see if you can still scream with your tongue ripped out."

Just like that, Brackett bit the tongue he was trying to keep in an effort to quiet his own yelling. He replaced it with a dull moan as the wooden table was starting to absorb the blood like a gothic stain.

"That's better," Oscar drawls, smiling as Brackett takes a massive breath when the towel is removed from his mouth.

I feel I've done what needs to be done. Letting him live is gracious of me. It takes more control on my part to let him live than it does to kill him. He'll live the rest of his life with a new understanding.

After wiping the blade on the table's green runner, I look at my handiwork, as does Gordy, who finally lets go of the professor. Brackett had been leaning heavily to his right against Gordy, so when Gordy removed his grip, the older man goes tumbling to the floor.

It's all too perfect. I think I actually like the idea of kicking a man when he's down. Brackett moans as he brings his chopped hand back into his body. Quietly, he promises, "I won't touch anybody again." He's covered in his own blood, looking

254

like a toddler who can't control themselves with finger paint. Brackett has blood on his chin that's being ground into the carpet as he writhes on the floor.

"Hm," I say, thinking about whether I want to be done again. I look up at the ceiling, which is popcorned in off-white paint. "You know what, Brackett? I'm remembering more of the story now. You actually used two hands in the classroom, didn't you?"

Brackett starts whimpering.

"Two hands," I reiterate. "One on her dress, one her arm. So really, there's two hands that need to learn a lesson, right?"

Behind me, Luis chuckles. "Boy Scout's earning some badges tonight."

Brackett is crying. Crying. Tears and everything. Tears, blood, and whimpers. In truth, I think I am ready to take Liling home but I promised she was going to be given the respect she deserves.

"I'll make you a deal, Brackett." I love making deals. I turn my torso so I can look at my beautiful Liling behind me. Her eyes are blazing in triumph; we're bringing down our enemies together. The tips of my fingers are stained in blood, but when I hold my hand out to her, she takes confident steps forward in her brown heeled shoes until she's clutching my hand back.

I'll always remember the sight of my queen looking down at the monster I slayed for her. I'll remember the way her hair fell over her shoulder, the way the puffy white blouse rose and fell with her breathing, the emeralds at the top of her chest catching the light.

"I'll make you a deal, Brackett. I like to be fair, I really do." I feel tired all of the sudden, this is tiring work. "I'll let you keep your other fingers, but only if you apologize to Liling." It's worded like an offer, but toned as a threat.

Brackett is half on his side, legs curled up, his bad hand stuffed under his other arm. He looks up through his sweat, starting to shake. He's looking at me when he says, "I'm sorry, I'm so, so sorry! Really!"

Not good enough. I'm shaking my head in disappointment. "Not me." I nod at Liling squeezing her hand. "Liling," I command.

I wait for Bracket's dull green eyes to move a few inches to his right, when I know he's meeting my queen's line of vision.

"Beg for her."

This is the most powerful I've ever felt. I'm drunk on this feeling. I'm a damn legend, a god. Behind me, I have an armed cartel, working in *my* favor. In front of me, I have the shell of the man I've broken, and I've got him begging and groveling at our feet. Next to me, I have an empress, a goddess, an apex predator of a woman.

I want Brackett to keep going. I want him to know he isn't safe yet, not until he's properly groveled for Liling's forgiveness. I continue to encourage him by forcefully repeating my order. "Beg. For. Her."

She's so beautiful when she's cruel. She's so beautiful when she smiles at the man basking at her feet. We let the begging go on long enough, offering him no encouragement, taking glee as he gets more and more desperate. The only sounds in the room are a ticking grandfather clock and a man crumbling in pain and humility on the floor.

Liling continues to look downward with regality. It's only when his cracked lips are about to reach her shoe that her face sours and she takes a step back.

With a sigh, Liling tells me, "He can keep his hand. I'll allow it."

The queen has spoken.

I hold the machete to my right, turning for Diego who comes to retrieve his weapon. Once he has the machete sheathed, he returns to flanking the door while Luis replaces the spot on my right.

Crouching in front of the disgusting man in front of us, Luis says, "Hey, look at me now." And pulls Brackett's attention with a sharp slap to the face. "We're going to talk about how you can keep the rest of your body parts."

You'd think Brackett was a toddler from the amount of crying and whimpering. He'll be fine, in the long term. I took his left hand, so he can probably still write and hold things, and live the rest of his miserable life in semi-peace.

Luis is quiet, his sharp cheekbones protruding against the harsh light of the lamp. "First, I think you should thank our Diamond for letting you keep your hand, because if you pulled this shit with my girl?" Luis laughs while shaking his hand. "Shit, I crucified the last person to disrespect my Blanca." In the pause, Luis barks, "Are you going to thank her?"

"Thank you, Liling," Brackett says like the words are being pulled from him. He's fading. Luis gives Brackett a speech about discretion, and even provides an alibi for what he can say when he takes himself to the emergency room.

Before we leave, we check out everything that the professor's house has to offer. At some point, he must've had a wife or something, because his bedroom has a dresser full of jewelry. I take a diamond tennis bracelet for Liling, and I know she'll wear it. I think we'll both want to remember this victory-how we brought down an enemy. We're taking what's ours, and even things that don't belong to us.

One more time, I'm overcome by Liling. I'm proud of her, and I'm proud of myself. I can do anything I set my mind to. Beyond that, I can do anything that Liling sets my mind to.

Professor Bracket will not be the first person I'll make beg at her feet. This will not be the first monster that I slay in her honor.

Through Liling, all things are possible.

LILING

Beg for her.

The way my body reacts when I remember Randall utter those words is positively sinful.

The first thing I do when Randall brings me back to his apartment is take a shower, with the water nearly as hot as I can get it. Randall wants to talk, because he's worrying that I'm not as alright as I insist that I am. He's so good at reading me now.

Still, I insist that the first thing I need to do is feel clean. Sometimes, I allow Randall in the bathroom while I shower, and he pretends that he isn't looking while we continue conversation between thick bouts of steam. This will not be one of the nights. I want to be alone while I wash away the professor's touch as well as his blood. I want to be alone as I think of Randall's arms breaking somebody down into nothing.

Randall Persch.

A knight in shining armor. A soldier.

A man.

Randall listens to me. People that make themselves an enemy to me have made themselves an enemy to Randall. Someone disrespected me and Randall corrected it. Some men can only offer love, but Randall offers so much more. Randall gives me respect, and power, and a love that is boundless.

Randall isn't afraid to throw his weight around. He understands that there are some people who don't listen to logic and reason but they listen to pain and humiliation.

Randall Persch: *that's* a man.

If Randall saw me in the shower right now, he might not ever recover from how my hands move.

Beg for her.

It's easy to ignore the sins I'm committing when I remember I'm gaining so much more than I'm losing right now.

Beg for her.

I imagine how Randall might react if I let him watch.

Beg for her.

I left the door unlocked, he'd come running if I called.

Beg for her.

There it is; the ecstasy, the sin, the pleasure. I'll ask for forgiveness later. Until then, I'm going to lean my head back under the faucet, letting the hot water roll over my face and down my body.

I exhale, releasing the pressure of the day and the joy of my thoughts.

Randall Persch: now that's a man.

LILING

I'm fine. I'm absolutely fine. I was fine watching Randall work for me, I was fine when we got back to his apartment, very fine in the shower, and I am still fine. As I'm rolling lotion over my skin in the humidity of the bathroom, my thoughts start to wander away from Randall and I'm thinking about the dark lecture hall.

It doesn't make sense to be thinking about it. Randall took care of it. That man is now sitting in agony somewhere because of what he attempted to do. No, he's in agony because of what he *did* do. For a brief period, I was wildly uncomfortable inside, pushing against how small Brackett made me feel.

It's over now. I need to focus on anything else. I'll focus on Randall. Keeping this thought in mind, I abandon lotioning the rest of my body. Leaving the quiet bathroom and turning off the fan, Randall is in the bedroom, sitting at the desk chair on the right side of the room on the back wall.

Randall notices me coming in, wearing what I wear almost every night for sleep, a long night gown that is truly meant for sleep and *nothing* else. It's white with purple flowers and closely resembles what my mother wears to sleep. Still, Randall

261

says what he almost always says at least once a day, "God, you're going to kill me looking like that."

This is enough. Enough to focus on right now, enough to pull my lips up into a smile when I see my beautiful soldier. As I approach the chair, Randall's legs open up and I rest my right knee on the space he's provided. "You seem pretty pleased with yourself," I tell him, wrapping my arms behind his neck as his hands are placed on my waste.

He grins. "*You* seem pretty pleased with me."

Maybe I am, and maybe our conversation gets lost between crushing lips and wandering hands for a while until I'm too tired to be able to carry on my enthusiasm. I felt a quick charge when I saw Randall waiting for me, but now the sinking feeling has returned. I'll sleep it away, and I'll wake up and everything will be fine.

Ten minutes later, Randall has climbed into the bed while I'm putting moisturizer on my face using the mirror that's on the back of the door on the dresser. When I lift my hand to rub the thick cream onto my forehead, my eyes catch the angry purple bruise that's been left on my wrist.

A man touched me today. Hurt me.

But I'm being dramatic. It could have been a lot worse. Many women have been through things that actually deserve tears. I need to stop this. It's fine. It's fine. It's-

"Are you ok, Liling?"

I tear my eyes away from my skin and continue rubbing my forehead as I turn toward him. "Hm?"

Randall's already pulled the covers back for me, waiting patiently. "Are you ok?" He asks again.

I take a deep, sharp breath that causes Randall to jump out of the bed before I even realize that my emotions have betrayed me once again. "I'm fine," I argue, using the bottom of my wrist

262

to dab my eyes in a way that doesn't make it seem like I'm crying again.

"What can I do?" Randall asks. "Don't think I won't go back-"

"I'm fine." My voice is harder now. "It was just stressful and I'm being dramatic. I don't even know what's going on with me. You handled it, it's over now, and I'm fine." I feel like I'm trying to convince both Randall and myself.

Randall's lowering his head, trying to meet my eyes but I'm focused only on putting my lotion away. "It's ok to not be ok, Liling." Randall trails me back to the desk.

"There's no reason not to be ok," I snip.

He hesitates to speak, but not to touch my shoulder. "Liling, it's not your fault Brackett targeted you today. You didn't make any sort of mistake. You were alone with a man three times your age, twice your size, and he took advantage of that. Sure, we handled it, but it's still-" My gasp of breath that followed stopped Randall immediately as he took a big step forward to wrap himself around me again. "Ok, I'm sorry. I'm not trying to upset you again, I just want you to know you can have feelings, Liling." He's trying to combat my sudden depression with a light tone.

I'm tense in his arms, saying, "I don't want to have a reputation of being a crying little girl. It's not who I want to be." People call me a diamond now. Diamonds are hard, diamonds can't crack under pressure.

Somehow, Randall finds it in himself to chuckle at this, and I shoot him a venomous look. He loosens his grip so that he can make a show of looking around.

"What are you doing?" I growl into his shoulder.

"Looking for all the people that are watching you cry right now. You know, the ones that are going to use this exact moment to craft your reputation?"

263

"Randall."

Taking me by both shoulders, Randall looks at me patiently. "Liling. If you feel like crying, then just do it. You'll feel better."

"But-"

"Look at it this way." Randall has turned me and is leading me back toward the bed. "If you cry now, nobody will ever know, except for me. You know I won't say anything, of course. Right now is your time to vent, to cry, to do or say whatever you want and still keep whatever image you want to the outside world. You don't have to be strong every minute of your life, and crying for some of those minutes doesn't make you weak."

He really is too kind to me. He's going to get me emotional again. The mattress squeaks a little as we both settle into it, with Randall on the right and me on the left.

At first, I only think about what Randall says, laying on my back and looking at the ceiling. The neighbors above us are making a racket and the air conditioning is rattling in the windowsill. The faded smell of his sharp cinnamon bark cologne from the bathroom where Randall applies it drifts from the bathroom as I continue to knead the blankets between my fingers.

Randall Persch.

Just when I think he can't be any better of a man, he surprises me.

Still staring at the ceiling, I quietly murmur into the darkness, "I want you to say it first."

I feel the bed shift again, and I won't turn my head because I know there's enough light in the room that I'd be able to see his face if I did. "What?"

I'm glad he can't make out the heat in my cheeks. "You say it first." My voice barely makes it above the rustle of the sheets.

There's a pause that's painfully, embarrassingly long. I don't know if it would be worse for Randall to not know what I'm talking about or for him to know and decide to stay quiet.

I'm gripping the blankets so tight when the bed shifts again and I can feel his heat on the side of my face. "I love you, Liling."

His voice is as sweet and warm as a promise, sharing nothing but truth. When my cheeks raise into a smile, I feel his lips there to meet them. With his lips pressed to my face, I murmur, "I love you, Randall." Feeling his reciprocating smile against my own sends my heart into a flutter and my brain reeling into the future.

I don't think I'll need to cry again tonight but if I do, I think it will be ok to do in just Randall's presence. Maybe here, I can be a different sort of Liling. I don't want to focus on all of the things that I have to do for just a few quiet hours.

Right now, I don't want to be a strong woman. I want to just be Liling. I want to be a girl who is occasionally sad, but it's ok.

I'm going to be a girl who wants to be held.

49.

RANDALL

Luis says he'll come find me later. Whatever he had come by for last night, he decided to let it wait. Luis is gradually getting friendlier, but there's something unnerving about his stillness. Maybe it's just because he's a weird combination of tall and skinny that when he has the habit of standing so still, he reminds me of those creepy stone statues that guard old churches.

Until Luis calls on me, I'm making sure Liling is alright. This morning, she's ignoring yesterday's trauma completely in a bid to convince me she's absolutely fine. Liling doesn't like dwelling. For now, I'll let her move on, and if she wants to talk later, I'll be ready for her.

Right now, I'm ready for her to go further. We've come so far from the Liling who gets flustered when I stand too close to her, but not so far that Liling can't claim a portion of that virginity she's hanging onto. It's hanging by the thinnest of threads.

The whole waiting until marriage thing is admirable, but it's killing me. We do most everything else, just not *it*. I'm convinced she does things on her own, when the shower runs, and I hope and pray she's thinking about me.

I'm getting ready to go spend the second half of my day and a part of my evening working at the hotel. The job is a joke, with how much I make working for Luis. Before, I was making hundreds and thought I was doing ok for myself. Luis makes me thousands. To hell with the drug addicts, I'm getting rich.

Not a single one of my sellers has stepped out of line yet. Not even Craig. After news about Yogesh got around, no one dared to not have their sales ready. I have no idea what Luis did with Yogesh's body, but it hasn't been found. There wasn't even that much chatter about his disappearance in the first place.

I was planning on wearing a slightly-wrinkled light-yellow button up to work but Liling took it off me and said I could not go out looking like that. Now, Liling is standing in front of a stained ironing board, working on my shirt while I'm standing behind her, hanging on for dear life.

"You're going to get burned," Liling says, bowing her head so that her chin moves against my arm as she talks.

I smell her hair before moving it so I have neck access. "I'll let you hurt me."

Her arm moves down the shirt pinned on the board, smoothing it with every pass over. "I don't even know what you're implying but you need to leave soon."

Into her neck, I tell her, "I can be a little late, they love me there."

"Of course they do."

"Give me ten seconds."

That manifests the midnight honey laugh of hers. "Randall, no."

"Ten minutes." When she laughs in response again, I reach over her shoulder, peeling her fingers off of the iron and sitting it up so that it's not on my shirt.

"I don't know what you're planning but-" She's struggling to maintain control of the iron when I snatch her hand back and pull her away from the heat. She squeaks a little from the intensity that I whirl her around with.

When she's looking at me with startled amusement, I tell her, "Ten minutes."

In response, she kisses me long and sweetly. "I'll give you five." She knows I can't get anything permanent done in five minutes, but I can get us halfway there.

The only good thing about waiting is I'm learning all the things that make Liling tick, so to speak. By the time she's ready to blow, I'll know exactly what gets her heated. She likes a show of strength, but she also loves to direct. I told her I'd make a movie with her but she shot me down.

I carry Liling with her legs wrapped around my waist back into my bedroom. I'm a professional at carrying her through this apartment while my vision is limited with Liling's face in mine. By the time I make it to the bed, my hair is already shot. Liling loves my hair.

After throwing Liling on the bed, I'm over her instantly, pressing down into her. She's taking full advantage of my shirtlessness, setting off my skin in pins everywhere she touches me. I have my hand cupping between her jeans, trying my best to work with the stiff fabric. Liling is weird like this, when it comes to getting her clothes off. Typically, if she doesn't initiate it, she'll shut me down.

I think I might have set off one of her virginity triggers when she clenches her legs and I nearly lose a hand. "I'll keep it down there, if you want," I say into her mouth.

She laughs, and I feel her teeth on her cheek. "Roll over."

I do anything Liling says. We shift until I'm laying with my back on the bed and she straddles me. She likes this control because it's harder for me to get away with things from this position.

She's going to kill me like this. I'm going to die with her legs pinching my hips, her breasts hovering as she crouches over me to kiss my mouth. I wonder what our time is at.

I told her I loved her last night. She basically asked me to. I said it back. It was easy to say. I've loved her, really loved her beyond that instant infatuation for a while now. I just didn't want to scare her off.

Now I know Liling doesn't scare easily.

50.

RANDALL

Honestly, the hotel gig isn't that bad. Not as an assistant manager. I keep customers happy, make employees feel cared for, and it's smooth sailing. It's as easy as remembering which recurring visitors are cheating on a wife and need extra discretion and which employees would appreciate leaving ten minutes early so they can make their kid's birthday party on time.

Give a shit about the small things and you can get away with the big things. That's why I've added one new seller, a bellhop who caters directly to our guests. More money for me means I'm making Luis more money, thus, I'm still on his good side.

The night manager is late, but so was I. Liling and I took more than five minutes but I showed up with a wrinkle-free shirt and freshly combed hair. There's usually about half an hour of overlap between the night manager arriving and me leaving. I'll let her know about anything that's going on before I head out.

While talking about an issue with the night manager about an ink pen that was in the laundry with bed sheets, her entire body stiffens when her eyes focus behind me. Stopping my story, I look to see who's coming through the revolving glass doors with gold trim.

Of course, he's found me here - or they did.

Luis, Diego, and Rogelio are coming through the doors, checking out the lobby as they enter. Rogelio sees me first, giving me a nod.

The night manager is a woman in her forties with box-blonde hair and dark eyebrows that haven't been notified of the color change. She's got a smoker's voice packed into a frumpy body that's been doing no favors in a tight-fitting orange dress. "We should call the cops," she says, as soon as they come in.

It actually makes me laugh, how instantly scared she is of these people who have done nothing. Sure, they're not an inconspicuous bunch. They look like people that are packing something, even if you can't see what it is. Diego's wearing his oversized leather jacket, and now I know why.

To be fair, Diego alone is terrifying. Even though he's not as skinny as Luis is, the way his eyes stick out from the black ink of insect tattoos makes him look almost skeletal. I would definitely understand crossing the street to not walk by this bunch that travel as if they own the ground they walk on.

I look back at Stacy, who's frowning at the group of men who have noticed me but are deciding to go sit in the plush green chairs at the far end of the lobby, by the stairs to the second level. "Why would we call the cops?"

She huffs like I'm being stupid. "Randall, look at them." Stacy's a little racist, sure. She thinks *people should just stick with their own kind.* It's great that she doesn't do the hiring here, otherwise our staff would look like a Willie Nelson concert.

I sigh, looking back at the group. Luis and Rogelio have sat down but Diego stands by, looking around, as if he's waiting for something to happen. In all honesty, they're not doing a great job at not being a cartel. "I'll take care of it."

She blinks, frowning. "Ok, but I'll call the cops if they start something in my lobby." I'll never meet someone more proud of being the night manager at a small family owned motel than Stacy.

I walk over the shined linoleum and the green runner to where the group sits.

Rogelio looks at my clothes and chuckles. "Playing dress up?" I'm most comfortable with Rogelio so I flip him off with my hand close to my body and hope he won't beat me up here in the lobby.

I ignore his response and look at Luis. "Sir, I'm going to have to ask you to leave," I say with mock authority.

The stone face smirks back at me. "Yeah, what, is this loitering?"

"You just scare the other manager," I chide.

Luis cranes his head to look around me at Stacy who I know has a hand resting on the phone. "What's her problem?"

"She voted for stronger border control," I reply, making Rogelio laugh and Diego smirk.

"Nah, she'd open up her borders for me," Rogelio grins.

I shake my head. "She'd shove her NRA card down your throat."

Luis stands, stretching his arms. "Got a job for you," he says, face settling back on his normal, sour disposition. "Different from what I came by yesterday for."

I put my hands in my pockets. "So there's two jobs, then?"

Luis takes a cigarette out of his pocket, and I know better than to try to tell him he can't smoke in here. "One job, one opportunity," he corrects, lighting his cigarette and pulling from it. "You do good today, I'll make sure you do good tomorrow."

"Your opportunities sound a lot like threats," I joke, but he doesn't give me a smile this time. "What is it?"

Luis opens his mouth, letting the gray smoke fan out into the lobby. I might have heard Stacy hiss my name behind me, but I'm not sure. "You notice anything different?"

They're down by one today. "Oscar's gone."

"Oscar's in jail," he corrects.

Whatever I'm about to get into sounds like it could get me into more trouble than I'm already involved with. "What happened?"

Luis shrugs. "They said soliciting, which is shit because *my* boys don't sell. That's what I have you for. They're like her." He nods his head toward Stacy. "They see a big brown person and get scared. Then, that idiot starts fighting back when he's questioned, and now he's got that charge too."

Rogelio adds, "But he got the best of one of the officers. It took three to take him down. He's in it good, now."

I don't see what a twenty-two year old college student can do about this. "Alright, what do you need from me, then?"

"Rogelio will drive you to Judge Peterson's house. You should bring that friend with you, the ugly one."

"Gordy."

"Sure." Luis takes another drag. "Does he have priors? I need someone I can get out if shit goes south. Do *you* have priors?"

"Are you going to get me arrested?" I really don't want to go to jail. That would really be pushing what Liling is able to forgive me for.

"If you do your job right, Boy Scout, you'll be fine," Luis promises with a smirk. "Plus, with that pretty, white, face of yours? You'd be out in minutes. You look like the damn poster child for some church youth group."

I have more questions which I know tends to annoy Luis. "Why can't Rogelio or Diego go threaten a sitting judge?"

"Status, Boy Scout," Rogelio says gruffly. "If we get arrested, we," Rogelio gestures between himself and Diego. "Get deported."

"And I would just go to jail for a very long time," Luis says in a low tone. "I think they've been trying to pin me with just about every crime they can." Luis starts counting reasons on his fingers. "Murder. Soliciting. Attempted murder. Kidnapping. Attempted kidnapping. Racketeering." He spreads his hands out in exasperation. "I don't even know what the fuck that is!"

The lobby phone rings and I jump, remembering that Stacy did threaten to call the police. Stacy, clearly unhappy, flags me down, trying to see what's going on. She wouldn't glare at Luis if she knew what he'd happily do to her.

I nod with a wave. "Give me ten minutes," I say. "I'm almost off, then I'll meet you outside."

"You want me to wait?" Luis asks impatiently.

"I want you to wait outside," I clarify, feeling a drop in my stomach when he shifts his weight. By the look on Rogelio's face, I'm starting to push Luis too far.

Luis stares at me for a moment, before saying, "You're lucky you make me a lot of money, Persch. Take your phone call. Get outside."

I nod. "I'll miss you too."

He growls at me as he leaves. Rogelio bumps into my shoulder as he passes. "You're an idiot," he grumbles. Diego says a single word that likely reflects that feeling.

Whatever Luis is going to have me do tonight, it's probably going to take a call, so I first call my own apartment, hoping Liling is there. It's a running joke that she won't just move out of her dorm and live with me already.

Liling is there, so I let her know I'll be back late, purposely being vague on exactly what I'm doing. Right before I'm ready to hang up, I ask her, "Hey, do you know what racketeering is?"

She takes this question pretty seriously. "Randall, what did you do?"

"Nothing, Gumdrop," I promise her over the phone.

"Don't call me that." She never got around to letting me call her by any pet names. "Be smart, be safe, and come back to me."

51.

[RANDALL]

"Do you understand what you're doing here?" Judge Peterson asks through a broken lip. "And I'm not talking about whether you understand how serious a crime assault and battery of a judge is." When he coughs, blood sprays the collar of his shirt.

"I know what I'm doing." Gordy and I are in the home of the judge that's going to be presiding over Oscar's preliminary hearing. Tomorrow, he can decide to try Oscar for a list of crimes that runs a mile long, or he can decide there's no probable cause for a trial and send Oscar on his way. Just like that.

But he's being difficult. He's got values, thinks himself to be a respectable man, and doesn't want to give in to cartel-sympathizers who have broken into his home. His wife and kids are locked in a room deeper in the house. I'm going to leave them alone, I just need the man of the house here to cooperate.

Judge Peterson is a black man in his forties, with a short build and petite frame. Right now, he's sitting on the floor with his back against a dark wooden desk fresh with polish. We've only hit him once so he'd listen to reason. Now he's trying to shame us.

"I'm asking if you understand who this makes you as a person." He's got a deep, authoritative voice that sounds like it was made to give speeches. His diction is slow and purposeful. "I'm asking if you understand what this is going to do to your life- because young man, I can tell you that people in your world rarely make it to a federal prison."

I'm interested in this conversation. "Judge Peterson," I sigh, pacing with my hands in my pocket, walking past Gordy, who stays close to the judge. "I know what the risks are. It's my own problem now, and I understand it. I'm here to make sure you understand what we need to happen tomorrow."

"I can't do what you're asking."

I want to go back to my apartment where Liling is waiting for me. "Do *you* understand what happens if you don't do what I ask?" My feet bring me back in front of the Judge, so I crouch down in front of him. "We're not going to do anything to you today." Other than the lip, which is probably going to just look like a small cut by tomorrow. We need it to not look like he's been approached by anyone in Luis' party.

Judge Peterson is brave, I'll give him that. He doesn't seem all that afraid of me. "I have values," he seethes.

"You have a family," I correct. Something in Peterson's eyes changes. "Me? I'm a nice guy, I really am. I don't want to involve them. But if I have a guess, they might get involved if Oscar's friends feel the need to retaliate. I can't say for sure, but I'd hate to see them involved when what we're asking you to do is so easy."

From the floor, Judge Peterson is starting to grapple with his options. "You're asking me to put a murderer back on the street."

I shrug. "Listen, we deal with other criminals, frankly. We're not interested in your family. We're interested in

277

competitors, threats." I reach my hand out and ruffle his tight curled hair. "Judges who are going to put our friends away."

The judge stares back at me with his brown eyes. "And when the state comes for you, for people in your situation, they don't just come for you. Do you have a family, young man? A partner? If you do, they get wrapped up in these things too. Putting yourself in danger is one thing, but are you ok with putting the rest of your family in danger?"

I don't respond. I know Liling is implicated by my own actions. I also know that I'm going to be able to give her so much because of my actions. For the record, Liling isn't perfect either. I've got drugs, Liling writes papers and has started doing personal loans that's quickly going to result in her claiming the title of a loan shark.

Liling already has a small clientele base. She weighs the risk, assigns interest based on the risk to her. She's already sent me out after some guy named Kieran, who started messing up as soon as he missed a payment to Liling.

At the end of the day, this still isn't something I can just walk out of. The judge made an offer of what my options are, talked about the protections that state can offer, but to me, that's an even bigger risk.

Luis already told me that walking away from this isn't usually an option. At this point, I made sure of that myself. I started a dangerous life for myself, willingly. I put myself in front of Luis to grab his attention. Liling has decided to join me, willingly. Sure, she's not directly involved but she knows what's going on and she's even supportive of me. That's why Liling is so perfect.

I'm going to look danger right in the eyes. I'm looking danger in the eyes and telling it what to do. Randall Persch isn't a coward, and he doesn't back down.

LILING

To no one's surprise, I finished the summer semester with a 4.0 in my International Business III course. Professor Brackett did not return for the last week of class, but I received an excellent score, as well as a glowing letter of recommendation on my file.

We're into the fall semester, back into football season. Randall and I still have our matching coats. Randall's moving up, so to speak, in the fast and dangerous world he's in. Randall's taken over another one of Luis' territories after the *termination* of whoever had been doing it before.

I haven't been to my dorm in weeks for more than a few minutes. As much as I hate to admit that I've turned into one of those girls, it feels like my entire life is revolving around my relationship; around Randall. I start my day with Randall, and his overly-affectionate pillow talk. During the day, when we split ways for our classes or for work, I think about all the things I want to tell Randall but have to wait because there's no way to talk to him for hours at a time. Too many hours.

In the evenings, we alternate between going out to dinner or we may stay home while I teach Randall how to cook. He thinks he can do it, but he also thinks a roast only needs salt. I also help

Randall with his sales- I keep track of his records, how much money he needs to bring for Luis, and how much is his to keep.

Randall is already making an unfathomable amount of money.

He works so hard for himself, but he works even harder for me.

53.

LILING

I'm feeling weighted today. There's no precise reason for it, there's just an ache inside of me I can't place. It's likely nothing more than the stress of classes and work and all of the papers I need to write. It doesn't matter why I feel like this, but I can easily let this mood make me a shut in. I could easily let this ruin my day.

But when I hear the door open and I know Randall is back, my entire mood has improved. There's nothing wrong. Randall is here with me.

I leave the counter, where I'd been wiping away some grime from the dinner I'd made myself to meet Randall at the door. He's covered in blood.

I stare at him, and he's too busy shedding layers of soiled clothing and his shoes to notice that I'm staring at him in horror. His plaid shirt has a large stain at the bottom, his jeans are speckled. Even the tips of his hair looks as though it's been dipped in red.

He starts a little when he notices me planted by the kitchen entrance. He starts to smile until he sees the horror on my face. He raises his hands in what's meant to be a *settle down* motion, but it only makes me notice that his hands are stained too. "I'm fine," he promises. "It's not mine, mostly."

"Mostly?" I half-shriek. He's disgusting. "Then who? What *is* yours? Randall!"

Randall's stripped down to just his boxers and his black socks. "It's a long story. Gordy and I handled it."

I'm up close to him now, inspecting his annoyingly-smooth, blemish-free skin. It really does appear that all this dirt, blood, and grime are just stuck-on messes. He doesn't seem hurt, except for a purple bruise that's near his hairline. Tenderly, I move his waves away so I can inspect this.

"I took one hit," Randall winces. "I just need to shower. I'll be fine."

I've never considered myself to have deep maternal instincts beforehand, but they've started to surface now that I'm dating Randall. He needs someone to look after him. While Randall picks himself out some clean clothes, I'm in the bathroom, letting the water in the shower heat and getting out a wash rag and a towel.

As Randall showers, I stay perched near the end of the tub in a small opening in the curtain while he tells me about the events that lead to the disgusting state he came back in. Randall's into a lot more than just selling drugs at this point. He's been taking on a lot of extra *tasks* for Luis in his bid to make himself an asset. So far, Randall's plan is working quite well.

I tell myself I'm only watching Randall so closely because I need to make sure he's not hurt anywhere else but… my gaze has turned sinful. His arms are fine. They're chiseled like a Greek statue of marble, using a wash rag to wipe away clouds of dirt from his skin. I watch water rivet off his skin, down his body.

There's no need for me to still be in the corner of the shower curtain. He's fine. There are no sores on his hard chest, or his stomach, or… I should not be seeing these things. I'm not meant to be seeing Randall.

But he's too pretty to look away.

His body is clean now, and he's moved onto his hair. I love that silly boy band hair of his. Randall's pinching his eyes shut while he washes the shampoo out. When he opens his eyes and he looks at me, I find myself blushing. I bite my lip to hide the smile, but he's grinning too broadly. "Do you like the show, Gumdrop?"

"Randall."

He beams at me. "Keep watching, baby. I think I want to just sear my skin in some hot water for a while," he says, lifting his head into the shower head and closing his eyes. "That, or I need to just marinate myself in the tub."

"Are you going to make a mess in my tub?" I ask him playfully. "I just cleaned it."

"Your tub?" He teases. "Is it your tub now?"

"I'm clearly the only one that cleans it."

"It gets cleaned when we shower in it." He steps on the drain to start plugging the water, making his decision.

Now that Randall has turned off the shower head so he can let the faucet fill the tub faster, I go to grab an extra towel because I know that Randall does not have the ability to not get water on the floor.

"You're going to stay and keep me company, right?" Randall pulls the shower curtain open to one side so that the filling tub as well as himself is exposed to the rest of the bathroom.

"If you behave yourself." I lay the towel out on the floor by the tub.

Randall has eased himself into the tub but the water hasn't risen enough to fully cover himself yet. He groans as he settles in the water that steams from the faucet. "I'm going to miss this," Randall tells me, leaning his head into the wall of the shower.

The water level has risen to his naval. "Miss what?" I sit on the edge of the tub, my fingers skimming over the warm water as it rises.

I know he isn't being serious by the smile that's pushing his cheeks up. "Miss you, when you dump me at the end of the school year."

I roll my eyes. "Hm." I don't know what to say to that. In my head, I've been planning a very different outcome. One that makes my parents disappointed in me.

He peaks one eye open. "Unless?" He can't take anything seriously.

I bat my eyes at him with the pinched smile that I know gets him on his worst behavior. "What? How long did you see this going on for?"

"Hm." Randall closes his eyes again, pantomiming deep thought. "I already told you that I'm going to marry you, so if you try to break up with me, you're just going to complicate things."

Randall shuts the water off by pushing the handle of the faucet down with his foot. It's quiet in the bathroom now, with the only sound being the water as it churns in the tub around Randall's body.

"Marrying you would complicate things with my parents." It's a real concern, but I say it lightly enough that Randall is still smiling to himself when he looks at me.

"I think you love me too much to listen to your parents at this point."

Ever since I told him I loved him, he's let it go to his head. He was walking on clouds for a week, beating the phrase until it's dead. "Is that what you think?"

He sits up, the water parting around him and my eyes dart to his stomach. "Remember when you told me I'm none of the things you want?"

I roll my eyes, but I'm leaning down closer to him. "I don't recall."

When he kisses me, I end up with wet cheeks and a wet chin. "Remember when you wouldn't let me kiss you?" He reaches his arm out to move my bangs, water running off of his arms and in a single trail down the side of my face. "Remember when you wouldn't let me touch you?"

"I don't think I remember who I was before," I say softly with a smile. I really don't. That's a different Liling.

"Before?" He asks, practically speaking the words straight into my mouth.

Our foreheads meet, breaths starting to escalate together. "I don't know who I was before I loved you."

My shirt was already wet from the kiss before. I was already falling in love with him for the third time today before we started melding our mouths together. Maybe that's how I end up inside the tub on top of Randall with all my clothes on. Maybe that's why I let his arms hold me against him in the warm water while my legs are pressed against the side of the tub, hugging his lap.

I'm in a daze. Water is violently escaping the tub as we move together, arms enclosed and exploring each other. I'm practically drinking water off his face. My hair is wet, sticking in black strings on my shoulders and Randall's chest. The periwinkle blouse I'm wearing is sticking uncomfortably to my skin, so it's discarded on the bathroom floor.

Almost. I almost stop myself. Stop this. I have a moment of Christian clarity. I'm in a bathtub topless, on top of a fully

286

naked man that is *not* my husband. Mama used to tell me that if something feels sinful, then it is.

The way Randall touches me is absolutely sinful, and the way I let him is damning.

I was not planning on getting into a tub with Randall fully clothed when I got dressed today, but I'm in the wrong outfit to preserve what I told myself I needed to keep intact. My beige corduroy skirt is wrangled up to my thighs, and I can feel *everything* Randall is thinking on my leg.

I may have been sheltered, but I'm not stupid.

I know what's happening beneath me, and I know what's going to happen when my underwear ends up in a sopping wet pile on top of my blouse. I know what's happening when I'm kissing Randall's neck and he's positioning himself. I *feel* what's happening; I feel it with every rise, every push, every time he moans my name into my chest.

This is always going to be what my first time sounds like. It sounds like water slapping frantically between thighs and echoed moaning as our ecstasy bounces off the tile. It feels like droplets dripping from my lashes and onto Randall's nose. It tastes like Randall, it looks like Randall; love *is* Randall.

I don't think I fully realize what I've accomplished, what I've done, until we've both finished. I'm still sitting on Randall with my arms wrapped around his shoulders, my head bowed between my arm and his neck. The sinful pleasure still radiates within me; what I've gained for a few fleeting moments after losing something that's left me forever.

As what's left of the water cools, Randall pets my wet hair away from his face. "Hey," he says softly, waiting for me to sit back to look at him after releasing his shoulders.

There's drops of water still rolling down his face as his breath steadies.

287

"Hi," I say softly, our eyes searching each other as if we're both accepting what we've just done.

He's so sweet, so soft, so loving. "I don't know who I was before I loved you either, but I'm glad he's gone."

54.

[RANDALL]

I can't believe we fucking did that.

I love her so much.

Liling.

55.

[RANDALL]

There aren't enough towels in the world to clean up the mess we made. There's water pooling on the floor, soaking everything in what Liling's forbidden me from calling our *love current.*

If it weren't for *how* we flooded the bathroom, Liling would've just let me call the landlord. I don't think Liling is even ready to admit to herself what we did in that bathtub, so she sure as hell isn't going to let me explain in any capacity that we had a tub overflow in the first place. I've got four towels that aren't up for the job, and I even resorted to using a blanket while Liling goes to the closest home store and buys towels after putting on fresh, dry clothes.

An hour and a half later, the floor is as dry as it's going to be for the night. At the very least, there aren't pools of water on the floor. Liling and I load up the in-unit washing machine with the sopping wet blankets and towels and the poor thing is fighting for its life to accommodate the weight of the wet blankets.

Once we're both in dry clothes, we sit on my couch with the TV on mute, listening to the hum of the washing machine.

Personally, I'm ecstatic about what happened less than two hours ago. Heck, I've got a dry bed that I'm ready to use properly.

Liling's looking ahead at the TV but I can tell she's not really watching Saturday Night Live. "Are you... alright?" I ask her.

I almost don't want to ask it at all because I'm afraid she'll say anything that sounds regretful to what we just did. It always feels like Liling is trying to convince herself that she's the good Christian girl that her parents want her to be. She knows she's slipping from that image but she had one last card to hold onto to prove to herself that she's the woman she thinks she needs to be. Now that card is gone.

Moments later, she still hasn't said anything. "Liling?"

Her head lifts higher as she comes back into full consciousness. "Hm?" She looks at me, still kind of dazed by her own thoughts.

"Are you alright?" I ask again with a doubtful tone. I don't know if I should crack a joke or be serious or... this is a big deal, especially for Liling. To Liling, it isn't just sex. It's... I don't know what to call it other than permanent.

She's pulling her face back into a polite, calm smile like what she does when there's a lot of people around. "I'm fine, I think I'm just tired."

"Oh, ok." I crane my head around Liling to look at the kitchen where the washing machine continues to fight the good fight. "You can go to sleep, if you want. I'll wait for the washing machine to be done and switch the blankets over."

Liling bites her lip before standing up. "Fine, thank you," she says stiffly.

Liling walks toward the bedroom, and I unmute the TV and lower the volume.

"Randall?"

291

I pull my eyes from the television to see Liling standing in an oversized t-shirt by the frame that leads into the hallway. "Yeah?"

Her brown eyes bare into me, my beautiful Liling. "You're all the things I want now."

56.

LILING

I've officially stopped trying to be the Liling Zhu that I was raised to be. The good Liling Zhu died fornicating in a bathtub two weeks ago. I have a boyfriend. I decided that, if I'm going to hell for premarital sex, then the damage is done and I may as well enjoy the wonder that is Randall Persch in all of his glory. Randall has a lot of friends, but no one gets Randall in the way I get Randall. I know that I have all of him, and I love that every piece of him belongs to me. I've given him all of my pieces now too.

Another dangerous rationalization has come to mind, one that Randall attempted to use long ago to get me into bed. In a way, he's right. If I do marry Randall at some point in our lives, then still, I'll only have ever been with one man. That's not so bad, is it?

Lishui is a college freshman now, and we'll share this campus for one year. It's two days before the first classes start, and I've promised Mama I'll show Lishui around campus. The plan was to get back to my dorm early in the morning, so when Lishui arrives I can pretend that it's where I sleep but Lishui is early, and her face tells me that she knows more than I'm telling her.

Lishui is wearing a green romper-dress with a white t-shirt under it and black converse sneakers. She looks up from a welcome-week pamphlet as I walk toward her. Lishui's always been a little ray of light; easily the friendliest of the three of us. "Morning!"

"Morning, Lish." I offer my younger sister a warm hug before fishing my keys out of my backpack. "Sorry, I just stepped out for a minute, I thought I could beat you back." I think lying is the least of my sins now.

"It's no problem., Lishui offers, following me into my dorm that feels like a foreign land at this point. I'm hoping Lishui won't notice the dust that's settled on my work desk.

"I just want to drop off my backpack and we can go." We only stay in my dorm for a minute and a half, before Lishui can do too much inspecting. Randall's books, a sweater, the feeling that this room hasn't been fully occupied in months- there's many signs that the old Liling has been gone.

It feels too cold for this early in the fall. It makes the task of walking Lishui around campus a lot less enjoyable. I think about how, if it weren't for my current infatuation with a certain red-haired boy-band member, I'd spend most of my senior year walking around with my sister on campus.

I show Lishui the library, the cafeteria, the buildings where her classes will be, and the coffee shop. Both of our toes have started to freeze and we're making a beeline back toward my dorm.

Lishui and I are holding arms like we used to do growing up. "So." Lishui uses her free hand to tug a pink knitted cap down over the top of her ears. "Are you still dating the cute pizza boy?"

"His name is Randall," I say patiently. "And he doesn't work there anymore. And yes."

Lishui beams up at me, happily walking along with me. "I hope I can have a boyfriend before Papa finds some boring guy from our church. At least you get to have a little bit of fun before you have to turn into Mama."

Fun, yes, I've been having a lot of fun. While Lishui is much more accepting and kind than Lhasa and the rest of my family, she's still in the mindset that our parents have the final say over everything in our lives.

We were raised that our parents make all our important decisions until we're married. Then, our husbands make those decisions. I wonder what Papa would think of Randall, who wouldn't dream of attempting to hush my independent thoughts.

If there's a person to voice my intrusive, independent thoughts with, other than Randall, it's Lishui. "What if... what if I don't let Mama and Papa choose someone for me?"

My sister's eyes get big as she contemplates. "You mean... find someone on your own?"

"I mean, what if I already found my someone?"

Lishui's little mouth parts. "Liling, he's... ok he's pretty, but..."

I sigh. "It's hard to understand if you haven't..." I trail off, cheeks reddening as I was about to say something gushy and emotional.

Lishui tugs on my arm in excitement. "If? If what?"

"I think I know why Mama and Papa try so hard to make sure we stay focused on anything other than boys," I lament with a smile. "Why they warn us about how easy it is to fall into sin, or to get lost." We've endured a lifetime of bible lessons tailored toward the concept of a good, chaste woman.

"Are you... lost?" Lishui asks in a confused whisper.

I partially ignore this question, still holding Lishui's arm. "They want us to stay focused on all other things they told us so

295

they can pick for us," I state. "And they know that, if we find a way to fall in love, despite their warnings, it's all over."

"It's over?"

"It's over," I repeat.

Lishui looks more worried than she does supportive. "I think… Liling, I'm happy for you but I don't know about making this guy your whole future just because you like him."

I bite back the urge to correct her usage of the word 'like.' "So we should let our parents pick our entire future? It's the nineties, Lish. We don't have to live like our parents did."

"But is it worth facing Papa's wrath?" Lishui asks me.

"What can they do?" I challenge. "What can they really do about it? I'm an adult. I can be my own person."

"They can excommunicate you from the family."

I hadn't thought about that. "Well… if they'd really do that, I don't need them, then."

"Liling," Lishui whispers.

I'm not really sure about my stance. "I don't know," I sigh. "I guess I'll worry about it when it's a problem."

Lishui laughs. "I think you already have a problem on your hands." Her eyes light up. "Do you *hold hands* with him?"

I miss when I had this sort of innocence. "Yes, Lishui. I hold hands with him."

57.

[RANDALL]

If there's one man that knows how to threaten a judge, it's this guy. Gordy and I were able to bring Judge Peterson to his senses, and Luis is pleased with our work. Oscar was released a while ago, not that I've seen him around. He might not be in Luis' good graces temporarily for getting himself arrested in the first place.

I'm now responsible for thirteen sellers, making more money than I thought was possible at this point in my life. At any point in my life. Everything's going perfectly, in terms of selling coke. My sellers are in line, my records are in order, and I've got a friend in the cartel.

I've got my best friend working with me now, too. Gordy doesn't mind the kind of work we do. He's always been a brute, and now he makes good money doing it. I pay Gordy anytime I need him to come help me with something. It's more than he can make selling pizzas.

Gordy's the kind of guy that would have no career path otherwise; he's barely got a high school diploma, and he's mean so it's hard for him to climb the ladder through social skills. He's also ugly, he's poor, and so far, my little empire that I'm building under the Padillas seems like his best chance at ever having anything nice in his life.

Today is the first day of classes for the fall semester. Liling has three classes today, with my first class not starting until tomorrow. Honestly, college is starting to feel pointless for me. I'm making my own career path. Classes are getting in the way. At this point, I might as well keep going but I think this degree is going to be an expensive point to make.

Liling didn't stay over last night, since her class is at eight in the morning and she'd have to leave my place really early to get to her course in time. I don't like sleeping without Liling next to me. I have to remind myself that eventually we'll have every night together. Liling Persch, that's what I'm working toward.

I spent my day collecting from my dealers and figuring out who's ready for new product. I don't see Luis all that often- but I make calls with someone who works for him- Jorge- and he makes sure I get the product I need and helps coordinate pickup. With the amount I need between all my sellers, I'm going to have to start working out a storage solution soon.

I've been busy, but I'm never going to let myself get to a point where I don't have time for Liling. All of this is for her, now. I'm not going to stop until I've got her dripping in jewels, sitting in a huge house with everything she could ever want.

I stop at my favorite florist that's on the edge of campus, picking up white and pink lilies with a few red roses thrown into an arrangement. It's six in the evening, and Liling should be back to her dorm by now.

I walk down the familiar green carpeted hallway of the girl's dormitory. After I turn the corner and I'm on the last hall that will take me down to Liling, I notice there's someone coming out of her dorm: the elusive roommate, Britney.

It's been a while since I've seen Britney. Her hair looks even blonder than the last time I'd seen her. She's got her boyfriend in tow behind her as she notices me coming her way. Britney's got on a pink jacket that looks more like a rain jacket than one meant for the fall wind and jeans. She's got a big, blonde hulk of a boyfriend that I think might play on the football team trailing toward me behind Britney.

I'm ready to politely greet Liling's roommate in the hallway, saying, "Hi Britney, how are you?" as the distance is closed between us.

Britney responds by slapping me across the face.

I blink the sting away, stunned. "Hey, what the hell was that for?" She's got tiny, cold hands so it wasn't like it hurt that much but it was completely uncalled for.

Britney, face pinched in a scowl, answers with another question. "What did you do to her?"

"What?"

"What did you do to her?" Britney asks again, louder. I don't know what's going on but from here, someone could be convinced that Britney is a loyal, longtime friend of Liling.

"Who?" I ask. "Liling?" Who else could we be talking about?

"Yes, Einstein! What did you do to her?"

I had to think, because as far as I know, I haven't done anything. Plus, Liling isn't really the type of person to air out the laundry in public, even if she is mad at me. "Gee, I don't know. Is she-"

"She's a wreck!" Britney hisses. "I've never seen her like this. I don't know what you did, but you need to leave, *now.*"

It's laughable that she thinks she can tell me what to do. She tells me Liling is apparently 'a wreck' and then expects me to leave? I don't even know that I believe her in the first place.

299

Liling's always been so composed. Liling doesn't crash. *Especially* when there's an audience.

"I don't know what you're talking about," I say calmly, but wearing a frown. "I saw her a couple days ago, and she was fine." Britney stops by her dorm maybe once a month, and she's going to stop in and act like she's Liling's friend and she knows what's going on? If I don't know what's going on, I don't see how Britney would.

Britney's a little dramatic in her emotions- she squints at me, hand on her hip, throwing her weight to one leg. "You know what? You must be some sort of snake, Randall Persch." I feel my blood pressure rising. Britney points a finger at me as she continues her little tirade. "I have never seen that woman be anything less than a perfect, composed, strong boss-lady type and now-" She falters, slapping her own thigh. "I know heartbreak when I see it." Behind her, her boyfriend lifts a brow.

Heartbreak. There's no way. Break Liling's heart is the one thing I could never, would never do. "What did she say?" I press.

Britney flips a hand dismissively. "She won't talk to me."

"Then, how do you know anything is wrong?"

I hate how she looks at me like I'm stupid. "Because she's a crying wreck, you jerk!"

"She's crying?" I start to step around her because so far this has been a colossal waste of time but Britney steps in time with me so the bitch is blocking me.

"No. Not right now," she quips.

"I have to see what's wrong." I argue, gesturing at the door that's just a few feet away. The walls are paper thin, surely Liling can hear all of this.

Britney eyes my flowers. "It seems like you know something is wrong already."

I also look at the flowers that I've brought. "These are *not* apology flowers. Believe me, if I had something to apologize for, I would've brought a whole lot more." Now I'm nervous that maybe I do have something to be sorry for. I'm trying to replay the last few days in my head, but I can't think of anything.

Both hands on her hips, Britney directs me backward with a hand pushing back on my shoulder. This bitch has two seconds to-

"Come on, man." Her boyfriend has a deep voice of someone who I can't match physically. "Just clear out for a while."

I look up at the behemoth of a man. "I have no idea who you are, but I don't need your involvement in this either." I send a pointed look to Britney. "You two have a good day."

Britney's boyfriend, Brock, is apparently a lot like me; he'll do basically anything his girlfriend tells him to. Not only would the two of them not let me through, but Brock personally escorted me out of the building and waited until it looked like I walked away to leave the doorway. Brock is twice my size, and I don't have Gordy with me so it was easier to lie low for fifteen minutes before heading back in.

Either way, I hope it was worth it, because Brock and Britney are on my list now.

By the time I'm back in the dorm building, I'm in a mood. My shirt is wrinkled, my flowers are bent, and I don't think my hair is how I had it this morning.

I only knock on the door because of Britney's intel but no one answers so I try the handle, knowing Britney is notorious for never locking the door behind her. Thankfully, the door opens into a dark dorm room, the only light coming through a half-open blind from the window.

Inside, sits a woman I've never seen before; she looks like Liling but she's a version of her that I don't know. Whoever is sitting on Liling's bed with red, teared stained eyes, is someone who looks at me like they've never loved me a day in her life.

58.

[RANDALL]

I've never seen Liling like this. I've never seen Liling look at me like that. Cautiously, I step into the dark dorm room, shutting the door behind me, killing a ray of light that comes in from the hallway.

Liling is perched on her bed, back against the wall with one leg folded to her chest, the other thrown in front of her. Her black hair is messed up and out of place.

"Liling," I ask in quiet alarm. "What happened?"

I take a step forward but she growls at me. "Don't."

I stop in my tracks. She's still in her sleep clothes: a large white t-shirt that we got during MSU's welcome week before classes start and gray pajama bottoms with a drawstring.

Her eyes aren't looking at me after I shut the door, but when I dare to say her name again, I'm met with those brown rage-filled eyes that shrivel up my insides. "What's going on?" Instead of moving directly toward her, I make lateral steps toward the work desk, setting down the flowers on top of a new textbook.

"Did… did something happen at one of your classes?" It doesn't look like she's left this room at all. There's a pack of unopened pencils next to her book, and a red backpack that still has the tag on it.

Liling doesn't answer me, so I start taking another step in her direction, despite the feral energy that's pouring out of her. She looks more upset now than she had coming back from Professor Brackett's classroom.

This is a woman of despair.

I need a name. I need a name to put to whoever brought her to this. Once I know that, I can make them count their days. I can make them beg. I'll fix this.

I'm at the foot of her bed now, my fingers resting on the red blanket that's been kicked to the end of the mattress. "Liling." I'm using a more forceful voice now. She's clearly got a problem that I'm going to fix. "Tell me what's going on."

She stares at me with foreign, cold eyes. These aren't the eyes that tell me they love me or the ones that are proud of me. These are the eyes of the woman who told me last year that I'm none of the things she wants.

Her quiet voice is broken but holds enough strength to send another rivet through my stomach. "I want you to leave, Randall."

She's so damn stubborn, sometimes. She never wants help. "No."

The look she gives me could rival Medusa. I might not make it out of here alive.

"Liling, tell me what the big problem is, and I'll take care of it," I promise.

Keeping her eyes on me, she shifts her weight to her left, reaching her hand into the small table that sits between her bed and Britney's bed. The table drawer, last time I checked, only has a small book of phone numbers and a pen, but she pulls something else out, something long and white, made of plastic.

Liling Zhu is handing me a pregnancy test.

I know what it is before it's fully extended toward me, and I know what it's going to say before I cautiously take it from her.

I look at the plastic tube, capped at the end. At the center of the wand, there's a small white window that has two blue lines that intersect each other to make a cross. The legend is clearly printed on the right side of the wand.

She's pregnant.

Liling is pregnant. Liling is pregnant. Liling is pregnant.

Liling is pregnant, and I know she isn't going to forgive me for this one.

A balloon's worth of air escapes my chest as my mind is reeling. Shit.

"Ok," I say, as if I know where the sentence is going. Ok. Liling is pregnant. I'm going to be a father. This time next year, I'm going to be responsible for a small human. I know nothing about kids. We haven't finished school yet. I'm selling cocaine. We're not married. We don't have a place to live. I work for a cartel. The apartment? How do we get a stroller up four flights of stairs? Why can't babies drink water? Liling is pregnant.

Shit.

"You can leave now," Liling says, her voice dead with self-loathing that likely extends to me.

"Leave?" I ask, my mind firing back up. "I, I'm not leaving, Liling. This is-" I smooth my hair back. Shit. Liling is pregnant. "We'll figure this out."

"Figure this out?" Liling snaps, looking the most animated I've seen her so far. Her voice is so, so cruel, and it's sending all of its poison my way. "How are you going to figure this one out, Randall?"

"I don't know," I fire back, setting the test back down on the edge of the bed. I really don't know. This is just my fucking luck. One time. *One* time. One time where I wasn't wrapped and ready and I knocked someone up. "I'll-"

She isn't going to let me finish the plan I didn't have anyways. "No," she snaps at me. "I want you to leave me alone, Randall. Just leave, and don't come back."

She's almost funny. She almost sounds like she's going to tell me she's pregnant and then break up with me. "You're out of your mind if you think I'm going to just walk away. You couldn't get rid of me before, and now." I shake my head. "I'm going to help you through this. You're going to help *me* through this."

"I. Don't. Want. You. Here. Randall," Liling yells.

"Why the fuck not!" I yell back, slapping my hands against my pants. "I don't know what we're going to do either, but we're going to do it together." It's rare that I get to tell Liling what's going to happen. What's not going to happen is me leaving and never coming back.

"No. We won't," she states with finality. "You're going to leave me alone. I'm going to handle this myself."

"Handle this yourself," I repeat, crossing my arms. "Why would that make any sense, Liling. Lil, you can be mad but it doesn't make any sense to shut me out. You're going to need m-"

"Do not *dare* tell me that I need you, Randall Persch, because I don't." This entire time, only one tear has escaped her red, puffy eyes. It's like she's in such a fit of rage that she's restricted her body completely. Rage. She wants rage right now, not sorrow. She wants me to wither under that rage, and it's working so far.

"Listen, you're pregnant." The words almost make her flinch. "You're pregnant, and there's nothing we can do about that now. It is what it is."

That may have been the wrong thing to say. "It is. What. It is?" Liling's smooth honey voice hardens into fucking terrifying shards of amber when she wants it to.

I put a hand out, as if calming a bull. "What I mean is… I don't even know what I mean, but we need to do this together. We need to plan, or something."

"I will do everything on my own."

"You will *not.*"

She's up from the bed now, taking two stomps over to me until she's just a few inches from me. She really hates me right now. I can feel it. "No more," she seethes. "I'm not letting *you* ruin my life any more than you already have."

"That's not fair-"

"You knew-" She interrupts me. "I told you I was waiting! I tell you over and over what parts of my faith, of my upbringing are important to me and you stomp over it- over and over, Randall! Now, I'm going to be responsible for upbringing a *baby* and this is the one thing I have to do right, now. This is the last thing I have to keep you from ruining."

I might hate her a little bit now, too. I point a finger at her. "Listen, you can be mad about the outcome, but you can't be mad about the circumstance. I *never* made you do anything you didn't want to do. You might have regrets now, but don't you dare act for one minute like you didn't want to have sex with me. You took your clothes off. You let me pull you in the tub with me."

I see the angry tears that are stuck in her lashes, getting captured before they can escape. I'm going to drive this point home. "You weren't sorry about it then, or any of the times after that. *We* could have been more careful, sure. But *I* did not ruin anything."

She tries to push me back with her hands but I catch them and let her have them back. "Leave!" She repeats.

307

"No!" I tell her, wanting to grab her hands again. "You're going to need me, Liling. This isn't something you can do alone. I'm the father, and I'm going to act like it."

She lets out a cruel laugh, arms crossed. "You know what you are, Randall?" I'm really in for it now. She was just warming up before. She pokes me in the chest. "You're the one that's made me everything I never wanted to be. You made me a slut. You made me leave my values."

Before I can respond, she's poking at my chest again, continuing to tear me down. "Worse than that, you made me a stereotype. Now, I'm going to be a college dropout. The woman in the business school that couldn't make it with all of the men. All of those white men that look at me and think I didn't belong- well, now they get to be right about it."

"Don't do that to me," I bite. "We made one mistake and-"

"I don't get to make mistakes, Randall!" Liling spits out. "There's no second chance for me. Now, my only identity is a college mother who's a dropout. You- people who look like you- you're free to live your life and do whatever you want."

"Liling, you're not a stereotype, ok?" I ask, not sure how we even got into this territory. "Being Asian has nothing to do with it."

She pushes me again for saying that. "You've seen my business classes, Randall. How many?"

"What?"

"How many?" She repeats. "How many other women, in a class of hundreds do you see? How many minority women? You don't get to tell me it doesn't matter, Randall. I have worked so hard to be the exception, to be the success story that's fighting adversity, and now all of it's gone. Four years of work to prove that I belong there only to be proven wrong."

308

I've never taken the time to gauge out the school demographics, I never thought to. Sure, Liling is one of few, but I didn't think it was ever a big deal. "It's not like you aren't tough enough to make it through this program, Liling. These are special circumstances-"

Liling is a storm, and I'm getting blown the fuck away. "I don't get to have special circumstances! Now, I'm just the girl whose life is ruined because she couldn't keep her legs closed. The girl who gets pregnant with the first guy she's with. You've made me a failure, Randall, and I will *never* forgive you for that."

I don't even know what to say to all of that. I only ever wanted to build her up. "Fine," I say. "Don't forgive me, then. I'm still not leaving."

"Randall," she says, still just as angry but her voice is getting thin. "You once told me that you'd always do what I ask you to do. Right now, I'm asking you to leave and not come back. I would rather do all of this alone than do any of it with *you.*"

She doesn't mean that. She's too proud to admit that she can't do this alone. Even if she could, I won't let her, but I'm tired. I'm suddenly drained of all of my energy, all the spirit having been sucked into Liling's swirling vortex of hate and misery.

"Find someone else's life to ruin," Liling snarls, still standing inches away from me.

If she wants to be nasty, fine. By the end of the day, we're both going to have some apologizing and forgiving to do. I lean down a little, so that our faces are even closer, making sure she can look right in my fucking eyes.

I speak to her quietly, in a voice I usually reserve for people that are out of options. "You know, Liling. You're lucky you have me. You're lucky I'm willing to put up with you because I don't think there's anybody else that would want to deal with

309

you." I'm trembling, and I don't know if it's because I'm so angry or because I'm scared of talking to Liling like this.

"You're mean, Liling. You're a prude, self-righteous person. So if I were you, I'd be real fucking wary about how you speak to me and about pushing away the only person that's ever going to love you the way you are. I can't think of a goddamn person in this world that would put up with this much of your shit."

I'm already so close, I raise myself just a few inches, placing a kiss colder than Judas on her forehead. She doesn't budge, but she's practically shaking with how much she hates me right now.

"I'll let you be by yourself tonight," I say quietly. "You can think about how you know, deep, deep, down, that you can't do this by yourself and you don't want to do it by yourself. I'll come back in a couple days."

"Don't come back," she says, voice trembling as I'm stepping away from her.

I think the half smile I give her looks like one of pity, and that's what it feels like. I hope she feels it. She's strong, but she's stronger when I'm supporting her. "I'll always come back, Liling."

LILING

I'm pregnant. I've become the ultimate failure. All my hard work, gone. Over two decades of working myself ragged trying to be the person I'm supposed to be; squandered.

All of it, gone because of pretty blue eyes and a sweet voice.

I let myself be tempted, seduced. I forgot my own work ethic, my morals, my way. I'm furious at Randall but I'm even angrier at myself. I made these choices. Now, I'll have to live with them forever.

There is a person growing inside of me.

The absolute worst part of this will be the embarrassment. The disappointment. It'll be the look Papa gives me, and the screaming that will come after. It'll be the final fallen chess piece in becoming the disappointment child, with my sisters surpassing me. It'll be canceling all my classes because I know I can't finish this degree while I'm preparing to raise a child.

The failure. That's what I hate the most about all of this.

I staked my claim with Randall. I told my parents he was what I wanted. They warned me about him, and I didn't listen. Now he's gone.

311

I haven't seen Randall since yesterday. I don't think Randall has ever been truly angry with me. Randall's never tried to hurt me with his words before. As soon as he left, I locked my door and broke down crying under my blankets. Pathetic little Liling, all alone in her room. No one to hold her because there's no one that would want to do it.

Actually, I'm not alone. Inside a marriage, a child is supposed to be a gift. In the lines of sin I've sewn this seed in, this child is a curse. No matter what, I can never do this the right way. Never.

I keep changing my mind on what the worst part is. As I sit alone in my dorm room, I think the worst part is that my weakened mental state just tells me how much I don't want to be alone. Being alone is not my way anymore. My way is Randall and his hard arms that wrap around me and his soft hair that tickles my neck.

I sit here alone, wanting comfort from someone I told myself I need to cut from my life. My mind keeps pleading with me – If Randall has already dragged me so low, why not let him meet me at the bottom?

I told him not to come back. Ever. I'm terrified he's going to do what he always does, which is anything that I ask him to do.

Randall Persch. I need him.

Is there a point in pushing him away? Is there a point in doing this alone? Maybe it would be better to let him stand by me, if that's what he wants to do. What's more pathetic- a single mother and college dropout, or a college dropout who stayed with the loser who knocked her up in the first place?

My pride wants to prove I can do this alone, that I can fix my own mistakes. My heart wants to step aside and let Randall come in and fix my problems. I don't want to stand on my own, I want to be swept off my feet.

There is a person inside of me. I've already failed this little person.

I don't know what I'm going to do. For now, I'm going to wallow. I'm going to sit alone in the dark and cry and sleep and cry some more. The only comfort I have right now is staying in this room and hiding myself away from the world.

This isn't how I wanted things to go; I wanted the world to hide from me.

60

[RANDALL]

I don't know what the hell to do. Liling is pregnant. She won't talk to me. I'm going to be a father. I have no idea how to fix this. Fix isn't the right word. I don't know how to move forward.

I said some real awful things to Liling.

I might be a piece of shit.

It wouldn't surprise me if she doesn't let me back into her dorm again, or if she doesn't come back to my apartment. Moving mountains would be easier than moving Liling.

My old man was only nineteen when he knocked my mom up when she was eighteen, and I obviously didn't learn the importance of contraception. My parents also aren't great examples of the strength of a marriage that starts too young purely for the sake of trying to raise a kid together. My parents divorced when I was seven, and I lived with my dad until I moved out for college.

I have to do this better than my dad did.

I'm still formulating a plan, figuring out what I'm going to do. That's going to start with bringing a pack of beer over to Gordy's shitty apartment.

Gordy lives in a building that has a deli on the lower level with three apartment units on the third floor. It's a single bedroom; single meaning there is literally one room where each corner is a different function. One corner is a kitchen, one is a bedroom, one is a living room, and one corner has nothing more than a half table that's littered with Gordy's junk.

I pass the shared bathroom in the hallway, knocking on a green door with chipped green paint and a number '3' in faded gold spray-paint. Gordy isn't the type to answer the door unless he's expecting somebody, which he isn't.

I knock on the door again. If he isn't here, I'll sit here in the hallway and wait. "Gordy," I call.

Gordy is such a loud person that I hear his gorilla steps lumber toward the door. Gordy answers the door, shirt off and looking like he needs some sleep and a shave. I watch the smug quip die on his lips when he takes one look at me. "What the hell is wrong with you?"

He lets me in, and I walk past him wordlessly, setting the pack of beer down on an old countertop that is dying for someone to wipe it down. I open the pack and have a can opened while Gordy watches like I've grown another head. "Hey- what's going on?" Gordy barks indelicately. "You got a job or something for me or-"

"Liling's pregnant."

Gordy stalls, staring at me directly. After another moment of stunned silence, he rubs his eye and growls, "You fucking idiot."

I lean my head back, looking up at a stained popcorn ceiling. "I know."

"You're stuck with her now."

"Gordy," I eye him. "That's not helpful."

315

Gordy walks up to the pack and takes a can of beer out for himself. "So, what are you going to do?"

"I don't know." If I knew, maybe I wouldn't be here talking to my idiot friend. "She's so mad at me, Gordy."

"Why?" my friend asks. "Did you accidentally fall into her or something?"

"No."

Gordy shrugs. "She's always got a stick up her ass about something."

"Gordy," I warn again. "I get why she's upset. I just wish she wasn't upset with me."

"What are you going to do?" Gordy asks again, slowly starting to migrate toward a beat-up loveseat that faces a minuscule television set.

"I don't know." I start to follow Gordy, bringing the entire case of beer with me. "I'm going to give her a day or so to calm down, and when I go back, I need a plan."

"You're going to need money," Gordy corrects, sitting himself heavily on the loveseat. I swear a cloud of dust puffs out of the cushion.

"I have a lot saved," I say.

"Yeah, but you're going to need a lot, since you ain't got insurance. All those doctor appointments? Plus all the shit babies need."

Insurance. I don't have any yet. That's what's going to kill me. I wonder what a doctor is going to think when I try to pay for a thousand dollar ultrasound with cash. Liling is depending on me. There's a kid that has my genes and my blood that needs me to get this right.

Maybe this is the ultimate test. How I respond now is important, and it's going to define what sort of man I am for the rest of my life. This whole time, I've been so focused on Liling's life - on giving her everything. Now there's two people two worry about. This little Persch that grows inside of Liling, I'm going to give them everything too.

My kid will want for nothing.

61.

[RANDALL]

Money. That's the first thing I'll need. I'm making good cash now, but is it enough? In my head, I need so much more than enough to pay month-to-month. All the things I had already wanted to give Liling before: those things are due now.

I've got a plan for Liling, for us. The three of us. Overnight, I got the motivation I needed. I'm done with the panicking and now I'm going to plan.

Today, I'm making big, bold moves.

It's a drop off day for me, meaning I take all the money I've collected from the sellers, minus their cuts, and deliver it to the Padilla cartel so I can get my cut. I called Jorge ahead, asking if he has more on hand that I can sell, more than what he normally has ready for me.

"You have a place to store all of that *candy?*" Jorge asks over the phone.

"I'm about to," I promise.

There's hesitation on the other end. "Man, you already take a lot more than everybody else. I'll have to check in with the boss." It's been a few weeks since I've seen or talked to Luis who lives over in Detroit. Now that I've got the area under control, he doesn't need to come around as often.

"Of course," I offer pleasantly. "I appreciate it."

There's laughter on the other end. "You sure are the nicest candy dealer, Boy Scout." Somehow, the nickname has spread wide amongst Luis' workers.

Move one, in motion. Sell more, make more. Gordy is going to scout, find a couple more people to sell for me. High risk, high reward.

Next, I'm going to the motel, where I've been working as an assistant manager. I'm done doing that, and I'm going to go speak with the owner about it. It's a small family-owned motel, with thirty units or so. It's not a bad place to work, but I can't get where I need to go by working the counter.

■■■

I usually meet Jorge at a storage unit lot in Fowlerville. Luis owns three of these lots, the other two located in Detroit and Flint. I always get there first, driving a used SUV I bought myself a month back. It's not the fancy car I wanted, but it's a step in the right direction. At this rate, I can get myself a nice car next year, after making sure Liling has a good, safe car that'll fit an infant car seat.

I'm leaning against the hood of my car, hunching my shoulders in against the vicious fall breeze that's trying to tear me apart. It's as I'm contemplating waiting inside my car that I hear a car traveling down to the end of the rows of storage units, where only the illegal workings take place. This is still a legitimate business; there are people who rent these units to store their furniture, or their cars and vehicles. They just don't know that some of these units might have cocaine, weapons, bodies, prisoners.

A black SUV pulls up next to me, but I immediately see that it isn't Jorge getting out, it's Luis. Luis, just as thin as ever, gets out wearing a black jacket that looks like it's lined by fleece

319

on the inside. His jeans lead to brown leather shoes with a pointed toe. "Persch," he says as a greeting.

I actually like Luis, even though he's always stiff at first. Every time I see him, it takes him a few minutes to start remembering that he likes me too. "I don't think I've ever seen you alone," I say as my own greeting when Luis leans against the hood of my car next to me.

Luis smirks, gesturing around the lot. "Don't get it confused, Boy Scout. We're not alone right now." With what Luis is hiding in these storage units, I have no doubt it's crawling with Luis' men who are armed and ready.

"Jorge tells me you want more."

I nod, digging my hands into my pockets because my fingers are about to fall off. "So, you wanted to come check on me?" I nod towards my car, where I've got several large leather bags of cash ready for Luis.

Luis, thin as the cigarette he's pulling out of his jacket, says, "You do good work, Persch, but I want to know why you need so much and how you plan to handle that much." He nods at his car. "The more you got, the more you got to lose." He takes a deep breath out, smoke mixing in with the fog of his breath in the cold. "Let's start with the why."

I sigh. I'm not even on speaking terms with Liling for the next 48 hours or so. I'm sure she doesn't want anybody to know, but she's going to have to toughen up. We both do. I only learned that I'm going to be a father yesterday. For once, I'm going to be more like Liling, when she's not even acting like herself. Liling doesn't wait for things to happen. She sees a threat and she pounces. Right now the biggest threat is my financial situation.

"Hey," Luis snaps. "Why are you trying to push so much product, Boy Scout?"

Still, I'm hesitating, passing over the first bag of Luis' money over to him. He's glaring at me by the time he takes the bag ."Liling is pregnant," I say. The first person I ever told I'm going to be a father was my best friend, the second is a drug lord.

Luis stalls, clutching the bag and letting his breath hitch on what turns out to be a laugh. "Shit, Boy Scout." He bows his head with a smile. "You're supposed to lock it down first." He gives me a playful shove. "Ring first, Romeo."

"I was going to wait until we graduated," I mumble into the cold, getting the next bag. Luis isn't bothering to count it right now. We both know our roles.

"What are you even wasting your time in school for anyway?" Luis asks. "You keep doing what you're doing, and I'll make you more than any fucker with a piece of paper."

I've thought about dropping out time after time. "At this point, I'm so close I might as well finish," I say, knowing maybe Liling would rather have a college-educated drug-seller over a dropout who sells drugs.

Luis shakes his head, looking straight forward towards a closed storage unit. Somewhere in the distance, there's a metallic knocking or something, making me turn my head.

"Just business," Luis says dismissively, as if knowing what I hear.

Whatever, as long as it's not me locked in a storage unit. "So, what do you need to hear to give me more to sell?"

The drug lord shrugs. "You got a place to put everything?"

"I have it worked out. Lots of space," I promise. "I'm being careful, I swear."

Luis looks at me with his dark eyes, hardening. "You better be careful. Any of this comes back on me, you're going to pray for incarceration where I have a harder time getting to you."

A chill runs through me. Luis Padilla: no more needs to be said.

Luis has almost double the amount I normally take to sell stored in a storage unit with a fake rolling door, so that unit looks empty save for some old furniture when we first come in. What looks like the back garage door or an alternative exit is really just concealing a crap-ton of cocaine.

I've got so much that it'll barely fit in my car, and I just have to hope I don't get pulled over until I can move it all. Luis isn't impressed by my transportation. I'll get better at it, someday.

"This is the most I can give you at once," Luis says, moving a brick of white powder into my car. Because I'm ordering so much, it's coming to me in bulk. I think I'm going to need to find someone that can take all of this and portion it so it can go to my sellers. I'm about to have a full staff to support this enterprise.

"Am I exceeding my limits?"

Luis shakes his head. "Supply isn't my problem." He wipes his hands on his pants. "It's a risk, at this point, Boy Scout. If you pull a Toby, I'm out over two hundred thousand."

As far as I know, Toby still hasn't been found. "It's about risk," I repeat, shutting my trunk. "So if I want more…" Someday, I'm going to need even more. I'll sell everything Luis has got. "What if I start paying up front?"

Luis raises a brow. "You got that kind of cash?"

Stupid money. That's what I've got just from some white dust. "I will by the time I need to start selling more. And I have other things in the works."

He stares at me, a small smile on his face like a proud father. "You're impressive, Boy Scout, I'll give you that." He shakes his head. "Other things in the works, ok, ok."

I grin at him. "I'm nothing if not ambitious."

Luis laughs, slapping my back. "Ambitious, or crazy?" He asks, before straightening his face and pointing a finger at me. "You better do right by Liling, you hear me? You better give The Diamond a diamond."

62.

LILING

I've spent the last two days holed up in my dorm room, a space that doesn't even feel like mine anymore. Randall's place, that feels like my place. But I haven't seen him in days. Maybe I pushed him too far. He's always so patient with me, but that's when I'm telling him that I love him and saying sweet things that he wants to hear.

I said some terrible things to Randall.

I pushed him so far that he said some terrible things back. I don't even think he said anything untrue. I don't think I ever deserved someone like Randall Persch.

I haven't had the courage to leave my room beyond going to the bathroom as necessary. I've now known that I'm pregnant for four days, and the only reason I'm leaving my dorm now is to shower because there's a nagging feeling that tells me Randall is going to continue to do as he says, and he'll be showing up at my door today.

Walking through the hallway in blue plastic flip flops, I'm clutching a bath towel and my fresh clothes to my stomach, as if my body has already changed.

Dread. That's what I feel when I remember there's no way to pretend like this isn't happening. I can pretend I don't write papers for other students, or that my boyfriend isn't a drug dealer, or that I'm a good person, but I can't pretend to not be pregnant. Not for more than a month or so.

The towel and the clothes do not leave my stomach until I'm concealed behind a disgusting green shower curtain in a white tiled shower with yellowing grout and hair on the walls. In the luxury of a private bathroom at Randall's apartment, I'd forgotten how vile the dorm showers are.

I'm going to take the fastest shower possible. The water isn't hot enough, this bathroom doesn't feel private, and I'm just going to get clean enough to not be repulsive. There are at least two other girls in the bathroom, standing by the mirrors and talking about a tailgate that's happening at the next football game.

I listen to their babble, wishing that it was something that I could worry about. My hand falls to my stomach, even though there's really nothing to feel yet. My stomach is still flat, and I still feel just as empty as ever.

I take a deep breath and pinch my eyes shut. *No more crying, Liling.* I looked like a disaster last time Randall saw me. Instead, I'm going to be put together; I'm still furious at Randall, I'm annoyed with him, and the things he spat at me still haunt me.

I'll probably forgive him as soon as he walks through the door, but I'll torture him just a little by trying to make myself look as stunning as possible in a way that doesn't make it look like I'm trying. Weaponized beauty. Good hair, good genes, and good planning is all it takes to fool a man.

Randall likes me in red, even though I'm partial to green. I've got on a thick red knitted sweater with stone wash jeans and black boots. My hair is big and blown out, pouty red lips and thick black eyeliner that would make my mother frown. Looking at my work in the mirror, I again thank God for being pretty.

In the next hour, I have the dorm cleaned, my desk dusted, and I'm ready to have whatever conversation Randall wants to have.

Until he shows up.

All the prep that I did to appear put together, but as soon as he knocks on the door, my heart shrivels up and I'm pinned against the wall. When Randall knocks on the door again, I hear his muffled voice behind the door. "Lil, if you don't let me in, this whole dorm is about to hear what I have to say."

God, I love his voice.

Cautiously, I walk to the door, leaning my face against the wood. I have no doubt Randall will one hundred percent embarrass me. I just haven't decided if I still want to be mad at him or not.

"Liling?" Randall calls, softer. "I know you're in there."

With perhaps a small smile through the door, I say, "Randall Persch, what makes you think I have nothing better to do than wait around for you to come sweep me off my feet?"

I'm grinning like an idiot, alone in this room, because I know he's smiling on the other side. "You've got it turned around." I roll my eyes, hearing Randall's smooth, sweet voice that could talk a fish out of water. "*I've* got nothing better to do than sweep you off of your feet."

With a small laugh I make sure has dissipated before the door opens, I decide the other women of this dorm aren't going to get anything more from our brief performance.

Gently, I peel the door open, hearing the soft click of the door handle. Randall is there, waiting, wearing a cream-color sweater with a collar over brown dress pants. His hair is gelled back in brown-red curls that sits above the beautiful, loving smiling face of Randall Persch.

Once the door is open, his blue eyes are scanning me, trying to see what sort of mood I'm in, if I look like I've been crying, and if I'm going to let him into this room. He lights up in an even broader grin, as if relieved to see that I look like myself.

"Hi, Liling." As soon as I smell his cinnamon-dusted scent, I realize how much I missed this silly, goofy man I've been calling mine. "God, you're going to kill me looking like that."

I'm still standing in the small space of an open doorway, resting on the door. "Hi, Randall." I'll just ignore Randall's comment. My eyes travel down his arms, noticing that, in one hand, he's got a big white plastic bag full of the only takeout I actually like; the only place that reminds me of Mama's cooking. It can't come close to what Mama would make but there's enjoyment in the familiarity of the dishes.

"Hungry?" Randall offers, holding up the bag once he notices where my eyes have fallen.

Instead, I question what he's lugging in his other arm. "What is the suitcase for?"

"Let me in, and I'll show you."

It's so hard to stay cross with him for more than a minute with that charming face of his. These last two days have been a record. My biggest urge, once the door is shut and I'm alone with Randall, is to just go straight into his arms but I need to act like I haven't been falling apart for the past few days. Even if Randall is here to help me, and even if I'm going to let him, I need to keep my composure. Image is everything.

Randall sets the food on my desk and leans the army-green suitcase against the bed. Randall stands just a few steps away, a bit awkwardly, with his hands on his waist. I'm almost going to cross the gap and forget composure anyways when his eyes drift down my body.

"Randall," I snap, resisting the urge to cover myself. "Don't start that, there's nothing to see."

He has the nerve to laugh at me. "What? I can't look at you?"

"No. Not like that."

Randall nods, looking around the dorm. "Fine, no looking." I narrow my eyes at him when he takes a cautious step in my direction. "But touching-"

"You are out of your mind," I interject, hiding the amusement. "That's what got me into this situation."

One more step forward, and I can smell his cologne. "Us," he corrects, smoothing his hair back in habit. "And us? We?" He begins gesturing between my body and his own. "We can't do this again."

I raise a brow at him. "Do what?" If 'this' is to have sex, then I'm ready to whole-heartedly agree with him.

"Fight," Randall states. "Be apart. It was good we had that argument, because every couple needs to have at least one. Now, we can say we've had a fight and agree not to do it again."

"All couples fight," I say slowly.

He shakes his head. "Well, fine. We can fight, on occasion, but the separation thing?" He slices his hand through the air. "I can't do that again. Can't do it. I need you, Liling. You can be as independent as you like, but I need you. I need you next to me, I need you to eat dinner with me. I need you to tell me what to do with my life because I don't know what the hell I'm doing otherwise. From now on, we're going to be doing everything together. Everything, Liling."

There's a warmth inside of me, thinking about what my little Prince Charming is telling me. I do love my independence,

328

but I love being needed even more. "It's hard for me to think past the next nine months," I say, not ready to agree to not ever needing time apart from Randall. I want to be careful about saying anything that would imply I'm planning for a lifetime with Randall.

Randall smiles, now turning towards the bag of food. "That's ok too. You can think short term, I'll think long term." He pulls a white Styrofoam box out of the bag. "But I've got it all planned out."

"All of what?" I ask, inching a little closer to him and the food. I've got my arms crossed close to my chest, but I'm secretly hoping Randall is going to officially end this separation and be the first one to reach for me.

Randall takes another box out of the bag. "How we're going to survive the next nine months," he says confidently, handing me a plastic plate. "Take your seat ma'am, my monologue is about to start."

I really do think Randall just likes to talk. Still, he makes me laugh, and I take a plate and load it up with my favorite comfort food. Randall has also made himself a plate, but he's hovering in front of the bed, waiting for me to sit as though he's really about to give a lecture.

On the bed, I sit with a plate of food on my lap, the heat seeping through to my jeans. Randal shovels a massive heaping of rice into his mouth. "First," Randall says through a mouthful of rice, "Let's get the biggest thing out of the way." Randall sets his plate down at the end of the bed before reaching for the suitcase and laying it down flat. I lean forward to see what's in the suitcase.

"So we're going to have a baby," Randall states definitively, making my stomach lurch. I'm going to have a baby. There's something growing inside of me. "We're going to have a baby, and we're going to need money." He unzips the suitcase, and it's completely bursting with stacks of money. Thousands of dollars, being lugged around in this ratty suitcase.

"Randall," I whisper. "Where did you get all of this?"

"I've been selling. A lot," Randall says with a shrug. "Or my sellers have been selling. And I talked to Luis. I'm going to start pushing even more."

"More?" I ask, voice slightly rising. I've seen Randall's records. Should he ever get caught, he's looking at a federal charge. He's dangerous.

"I'm going to start paying up front."

"Paying-"

"For the cocaine." I hope the walls aren't too thin. "I pay up front, so Luis can give me more to sell. Then, I keep any money I make from our sellers, minus their portion of course."

"Hm." I'm dating a drug lord. A beautiful, goofy drug lord.

"It's better this way, anyway. If I have a problem with a seller and their finances, I don't have Luis breathing down my back because he's already been paid. It gives me freedom and time to handle things... however I want to handle them."

I don't know what that means, but Randall seems to pick up on this. I also don't know what to do with all this cash. "You shouldn't carry around this much cash, even to make a point," I scold.

Randall chuckles, flipping the suitcase shut and picking his plate back up. "One time you told me something about needing legitimate income... or something?"

Slowly, I nod. "You can't put all of *this*," I gesture at the luggage. "In the bank without someone asking questions. Not without-"

"It's called laundering, isn't it?" Randall asks. "I read about it in one of my classes. Usually, it's in the context of being illegal and something we shouldn't be doing but… I mean, hey, I guess I am learning things in school."

"How are… How are you going to launder it?"

He beams at me, proud of himself. "I bought the motel." When I only tilt my head and squint my eyes in response. "The one I've been working at. I bought it."

"It was for sale?" I ask. "You had enough money to buy a business?"

"It was for sale… when Gordy and I asked for it to be." Randall shrugs. "We got a good deal. Cash offer. Papers are signed, I now own a motel. We can run *this.*" He gestures at the suitcase too. "Through it, right?"

I'm thinking; I've never done this before. "If we… yes. We have to make it look like it's coming through as profits earned by the hotel… once the money is clean… you can put it in your account as you please."

Randall nods before shrugging. I think he has a broad grasp but I don't have confidence he actually knows what to do. "Sure. Plus, the motel has a lot of storage space." He grins, the small gap in his teeth present. "We're business owners!"

We.

"Your parents might like your boyfriend more if he has a profitable business, huh?"

This is when I feel my face souring. My parents. Randall can be successful, but he will never be what my parents want from me. He will always be the man who impregnated their unmarried daughter and brought her to a life of debauchery.

"I fully believe that you can…" I'm struggling to find words of intimacy amongst the words of fear that populate in my head when I think about my parents. "I know you can do great things, Randall. It's… everything else is going to be so hard." I swallow hard. I shake the weakness from my head. "We made a mistake, Randall," I say, looking at him. "We made a mistake, and I don't want to tell the world about it."

The amount of time it takes Randall to chew the piece of chicken in his mouth leaves an uncomfortable silence. Eventually, he shakes his head. "See, I've thought about that too."

Randall sets his plate down on the desk, and I put my plate down too. He then comes back to the bed, climbing up until he's sitting on his knees in front of me. "I know... I know this isn't the ideal way for us to start our family." He smiles softly, reaching for my hand. "But this is an opportunity for us."

"An opportunity?" I don't know that I would call an unplanned pregnancy that's going to bring me shame an opportunity.

Randall nods. "This is our chance- *your* chance - to prove what you can accomplish despite this... unexpected opportunity," Randall explains. "I can't tell you what to do, but I can tell you what you're going to do."

"That doesn't make any sense."

"You're going to finish your classes, and graduate." Randall tells me. "You're going to do all of that while being pregnant. You're going to have a baby. You're going to be the person that graduated while being pregnant. You're going to be the person that has an amazing career while being a mother. All of it, Liling. You're going to do it, no matter what anybody tells you."

"Randall-"

He's steam-rolling ahead, not stopping to let me speak. "You *can* have it all, Liling. Do you know how hard that's going to be?" He squeezes my hand with a shrug. "Still, you're going to do it. We're going to do it. You're going to prove how much stronger you are than everyone else. Not everyone can do it, but you can."

I bite my lip, knowing there is no other path for me than the man that's right in front of me. This is who I want- the one that builds me up after I've torn myself down. The one that keeps me from falling in the first place.

Gently, Randall reaches out to touch my chin, my skin lights up in the warmth of Randall's love. "No more self-doubt, ok?" He asks, before dramatically furrowing his brow. "And if anyone tries to make you feel like a stereotype, let me know and I'll kick their ass."

At this, even with his vulgar language, I laugh, and return the touch to Randall's face. The face, the father, the great love of my life. No one will deprive me of this. No one will tell me that Randall isn't mine. No one will tell me that I've made mistakes.

He's right. I will do all of the things I told myself I wanted to do. I'll graduate. I'll be a successful business woman. I'll be a good mother. I will do everything, and anything, I want. In front of me, I have all of the support that I need.

Anyone that gets in our way... God help them.

**

Quietly, for hours and hours, we talk in a warm dorm room. It's too early to talk about being parents, to talk about babies. It's alright, though. Just two days apart, and we have so much to tell each other.

We talk for so long, wrapped into each other's arms and worlds. Randall's soap hasn't changed. His arms feel the same, his voice is just as sweet, and he's still mine.

Until tomorrow, when I officially pursue the career Randall knows I can have, I'm going to remain a girl. Just a girl that wants to be held by her boyfriend. It's an ok thing to be.

Right here, with Randall, this is safety. Happiness. Worth. Potential. Love.

Randall Persch: what a man.

63.

[RANDALL]

I've got Liling back at my place. Our place. She's still a little touchy; she doesn't really want to talk about anything that has to do with being pregnant just yet. I'm ok with it, only for another week or so. Then, I'll want to talk. Now that Liling isn't as cross with me and I've got our future planned out, I want to start planning a life with Liling.

Father. I'm going to be a father. I'm going to be half of a permanent partnership with Liling. *You better give The Diamond a diamond.* Other than the timing, this pregnancy is mostly complicating my plans to propose to Liling. In all honesty, I could have done it months ago. I've been there. I know it's soon, but there are plenty of people who get married with even less time than Liling and I have put in.

Technically, (if you ask Liling) January would be one year of dating. We're in late September right now, so by Liling's calendar, we've only been dating for eight months. If you go by my calendar, we're just about to be at a year. This time last year, I was already taking Liling to football games, going to church with her, and working on extracurriculars in her dorm.

Either way, I was so sure that, by the time we graduated, I would have fulfilled both my and Liling's timeframe with dating for it to be acceptable for her to accept my proposal. Sure it's a cliché, but I had this dream of taking her on a walk through the MSU gardens while we're still wearing our green and white gowns and I'd find a quiet corner between the rhododendrons and propose to her.

I still want to propose to Liling. Now, the problem is when. I don't think Liling is too perceptive at this very minute. Still, I'd propose tomorrow if I could. But now Liling is pregnant. I don't want it to seem like I'm only proposing because I think I have to, because I knocked her up. I don't want a shotgun wedding, and I don't want there to be any confusion on why I want to marry Liling. It's because I love her first, and because I love the future family we'll have together second.

■■■

By mid-November, the embargo on baby-talk is officially over. We think Liling is around ten weeks pregnant, and we're doing our first ultrasound. Personally, I'm ecstatic. It's been our little secret, aside from Gordy and Luis. Today, we get to go... I don't even really know what's happening but I'm excited Liling is letting me come.

The air is cool but when the sun is able to get around the clouds, the weather isn't too bad. Fall decorations are starting to be replaced with Christmas decorations - pumpkins giving way to elves and snowflakes.

I'm sitting next to Liling in an OBGYN office that is too cold, watching her fill out paperwork before we can see an actual doctor. Liling has been very quiet today, like this is the last day she can pretend she isn't pregnant.

When we're filling out the paperwork together, it does feel like we're doing things out of order. It takes both of us together to fill out our family medical histories, since it isn't something we ever got around to discussing before jumping in a bathtub together.

Liling keeps her voice quiet in the office where there aren't many sounds competing for attention. "I think I'm behind."

I've got one hand resting on her knee, rubbing my thumb over the curve of her leg. "Behind what?"

"Whatever I'm supposed to be doing." She looks at me, the pen tapping on the clipboard. "I'm sure there's something I don't know about- something I'm supposed to be doing, or something I'm not supposed to be doing."

"That's what we can figure out while we're here," I reason. "You don't need to know everything."

She huffs quietly. "This is important," she says through lips that are barely parted. "I could mess up our child before it's even born."

On one hand, she's already holding herself to perfection. I wonder what kind of mother she'll be like. I wonder if she'll find a way to make even motherhood a competition.

On the other hand, she just used the phrase *our child.* The little phrase has me forgetting her actual concern and trying to hide a pleased smile. Liling clocks this and frowns at me. "You need to be a lot less excited that we're experiencing an accidental pregnancy."

I chuckle. "You need to be more excited. It's not the timing we would have chosen, so what? In the grand scheme of things, will it really matter? Two years from now- will it matter, or will we have an adorable toddler? Ten years from now, will it matter, or will we have a kid graduating from elementary school?"

"I'm not focused on ten years from now, I'm focused on right now."

I lean back in my chair, looking wistfully at the ceiling. "Ok, let's focus on now," I agree. "This is the very first time you're pregnant. Your only first time. And this-" I spread my arms to gesture at the office. "This is our first time getting an ultrasound done. Just let yourself enjoy it, Liling, because I know you wanted to be a mom someday anyway. When you look back on this time, I don't want you to remember being miserable, I want you to remember that we started a life when we wanted, how we wanted."

She's trying to pretend like I'm not right about this. "Is this how and when we wanted to start our lives?"

I give her knee a squeeze, taking in her brown eyes and the rest of her pretty face. "We're ahead of schedule, no big deal."

Liling looks back down at her paper, flipping it to fill out the last round of questions that ask about symptoms she's currently experiencing. "It is a big deal," she grumbles.

I'll risk a joke. "You know what else?"

"Hm?" Liling fills in a square next to *morning sickness.*

"When Lhasa gets pregnant." The pen stops moving on the paper. "She might have to come to you to ask questions," I say nonchalantly. "Because you will *always* have more experience than her in terms of motherhood."

She's stretching her jaw. "You're ridiculous." I think she secretly likes the point I've made. It keeps her in a pleasant mood until it's our turn to go in.

Our physician is a very nice woman with blonde hair and rosy cheeks. She's short in stature and has a quiet, gentle voice that sounds like it belongs to a nursery teacher. She's very positive and hasn't said a word to suggest that two unmarried kids in school have made a big mistake.

Dr. Kinsey has been asking Liling about how she's feeling, if she's experiencing pain, and about her sleep. My role is mostly to be quietly supportive. While Liling speaks, Dr. Kinsey nods with a kind smile, taking notes with a little pink pen.

After fifteen minutes of talking and questions, Liling rolls up her shirt and unbuttons her pants so that a clear gel can be spread over her abdomen. Liling flinches when the cream first goes over her skin.

There's a thick computer screen that's on a cart of sorts, sitting over hard white plastic that's fitted with various buttons and cords that I could never learn to use. There's a long white cord that connects to a thick stylus that's sort of hammer shaped at the end. Once the gel has been applied, Dr. Kinsey smoothly glides it over Liling's stomach.

I find myself desperately looking at the screen that's connected to the stylus that's being rolled over Liling. Liling looks nervous too, as if there's something wrong she could do at this moment. We both look at the screen - a blur of wavy black and gray lines. None of it looks like anything.

"What am I looking at, Doc?" I ask, clutching Liling's hand.

Dr. Kinsey points a manicured nail at the screen, pointing at a collection of lines that maybe looks more like a peanut than the rest of the blurry lines. "This." Dr. Kinsey pushes a button on her computer, and the image gets slightly bigger over where she's pointing. "Is your baby."

Liling doesn't say anything, so I keep talking. "That hamster-looking thing?" I tilt my head, thinking maybe the baby is upside down and it'll look more like a baby at a different angle. Oh God, is the baby upside down? Is that ok?

Dr. Kinsey chuckles, lowering her hand and looking between me and Liling. "Hamster, that's funny." She looks at Liling.

"He seems to think so," Liling says a little impatiently.

Dr. Kinsey doesn't seem to pick up on Liling being less than amused with me. The Dr. turns back to the screen, raising her hand again to point at one side of the blob. "This is the head," she explains. Maybe, just maybe, I can see the baby. My baby.

"Does everything look ok?" Liling asks. "Normal?"

Dr. Kinsey nods enthusiastically. "I don't see anything of concern. But we're not even at the best part yet." She slightly moves the stylus on Liling's stomach again, using her free hand to hit a button on her computer.

The room is filled with the steady beating sound of our child's heart.

With the sound of the heartbeat, the first real emotion is seen from Liling since we've entered the room. She lets out a little choke that's between a laugh, a sigh of relief, and a sob. Now, she's squeezing my hand too.

I could listen to this heartbeat all day. We did this. We're doing this. Our baby. "When can we find out what it is?" I ask excitedly.

"It's a little early for that," Dr. Kinsey says, removing her hand from Liling's stomach, silencing the heartbeat that was echoing in the room. "We'll get you scheduled for another visit around twenty weeks and hopefully then we can give you an answer. But for today, I can send you home with a picture of your baby." A hopeful smile enters my face.

True to her word, Dr. Kinsey sends us home with another appointment, a plan of action for Liling in the meantime, and two copies of an ultrasound picture of our future child. The picture doesn't leave Liling's line of sight the entire drive home.

"I think…" Liling hesitates. "I think I want to be excited about this." She runs her thumb over what I think is supposed to be the baby's head in the picture. "I'm petrified about telling my parents at some point, but until then…"

"Let's go to the bookstore," I say, seeing Liling's head pop up in my peripheral vision at the mention of her favorite place.

"We'll pick up some pregnancy books or something." I know that being unprepared is something Liling hates, so maybe if we get some reading material I can get her to have a little more confidence.

"Maybe there's a dad book," I continue, turning the wheel. "You think there's a pre-dad book out there?"

Liling leans over, stretching against her seatbelt to kiss my temple. I bend my head into it. "I love you, Randall Persch."

64.

[RANDALL]

For the next week, we're letting ourselves be happy as future parents while ignoring any responsibility to tell our own parents. We figure we'll wait a while… Liling won't start showing for another month or so, according to the books we've been reading. Liling's made research a part time job. I shouldn't be surprised. This pregnancy is a task and Liling is going to do it to the best of her ability.

The week is over, and Liling and I are going to meet our friends (or my friends, at least) at a football game. We've got the same coats that I bought us last year, and as we walk through campus, I wonder how long the coat will fit her. I've got a little plastic Nikon camera that I'll have Gordy use to take a picture of me and Liling. I had one taken last year too. Someday, there will be a whole album of the two of us.

It's the same group as last year, plus Stoner Greg. Liling never really told me what happened between her and Natalia but said it's ok if she's around as long as Natalia "behaves herself." I don't know what that means, but Liling is extra lovey-dovey when she's keeping me on lockdown. I have no complaints. For all I care, she can tattoo 'property of Liling' on my wrist and I'd be thankful to have a piece of her everywhere I go.

This year, we've got better seats closer to the field. This is a big game; the stadium is almost split down the middle with fans in green and white on one side and blue and yellow on the other. The weather is being forgiving. I've got a hotdog in one hand, and the mother of my child standing next to me. Life is good.

I wonder if I'll have a son. I wonder if he'll want to watch games with me. I wonder if he'll play sports. Would Liling let our son play football? Probably not, with the rate of concussions being so high.

Maybe I'll have a daughter. Maybe she'll be Liling's perfect little clone. Maybe I can impart my sense of humor, or my positive outlook on life. I want to teach my kids so much.

I'm not paying too close attention to the game; I'm too busy daydreaming about my future with Liling the entire time. Still, I'm happy to be out. This is probably one of the last times this year we'll be able to be outside for a while without being miserable from the cold.

When the game is over, and our team has lost, we're all quick to try to distance ourselves from the stadium. It's a rowdy, drunk crowd. We let the girls walk in between us all and make a buffer between all the shoving students that threaten to separate someone in the crowd. Navigating our way through swarms of people, we push through the smell of beer and cigarettes and sweat. Somewhere on campus, I'm sure couches are going to be burned tonight.

The plan after the game is for everyone to go to mine (and Liling's) apartment for a small gathering. Gordy rented some movies from BlockBuster and Liling stocked our place with snacks. We have hidden all evidence of pregnancy from prying eyes and we're ready to entertain.

We take two cars back to our place, and it looks like our complex as a whole isn't immune to the effects of the big game. We'll have to contend with raging parties here too; the parking lot is nearly full and it's littered, as if parties have already begun.

Ginger is talking about an internship she's starting in January, sparring with Gordy on whether it's a legitimate position or not, since a lot of the circumstances of how she acquired the role are sort of weird. We're all a little out of breath when we've hiked up the three floors, but Ginger and Gordy are still animated in their discussion.

At the top of the stairs, Natalia looks down the hallway, pulling her attention away from the story and mutters just loud enough to pause Ginger's chatter. "Oh, fuck me." This is probably why Liling doesn't like Natalia all that much. I follow Natalia's line of vision, just as she adds, "Hard."

Waiting by the door is a great bear of a man with tatted knuckles and a small patch of scruff on his chin. Next to him, a ghoul of a man, more ink than skin. Seeing us, the man of ink tugs his long coat tighter into his body.

Ginger leans over as we walk and looks at me. "Randall, do you know them?" She whispers.

"Are you in a gang?" Natalia whispers next, eyeing Diego as we approach. Diego doesn't look like someone who works an office job, or any job that's customer facing. The joke is a little close to home, and I don't know how to respond to that offhand.

"They're friends," I say lightly. "From work."

"What kind of work are you up to?" Greg mutters.

I look at him, lowering my voice. "Remember our old boss?" Greg nods mutely. "You know *his* boss?" Greg's eyes widen. "These are his friends. My friends, now, really."

Greg swallows hard. "Right. Cool. Cool. Cool. Casual."

Now, we're close enough to Rogelio and Diego, and I'm glad we're not dealing with the entire lot of Luis and his men… unless they're around here somewhere. For people that supposedly live an hour and a half away, they seem to have no problem driving down to check up on me.

Rogelio nods as I'm pulling my keys out. "Looks like we're just in time," Rogelio says, his light accent lilting his speech. Gordy is lugging a case of beer in one hand, BlockBuster VHS cases in the other. Natalia has a tray of cold cuts and crackers stored in the car during the game and Ginger has cookies. It doesn't look like we're having a rager but it's clear that I wasn't planning on spending the night alone with Liling.

"Ready for movie night, Ro?" I ask with a grin. Behind Jorge, I see Rogelio the most. Sometimes Luis asks if I can do different odds and ends jobs, and Rogelio sometimes comes down to help coordinate whatever it is. Lately, Luis is using me to help keep his control over the area without having to drive down from Detroit. But now, Diego is here too. Whatever Luis wants, it might be a little more involved than our regular criminal shenanigans.

Rogelio looks at Diego just as I get the door open, holding it open for everyone. "What's the movie?"

Gordy, who's met Rogelio several times, stops and says "I've got Scar Face and…" He eyes Natalia, who clearly had a hand in picking out the other movie, "While You Were Sleeping."

Rogelio chuckles, looking at me. "You two Sandra Bullock fans?"

"I am." Natalia slides in next to me, smiling a smile I've seen too many times. I'm going to have to watch this girl closely tonight and send Gordy in to cool her off as needed. I know a bad idea when I see one.

Rogelio, however, knows a pretty girl when he sees one. "Who's your pretty friend, Boy Scout?"

I roll my eyes. "Rogelio, this is Natalia, Natalia, this is Rogelio." These two idiots are grinning wide at each other. "And that's Diego," I mumble, although Natalia, understandably, isn't as taken with the haunting man next to Rogelio.

Liling, my Wonder Woman, clicks her tongue and says, "Natalia, you can come put that tray down inside." She lets herself in, waiting with her hand on the edge of the door.

Natalia's eyes flick toward Liling before returning her sultry smile at the mountain in front of us. "Nice to meet you," she says lightly, clutching the tray to her chest. I roll my eyes again, waiting for her and Ginger to file into my apartment, Gordy follows behind, knowing to shut the door behind him.

Diego mutters something in Spanish and Rogelio replies, "You think she wants to be bilingual?"

"Natalia's messy," I warn. "She's fun, sure, if that's all you're looking for." Natalia isn't someone I would ever count on for anything beyond a good time. I figure, when there are women out there like Liling, girls like Natalia are pretty much worthless.

Rogelio laughs. "Ah, I've had a girl for a long time, anyway." He grins. "But I like to be reminded how handsome I am." I roll my eyes at this, but Rogelio is definitely the best looking of Luis' bunch.

Rogelio scratches his chin. "You have a way of surrounding yourself with beautiful women, eh Persch?"

I shrug, as there's only one beautiful person that really matters to me. "So are we all going to snuggle up and watch a movie or did you two need something?"

"Luis put us to work in the area," Rogelio explains. "A little above your pay grade so he sent up the big guns. We're just checking in."

Maybe if I had just met Luis and his men I'd be scared, but I have a good reading on them now. They don't bother pretending to be nice when they're about to get violent. "Don't you guys ever call ahead?"

Rogelio shakes his head. "People run when they know we're coming," he says with an amused gleam in his eye.

"What, you don't think we're friends yet?" I joke. Rogelio seems to be a lot easier going than Luis and Diego are, but I've seen him snap into his violent alternate personality in half a second when called to.

"I guess we could start giving you a heads up, Boy Scout," Rogelio sighs, arching his back against the hallway wall. "Diego and I were handling something in the area. Luis wanted us to stop by while we were close, make sure you get your verbal party invitation, since we don't like to put things on paper."

I chuckle. "In the area? Doing what?"

Rogelio looks at Diego before saying, "We've got some round ups to do, party prep. You'll see."

"I'll see what?"

Rogelio looks at the door, like he's making sure it's actually shut. "You know what, Randall?"

I blink at Rogelio, not used to hearing my first name that much when working with anyone from the cartel. "Hm?"

"Luis likes you," Rogelio states. When he says this, Diego slightly turns his head, but as usual, stays quiet.

"You already got a reputation with *our* people. You know that? One to watch."

"Aren't you glad you didn't shoot me that day in Toby's bathroom?" I jest. I like the idea of having a reputation. I work hard, and it seems that people are starting to notice.

Rogelio gives me a look of feigned annoyance. "No, I regret not doing it." I laugh before he continues. "I'm just saying,

347

when you become one of Luis' favorites, you stand to be set up pretty good, you know? Anything you want, you can get. All you have to do - just one thing."

I start to unzip my coat, getting hot wearing it inside. "Let me guess- is that one thing to do whatever Luis says? Or to not try to fuck him over?"

Rogelio laughs. "Shit, maybe you only have to do two things. See? That's why you're getting ahead so fast."

"But it sounded like you were about to warn me, either way," I lead on.

"Just reminding you, that if Luis throws any tests at you, which he likes to do, make sure you're ready to pass," Rogelio says in his whiskey smooth voice.

I nod, thinking about this. Luis has given me too much to turn him away. So, I'm a terrible person, sure. I don't care if I'm getting what I want, which is everything. "How will I know if I failed?" I ask, putting my handle on the doorknob.

"You'll know." Rogelio smiles." He checks a gold watch after rolling his sleeve up. "December fifteenth. Six o'clock. Bring your diamond. You still got Luis' address memorized?"

I tap my forehead. "Got it. You two want to come in for some food? A drink?" Breaking bread with the cartel, all in a day's work.

Rogelio and Diego take me up on my offer, but only Rogelio grabs a cookie and holds a quick conversation with Liling before they start making plans to leave. Diego stands by the door the entire time, not doing a great job at looking like anything other than a hired gun who's ready to shoot.

Natalia has been unhappily watching Rogelio talk with Liling before she turns her attention to me. "Randall," she calls. I'm sitting on the couch next to Greg.

"Yeah?" I ask, turning my head.

"How do you know these two again?" she asks sweetly. I see Rogelio's attention has been pulled, waiting to see how I answer.

"They work at the motel with me," I say, the lie falling effortlessly from my lips.

Natalia raises a brow, her eyes falling to Diego by the door. "*You* work at the motel with Randall?" Diego looks like someone who can only be a murderer or a freak show performer.

Diego only moves his head a millimeter, and I find it very unnerving. Diego's soulless brown eyes return Natalia's gaze. He opens his coat up, and I flinch, knowing what I've seen come out of that coat before. He puts his arm through the opening at the top, rifling without taking his eyes off Natalia. At last, Diego pulls out a rusted silver wrench, looking large and heavy in his inky fingers.

Diego's black-lined lips utter a single word in a thick Columbian accent. "Maintenance.*"*

The room is dead silent. Diego talking is something of an omen. I'm sure he's fixed a lot of things with that wrench.

Rogelio clears his throat. "When he starts pulling things out of his coat like it's Mary Poppins' bag, it's time to go." Diego slips the wrench back into his coat as I stand to walk them out.

Diego and Rogelio leave, saying goodbye to Liling and politely nodding at Natalia, who isn't happy to see them go. I'm sure she'll corner me later for information on them.

In the lot, I note that it's already way colder outside than it was during the game. Still, there's more than one group congregating outside around cars in some sort of drunken stupor. Rogelio and Diego have a parked car near the back of the lot, looking out of place among all the beater cars.

"See you in a couple weeks, Boy Scout," Rogelio says while he loads himself into the car.

With a wave, I say, "Bye Ro, Diego." Diego, of course, doesn't say anything.

It is way too cold out, so I turn on my heel and start heading back to the apartment. There's a holler of drunken energy a ways down the lot, and I look to see what idiots are partying in a parking lot when it's not even forty degrees outside.

For the amount of noise, I was expecting more people but it's a group of only four guys acting reckless. Whatever kind of idiots they want to be, I don't care all that much because they're not by my car.

My attention is back on getting inside, only hurrying when I hear the group of guys is also ready to go inside so I don't get stuck on the stairs with them all. By the sound of it, they might not even make it up the stairs.

There's two cement steps to get back into the building. Hands in my pocket, I'm on the second step with my hand on the brass doorknob when a hand plants itself on my shoulder and I'm spun around.

Kieran Smith, count your fucking days.

I know this drunk. He's a new client of Liling's. He messed up early on, and had to deal with myself and Gordy early on. I wouldn't say we're friends.

Out of all the idiots and all the parking lots of the world, Kieran Smith finds himself in the same one I'm in, and this time he's not alone. He clearly remembers our last interaction. "Hey, Randall, man," Kieran slurs. Kieran is dressed only in a thin long-sleeved shirt and jeans with white sneakers and a red winter cap.

I blink, adjusting to being spun so fast. "Kieran, what is wrong with you?" I flip my hair away from my eye. I'm very aware that Kieran hates me and he and his three friends are standing in a semi-circle in front of me, the building door is pressing against my back.

Kieran pokes my shoulder. "I just wanted my friends to meet you." He waves his hands, wiggling his fingers in the air like he's telling a scary story. "Randall Persch: debt collector."

I raise my brow. "And what of it?"

One of Kieran's friends, a stocky guy with chopped black hair says, "So last time you came over, you had a friend with you, right?"

"You want me to go get him?" I offer through gritted teeth.

Kieran slams me back against the door, the knob painfully digs into my muscle. I catch Kieran's arm, our arms locked against each other so that he can't choke me out.

I huff out, struggling against Kieran who is taller than me. I've got anger and fear on my side, but that will only get me so far. "Kieran, you're about to make the biggest mistake of your life," I promise. In the back of my head, I'm praying that Gordy comes to check the lot. Two against four isn't great but with one versus four, I'm about to get my ass beat.

Kieran laughs, looking at the friend to his right. "See? This guy, unbelievable! He totally is like extorting me- he and his ugly friend."

"Me and my ugly friend know where you live," I remind him, shaking Kieran off of me.

The dark-haired friend takes over for Kieran, grabbing me by the coat and pulling me forward. "So, let's stop beating around the bush. The four of us are going to beat the shit out of you right now, and since we all know where *you* live, we can make sure you give Kieran his money back, yeah?"

I know I'm about to be unconscious in another minute. "Fat chance." I might need to take one beating before I can retaliate with Gordy, but shit, this is going to hurt.

As soon as I start to pull myself back, Kieran's friend helps me by throwing me back into the door and immediately punching me in the gut. I double over with a grunt, but I'm going to fight for as long as my eyes aren't swollen shut. While doubled over, I launch myself at the dark-haired friend like a wrestler, sending him back over the step.

The two of us both roll down two steps. My ankle is bit by the hard cement on our way down as the two of us grapple until I'm on top, punching this stranger beneath me. I get two solid hits in before Kieran and his other two friends pull me off. I don't even make it in a full standing position before I'm hit again and my back hits the ground.

Once I'm on the ground, I know that's when it's hard to recover. With four of them, it's easy for them to pull me up just to hit me back down. By the third time I've been pulled up and punched down, I'm ready to tap out.

"You still Mr. Tough Guy?" Kieran asks while his friend brings me up again. I'm on my feet now, wobbly and in pain. Kieran strikes me down again, his fist slamming into the side of my face. This time, I land on my shoulder, back against someone's feet as I realize with dread that more of Kieran's friends have arrived. Six against one? I might just die tonight.

From the chilled pavement, the world is still moving even though I'm stationary. I blink up, my head is still against someone's foot. Above me stands some sort of demon in black.

I don't know if I'm hallucinating for a quick second, but to the figure standing over me, I mumble, "Hi Diego, thanks for coming."

"Who the fuck are you?" Kieran asks.

Without a word, Diego bends over and pulls me off the ground while I furiously blink until something makes more sense. It's not until I'm back on my feet that I fully comprehend that I'm not alone; both Diego and Rogelio are here now. Thank God, because I was about to get all of my teeth kicked out of my head.

Rogelio roughly grabs my shoulder so I face him. "Ey, Boy Scout, you alright?" He smirks. "Tell Daddy which one hurt you."

"Go to Hell," I mutter, holding a hand to my head.

Rogelio laughs, stepping around me, facing Kieran and his friends. "Someone want to tell me what's going on here?" He nods at me. "This, here, is our boy."

Kieran's friends are going to let him talk. They still have an advantage with one extra person, but it's clear that Rogelio himself makes up for at least three people, and Diego might not even be human. "Just a score to settle," Kieran says.

Rogelio turns to look at me, raising his brow in question. "He can't settle his debt so he's trying to pull this," I say.

Rogelio chuckles. "Of course, you're a loan shark too, huh?" Rogelio looks back at Kieran and his friends, cracking his knuckles like he's a mobster in a movie. "But if you want to settle the score." He spreads his arms. "Fine, let's go."

"You're outnumbered." The dark-haired friend points out.

Rogelio takes a fighter's stance, spreading his legs and raising his fists. "You and me then, let's go." Even with a few screws being knocked loose, I can see that Rogelio is not someone I would ever choose to fight. This other guy, however, is an idiot, and he takes a fighting stance too.

Next to me, Diego makes something between a growl and a laugh. He elbows me. "M-M-A."

Looking at Rogelio, he does look like someone who was, or is, a fighter. Rogelio looks ahead in anticipation, like he's got complete confidence that he's getting ready to dominate. "You ready?"

353

Fist raised, Kieran's friend moves his head in a nod, and before he's even really done with the movement, Rogelio has struck out a massive fist square in the face. Ro's fist lands with a heavy thud and the dark-haired friend is knocked out cold. Rogelio turns off his fighting stance, lowering his fists. "Looks like we're evenly matched now, huh? Who's next?"

This is when the apartment complex door opens. Gordy comes out, wearing a red coat and cussing under his breath. Gordy blanches at us all, taking in the situation with a furrowed brow. He first sees the guy out cold on the ground, the poor guy is bleeding somewhere from his head but he's face down and his worthless friends haven't helped him up yet.

Gordy keeps moving, face lifting when he sees who is standing in front of him. Then he sees me, and I have to imagine that I've been hit too many times to not have some sort of mark on my face. "Shit," he growls. "You ok?" He starts down the two steps to come see me, Diego steps out of the way.

"I'm fine.," I say, shaking Gordy's hand away from my temple that's throbbing.

Gordy leans around me now, noticing Kieran. "You're in for it now, asshole."

He really is.

Rogelio faces Diego, and asks a question in Spanish, which results in Diego nodding. Rogelio crosses his arms, and in the silence Kieran starts to try to mumble his way out of trouble and getting his own assed kicked. "Look, fine, I'll work it out." Now, Kieran is looking at me. "Randall, I'm sorry, I can finish out the payments."

It's hard to try to maintain control when I know I probably have a bruised face already. Still, everyone's eyes are on me, waiting for my call. Right now, I can do whatever I want, and I'd have several sets of hands to help me do it.

I run a tongue over my busted lip. "You know, Kieran, I'm trying to be a businessman, someday." I don't need to turn my head to know Gordy is rolling his eyes. "And I know it doesn't make good business sense to destroy my investment." I'm making interest here, after all.

Kieran nods vigorously. "Yeah-I- you know, I'm just drunk, that's all it is." Kieran's other two friends start to pull up the fourth person off the ground.

Gordy huffs next to me. "Oh, that's all?" Kieran nods, unsure of who's making the calls.

It's me. I'm making the calls, and I'm still angry about what they tried to do. I'm forgiving, but I'm not forgetful.

"Hey Ro." I stuff my hands into a pocket, more out of habit than to chase away the cold.

Rogelio's breath puffs out in front of him. With another look at him, I'm damn grateful he's my friend. "What are you thinking about? You need help tying up some loose ends?"

'Loose ends' is a common phrase with Luis. It meant eliminating problems, threats. Sometimes, it meant beating someone into submission, so that they're too afraid to step out of line again. Sometimes, it meant cutting out someone's tongue. Sometimes, it meant murder.

I nod. "Is there any free space in Fowlerville?" One of Luis' storage units.

"Oh, plenty of space, Boy Scout."

"What's…. What's in Fowlerville?" Kieran asks.

I look at Kieran, debating whether it's better to tell him now and let him be scared or if it's better to say nothing and see if it's easier to get him into a car. "I just want to make sure everybody is on the same page." Kieran will be on the same page as me after a few days of bleeding in an ice-cold storage unit.

Rogelio starts pointing to each man, counting in Spanish under his breath. "I'll tell you what, I'll call up someone from the lot to bring them in, because Diego and I need to get back soon. You can drive yourself up when you feel like it, do whatever *settles the score.*" His eyes flick to Kieran, who has paled considerably.

"Wait, what are we talking about?" Kieran asks.

Rogelio ignores him and continues to talk to me. "When you're done, let Raul know and he can help get everyone loaded back up and sent on their way."

When I grin at Rogelio, I feel a new sore in my cheeks. "I appreciate it."

Rogelio shakes his head. "You know what, Boy Scout? You're welcome. Don't forget about me when you make it to the top, okay?"

65.

LILING

Randall has a way of getting himself into trouble when I'm not around to monitor his activity. I'm getting used to Randall disappearing with little warning when it comes to anything to do with the Padilla cartel. I'm not concerned when Rogelio and Diego arrive unexpectedly, and I'm not worried when Randall goes to see them off. As I've said before, everyone likes Randall - even the cartel.

It's when it's been almost fifteen minutes and Randall hasn't come inside yet that I start to wonder what he's gotten into. It's a bit cold to be congregating outside for too long after how long we'd already been out. I'm half-listening to Natalia and Greg prattle on about their plans after they graduate but I'm wondering if I should go outside and check on Randall.

I catch Gordy's eye, and after months of being in a sort of forced acquaintanceship through Randall, I think Gordy knows when I want something. He also knows it isn't worth the argument with me in resisting. Gordy gives me a subtle nod before rising from the couch and discreetly slipping out once he's grabbed his coat.

"What are you doing after college, Liling?" Ginger asks me.

It takes a moment to process that I've been reeled into a conversation. It takes another moment to think of what I'm actually going to say. That plan has changed drastically in the past few weeks.

"I've applied for some internships for the spring semester," I inform Ginger, reciting the plans I made pre-pregnancy because now is not the time for any sort of announcement. I'm not sure how I feel about Natalia knowing. It's either going to fill me with a fresh bout of shame because everyone will know this is an accident, or it will fill her with jealousy because she'll know that if Randall wasn't mine before, he certainly is now.

Ginger, who has been much friendlier after I called her a doormat months ago, smiles enthusiastically. "I bet you've got the grades that will land you something good, huh?"

I nod. "And I've got quite the recommendation from one of my summer professors." It's fortunate that Brackett is right-handed, and he had the sense to do what he must to make sure Randall doesn't return.

Natalia sounds like she's bored now that there's no men to stare at her in the room. "And what's Randall doing after graduating?" It's a test. No one really expects a relationship to make it out of college. There's a stigma around the concept for a reason.

"Randall…" For the moment, we're not advertising that Randall, at the age of twenty-two, has found a way to purchase an entire business. That would open us up to questions as to how he got the funds. "Randall works as an assistant manager at the motel. He's hoping he can be promoted."

There's a lag in the room until Ginger wisely moves onto Greg. "What are you going to be up to?"

Greg is slumped on the couch, and I wonder if he's taken something while no one was watching. "I dunno," Greg shrugs.

"You don't have any plans?" Ginger presses.

"People call me Stoner Greg," he drawls. "I think I'll go exactly as far as anyone would expect me to." This spins the conversation toward lighter topics that I completely disengage myself from. Now, Gordy has been gone for ten minutes.

After it's been almost forty minutes and no one has come back, even Ginger and Natalia are wondering what's happened to the other half of the party. Ginger asks if Randall and Gordy went to the store. I'm at the door, putting my shoes on, when I hear them in the hallway.

Barefoot, I rip the door open and step into the hallway as I see the top of Randall's head as he steps up the stairs. My heart convulses at the sight of my charming prince with a split lip and several nasty bruises on his face. Randall's coat is covered in dirt and his hair is disheveled.

When I gasp, Randall's face immediately lights in worry as he quickly spits out, "Hey, I'm fine." I don't know why I'm blinking so hard, but Randall continues to sputter out words. "I'm fine. What- does it look bad?"

"You look like shit," Gordy grumbles as Randall closes the distance between us.

When Randall and I are holding each other and I'm gently poking at his face while he squints through it all, I ask, "What happened?"

Randall rubs his thumb over my shoulder. "You know Kieran? He is- or he was- out there with his friends. They're all drunk and they picked a fight."

"Got his ass whooped," Gordy says from behind Randall.

Randall turns his head with a smile that I'm not sure where he's pulling from. "Do you think you're helping?"

"So, what happened?" I say, tugging on Randall's shoulder. "How many were there? Where are they now?"

"There was four of them. Now they're…" Randall falters, thinking.

"How did you manage four of them?" I continue to pepper him with questions.

Randall grins at this, kissing my forehead. "Are you saying you don't think I can fight off four guys alone?" Randall, while not necessarily short, is not especially tall and is not especially large. Randall is nice and he's pretty, and that's how he gets by.

My eyes flit to Gordy. "His friends hadn't actually left yet. They were in the lot, and stopped him from getting his skull caved in."

"Rogelio and Diego stepped in?" I direct this at Randall.

Randall nods. "They've got Kieran and his friends." Randall looks over at Gordy. "We're going to go visit them- tomorrow, maybe. Make sure everything is worked out." He kisses my head again. "Don't worry about it, Gumdrop."

Randall starts to head toward the apartment door but I snatch his wrist. "What are you going to do to them?"

"I don't know yet." Randall shrugs. "But… you know how I handle things."

I have no problem with the way Randall handles things. "Make sure they understand *very* clearly."

A devilish grin lights up Randall's face as he pulls himself back into me. "I think you like it when I'm mean," he says an inch from my mouth.

I don't know if it's too soon to start blaming things on my hormones but I need something to justify the feeling that runs through me just before I have Randall's face all over mine.

"You two are meant for each other," Gordy mutters, squeezing past me and letting himself back inside.

Randall and I take another moment alone outside the apartment before we go back inside, explaining that Randall got in a fight in the parking lot without getting into too many details. It's just after a football game and nearly every student in the city is drunk is explanation enough.

Even with the events that took place, movie night still happens, and Natalia and Ginger won in their pitch to watch *While You Were Sleeping*. After the movie, Ginger and Natalia drive Greg back to his own place. Gordy, as he has before, falls asleep with his legs wide open on the decrepit recliner.

It's late now, and I'm sitting with my legs crossed on the couch. Randall's head is in my lap. I've been stroking my fingers through his hair for some time now, and he's been sleeping soundly.

I have that feeling again; like I'm recognizing love. The first time I felt it, love was the sound of Randall's song on the freeway and sweltering heat with Randall's hand on my thigh. Now, it's much different, much more intimate, much more permanent.

Now, love feels like sharing Randall's warmth after a cold day outside while Randall sleeps in my lap. Love is the feeling of Randall's chest rising and falling, his head gently pressing into my lap while his hair slips between my fingers. This is my most recent association of what love is, what it feels like.

One thing still has not been changed, and I don't think it's likely to change anytime soon: Randall Persch. Randall Persch is still, and will always be, what I associate love with.

66.

[RANDALL]

Gordy and I take our time with Kieran and his friends. Initially, Kieran was the only one who owed us money. By the end, all four of them walk out with fresh agreements. Honestly, getting my ass kicked was worth it with how much money we're going to make off them.

I've got so much going for me right now. So much going on that I can't even tell the world about, not yet. I think I'm going to wait to tell anyone (other than Liling) that I own a motel. It's not something that somebody my age could normally pull off. I only pulled that off because I sell cocaine. The cocaine is another thing I can't tell people about.

I can't tell people I work for a cartel, or any of the things that I do for, or with, them. I'm going to be a father, and we're not ready to tell the world about that either.

Now, thanks to Kieran, I do think I'll find a way to get into personal loans. I've got more money than I know what to do with. The way I see it, I can help people do the things they need. Money is such a simple problem. Easily solved. All I needed was a little so I could get a lot.

Of course, I run everything I do by Liling. She's so smart. I think I would've been arrested by now if it weren't for her thinking about everything. She knows how to deposit the cash I get as revenue from the motel so that it looks legitimate. Liling knows who we can give loans to, and how much interest to charge to make the risk worth it.

Everything I do, all the risk I incur, all of it is worth it. Every dollar I make is a dollar I can spend on Liling, on the life we're going to make. There are people that are going to live their whole lives never seeing anything near what I've already seen. There are people that are never going to love the way I love Liling, and are never going to be loved by someone like Liling.

Everything. Liling is worth everything.
■■

By the first week of December, I already have a closet full of presents for Liling. Christmas is Liling's favorite holiday, and we had a tree up at my apartment just a few days after Thanksgiving.

Liling is at class, but I'm going to meet her at her dorm in some of the spare time she has before the next one starts. In the morning, I met with Jorge to do some exchanges and then met up with Gordy to pay him as well.

Now, Gordy and I are in a *Babies R Us* because I want to talk to Liling about talking to our families, and I'm going to approach this topic with a baby present. She's three months pregnant now, and we're lucky it's oversized sweater and coat season. Sometimes, when Liling stretches, if she's not wearing anything too bulky, I see it - our child.

Pregnant Liling is already something of a beast. She hurls in the morning, could out eat a small family by evening, and surprisingly, is incredibly happy. I thought pregnant Liling might be... irritable. She's actually the opposite, as she's not stressing about telling her parents. Pregnant Liling is joyful.

We both want to be happy about this pregnancy. We're over the shock, and we just have to get around to telling the world. We've already let a few people know- Gordy, Luis, and presumably Rogelio, Diego, and Oscar. Natalia figured it out, meaning Ginger probably knows too, which Liling initially wasn't too pleased about.

"Of course *she* would notice my stomach," Liling said in bed one night, arms crossed. We got a card from Ginger shortly after. With the way Natalia's mouth never stops moving, I'll go ahead and assume Greg knows too.

That's why I'm at a baby department store looking at unisex baby onesies with Gordy. Gordy did a lot of grumbling when I dragged him in here. He's not doing too much looking, mostly trailing behind me while I try to pick out something Liling would agree to put our child in.

"You think you're going to be ready?" Gordy asks, hands in his pockets as he shuffles behind me.

I look at an orange onesie that says *PROFESSIONAL NAPPER* that I know Liling would just hate. "I mean, I want to be ready," I say, wandering to another rack of onesies. "I don't know what I don't know, I guess. But I'm reading- trying to keep up with Liling."

Now, I've found a blue onesie with striped arms that reminds me of a little baby sailor. I smile at the thought of that- a little classy baby on a little classy boat. Voyageur baby.

"You ready to be with Liling for the rest of your life?"

I freeze, this comment instantly souring my mood. "What the hell does that mean?" I ask, forgetting about the little sailor baby for the moment.

Gordy hesitates, knowing I tend to lose my patience when it comes to anyone saying anything less than positive about Liling.

My Liling. "I mean…" He shakes his head. "I can see it in your eyes- I know the kind of man you are, Randall."

"Yeah? What kind of man am I?"

Gordy puts a finger up. "First of all, jackass, don't act like you're going to punch my lights out in front of a rack of Sesame Street pajamas. Second of all, I mean… it's the nineties, you know?"

He's ruining the Christmas baby buzz I was working through. "I know what year it is."

Gordy sighs, propping an elbow up on a rack of seasonal pajamas that bends forward under his weight. "I mean- just because you knocked her up doesn't mean you gotta marry her. You don't have to spend the rest of your life with her just because you think you have to."

"I have to?" I ask incredulously. "What am I doing to make you think I'm in this relationship under duress?"

"Your fucking baby!" Gordy snarls. "I just think it's too soon to say Liling is it for you, ok?"

"No, not ok!" I hiss. We're drawing the attention of mothers who are circling the store with strollers and toddlers. "Liling *is* it for me. And what's your solution here? Just leave Liling with the baby?"

Gordy shrugs. "Acts like she knows everything. She'll figure it out."

"And what kind of man does that make me?"

Gordy shrugs again. "A smart one."

Maybe I need more friends. Better friends. "You have a piece of shit dad. I have a *you're on your own* kind of dad and an absent, shitty mom. I don't want to be like that."

"We're fine," Gordy says dismissively. "You own a business. You got a car. I bet you can buy yourself a house soon. All that with shitty parents."

"My kid is going to have everything they'll ever need," I say, angrily flipping through clothes that I'm not really looking at anymore. "Everything. That includes two loving, supportive parents." I shake my head. "Are you testing the product? What the hell is wrong with you?"

Gordy rolls his eyes as if I'm being dramatic. "Fine, fine. I just… I don't get her."

"I know you don't," I say, trying to level my voice. I pull a green onesie with caterpillars on it. I mutter as I look at the price tag. "I don't like your girlfriend either."

Gordy meets my eyes, knowing I'm ready to move on. We do this from time to time- we'll get into an argument that will last all of five minutes. We say some rotten things, then we're over it. "Funny. You know, I could get a girlfriend if I stopped playing hard to get."

"You're playing hard to get away from."

He huffs a laugh, flinging a pack of baby socks at me. "Fine, fine, you know what? I'm sorry I opened my fat mouth, and I won't say nothing else about dumping her ass."

"I'm not going to leave Liling," I say, tucking the socks under my arm. Liling loves practical things. If our baby is going to be on a boat at any time, it'll probably need socks.

"Damn," Gordy says under his breath, shaking his head. "You're going to have me working for her eventually, aren't you?"

This poor, poor idiot. "Gordy, you already work for her."

366

LILING

I don't know why my feet hurt so much when I'm not even standing. I'm three months pregnant- not even *that* pregnant. I want to tell my body it's being dramatic. It's too soon to really be feeling anything, isn't it? Still, my hand seems to find its way to rest on my stomach, feeling.

If it weren't for the weight gain, I almost wouldn't believe I'm actually expecting. The weight gain, God, I already hate it. I look at myself in the mirror and know that there's no coming back from this one.

I wish there was someone I knew that I could ask about pregnancy. I need to know what I should be feeling, doing, preparing for. I have books, I have a doctor, but sometimes I just want to talk to someone. My mama is the only person I can think of, but I have a feeling it won't be an option. She's going to be so disappointed in me.

"Hey," Randall calls down the hallway, and my thoughts snap to the one person who I truly believe will never abandon me. "How was class?"

I smile as we close the distance. Standing in front of my seldom-used dorm, Randall looks like a heartthrob straight from a romantic-comedy. Randall's already shed his coat and has it folded over his arm, showing that he's wearing a sand-colored sweater with a white collar and blue dress pants. His red-brown hair is fluffed and kissing the top of his head, as I will be doing soon.

"Classes were fine," I say, not too interested in giving him more than that because I'm going to be unashamedly kissing him for a considerable amount of time before I notice the bag that keeps hitting my leg.

"What is that?" I say, arms over his neck, my head bowed to look at the bag.

Randall looks down too. He's got one of his legs folded up against the door, a white bag with purple *Babies R Us* lettering in hand. "I went shopping with Gordy."

The idea of Gordy trailing behind Randall at a baby store makes me laugh, and I pull Randall back in. "What did you buy?" I straighten his collar. "We don't even know what we're having yet."

"You want me to show you out here or-"

I quickly shake my head. Once I tell my parents- the worst of it- then we can tell the world. When we're inside my dorm, Randall sets the bag on my bed and starts pulling out at least a dozen baby onesies in a multitude of colors.

"Randall," I say with a giggle. I'm pulled in by these tiny, miniature clothes. I can see Randall tried his hardest to pick out gender neutral clothing, with the exception of something that looks like an infant sailor's uniform.

"I know it's early but..." Randall trails off, holding an orange pajama set in his hands. "I want to be excited, Lil. I want to start thinking about raising a baby with you."

When Randall's smile grows, I realize he's only mirroring my own, because I have that feeling again. That recognition that *this* is what love is. Love is a bed full of baby onesies. Leaning against Randall, I start going through what he's purchased. One outfit catches my eye- one that is in fact not at all neutral and makes a bold statement.

"Little Trucker," I read, unimpressed. It's a little white shirt with a blue pickup truck on it. The outfit has white pants with blue spots on it.

"Gordy picked that one," Randall explains.

"Hm." I put that one back and continue to browse, holding a soft yellow cover that looks like a little ducky meant for after bath time. I like this one. I imagine myself in the future- even this time next year. I'll have this little human, this baby that will be mine. Ours. We're going to have to learn to change a diaper, and how to get tiny feet into a onesie without catching their skin as they squirm.

"We'll figure it all out." I really need to know how he can read my thoughts now. "We're going to figure all of it out." Randall's arm is around my shoulder and he's resting his head on mine when someone knocks on the door.

"Expecting someone?" Randall asks.

"Britney's been by more often lately." Britney usually checks to see if I'm here before bothering to get her key out.

"Just protect me from her backhand," Randall mutters behind me as I'm approaching the door.

This comment confuses me and I'll have to ask him about it later after Britney leaves-

It isn't Britney on the other side of the door, it's Lishui. Lishui's excited face freezes in place- her greeting stuck in her throat as her eyes instantly catch what I'm still holding.

One little ducky towel cover, and my secret is out.

Lishui's eyes could just about pop out of her head. "What is that?"

There's no point in lying, not when behind me I have a boyfriend standing in front of a collection of baby apparel.

I let out an exasperated sigh, rubbing my temple with my free hand. "Alright, just calm down for a moment-"

"Liling!" Lishui gasps, now leaning around me to take in the nonsense we've got on the bed. Randall really did buy a lot of clothes. Lishui's brown eyes meet mine. "Please tell me-"

"I'm pregnant," I choke out.

The pause is just as pregnant as I am as Lishui's wide, scared eyes stare back at me, like she's waiting for me to take back the sentiment. "Oh, God." Lishui cries in something of stunned horror. "Oh God, oh God, Oh-"

I sigh, turning to Randall while Lishui consults with the Lord. I toss him the hooded duck towel before facing Lishui again. "Let's talk out here." I put my hands on her shoulders and gently move her into the hallway. "Calm down," I say again once the door is shut. I don't know what Lishui is going to say, and just in case she feels the same as the rest of my family does about Randall, I'd rather not have the blow to his confidence.

"Liling!" Lishui whispers in a worried hiss. Mama taught us to keep our problems to ourselves. "Liling!" She hysterically whisper-cries again.

"Lishui, I know, I know," I say soothingly, seeing my little sister is about to start crying. Lishui has always taken everyone else's problems to heart. Lishui knows the kind of trouble I'm about to be in and it's already tearing her apart.

"You're pregnant!" Lishui's frantic whisper sounds from her wavering lips.

"Yes," I say calmly. I remind myself that telling Lishui will be the easiest, kindest reveal of anyone in my family.

"You're having a baby."

"Yes."

"But you're not even married so-"

Mama is going to rip me to pieces. "I'm not married."

Lishui's face lights up in near fear, sharing my exact thoughts. "Mama- oh, God. Do Mama and Papa know?"

"No." I nod gravely. "Soon, we'll tell them soon."

"We…" Lishui whispers, furring her brow while she throws some flyaway airs back behind her head. "What- Liling how did this happen?"

I raise a brow. She knows at least that much.

"Was- like-" I can see Lishui's mind spinning. "Was this like a one night stand thing? Oh God, Mama was right! You have sex one time and your whole life is ruined!"

"I-" Mama has us all brainwashed, and I'm struggling to reason with Lishui. "No, it wasn't a… he's my boyfriend, Lish." The inference has my cheeks reddening slightly, the warmth heating my face.

For some reason, this sets off a newly charged round of frantic whisper yelling with Lishui. "You can't have a baby with him!" She throws her hand in a gesture to the door.

"It's… too late for that," I say softly, wondering how much of this Randall is catching.

"But you're not married!" Lishui says again. I sigh at this. Even quieter, she whispers, "He's white!"

I roll my eyes. "Yes, I know."

"Like, super white! His hair is practically red. You're having a baby with the whitest of white men- oh, God!"

"Stop saying that," I scold.

Now Lishui, eyes barely concealed into her head, puts both hands on her head. "Liling, is he even a Christian?"

That's… debatable. "He comes to church with me every week."

Lishui pauses, mouth open before jumping around me to whip the dorm room open. Randall is on the bed, looking startled by the force with which Lishui has opened the door. "You!" She snaps in her perky little voice.

"Hi, Lishui," Randall says with a bit of a stunned smile.

She shakes her head with a flip of her hand, like they're wasting time. "John 3:16."

"What?" Randall asks, eyes flitting in my direction.

Oh, God, I think for myself. He's going to embarrass me.

"John 3:16," Lishui repeats again. "Say it!"

Randall clearly doesn't know what to do. I don't think he even knows what she's talking about. "Is that-"

"Oh, God!" Lishui cries again before slamming the door again, leaving Randall alone inside. She looks at me again. "You can't take him to Mama and Papa! He's not even- he doesn't know the most basic bible verse!"

"Lishui-"

"Atheists know that verse! And they're going to hell! Liling, oh my gosh are you-"

"Ok," I interject. "How about we go out to dinner?" Before Lishui can argue or use the Lord's name in vain one more time, I swing the door behind me back open. Randall, to my great amusement, has fished out a bible and is flipping aimlessly through it.

My lips catch in a smile while I shield him from Lishui in the hall. "What are you doing?"

Head still bowed to the sacred text, Randall replies, "Whatever she said sounded familiar."

"You can learn that later," I tell him. "Let's go find something to eat."

Randall's face lights up, shutting the Bible and putting it back in the drawer of the bedside table. "I'll have this down by the time the baby comes. Promise."

I roll my eyes lovingly. "Good, because we are raising him or her to be a good Christian child."

"Just like me." Randall grins.

I laugh, but I think I'd love to have whoever our future child is to be just like Randall.

68.

[RANDALL]

It's the fifteenth of December, and Liling and I have a party to go to. We've been invited by Luis, so we obviously can't miss it. I don't mind. I like parties. For Liling, it depends on the crowd. Something tells me she'll shine amongst this one.

I called Rogelio ahead of time so I know what to expect. Rogelio starts with saying, "I promise you, you'll be the only white guy there, besides Gretch. Best behavior, Boy Scout, represent your people. No stealing shit."

I'm not worried about it. I can make friends as easily as I can breathe. Rogelio already warned me a few weeks ago that this party, while a party, is likely to have some sort of cartel team-bonding activity. Luis likes to make public examples, and sometimes he asks for volunteers. I think.

I already know there will be a lot of eyes on me tonight. I'm the new guy that's rapidly rising through the ranks. I'm going to show them why, and quiet any doubts that I can run with this crowd. It'll be easy with Liling at my side. Liling dazzles when she's with the right crowd. Natalia, Ginger, and Greg- that's not her crowd. The sort of people that will be at Luis Padilla's party- those are her people.

It's a formal dress code. "Really fucking fancy." Were Rogelio's exact words. I told him that, if he's pulling my leg, and I show up in a full suit while everyone else is wearing a Christmas sweater, I'd beat his ass. We both laughed over that because we both know Ro could fold me like a piece of paper.

I'm dressed in a full suit- black jacket with black pants and a white shirt that buttons too close to my chin. I've got my hair gelled and tousled in what Liling refers to as my "George Michael" style and I'm ready to go.

When Liling comes out of the bathroom, I know I'm going to spend the entire night beating all the other guys off with a stick.

Liling wears an emerald green dress that glistens slightly when it catches the light. It's got a high neckline and swooping back. It fits her snugly without being suggestive; she looks so damn classy. Liling's wearing the green emerald necklace I bought her and her long black hair playing across her back.

She's too perfect.

My favorite part of her dress is what I can see growing beneath the fabric. In this dress, there's no mistake what Liling's carrying with her. I'm staring at her in wonder as she leaves the bathroom. When she catches me staring at her, Liling instantly puts her hand to her stomach. "What?" She steps back in front of the mirror, turning to the side. "Should I-"

"Don't you dare." I'm over to her side where I belong in a heartbeat. Carefully, I move her hair over her shoulder so that I can put my arms around her and squeeze. "You look beautiful, Liling."

We're looking at each other in the mirror, and I can feel her heartbeat pulsating beneath my forearm that crosses her chest. "There's going to be a lot of people looking at us tonight," she says wistfully.

"There's going to be a lot of people looking at *you*," I correct. "You let me know if anyone looks too long."

Her sharp eyes find me in the mirror again, talking while I find spots to kiss her without messing up her makeup. "No macho-man tonight, Randall. Best behavior."

"Mhmm." She's ticklish at the back of her neck.

Liling squirms. "Randall,"

I pinch her in tighter. "Mmhm."

She sighs, flexing her shoulders beneath my hold on her. "Are you listening?" When I bite her neck in response, she gasps and swats me away. "No- bad!" She hisses at me like I'm a Rottweiler. She bends in close to the mirror. "If you left a mark-"

"I've got a surprise for you."

Liling pauses, giving me a sour face. "Your last surprise was enough."

I laugh, slipping out a jewelry box from my back pocket and handing it to Liling. It's a pair of large emerald earrings to go with her necklace. I made *very* sure the box these were packed in looked nothing like a ring box. That's for later.

Liling's eyes dance over the velvety blue box while I grin at her. She's a very practical woman but has a vice for fine jewelry. Someday, I'll have her dripping in diamonds, and this is the next step toward that.

"What is this?" Liling says in a pleased purr.

"Like I said, there's going to be a lot of people looking at you tonight. I need to make sure you shine."

Liling shakes her head with a blush. "Too cheesy." She murmurs, her dark green nails clutching the box. I'm too excited as I watch her open the box, watching her eyes light up and her little pinched smile as she takes in the massive gems.

376

The earrings are each the size of a quarter. A large coin-sized emerald in a gold setting, failing to hold up to Liling's own beauty. "Randall these are huge," she gawks.

"Too big?"

She quickly shakes her head. "I didn't say that." Liling is long past pretending she doesn't want gifts from me, and she's taking the earrings out of the box to replace the small hoops she was already wearing.

Once the earrings are in, Liling pets her ear lobes, staring at herself in the mirror. "I know it's vain but... I really don't care. Randall, these are stunning."

She really is. Now, she's starting to look like the queen I've seen her as since the day I first met her. All she needs is a massive diamond around her finger. Again, that will come later.

I move her hair again to plant a small kiss on her back, between her shoulder blades. "After this, we're going to have to get you some more colors."

Liling turns to face me, straightening my collar. "And what do you want from all of this?"

That's easy. "The same thing I have wanted since the first time I saw you. I just want to give you a reason to smile when you see me."

[RANDALL]

Luis Padilla lives near Detroit, off a suburb called Royal Oak. It's the rich part of Detroit. Before we get to the house, we turn off a paved road that's flanked in willow trees before stopping at a large golden gate. I give my name at the gate so that I can drive down an incredibly long driveway.

The entire driveway is paved in red brick, and there's another security checkpoint further back, away from view of the road. This is the first indication of where we are. At the second checkpoint, there are two armed guards, massive guns strapped on their back.

I roll to a stop at the second gate, opening the window and letting in a blast of cold air. "Name?" Asks a guard with a thick, black beard.

"Randall Persch." When the man's eyes travel to the passenger seat, I add, "and Liling Zhu."

The guard goes back to the gates, where there's a small booth. He has a clipboard as he flips. He smirks as he comes back. "Randall Persch, ok." His eyes flit up to Liling. "I'm going to assume you're *the Diamond.*"

Liling blushes, while I ask, "Does it say that?" I don't understand how Liling was able to get that nickname after all of an hour with Luis. The name has stuck ever since that one day I went on a field trip with Diego.

The guard keeps his eyes on the clipboard. "We have to make sure we let in the right people. If there's no picture for a guest, Mr. Padilla has provided vague descriptions. It's a judgment call," he sighs.

I'm almost afraid to ask. "Yeah... and what's my vague description?"

The guard smirks. "*Duende.* Looks like he sells cookies."

Liling starts giggling in the seat next to me.

"What's that first word mean?" I ask.

"Leprechaun."

Liling's laughing even harder now.

"It's not that red," I mutter. My hair is brown. When it hits the light, it's a little bright but I am not the damn Lucky Charms Leprechaun. I sigh, pushing my head back into the seat. "See, so now if you let me through, that means you agree that I look like a leprechaun that sells cookies, and that's just not what I'm going for."

The guard laughs at that, holding up a *one second* finger at the car that's pulled up behind us. "Hey, if you're rolling with Mr. Padilla, I'm sure they're some tough-ass cookies. Have a good night, man."

We drive for a couple more minutes down a private drive. There's no other houses in view; just trees and lush green grass. When we finally come upon the house, I have another one of those feelings. It's the feeling that I'm seeing what I'm working toward. What Luis has? I want that too.

I've never seen the kind of wealth I'm seeing now as I pull my car around a massive stone fountain; off for the winter. It's a massive stucco-style house, orange-cream in color. It has a huge circular window at the top of the house, a large set of double glass doors and white columns on each side.

The house has white trim with peach colored shutters and roof tiles; dotted with snow. The most impressive aspect is that the house is absolutely surrounded by massive rhododendrons on all sides, making it look like the house is comfortably hidden inside of a massive jungle of trees. The bushes retain their leaves even in the winter, so the rhododendrons add a beautiful taste of green in an otherwise bleak winter. I imagine, that in the summer, the entire house is surrounded by large purple blooms.

There's four gloved valets waiting by the curved driveway that's between the front door and the massive fountain. When I pull up, they're quick to open Liling's door for her and run around the front to park my car for me after I give my name in return for a little piece of paper with a number on it.

Liling and I look up at the massive house, arm in arm. "What kind of house do you want? "I really am going to build this woman a huge house someday.

Liling thinks about it, huddling in close to me in the cold. "I just want to have somewhere safe for-" She pauses, as if she wasn't ready to speak so freely about our future. "Somewhere we can raise a happy child. Safely."

"That's pretty vague."

Liling kisses my cheek, starting to lead me towards the door, where someone is waiting to open it for us. "You once told me you'd build me a house somewhere private," Liling says thoughtfully. "I like that idea. Private. With a lot of trees."

My mind rolls back to that conversation we had. "Private house, so we can have sex in all the rooms, right?"

Her eyes widen. "Randall, shh! No, that's not what the privacy is for."

"What's it for, then?"

She shakes her head. "I'm already pregnant."

I laugh. "Eventually, you won't be."

"Then, we'll be new parents. There won't be time."

"Trust me," I say seriously, stopping just before the door. "We'll find time."

Liling laughs but slaps my shoulder as we're greeted at the door by someone dressed as a waiter. This is clearly going to be a catered party with wait-staff, attendants and whatever else Luis can dream up.

As soon as we're through the door, we're given a glass of champagne, which Liling denies, and we're welcomed into the house. My first impression of the house is that Luis is absolutely stupid rich. This house was designed with the thought "I'm a millionaire" in mind.

The house opens into a huge foyer with eccentric blue Spanish tile and wooden archways that tone down the pattern of the tile. There's shined tables of dark wood lining the walls, decorated with porcelain decorations of bulls and vases, along with glasses that have been left behind by party goers.

By the doorway, there's a winding staircase with black railing to the right. There's two people at each side of the staircase, arms crossed and looking as if it's their job to keep anyone from going upstairs.

We pass the stairs, heading further into the house. Just as I was told, it's a formal event and everyone is dressed in suits, women in dresses, and everyone is staring at me. We both stick out like a sore thumb, but I can say with full confidence that I'm the only white person here tonight.

We were right when we said all eyes would be on us. Maybe people are looking at me because I apparently really do look like I sell cookies, or maybe it's because I have a reputation already. I'm new here, but I'm already in Luis' good graces.

381

If anyone is staring at Liling, it's because she's the most beautiful person in this house. There's plenty of other women here, but none (in my biased opinion) come close to Liling in beauty. On second thought, if people are staring at me, maybe it's because I'm the only one here that gets to hold Liling's arm, or any other part of her.

On our way to where there's the heaviest congregation of people, I see Diego walking in the opposite direction. Even in a house full of cartel members, Diego is still the scariest person here. In passing, he gives me a nod, and I know that's pretty friendly for him. This is probably the only time I've seen the guy not dressed in a long coat that's concealing who knows what.

"There's so many people here," Liling whispers, taking in everything.

"I'm going to have to work overtime to get to know everybody," I reply.

"You can't possibly get to know all of these people."

I grin at her. "I love when you challenge me."

Further in the house, there's a large living room area. There's an old-school conversation pit in the center; retro orange couches sit around a square white table that's built into the floor. The couch is decorated in yellow and white pillows. In this room, the tile is still patterned but a little calmer in white and orange lines and designs.

In the back of the living room, nearly the entire wall is composed of large glass windows rimmed with a warm-colored wood, orange in hue. By the windows, stands the mountain of a man: Rogelio himself.

I feel the comfort of finally finding someone who I not only recognize, but someone who will talk to me. Rogelio is dressed in a suit just like nearly everyone else, glass of wine in hand, surrounded by other men that I don't know. One of the men standing around Rogelio notices me approaching first, the smile leaving his face as he murmurs something to the group. Now, they're all looking at us.

Rogelio lights up when he sees us, the sparkle of alcohol reddening his cheeks. "Hey! Boy Scout!" He roars, greeting both Liling and I with something of a hug. "Hey, hey, everyone shut up so you meet this guy!" As usual, Rogelio has a clean part on the side of his short, black hair glistening in the ambient Christmas lighting.

"Here we go," I mutter happily.

Rogelio's arm is still weighing over my shoulder. "Ok, this fucker right here is Randall Persch. He's making everyone a shit ton of money further down in the state." I see a few men exchange glances, and I think maybe people won't like me either because I'm new, I'm successful, or I'm different.

I was completely wrong about that initial thought.

Instead, I'm rapidly introduced to seven people. Carlos, Michael, Ernesto, Daniel, Alejandro, Jose, and Javi. I'm determined to remember the names of everyone I meet here tonight.

Each of the seven people are a lot more polite than I would have thought, and each of them are even more enthusiastic to meet Liling. Liling really is a diamond tonight, and she's shining.

After Rogelio loudly breaks the ice, people start coming out of the woodwork to introduce themselves. Maybe it's curiosity, maybe it's a *keep your friends close and enemies closer* thing, but I end up meeting at least a dozen more people in the span of half an hour.

At some point, Liling spots a waiter with water, and she excuses herself to grab a glass. In that time, I meet three more people and Liling is cornered by some dazzling woman in a red dress who looks like she could deliver a baby at any minute.

383

Rogelio follows my gaze as I watch Liling charm yet another new person. "That's Blanca." Rogelio finishes his glass. "Luis' wife. That means." Rogelio looks around, squinting. "He's close by." He cracks into a smile.

I figure I should probably pretend that I'm going to catch Liling and then introduce myself to Blanca. Luis is like me, I think. If you want to be in good with him, you have to be in good with his partner.

It's like Rogelio knows what I'm thinking. "I'll introduce you later. Let's go have a cigar outside."

I raise a brow. "It's thirty five degrees outside."

"We'll be quick. We want to be back inside before the show starts, anyway."

"Show?"

Rogelio, arm on my back, starts leading me toward where there's a glass door and someone waiting to open it for us. We're on a massive stone balcony that overlooks what's probably a topiary in the spring and summer. The balcony is almost empty when we get out there, with a few people smoking over the railing.

There's someone waiting by the door with a box of Cuban cigars. As far as I know, imports like these are still illegal, but so is pretty much everything else Luis brings into the country. I'm not much of a smoker. Liling hates the habit, but I think she'll forgive me for a social smoke.

The attendant lights our cigars for us. I follow Rogelio out to the curved railing. "There's a lot more people here than I thought," I say, noticing there's armed guards out in the perimeter of the yard as well.

"Luis does this once a year. Gets everyone together. It's good for morale, yeah? People want to see the boss. Know who they're working for. It's also good for people to be reminded *who* they're working for."

My mind goes back to when Rogelio invited me to this party. "What's the reminder going to be?"

Rogelio sighs, his smile falling a little. "No one is going to forget who's in charge after tonight."

"You're being cryptic, Ro."

"Don't chicken out on us tonight," Rogelio replies, not really addressing what I said last. "It's your big night, too."

"What does that mean?"

Rogelio thinks about this. "It's your first year here, Boy Scout. Your welcome into the Padilla world."

"Tell me more about the world, then." I need to know everything about the Padilla world, inside and out.

Rogelio chuckles at this. "Fine. Ok, so in the Padilla family, there's several big players. People that have earned respect and have Luis' ear."

"Like an inner circle," I supply.

Rogelio snaps his free hand. "Exactly. People Luis likes enough to not just look out for them, but make sure everyone knows they can be treated as extensions of himself. Diego, he's part of that circle. Diego could point at anyone here, give them a thumbs down, and Luis would shoot that person dead, no questions asked. Luis trusts his circle. Everyone knows to respect the circle."

I would think someone would know to respect Diego just by looking at him. "Alright, who is in the circle?" I should make it a point to meet anyone that's in Luis' short list of favorites.

"Well, yours truly, of course," Rogelio says with a proud smile. "I grew up with Luis. Here since the beginning."

"That doesn't surprise me. Who else?"

Rogelio thinks. "You know, it's a small circle, right now. Jorge is close, but he's not there yet. Maybe next year. Carlos, eventually, I'm sure."

"How do you know when someone is there?" I need to know so I can get there.

"The test," Rogelio explains. "These parties. Luis always picks his inner circle members for a test. It's an unofficial announcement of who's who."

"Has anyone ever failed this test? What happens then?"

"There have been people who have declined to do the test. Sometimes, Luis tries to make it personal," Ro says with a nod. "Just like that, they're not in the circle, and they usually don't get to be tested again."

I sigh. "Someday, I'll be up there with you, Ro." I promise.

Rogelio laughs at this. "I'm sure you will, Boy Scout. You work hard. You do what you're told. You're not a pussy. You make Luis a lot of money." Rogelio shrugs. "That's all there is to it."

"Does everyone else know who's being tested?"

"Me and Diego know, but Luis likes to keep it under wraps until he makes it public. Everyone else is placing bets on who Luis is going to test this year. He usually keeps three or four guys. He's only got two right now, me and Diego, so everyone is trying to guess who Luis will add." I wonder what happened to whoever the third person was.

Rogelio. Diego. We're missing someone. "Isn't Oscar in the circle? He's always with you guys."

Rogelio smirks, shaking his head. "No, he was close, but he doesn't have it. He has a problem with the *doing what he's told* bit. And the not being a pussy bit, otherwise, this would've been his year to be tested." He takes a long pull from his cigar.

"I'm guessing life is pretty good in that inner circle." I comment feverishly.

Rogelio nods again. "Of course, they're going to try to come kiss the ring. If you're in the circle, you're one of the people that can make their life hell, or take it away if you feel like it. No one's going to want to be on your bad side. Pass the test, and you're as safe as you can be in our world, brother. Assuming you don't get shot while working, no one can touch you. No one would even think about it." He nods back toward the house. "That goes for your family, too. Congrats, by the way."

"Thanks," I say absentmindedly. Inner circle. That's what I want to be. I am on my way to getting everything I've ever wanted. It feels like I'm almost there. I've got a bank account full of money. A beautiful, pregnant girlfriend who I'm ready to wife up. Respect.

I've done a lot to get here. I'm ready to do so much more.

LILING

I've been separated from Randall for all of a minute before I meet Blanca Padilla, Luis' wife. Blanca Padilla is one of the most divine, sultry beauties I've ever seen.

Blanca has pristine skin, absolutely no flaws marring her light brown skin, lightly sun kissed. Her dark brown eyes are rimmed with dark liner that gives her a very siren-like look under large lashes that have to have been installed. Blanca has dark brown hair that naturally falls in waves, reaching almost to her chin.

I know Blanca is coming before she's even reached me, because the party swirls around her, parting like the Red Sea. Blanca is outrageously pregnant, but only carries the weight in her stomach. I can already tell I'm not going to be blessed with that feature.

Coming toward me in a deep red dress with a hard shine, Blanca approaches with a genuine smile. "Hello," she greets in a warm, joyful voice. "You must be Liling." Blanca's accent is thicker than Luis or anyone else in his party. My name is pronounced more as Lee-ling coming from her beautiful mouth.

"And you have come with that Randall Persch I have been hearing so much about?"

The other women at this party are few and far between, and I'm interested to see who holds Luis' heart. Love has been a big interest to me of late. "Yes, hello, I'm Liling." When I extend my hand to her, she returns one with deep red nails and massive diamonds.

Blanca smiles radiantly at me. "Have you had time to enjoy yourself yet?"

"Oh, yes. We're trying to keep track of everyone we meet."

Blanca laughs with a nod. "Yes, everyone wants to get to know your Randall." She lowers her voice. "Luis likes him, so everyone else wants to like him too."

"I'll introduce you once I find him," I say, looking around. It seems Randall has disappeared from the room. If he weren't such an apparent favorite, I might worry.

Blanca flips a hand. "Oh, let the men be men for a little bit. Why don't we find somewhere to sit." She nods at my stomach. "If your feet feel like mine, I'm sure you wouldn't mind somewhere a little more quiet."

At this, I nod thankfully. I thought I wasn't so pregnant that I could stand a few hours in some green heels but I was very wrong about this. I'll never make this mistake again.

People watch us with great interest as we walk together. Blanca leads me to a narrow room with the same blue Spanish tile as what's at the doorway. The back wall is a dark bookshelf covered in books and figurines. There's a wide windowsill in front of a Spanish-colonial style window. The sill has a turquoise cushion and sits across from a pleated bench of the same color.

"When are you due?" Blanca asks, taking the seat in front of the window.

389

"June," I say, taking the bench. "Which feels so far away, but also like it's not enough to get ready."

"You are telling me!" Blanca agrees.

"Will this be your first?"

Blanca nods, beaming. "Yes, a boy!" She really is dazzling.

I beam at the thought. I've decided, without voicing this thought, that a boy is what I want first. I catch that thought too- *first*. "Have you decided on a name?"

"We will name him Rafael. Good name, yes?"

"It's a good name," I confirm. I really do like that name.

"And what about you? Have you picked a name yet?"

I shake my head. "We've talked very briefly about it, just a couple of times," I say. When we talk about it for too long, it gets daunting. It's when we start trying to name the baby that I realize there's a real human coming into our lives. "I think we're both trying to go in very different directions with names."

Blanca takes a sip of her water, gesturing with her free hand in a circular motion. "Tell me your names, then- let me hear!" She says once she's done drinking.

Suddenly, I'm feeling shy. Naming a child is an intimate, personal choice. "Randall likes-" I stop, trying to find a nice way of phrasing things. "Very traditional names."

Blanca does something of an eye roll. "John, Robert, Thomas," she says, trying to say it in a straight Mid-western American accent.

I nod. "He really likes the name Nicholas for a boy. He likes Cassandra and Emily for a girl."

"Hm," Blanca says with a nod. She narrows her eyes like she is thinking, finally shaking her head. "You can do better." She gestures at me again. "Ok, tell me *your* names."

It would be a lie to say I haven't given it much thought. "Me and all of my sisters have destination names," I start. "Lhasa, Liling, Lishui- they're all places. I think I like the idea of continuing that."

Blanca seems to hold onto this idea. "See? I already like where this is going. What's the name?"

"For a boy," I say cautiously, knowing the name I've had circulating my head is different, is unusual, but there's something about it that is a statement. "I really love the sound of Wuhan." In the immediate silence I add, "It's a city. Wuhan."

"Wuhan," repeats Blanca in thought. "Wuhan." She says again. After another moment of thinking she points at me with a nod. "That is a strong name. Good, strong name."

I *almost* startle when Luis Padilla has suddenly conjured himself in the arched opening of the room. He's loud, happily saying, "Oh, my heart!" He puts a hand on his chest. "If it isn't my ruby and my diamond together!"

Luis looks very handsome tonight, wearing a suit that is a deep purple, so dark that it almost shines black. After giving me a warm embrace, Luis crosses back to Blanca, standing next to her and draping an arm over her neck, hand resting at an almost scandalous spot. "And what are the precious jewels talking about?"

"Names," Blanca says, smiling at Luis.

Luis nods enthusiastically. "Rafael- *my* son! He's going to run this world." He sounds like Randall.

"And now we're talking about what Liling will name her baby," Blanca supplies.

"Yeah?" Luis asks. "Then let's hear it." This is when Randall, escorted by Rogelio, has found us. "Hey!" Luis hollers. "Boy Scout! Just in time. What are you naming that kid of yours?"

Randall blinks with an amused look of apprehension. "We haven't settled on anything." His eyes look at me, as if asking for permission.

Blanca starts pushing on Luis' arm. "Randall likes the boring names."

"I like names that aren't going to get my kids beat up in school," Randall points out.

"Beat up?" echoes Rogelio, from next to Randall. "Nah, you teach your kid to kick ass. Someone makes fun of your kid?" Rogelio punches the air a couple times. "*Nocaut.*"

Luis nods approvingly. "Then what is your name, Persch?"

"Something simple." Luis rolls his eyes when Randall says this. "I like the name Nick. Nicholas."

Blanca snorts. "You can do better." When she looks at me, Randall sighs, coming over to sit on the bench next to me.

"*She* likes the name Wuhan, for a boy." I do love how Randall listens to me. "I think the poor kid is going to get made fun of."

Luis, like Blanca, takes a minute to consider. "That your name, *Diamante?*"

I nod. "I'm starting to get attached to that one."

"Wuhan…" Luis mumbles. His voice changes to an excited whisper. "Now, that's a fucking name. That's a name people will know not to fuck with. That's a name you respect."

I smile at Randall, leaning into him. I know, now more than ever, he's losing this fight. I also know he'll let me choose whatever name I want.

"You really think that's *the* name?" Randall asks.

From the archway, Rogelio interjects. "Ok, you gonna name your kid something that makes a statement like Wuhan? Or you want him to name him something safe? We don't live in a safe world, Boy Scout."

"Nicholas," Luis laughs. "Get the fuck out of here."

"Rafael and Wuhan," Blanca says, as if this is all decided. "Our kids will be great friends, I'm sure."

"They'll burn the world down together," Rogelio adds.

"Rafael Padilla, and Wuhan fucking Persch," Luis says triumphantly before stopping himself, looking at me and then Randall. "Persch? Wuhan Persch?"

I can feel Randall squirm next to me. "I-"

Luis puts his hand on his waste. "Wait- where is her fucking diamond? Boy Scout- what did I tell you?"

Blanca starts laughing, swatting Luis again. "Leave them alone, Luis."

Luis shakes his head. "Oh, Diamante, I'm so sorry. I thought *this one*." He nods at Randall. "Was worth a shit."

Randall laughs. "Listen, I didn't know I'd be under attack tonight."

I have a massive blush burning at my cheeks too. The topic of a possible marriage, especially under the circumstances, is one that we've been skirting around for a while. I have no doubts that Randall wants to, and will, marry me.

The question is *when*.

"You better be careful, Randall," Luis warns light heartedly. "Liling could go out to the party and throw a rock and find someone willing to be that baby's daddy."

"Then go ahead, Liling," Randall says, looking at me. "Start throwing rocks, and let me talk to them."

Diego enters the room, looking out of place in a long black button up. He's left behind the jacket he was wearing earlier. Diego's head has been freshly shaved, showing off the tattoos that cover his entire head. There's a large moth on the right side of his

393

head, above his ear. While many of the tattoos are dark and artful, the moth continues to catch my attention. Diego mutters something to Rogelio, who nods.

"Everything's ready," Rogelio says to Luis, who seems to have some of the amusement leech out of his face.

"Well then, let's not wait. Get everyone rounded up," Luis orders.

Rogelio and Diego both nod, leaving the room. Luis looks at me again. "We're going to be doing something... indelicate, *Diamante*. You might want to wait in here, with My Ruby." Besides him, Blanca shares a knowing look.

Amused, hand on my stomach, I stand as Randall does. I grip his hand. "Diamonds don't crack under pressure, Luis."

At this, Luis tilts his head back in laughter before slapping Randall's back as he heads to the exit. "You've got yourself a fucking blood diamond, Persch."

71.

[RANDALL]

The test, whatever it is, is taking place in a large room with orange and white patterned tile that's large enough to be used as something of a ballroom. It's a space with the sole purpose of entertainment.

There's a few tables around the edge of the room, but it's been mostly cleared of furniture for the event. There's a large chandelier with big, ornamental bulbs hanging over the center of the room, over the swarms of Luis' cartel members.

By the time Liling and I make it to the large entertainment space, the room is full of what looks to be around forty to fifty people. Every single one of them looks like they belong here.

Holding Liling's hand, we start to settle near the back of the crowd. I notice that I've landed next to Jorge.

Jorge nods at me. "Hey, Persch, good to see you."

We shake hands, and I realize that, as soon as Jorge said my name, we start receiving sideways glances and whispers. I think I like having a reputation. "Hi, Jorge." I move my free hand to Liling's back. "Jorge, this is Liling. Liling, Jorge."

Liling knows Jorge by name only, and knows that I have a lot of contact with him on a weekly basis. "Hello, Jorge," Liling says warmly. She's literally sparkling right now.

"Liling." Jorge smiles. "This guy doesn't shut up about you, do you know that?"

Liling laughs, because she definitely knows this. I'm not even embarrassed about it. "That's why I love him."

Love.

Jorge steps aside, patting me on the back. "This is your first party, right? Why don't you get a better spot?" Even before Jorge says this, people began moving out of the way, opening up a place for us.

Whoever will be tested is not just going to be tested by Luis, but everyone else here too. Rogelio and Diego are leaders. People are going to be judging to see who else can be a leader.

In the front of the crowd, I can finally see what's in the center of the room. There's a large black tarp of plastic covering the tile. It's a major indicator about what's going to happen, and what the inner circle will be asked to do. Over the tarp sits three wooden chairs, paced about five feet apart from each other.

On the opposite side of the crowd, I pick out Rogelio standing with his hands in his pocket. He nods at me when we make eye contact. To my left a ways out, Diego also stands at the ready.

At first, I don't see Luis anywhere. Blanca has decided to stay out of this room. There are very few people talking in the room, but all of them stop when Luis cuts his way through the crowd, standing in the opening by the empty chairs.

Luis has settled down since our last conversation in the study. Now, he's closer to the Luis Padilla who was deciding whether to have me killed when we met at Toby's apartment. This version of Luis has very few friends.

"Let's get started." All sound in the room dies immediately. "If you've been here before, you know what we need to do before we really start to enjoy ourselves tonight. If you're new here, I'm sure you've been warned."

Looking around, I can tell who's ready for what's about to happen and who isn't. The people here are either indifferent or scared. Even now, as Luis speaks, there are people looking at me too, in the same way they're looking at Rogelio, or Diego. How do all of these people already know about me?

"All of us in this room stand to lose a lot. Our lives. Our freedom. Our family. Our money. That's why there's a lot of rules around here, yeah?" Luis circles the empty chairs as a few people in the room mutter words of agreement.

"So, when I get everyone here to celebrate all of our accomplishments, I don't want anyone to forget what we're fighting against. We all know about the fights outside the house-*policia,* the feds, immigration."

I think I'd be more nervous if it weren't for Liling standing next to me. She seems so calm. Regal. She doesn't even care how clammy my hand is getting.

Luis continues, walking in a large circle around the chairs, making eye contact with different people as he speaks. "But sometimes, these threats come from inside the house. They work to bring down our foundation from the inside. And when it's an inside job, we deal with it inside the house."

Luis turns his head and nods at someone I know I've met tonight... Carlos. His name is Carlos, and I think he's essentially a jailer for Luis, and works under Diego. Carlos disappears into the crowd, heading toward a door in the back of the room and knocking twice on it.

At first I can't see what's happening, not until the crowd parts again. Carlos is leading three hooded figures into the center of the room. My eyes dart to the tarp that crunches under their feet as they're led over it and into the chairs. My eyes find Rogelio again, who looks at me with a stone face.

Each figure, men based on their shape and stature, are heavily seated in their own chair. Even with the hoods still on, it's clear they've endured hours, maybe even days of torture before coming here. This, right now, is just the finale.

Carlos disappears again and comes back with... tools. He's got golf clubs, bats, knives, and more - just about everything being lugged by him and someone I don't know.

Luis grabs a bat from Carlos. It's a classic wooden bat, brown and splintering at the end. The wood looks like it's already been saturated with blood at some point.

Luis stops at the figure on my far right, at the end. He lets the bat rest on the person's shoulder. "This? I don't do this lightly. Every person in these chairs deserves to be here, yeah?"

He waits for the room to agree with him, and they do. "These people are trying to bring us down. We will stop them now." Luis first places his free hand on top of the first hooded head, he rubs his hand around, like he's petting the person.

Ripping the hood off, there are murmurs as Luis reveals the first person. The first terrified person is somewhere in their forties, black hair with gray on the sides. He's got one eye swollen completely shut, an open sore on his nose and he's missing several fingers. I'm noticing the smell now.

Luis starts walking again, using the bat like a cane. He stops at random, stopping in front of a tall Hispanic man in his fifties. He has long gray hair that's in a clean bun pulled tight over his head where a long vertical scar touches from his forehead to the bridge of his nose.

"Do you know who this is?" Luis asks.

The man with a scar looks at the first person with the hood removed. "Manny." He looks almost hopeful that Luis has stopped to talk to him. A few people start murmuring in the crowd.

Luis nods, moving on. "Manuel." He stops at another person, pointing with his bat, the man with the scar deflating slightly when he keeps walking. "Do you know what Manny did?"

The person Luis stops at seems fairly young, around my age. He shakes his head. "No, sir," he says quietly.

Luis nods with understanding, raising his voice to the rest of the group. "Manny's a thief. Manny's been doing a lot of pocketing, you know?" He shrugs. "Some money for a night out. A few grams for him and his friends. Worse yet, he let our sellers take the blame for shortages." Luis isn't very theatrical. He's direct, and he knows he doesn't need to do much to get his point across.

Manny has been breathing heavily in his chair. He isn't tied in, but he's surrounded by a mob. There's nothing he could do. "Diego." Luis' voice rings out.

Immediately, Diego steps out of the crowd. The whites of Diego's eyes standout between pools of ink that covers his face, his entire body.

Once Diego has made himself out of the crowd, Luis looks at him. "Handle it, Diego."

Diego nods, walking toward where Carlos is standing. Carlos is holding something familiar; a long, sheathed blade. Diego knew he would be tested tonight, just like he's probably been tested before. Diego came prepared with his own weapon.

Taking the blade from Carlos, Diego slowly unsheathes the machete. Diego is standing behind and to the left of Manny, but Manny hears the sound of *La Princesa* coming out of her cage.

Manny is being a lot calmer than I think I could be. He's keeping his eyes shut, and he's whispering prayers under his breath. Sweat has soaked through his shirt, blood stains every other part of his body.

When Diego's steps can be heard coming over the tarped tile, Manny's chanting increases. Diego stands behind Manny, and grabs the man by his hair, pulling Manny's head back. Diego looks emotionless, as he almost always does. Diego doesn't wait for any more direction from Luis, nor does he let Manny get out any more last words. In one clean swipe, Diego slashes his machete across Manny's throat.

There's a gurgle, and for half a second, it's like Manny's voice isn't coming from his mouth, but from the open hole in his neck. Blood splatters everywhere, the tarp being dotted with loud thunks as the blood pours out of Manny. Still emotionless, Diego lets go of Manny's head and lets the body fall out of the chair and onto the ground.

Diego steps back into the crowd, lowering the jeweled blade beneath his hands as it leaks Manny's blood on the floor.

Luis has returned to the chair and removed the next hood. The next person in the chair is another very young person. He's got lighter brown hair than everyone else, looking like he might not even be twenty. "This one?" Luis continues. "What did you do, Andres?"

Andres' face is tear-stained and bruised. He looks up at Luis with pleading eyes. "I'm sorry, Mr. Padilla, I can do better."

Luis shakes his head. "How can I hold my men to such high standards if there are no penalties?"

"I know- I'm asking for another penalty, anything," Andres pleads.

Luis responds by smashing the bat down on Andres' bent knee. Andres howls and clutches his malformed knee. The leg now lies awkwardly, bent in at an unnatural angle.

Luis calls over the noise. "Rogelio."

Across the room, Rogelio takes a deep breath, solemnly walking to stand in front of Andres. I know Rogelio will do what needs to be done, but he's going to be affected by this. When I watch Rogelio walk, I have this weird moment of re-realizing what a beast he is. It's a privilege to have that man as a friend and not an enemy.

"Rogelio does a lot of the training around here," Luis explains to the crowd. Moving next to Rogelio, he puts a hand on his friend's shoulder. "But we have to remove the rot before it infects everything else."

Rogelio being asked to kill someone he's trained; that must be what he meant when he told me that Luis tries to make things personal. Luis offers the bat to Ro but Rogelio shakes his head. "Don't need it," Rogelio says. Rogelio is taking this personally too.

"Rogelio, please," Andres says. He starts to act like he's going to try to stand, and in a way Rogelio helps him do this. I've joked that someone as large as Rogelio could break me with his bare hands, if he wanted. When I see Rogelio grab Andres by the throat and lift the kid straight in the air, I know the previous statement isn't an exaggeration.

As if Andres weighed nothing, Rogelio holds Andres by the neck, suspended in the air. Andres kicks and gurgles as he claws against Rogelio's grip but Rogelio does not drop him. One of Andres' shoes gets kicked off as he flails, blood starts trickling down one of Rogelio's hands where Andres has been attempting to claw himself free.

Rogelio grips harder, holding until Andres' face turns an unnatural shade of red until it's an unnatural shade of blue. Even when Andres stops moving, Rogelio holds on until his arms start to shake.

"He's gone, brother," Luis says softly. Andres' body hits the floor with a thud. Rogelio's hands are scratched, and he wipes his own blood off on one of the discarded hoods on the floor before throwing it over Andres.

Now there's only one hooded man left. My stomach rolls. In some ways, I want to be tested. I want that honor, that validation. In other ways, I'm hoping my name isn't called at all.

"This next one hurts," Luis says, making his way around a quaking figure that's breathing heavily through a cloak. "This next one could've been something. This next one, I let close to me, thinking he could've been one of my guys." He nods toward Diego. "But I guess it's better to find out now, but it's disappointing, still."

When Luis rips off the final hood, it's Oscar sitting in the chair.

"Oscar, here, got himself arrested a few months back." Oscar looks the worst of the three captives. His thick, curled hair is in mats. He's not only missing his thumbs, but he's missing an entire eye. There's a sickening, open hole where Oscar's right eye has been grotesquely gouged, the skin around the eye also looking damaged from the operation.

Oscar seems like he's barely conscious. Out of Luis' three men, Oscar had been one of the jolliest. Now he's nothing. "I'm not mad Oscar got his dumb ass arrested," Luis explains, beginning to circle the room again. "I'm mad about what he did while he was waiting to get out." Luis passes me without looking at me.

"You see, I take care of my people, don't I?" Luis asks the room. The room all agrees, giving enthusiastic sounds and words of encouragement. "So I sent someone else to go make sure that Oscar here got out with no charges. I risked someone I saw potential in just to get your ass out."

Oscar's head rolls forward, and he starts making something that sounds almost like a word. Liling leans into me, whispering very quietly, "His tongue has been removed."

As Luis continues to walk, I get even more anxious to get this over with. He's almost made another circle around the room, still holding a bat with fresh blood. "I think everyone here knows how seriously I take snitches. Everyone here knows there's nothing I hate more than a bitch with a loud mouth."

Luis, still circling, is getting ready to pass me again. I, along with everyone around me, tense. Just as Luis is about to walk by, he swings the bat out in line with my stomach, stopping just before it can make contact with me. He's so fast that I didn't even have time to flinch.

Luis' dark eyes stare back at my own, although I'm sure mine look a lot more bewildered. "Randall. Persch." Luis calls like an order. In the room, there's what sounds like a surprised murmur and words of disbelief.

I don't look around or wait for another reassuring nod from Rogelio. I don't wait. Still looking Luis in the eye, I release Liling's hand so I can grab the bat that's hovering just in front of my stomach. My fingers clutch over the bat, hand spreading over the preexisting blood.

With a small grin, Luis releases the bat and steps back. As I take short, lingering steps toward Oscar, who slowly lifts his head at my approach, Luis continues on. I catch Rogelio's eye too, and he gives me a smirk, because he knew this was happening the entire time. I'll give him crap about it later, if I pass this test.

"You see, while Randall did exactly as he was told, and was working to get Oscar out, Oscar was busy making himself a deal with the police." Luis shakes his head. "And you were working so damn fast, huh? I mean, Randall had you out in what—a couple days? It took less than forty eight hours for you to betray me, and less than two hours for Randall to do his job. You see the difference, Oscar?"

Unlike the others, Luis isn't done monologuing by the time he's called my name. I wait patiently, bat in hand in front of Oscar.

I hear Luis' steps behind me. "In case Boy Scout hasn't made his rounds yet," I take a deep breath to keep my face from getting warm, now that everyone knows the nickname I'll never shake with this crowd. "*This* is Randall fucking Persch. And you all better get to know him."

The king has spoken.

Luis looks at me expectedly, folding his hands in front of him, his massive golden rings glistening. I'm not going to wait for a nod, I'm not going to hesitate.

In front of me is a threat. He was ready to tell the Padilla's secrets. My secrets. In front of me, this ragged, bleeding shell is also an opportunity. This is my test.

It's a really easy test.

Gripping the bat, I kill Oscar with one fatal blow to the head. His head splits; his remaining eye is imploded by the bat when it smashes against his skull, and Oscar's nose is crushed into a mangled mess of skin and cartilage.

Behind me, Luis laughs, stepping up to me until his hand rests on my shoulder. Luis is a lot taller than me, his skinny frame hanging close behind me. He leans in, whispering in my ear. "Good job, Boy Scout. Welcome to the family, brother."

72.

[RANDALL]

The remainder of the night goes by quickly. The rest of the night goes by as if we're not all members of a drug-peddling cartel that watched performative murder earlier.

I don't know whose job it is to clean up, but it's not mine. Instead, there's a massive dining hall with about seven long tables spread in a square around the room. The tables are lined with a white cloth with orange trim and they're overflowing with trays of food. I sit next to Rogelio, with Liling on my other side. We dine, we drink (Liling doesn't drink, to be clear), we laugh. This is my life now.

Last year, I was a low-level cocaine dealer and part-time pizza boy. Now, I'm a drug-lord in training. That's progress.

When the party is nearing an end, we migrate to a darker room with a huge tropical fish tank and dark orange couches. Liling has gone off with Blanca to tour the house, leaving me with Diego, Carlos, Rogelio, and Luis

As the party begins to wind down, people trickle in to pay their respects to Luis before living. Many part with gifts left for Luis, and many stop to spare some kind words to me, as well as Rogelio and Diego. It feels like Luis is the king, and I'm in his court. I think my proximity to the throne is going to really work out for me.

It's well after midnight by now, and the house is quieter, but not empty. The remaining few are all now in the den space. I've been holding a conversation with Rogelio, and Luis has wandered out of the room.

In the corner, the man Luis talked to earlier during the executions, the one with the scar on his forehead, is having something of an argument with Jorge. They're arguing in Spanish, so I have no idea what it's about.

"What's that guy's story?" I ask Rogelio.

Rogelio is leaning over his knees on the couch, clearly more tired than he was when the party started. "That's Gael," Rogelio rumbles. "Nasty motherfucker. He does some of what you do now- without the extras. He's in charge of sellers in his area, and keeps them in line. He just doesn't do any of the bonus work for Luis that gives the opportunity to get ahead in our world."

"I haven't met him yet."

"He probably won't like even you, Boy Scout," Rogelio replies. "He used to be in the circle."

I thought it was hard to get out of the inner circle and live. "Luis kicked him out?"

Rogelio looks at Diego, who is sitting quietly on the other side of me. "Gael brought in Diego, almost a decade ago."

Diego nods, but offers no comment.

"For a while, it was me and Gael in Luis' circle. Then, Diego moves into the circle after about two years of working for Luis."

"What happened?" I ask.

Rogelio keeps his eyes trained on the man with the scar. "Gael just… you know, you need to kiss a little ass with Luis from time to time, right?"

406

"Sure."

"Gael doesn't get it. He doesn't always get that he is not in charge, every idea he has isn't good, and sometimes he can't do what he wants. He does good work, he just doesn't play nice with Luis, so Luis cut him back down just because he could."

"Pride," Diego mutters next to me. I'm not sure who he's talking about.

"So Gael didn't do anything that's going to get him killed, but his ego took a real blow. Everyone knows he got demoted, and Diego, who Gael brought in, has risen past him. And now, you're here."

Gael looks like he's in his fifties; I bet he hates someone like me coming in and taking his place. I meant to sneak one more glance at the scarred man but we catch each other's eyes and now Gael is on his way over, glass in hand.

"Diego, you still got the princess handy?" Rogelio mutters.

Gael first greets Rogelio, nodding at the giant man. Gael seems to prefer Spanish, because I don't catch any of the conversation. He does the same with Diego, who only responds with two words. It doesn't seem like a friendly conversation between someone and a past mentor.

When Gael is ready to face me, he has this smug smile that I instantly hate. He starts saying a flurry of words I don't understand, and I only catch a few words that I've learned just from being around Luis and Rogelio. For that matter, I think most of the Spanish words I've picked up are curse words.

I have no idea what Gael says, so with a wary tone that doesn't make me sound like the friendliest of people, I say, "Hi, I'm Randall. Randall Persch." I extend a hand. Maybe with this person, it'd be better to remember that I am in the inner circle now, and I don't need to be friends with everyone.

407

Gael laughs when I say this, shaking my hand with little grip. "What? No *habla espanol?"*

I shake my head. "Not enough."

Gael grins at Rogelio, who doesn't reciprocate. "How did you let this guy in?"

Rogelio meets Gael with a dead stare. "*I* didn't." I know Rogelio doesn't mean this at my expense. He's reminding Gael *who* let me in.

Gael looks down at me, one hand wrapped around his drink, the other in his pocket. "I just don't get it."

"What don't you get?" My own voice has turned. It's the voice I use when I'm speaking to someone who doesn't need a friend, they need a teacher.

"I don't get what's so special about you, frankly. I've been hearing about some *gringo*- some Persch for months- and you're it? I don't get it," Gael snaps.

I shrug. "I haven't heard anything about you at all, so I don't even know why you're talking to me. Who are you?"

Next to me, Diego seems amused. It's rare that I choose to be mean. Even when punishing someone, I remain pretty verbally cordial.

Gael holds his glass so tight that it cracks, and the alcohol starts leaking onto the floor, some dribbling over Ro's knee. Rogelio cusses, standing quickly. "Isn't it time you left?" When someone as large as Rogelio takes a fighting stance, the room takes notice.

Gael looks down at me, ignoring Ro. "You can't even fight your own fights, can you, boy?" Boy seems so much more disrespectful than Boy Scout, I can't explain it.

There's people looking, watching, some filling into the mouth of the room when they hear raised voices. This is another test, in a way. How do I respond when challenged by someone other than Luis? This isn't a time to buckle. I stand too. "You should sit down before you break a hip."

Gael responds by pushing at my pec, but I don't budge. Rogelio quickly steps in front of me, and he stares down at Gael, peering down at the scarred man with malice. Now, Gael can see how mismatched he is. There's no one in this house that could handle Rogelio.

The thing is, I want to handle it. We all know what Rogelio can do. "Ro, I got this."

Rogelio turns his head, looking amused. "Yeah? Well shit, go ahead then." He steps to his left, giving me space.

"I'm going to give you one pass," I say. "Because I don't really want to fight in Luis' house, I think it'd be disrespectful. How about you move on?"

Gael has long, gray eye lashes that stare up at me through pale green eyes. "A pass?" Gael laughs. "Rich, coming from some white-trash, piece of shit who's so cheap that he walks around with some pregnant Chinese whore-"

I think we all know where my snapping point is. Gael's snapping point was his nose when my fist slammed into the side of his face. He was so wholly unprepared that the impact spins him around and he crashes down onto the table before sliding off it, landing between the table and the couch. On his way down, he hits a tray of cold appetizers and ends up covered in food and alcohol.

The room reacts in a pulse of *oohs* and cusses and laughter. I hear my nickname reverberating around the audience. I really was only going to hit him once and be done with it, especially with the mess that was made. A room full of people just watched me strike someone down, but no one is going to move against me. No, they know who I am now.

409

"What's going on here, Boy Scout?" Luis drawls from the doorway.

Shit, he's got that tone.

Feeling a little bashful, I look at Luis, standing in his dark purple blazer, fresh drink in hand. "Settling a disagreement."

"Little bitch had it coming to him," Rogelio chimes in from the couch. Diego nods in agreement.

Gael is still on the floor as Luis steps closer, standing over him. "You being a little bitch again, Gael?"

Gael sits himself up, face reddening. "*He* does not belong here, Luis! He is not one of us! I've been working for you for *years.*"

"You've been annoying me for years. He's one of us because I say he is," Luis states, before raising his voice to the room. "Does anyone else here think Randall doesn't belong with us?" The room stays silent, so Luis asks another question. "Does anyone think Gael deserves a spot with Rogelio and Diego?" No one speaks.

Gael looks around the room incredulously. "What? *Everyone* is afraid?"

"Hm." Muses Luis. "You think everyone is afraid, or you think no one here wants to stand up for you?"

"Both." Mutters Rogelio, and the first sound from other people in the room is the sound of murmured agreement.

"Plus, Randall works a whole hell of a lot harder than you." Luis continues.

"Impossible."

"And he's not an asshole all of the time," Luis adds, looking at me with a sideways glance. "Just annoying as hell."

Gael laughs. "What? So I don't play nice enough for you? Because I won't get on my knees and suck your dick, you don't want me in your circle?"

410

Luis has lost all amusement now. "I would choose your next words very fucking carefully."

Gael sits himself up, slowly rising until he's almost standing at eye level with Luis. Rogelio tenses, and Diego stands and moves himself to Luis' left. The entire room has gone silent.

Gael stares back at Luis. "I won't get on my knees just to stay in your good graces. How often do you make this new guy suck your little dick to-"

Luis cuts Gael off by raising his glass and pouring it over Gael's head with a level of calm that chills me. Before Gael can even blink the alcohol out of his eyes, Luis grabs Gael by the throat with one hand, and smashes the empty glass into Gael's face with the other. The glass shatters and leaves wicked cuts on Gael's face. "Oh, you'll get on your fucking knees."

Gael starts furiously wiping off his face, blood and alcohol mixing into his cut skin. Wine is dripping off his brow and staining his shirt.

Luis snaps his fingers and points at the floor. "Knees. Floor. Now."

This is when Gael realizes his situation. He's gone too far, and he's pushed a drug-lord into a corner. Gael's made a scene, and now a scene is going to be made of him. "Luis, look-"

"You want to get kinky?" Luis asks. "Fine. Call me *daddy* and get on your fucking knees and apologize. Let's see how submissive you can be."

Shit.

Gael looks at Rogelio, as if Rogelio is going to interject. "I can put you down there myself," Rogelio growls. Diego sure as hell isn't going to do anything for Gael here. It's clear who Diego's loyal to, and it's not Gael.

Luis snaps his fingers again. "Knees."

411

Gael looks around the room, looking at faces that aren't going to help him. This time, Gael doesn't argue. He sinks to his knees, steadying himself with a hand on the carpet that's soiled with alcohol and crushed strawberries. "I didn't mean it," Gael says, looking at me for only half a second before looking at the real threat. "I'm sorry, Luis," Gael says with a nervous laugh.

"What did I tell you to call me?" Luis snaps. "My friends call me Luis. My workers call me Mr. Padilla. My bitches call me daddy." This man is amazing. I'm almost too amused and stunned to be scared of Luis.

Gael blanches. "Ok, Luis. I get it, you're in charge."

Luis steps forward, and Gael arches his back to accommodate the uncomfortable height he's at in relation to Luis' crotch. "You ready to fucking die on this hill?"

Gael locks his jaw, looking at the carpet, letting silence weigh down the room. After a moment of contemplation, he finally mutters what everyone is dying to hear. "I'm sorry, daddy."

I have to bite my lip to try to look serious about this. This moment is just too good. The rest of the room is so quiet you could hear a pin drop. No one really believes what we're watching.

"Fucking look at me when you're being my bitch," Luis barks, grabbing Gael by the graying bun at the top of his head.

Gael looks up, writhing against Luis' hold. "I'm sorry, daddy," he says again through a pained grunt.

Luis releases Gael's hair, nodding at Rogelio. "Now your other daddy."

Gael's face is flushed and pained. "I'm sorry, daddy."

Rogelio nods, amused. "Whenever I need to smile, I'm going to remember this moment." I will too.

"Now the spooky one."

Gael looks with shamed eyes at Diego, starting to tremble. His tone gets even heavier, like he can't bring himself to say it.

412

Diego seems indifferent, but still expectant. "Sorry, daddy," Gael mutters again.

"One more," Luis prompts, elbowing me lightly. "Ask your newest daddy for forgiveness. Let's hear some manners this time, yeah? Say please."

Gael's cold eyes look at me, and he swallows hard. "Please forgive me, daddy."

I look down at Gael with a smug smile. "I appreciate your humility."

Luis laughs, taking a step back. "Humility is a good teacher, but pain is better." Luis sits back down heavily on the end of the couch, legs spread wide. He gestures for Rogelio, Diego, and myself to sit down so we do. Diego returns to my right, with Rogelio sitting on my left.

"Men," Luis calls, snapping his fingers once, and everyone else in the room straightens up. "Give us a show. Let's see what you can teach Gael in the next five minutes."

Gael doesn't get out another word before he's dragged to the back of the room and beaten mercilessly. I watch the man get kicked against the wall, punched, spit on. It's like an offering for us. Everyone in this room understands how the game is played.

Slowly, Rogelio leans over to me, tapping my knee with his own. "And that's why everyone respects the fucking circle."

LILING

A boy. We know for sure now. Randall and I will be new parents to a baby boy. We're going to name him Wuhan. Randall and I are going to wait until after the holiday to tell my parents and not bring that issue up until the new year.

In the meantime, I'm avoiding my parents like the plague of Egypt. I've told my parents my final school year is busier than ever, and I'm not able to make the weekly drive to church and dinner right now. As long as I ensure my parents that I'm making time to visit my own local church on campus, my parents have agreed to the separation. Lishui has sworn herself to secrecy, and will keep her mouth closed while she continues to drive home on Sundays.

Until it's time to bring the family into the joint world Randall and I started, we're going to enjoy our joint world privately.

Randall Persch.

Every day, he's better than before. One honestly wouldn't know he's a drug dealer; his natural disposition is just so charming. He's been in the goofiest, happiest of moods lately. He's constantly asking what I need, what I want.

Looking under our Christmas tree, I can tell Randall is going overboard already. The tree is overflowing with not only presents for myself, but there are already presents labeled *Wu*.

"He won't even be born by Christmas," I point out.

Randall shrugs, sitting on the couch and looking at a report that has something to do with his motel operations. Randall's already making too much money via illegal Padilla operations that even filtering it through the motel doesn't seem feasible. We, Randall, may need to find another business to purchase to offset how much gets funneled through the newly named *Persch Inn*.

"I want to give my son everything the minute he's born," Randall explains.

"And we're already giving him a nickname?" I ask.

"You don't like Wu? I like the sound of it."

I consider it. "It's not bad. But I prefer his full name," I say, pushing a present further under the tree so that it's out of the way.

Looking at the tree we've decorated in red and gold, I think about how this is the last Christmas I will ever have where I'm not a mother. There will never be another year where I'm not helping a child open a present, or worrying about what my kids are doing on their holiday. Even now, even this Christmas, it's different.

"What are you thinking about?" Randall asks, jarring me from my thoughts. He puts the papers on the table that's across from the couch.

I make my way over to him, sitting next to him, leaning against Randall. "I've been doing a lot of thinking about what I'll be doing this time next year."

"We should have a six month old," Randall says warily. "We're going to be tired from parenting and working and running the world."

"Hm," I say with a chuckle. "I don't know what my career will even look like. At the time I graduate, I'll be far too pregnant to get a job. By the time Wu is born and we could consider a daycare, I'll have this big gap in my employment. That, and my Mama would scold me beyond recognition if I did anything to imply that I'd rather not give up my career in pursuit of being a mother.

"Well," Randall starts. "We'll work it out."

"There's nothing to work out," I explain. "I have a different reality now. We... I didn't do things in the order I was supposed to, and now I have to deal with the repercussions of that. It's fitting, I suppose."

Randall stiffens, moving back against the couch so that I have to lift my head to look at him. "Repercussions?" The tone in his voice sets off a little alarm. "Liling, I don't think you should say things like that."

"Why not?" I ask. "I'm not entitled to my feelings?"

"I don't think you should be *feeling* like our son is a punishment, no matter what the circumstances are."

"Well those are the circumstances, Randall," I snap. "He will always be born too soon. He will never be able to come into the world the right way. I have to live with that now."

When Randall removes his arm from my shoulders I know that he's very cross with me now. "But none of that is *his* fault."

"Did I say it was? It's our fault. My fault." I will never forget whose fault it is.

Randall stands and starts pacing. "I just need to make sure you're not bringing that sort of energy around our son. I won't allow it."

I raise a brow at the challenging, combative language. "Would you like to rephrase that?"

"No," he snaps. "I will never allow *my* son to feel like an accident, or like he isn't wanted."

I stand now too, crossing my arms. "Even if he doesn't hear it from us, he'll hear it from my parents. We can't protect him from everything."

"Easy fix," Randall bites. "Your parents? If that's how they'll act? Not allowed around my son."

"Randall," I warn.

"I'm going to protect my son from all of it. From your parents, from my dad, from-" Wisely, he stops himself. He shakes his head, starting to retreat to the bedroom. "Let me cool off."

"Randall," I start to follow him.

Randall sighs and stops at the doorway. "Yeah?"

I feel sheepish now, not really wanting anything other than for him not to be mad at me. "I'm sorry. I'll work on my attitude. Hormones."

Randall laughs softly, kissing my forehead. "If our son gets a fraction of your attitude, God help us all. We'll have to protect the world from *him*."

74.

[RANDALL]

Luis is the only person that ever calls me before seven in the morning. It doesn't matter what time it is, when Luis Padilla calls, you get to the phone. Liling is usually up already, but she's used to seeing me sprint out of the bed when the phone goes off.

Today, Luis is even earlier than normal; it's only six twenty nine in the morning. "You know, Detroit is in the same time zone so these early morning calls really don't make sense," I say groggily.

"Persch, you should be up making me money, anyway."

"Fine, fine. What's going on?"

I don't know why Luis sounds like he's running out of time this early in the morning. "Get a pen."

Luis does this all the time, and I've got a pen and paper waiting. "Go ahead."

Luis starts spewing off numbers and a street name. "It should be about half an hour from you. Get your ass there at ten AM and do what needs to be done. Got it?"

"No, don't got it," I say, capping the pen. "What needs to be done?"

"You'll figure it out when you get there," Luis says like it's an order.

I can usually tell when I'm out of annoying things to say when Luis is at his limit. We're not there yet. "Do I need to bring anything?"

"Look, Boy Scout," There it is, the limit. "Just show up, Ok? I'll follow up with you later. Leave *Diamante* at home." He hangs up.

There's several things of concern here. If I was still in the earlier phases of working with Luis, I'd be scared shitless. I've been around Luis enough to know how he operates. He doesn't send someone somewhere to trap them, he makes a direct house call. If anything, the lack of information is some sort of power move; a test. Luis likes to test his authority.

I decided not to bug Gordy, but I usually like to bring him with me if I don't know what I'm walking into. I can handle my sellers and their issues on my own, but when it comes to a side quest from Luis, I never know what to expect. At the very least, I'm armed now.

I'm not great with directions, but between the map I've got in the glovebox and a general knowledge of the town that Luis gave me, I find the address with ten minutes to spare.

When I arrive at the address Luis gave me and told me to go and "do what needs to be done," I had to double check that I had the right address. It's a jeweler. There's no way to contact Luis, even if I hadn't reached my limit with him for the day, but I can see there's someone waiting outside in a coat. Luis has a way of making people wait on him, so I know I'm in the right place.

It's just before I open the car door that I realize what I've walked into. *You better give the diamond a diamond.* I roll my eyes, even though there's no one here to see it. I know, wherever he is, he's pretty happy with himself.

419

Waiting for me by the door is a man with white-blonde hair pulled into a ponytail. He's got icy blue eyes and thin skin but greets me with a professional smile as he opens a glass door with bars for me. "Mr. Persch, welcome."

Mr. Persch. There's something amusing about it. Ever since I started working with Luis, I'm finally being treated like a real adult.

"Hi, you can call me Randall," I greet, stepping into the store. I find myself in a large jewelry store with dark green carpet, dark gray walls. There's cases of jewelry with blinding lights around the entire room. Behind the cases, there's six employees all spread around the store, waiting.

"You'll have the entire store to yourself today," the man with a ponytail, his name tag reading *Felix*, tells me. "We are Mr. Padilla's personal family jeweler, and we're so pleased to have you here today.

It feels like a dumb question to ask, because I think I know the answer. "What did *Mr. Padilla* tell you specifically about my visit today?"

There's something really performative about Felix that I don't like. The question throws him off. "Mr. Padilla said something about you needing a ring?" He says cautiously.

"Of course he did," I muse. "Well, he's right. I'm in the market for an engagement ring. A good one."

Felix nods enthusiastically, gesturing towards the cases to the right. "We have a large collection of fine jewelry- with the Padilla family discount, of course."

"Perfect," I say, knowing that I've got my work cut out for me. "What ring would be appropriate to give to the smartest, most beautiful, most driven woman in the world?"

420

The ring I found for Liling is magnificent. It's a giant pear-shaped diamond on a gold band surrounded by smaller diamonds bordering the brilliant stone. It costs as much as a house. It's the kind of ring a basketball wife would get after she catches her husband cheating; an apology ring.

In a way, this is an apology ring.

I'm going to propose soon, and we'll have a short engagement. We can get married before our son is born. Sure, that definitely makes whatever we'll have a shotgun wedding, but I think it's what we need.

He will never be able to come into this world the right way.

I'm trying to make sure I bring my son into this world the right way. I'm trying to get this world ready for Wuhan.

I understand the values Liling was raised with. I also understand how important appearances are to her. She's not mad about this pregnancy because she doesn't want to be a mother, or because she doesn't love me. She's mad about how it looks. She's mad because it's not the way she was told it had to be done.

It's not the exact way I wanted to marry this woman, but if entering motherhood as a married woman will make things a little easier for her, then so be it.

Liling's happiness first, always.

∎∎

Liling helps me set my alarm to six o'clock in the morning. I don't understand how to do anything with my new digital clock beyond looking at the time. The morning after I was told by Luis to "figure it out," I dial him up.

Luis has a housekeeper named Gretchen. She answers the phone, sounding sleep deprived herself. "Morning, Gretchen," I say into the phone, keeping quiet because even Liling is still asleep. "It's Randall, is Luis up?"

421

I have my answer when I can hear cussing in the background. "He is now," Gretchen mutters.

"Who the fuck is calling this early? We've got a fucking baby!" There's a shuffling sound of a cord as Luis must be snatching the phone from Gretchen. "Who the fuck is this?"

"Good morning, Luis," I say cheerily into the phone.

"Persch, you're going to eat shit next time I see you."

"Listen, you told me I should be up making you money, and I do as I'm told, so I'm up early today."

"I'll send Rogelio to come get your ass," Luis threatens.

I laugh. "Listen, I just wanted to let you know I'm taking care of it. What needs to be done."

Luis sighs with a growl. "Yeah? You going to take care of your diamond?"

"I'm taking care of it," I promise. "I just wanted to call you during your regular business hours."

Luis gives me a groggy laugh. "Fine, message received loud and fucking clear."

"You still sending Rogelio?"

"No, I'm going to wait until you have a two-week-old baby and then call you at the ass-crack of dawn. You just wait, Persch."

For that, I really can't wait.

LILING

Christmas was lovely. I spent most of it with Randall, who didn't even bother to visit his own family for the holiday. I did visit my own for Christmas service and present opening, but I got out of there as quickly as possible.

I spent the entire portion with my family buried under a massive sweater, feigning a chill and keeping myself buried under a blanket while at home, leaving my coat on while at church.

Christmas was two weeks ago, and now it's finally time to tell my parents what I've done. I'm starting to think I should have done this months ago. Even in the last two weeks, I feel like, even under a massive coat, there's no way to hide my stomach any more. It'll be hard to even have the conversation before my parents see what's happened for themselves.

As Randall drives us, I fiddle with the gargantuan rock on my finger.

Randall Persch has proposed to me.

I said yes.

I didn't even need to think about it. Even if I wasn't pregnant, I still would've been ready. Maybe Wuhan's timing isn't *that* far off.

He proposed on Christmas Day, as if I didn't love the holiday enough. I know why Randall is doing this now; he's doing this for me. Randall isn't as sneaky as he thinks he is. I know, because Randall had already made it abundantly clear, that Randall saw a future with me long before we knew I'd end up pregnant.

Randall has been very clear since the beginning; Liling Persch- that's what he's working toward. It's what I'm working toward as well.

I love that Randall's moved his own timeline for me. I love that I can go to my parents and have some semblance of a plan. I'll marry Randall, we'll have a respectable marriage, and we'll raise a respectable child.

Yes, that's what I'll focus on: my new plan of action. I've made a mistake, but I'm already working to correct it.

In other news, the ring Randall presented me with is spectacular. Looking at this ring lights up my thoughts like a Christmas tree. The pear-shaped diamond sits on my finger like the heaviest promise I've ever made. This is a ring that stops traffic, and I love it. Am I shallow? Perhaps. Do I care? Not when I look at this ring.

"Are you ready for this?" Randall asks, pulling into the quiet neighborhood where my parents live.

Dread. That's all I feel. I know, deep inside, this is going to be one of the worst conversations I will ever have. "I don't think you're ready for this."

"What does that mean?"

"You've never seen Papa when he's mad," I huff.

"We could always start with telling my dad," Randall offers. "He'll probably just call me an idiot and make sure I know he can't help me. It'll be a lot easier."

"We're already here." I fuss, using the mirror of the sun visor to fix my hair and lighten up my lipstick with a napkin. "Let's get this over with."

Mama knows I'm coming, but she doesn't know Randall is coming with me. I can see Mama waiting in the window, and I can see her frown when she realizes it's Randall's car pulling up.

"She looks happy," Randall mutters, putting the car into park.

I'm focused on the extra car that's already in the driveway. I don't recognize the car, but I pray it's not Lhasa's fiancé's car or anything like that. I really don't need the audience here.

When I see Mama running out in her slippers, I instinctively put my arms over my stomach. "What is she doing?" Randall asks.

"I guess I'll find out," I say, unbuckling my seat belt. "Give me a minute." Mama's got her *we need to keep a secret* face. It's bitterly cold outside, but I'm keeping my arms clutched over me more to cover myself than to protect from the chill.

"Mama, what's going on?" I ask, the air already biting at my cheeks.

Mama is impervious to the cold; she's clearly on a mission. "Why did you bring him?"

"I have something important to tell you and Papa," I explain. "I wanted Randall to come with me."

Mama sighs. "This is not good."

"What?"

"We have it arranged! Today!"

I hardly ever like Mama's arrangements. "What's arranged?"

"You want a boyfriend?" Mama asks. "We found you one. Good man. Michael Kang."

I sigh. "Mama, I don't need you to find me a boyfriend." Certainly not now.

"He is here!"

"Mama!" I hiss. "Why-" I almost pull my hands out to angrily gesture at my surroundings but I'm afraid of what Mama will see. "Well, make him leave. I'm not going to date Michael Kang."

"No!" Mama croons. "You can marry Michael. Perfect for you. He is a good man! It's already arranged," Mama insists, starting to count the reasons on her fingers. "He goes to church, has a college degree, very respectful."

"Mama," I plead. "I need to talk to you and Papa."

Mama nods enthusiastically. "Yes! You can talk to us and Michael inside."

"Randall is here, Mama." I gesture with my head to the car.

Mama looks at Randall through the windshield with a frown. "Yes, very awkward. You really should have let us know ahead of time, Liling."

I scowl, walking to the driver's seat with my arms crossed as Mama goes back inside. Randall gets out of the car, crossing his own arms. "What's going on?"

"It's a setup," I grumble.

Randall furrows his brow. "What's a setup?" Randall throws his arm over my shoulder and I let him, even though Mama is likely spying from the window. She's about to know that Randall has put a lot more than his arm on me.

"Well, while we go inside to tell my parents that I'm pregnant, we can also tell my other fiancé, Michael."

Randall frowns at me. "Who the hell is Michael?"

"Language."

Randall rolls his eyes. "Sorry. Who is Michael?"

I shrug. "I don't know, but apparently Mama and Papa have found me a good man to marry. I'm sorry you had to find out this way. I'm sorry I had to find out this way."

Randall sighs, starting to lead me to the door. "This is going to be fun."

Mama is waiting by the door, frowning as I lead Randall into the house. "Good morning, Mrs. Zhu," Randall greets cheerily as he stomps snow off his boots at the rug. Mama responds in something of a grunt.

Papa waits by the stairwell, arms crossed behind him, also frowning. I'm still religiously clutching my stomach while Randall crosses the room to shake his hand. Papa does so begrudgingly.

"Randall," Papa says icily. "We didn't know you were coming."

Randall grins, moving onto the next person in the room: my apparent perfect match, according to Mama. "Hi, I'm Randall." Randall shakes Michael's hand while I survey him from a distance.

Michael Kang might just be one of the most unattractive people I've ever seen. It's almost offensive that *this* is the person my parents settled on. By the way he greets Randall, I can also see he has the personality of a raisin.

Michael is short and plump, with small eyes and big glasses that do him no favors. He has oily black hair parted down the side, raging acne, and a flat pug-like nose.

"Hello, Randall," Michael says. God, Michael has this terribly whiny voice. "I wasn't expecting… I didn't know Liling was bringing…how do you know Liling?"

Randall laughs his charming laugh. I recognize the laugh too late, not ready to intercept Randall acting like Randall. "I'm her fiancé."

My mouth drops open, Mama shrieks, Papa does something of a guffaw. Randall has made this so incredibly awkward.

Michael's mouth also falls open, looking at Papa in confusion. "Oh, I, um-"

Papa's vicious frown snaps in my direction. "What is he talking about?"

Mama is quick to snatch my hand and I feel like I might be sick. My coat covers me- but not enough. Fortunately, Randall has given me the ring to end all rings. Mama looks at the diamond in disbelief, like even she might be willing to consider Randall if *this* is his idea of an engagement ring. "Liling," she whispers, shaking her head.

I blink hard a few times. "I'm happy, Mama." I whisper.

She looks at me with a heavy water line, and I don't know whether she's overcome with emotion of joy or if she's just disappointed. "No, no, Liling." She starts shaking her head and I have my answer. "Not him."

I sigh. "Mama-"

"Maybe I should leave," Michael says awkwardly, already grabbing his coat.

I look at him and nod. "Yes, I'm sorry Michael. But it was nice to meet you." I take one last look at Michael as he says quick goodbyes and I'm thankful for what I have.

Randall Persch. That's what I'm working for.

"We need to talk to Liling alone," My father tells Randall, sounding unhappy. I hear the edge in his voice. I hadn't thought there was a chance the engagement might backfire on us. This was not how I was going to tell them.

Randall looks at me, almost in permission. "I think I'd rather stay here, with Liling."

428

Papa looks at me now with a look that says *fix your mistake.* "We should go sit down," I say.

Only because my back is now turned to my parents, I grab Randall's hand and lead him into the sitting room, heart in my stomach. This level of stress can't possibly be good for my baby.

My baby.

I return my arms over my abdomen as Mama takes her small purple armchair, and Papa sits on the matching chair next to her. There's a little couch in front of the window where Randall takes a seat, but I remain standing. I realize that it doesn't matter how I phrase this, it doesn't matter what plan I present. Either way, this isn't going to go well. I'm going to rip the band aid off.

By that, I mean my coat.

Papa and Mama are looking at me in confusion, wondering why I haven't sat down yet. "What is going on?" Papa asks. He gestures at Randall. "Why bring *him?*"

"Her fiancé." Randall smiles back.

I send him a glare that snatches the smile right off his face. Papa looks at me, waiting for me to correct this statement. "Randall and I are getting married," I state.

"No, you're not." Papa demands.

"I'm an adult, Papa. You can't make this decision for me."

"Liling," Mama touts. "You don't understand-"

I unzip my coat and let it fall off of my shoulders. I've never felt so exposed. I never felt so much loathing for myself as I do now. I've never felt as much shame as I do now that Papa's eyes fall over my growing baby bump.

Mama lets out something of a strangled cry. I don't know what to say, since I don't want to say the obvious. Papa's hard face stares at me like he doesn't know who I am, and maybe I don't know who I am either.

"What have you done?" Papa asks in anguished whisper.

Still looking down, I nervously fidget, pushing hair back behind my ear. "I'm sorry, Papa."

Mama's crying now, and it's the only sound in the room, until Randall starts quickly talking behind me using his problem solving voice. "We're going to be ready," Randall vows, and Papa's stony gaze whips over to my fiancé. "I'm out of the dorms, so I already have a place to live- we already have a place to live."

No one responds to Randall, and my voice seems to have vanished. "And Liling isn't due until after graduation, she can still graduate, we both can. I already have a permanent job-"

"You think you can support a family working as a pizza delivery boy?" Papa asks.

"No, sir," Randall volleys back. "I have a motel, now."

"You work at a motel?"

"No, sir," Randall says patiently. "I *own* a motel." There's a part of me that wants Randall to stop talking about the motel. It makes me worry that perhaps Papa will somehow know how much one might make from owning a small motel- and start piecing things together. The motel itself is not abundantly profitable, despite what we're reporting to the federal government.

Papa leans back in his chair, resting a hand on his knee. "What do you have to say, Liling?"

There's no need to be crying right now, stop it. I have a plan. Focus on how I'm fixing this. "We're going to get married. We can-"

"You have already walked against the faith, what does that matter now?" His voice has elevated, and I know that Papa is about to start yelling.

"I'm sorry." I don't have much more of a plan than what I've already said.

"Sorry?" Repeats Papa, hitting his lap. "You're sorry, Liling? Do you see what you've done?" Mama is still crying.

430

"Papa, I'm going to do everything I can. It-" I'm stuttering. "We'll make things right."

Papa stands now, speaking down to me in the way he does when he is angriest, his voice ringing my ears. "You cannot make this right, Liling. There is no way to right your disgraceful behavior! You have brought so much shame to me and your mother." He slaps his legs again. "We tried to warn you months ago and look- you have defiled yourself!"

Behind me, I feel Randall shoot up. "That's enough." He's got an arm around my shoulder, but I don't feel like I'm fully present anymore.

"And *you,*" Papa spits. "Are you happy now that you've made her stray from her path? You've ruined her!"

"I love her, and she isn't ruined. And you know what? Yes, I'm happy for the path we're on now."

"*Love* does not justify sin," Papa directs, going back to yelling.

Randall raises his voice to match. "And nothing justifies you talking to her like that." There's a silence in the room after Randall's tone carries something of a warning.

I've been frozen for a while now, head bowed against the shame my father is pushing down on me. Mama is quieter now, but she hasn't said anything.

Randall lowers his head, quietly murmuring into my ear. "We should leave."

I stiffen, looking up at my Papa, who stares back at me with hard eyes. I know that he could not possibly be more disappointed in me. I feel Randall's arm, heavy on my shoulders and think *sometimes, Randall knows best.*

I nod. "Let's go." I look at Mama, talking softly, wanting her to say *something* to me. Mama was never a soft woman, but she has an ounce more patience than Papa has. "Mama? Can I call you later?"

It isn't Mama who speaks, but Papa. "No." Papa moves to stand in front of my mother, who looks at him with panicked eyes. "You do not call her. You do not talk to anyone."

"Papa," I reason. I was not planning on finishing this pregnancy without a mother. I've been desperately missing someone to talk to about this period of my life.

"No, Liling. *You* have no home here, anymore. You choose him?" Papa gestures at Randall. "You choose sin? Go live in it then."

LILING

I barely registered Randall pulling me out of my parent's house and getting me into the car. It must have been a fast transaction, as I end up riding in silence with my coat over my lap like a blanket.

I feel stupid, in all honesty. I'm not sure what I expected to happen. I showed up at home to see my very religious parents and announced an unplanned pregnancy outside of a marriage and expected... what did I expect?

Now I don't have a home.

We've driven in silence for the last twenty minutes. I think Randall asked once if I was ok and I didn't answer so he left me alone. The car feels too small to cry in. I hate crying. I absolutely despise that weakness. Randall's seen it before but I'm at a point where I'm too tired to cry. This baby is taking all of my energy, and now it's taken my parents as well.

I shouldn't think like that. *It's not his fault, it's yours.* I pinch my eyes shut and lean into the headrest, trying to get these thoughts out of my head. I'm so, so tired; physically and emotionally, spiritually.

The warmth of the car is lulling me into something close to a sleep, but at some point the drive feels too long, and the car hasn't stopped at a light or a sign in a while. When I open my eyes, I have no idea where we are, or where we're heading.

We're on a long road with sprawling farmland behind us, and we're traveling toward a much more forested path. Ahead of us, we're blanketed by trees on both sides. Randall reduces his speed as the road turns and it looks like perfect deer crossing territory.

"Where are we?" It's starting to snow, but almost none of it has made it through the tree line where it's significantly darker on this road.

Randall takes his eyes off the road to offer a small smile. "I want to show you something."

"Randall, I'm tired."

"I know, and you really deserve a nap. But I want to show you something first."

I bite back the response to ask if it's a Time Machine because I know that Randall is very sensitive about anything that sounds like regret when it comes to the topic of this pregnancy.

"It will make you feel better, I promise," Randall vows, slowing down even more, looking to his left for something. I won't argue the point anymore, because Randall's promises carry a lot of weight with me. I don't think he's ever broken a promise with me.

Randall turns left onto a path cut directly through an even thicker tree line. The path is unpaved, looking like it was only recently cleared. There's deep rivets from other tires in the dirt, but the trail goes deep enough back that I can't see where we're at yet.

I'm about to ask where we are again, but Randall has his little elfish smile on and it catches the words before they leave my lips. At what is apparently the end of the path, we're absolutely nowhere.

The path lets out into a large clearing. Trees have been cut and piles of logs remain, and there's various work equipment and vehicles parked neatly to the right.

"Put your coat back on," Randall tells me, stopping at the end of the path and putting the car into park. "Please," he adds, as an afterthought.

I do as he says, but I'm looking all around for context clues. "Where are we?"

Randall only smiles at me and leaves the car. He's all too happy when he's scheming. I zip my coat once I'm outside, and Randall comes around to meet me.

"Come on," he says, putting his arm around me and leading me toward the clearing. Once we're closer to the clearing, I see there are wooden markers sticking out of the ground, forming a perimeter. In addition to the markers, there's utility flags of various colors pressed into the dirt.

These are zoning markers. Someone is building a house here.

My head whips to Randall who is grinning wolfishly at me. "What do you think? My lips start to form a word, but I stop because I don't want to be wrong. Randall laughs, as if he knows exactly what's catching me. "It's ours, Liling."

I look back at the open space in a stupor. "Ours?"

Randall gestures to the spot in front of us. "I told you I'd build you a house. Didn't I?"

Randall Persch always does what he says he'll do.

Still, I'm not able to wrap my head around this. "This… is… you're building a house?"

"I'm building *you* a house. It's going to be whatever you want it to be." He steps further into the clearing. "How big is Lhasa's house going to be?"

Something about the mention of my older sister triggers the feral part of my brain so that I can start functioning again. "What?" Half-capacity, at least.

"You said you wanted a house bigger than your sister's." Randal spreads his arm out in the expanse. "I'm thinking five bedrooms, at least."

I laugh. "She hasn't bought a house. She's not married yet," I tease lightly.

Randall puts his hands on his hips. "Well, we can always add on to it. I've got what I want out of a house, anyway."

"What did you want out of a house?"

His wolfish grin is back. "Privacy? Remember?" *Every room of the house.*

I should be used to his charm and how he flirts by now, given my condition, but I still need to study the ground to keep from blushing.

"I want a pool, too," Randall continues.

"It's only warm enough to use a pool three months of the year." Sorting through Randall's foolishness is exactly the distraction that I needed.

Randall shrugs. "We'll build an indoor pool, then. It can be inside with big windows, and plants. I like plants."

He's going to keep talking while I think. "We're going to have a home office too." That catches my attention. "Because I was thinking… about what you were worried about- with working and all that. What if you… I'm going to need help, Liling."

"With what?" I ask cautiously.

"Everything." His voice is so honest. "I… I'm going to need someone to tell me I'm doing the right things. You already

436

know I'm running out of ideas on how to run that motel and make it look like the money I'm making from Luis is coming from that. I mean… it's going to need to be a family business. Plus, that way, your career is whatever you want it to be. It's going to be me and you doing things our way."

"You don't think you'd get tired of working with me *and* living with me?" I ask.

"Impossible," Randall says quickly. "I want to wake up every morning next to you, and then walk down to our office where we sit at desks right next to each other every day. In the house we're making."

A house. He's building me a house. The thought has started to sober and calm me. I look at the ground that was cleared at some point earlier in the season, but now is bare dirt that's whitening from falling snow.

"What do you think, Gumdrop?" I have my back turned to Randall so he doesn't see me hide my smile when he uses the stupidest of pet names. I still haven't given him what he wants: my approval.

I turn around, looking to where he stands but something else catches my eye. Not too far from where one of the sticks that outlines the potential home, there's a towering poplar tree, bare of leaves. Gravitating towards the tree, I stare up at this Goliath of nature. It must have been here for decades.

Standing directly under the massive tree, I think I see it; our future. Maybe.

I have a home now.

"What are you doing?" Randall is coming to join me, wondering why I'm lowering myself onto the bare earth to lay on my back. "Please don't have the baby out here."

I position my hair so I'm not laying on it, looking straight up into the tree. "I read a book that said when you're baby proofing

437

a home, you need to get down and try to see what the baby is going to see when they're crawling around."

Randall doesn't even question it, he gets down and lays next to me on the frozen ground. I find Randall's hand. It's cold and wet like mine is, red from the bite of winter. "It got me thinking about trying to see the world that Wuhan is going to see," I say thoughtfully. "He's going to see this." I keep looking up, imagining a warmer day, when the sunlight is being filtered through large green leaves and little yellow flowers of springtime.

"Someday," I say softly. "He's going to come out here and lay under this tree, and this is the sky he's going to see. We'll have the kitchen windows open, and he'll hear you singing while you make under-seasoned chicken."

"I'm using pepper now," Randall mutters. "*And* salt."

"And I'll be watching him from the back porch." I turn my head. "I want a deck in the back," I tell Randall quickly. "And then *I'll* think about the first time I ever saw this place; our home."

We're both looking at each other now, and I can see all the hope there is in the world right in Randall's eyes. It might just be reflecting off my own. "Please just tell me that you like it." Randall says a little desperately before spitting out more words. "If you don't, we can still live somewhere else. We can buy something already built, or -"

Kissing him is the most effective way to quiet him down. We're not all that good at it, because we're both smiling too much but the emotion is there.

We lay under the tree for a while longer, holding hands, even in the cold. Randall's cheeks have gotten rosy, and his cinnamon-stained scent is fleeting in the wind. "I think we should wait to get married."

I instantly sit up, looking down at him with incredulous eyes. "Excuse me?"

Randall has the audacity to laugh, continuing to stay down on the ground. "Hang on, hang on, I mean I don't think we should rush to get married before our baby gets here."

I don't like something with an indefinite time frame. "Don't you think we should be married if we're going to raise this baby together?"

"Eventually, sure," Randall says nonchalantly, shrugging his shoulders into the dirt.

"Eventually?" My voice is accusatory. "What's the benefit of waiting? Do you not want to marry me?"

I could slap him when he laughs at me again. "Of course that's not it."

"Randall."

He finds my hand again, dry from the cold we've been having. "Firstly, when I say wait, I mean just a few months, until we can do everything the right way."

"The right way is getting this done before Wuhan is born," I argue.

Randall shakes his head. "Why? Is our son going to check that our marriage records match up with his birth? How is he going to know the difference between us getting married now versus when he's eight months old? I mean, we'll be living together-here. And he's not going to remember. As far as he'll remember, he'll grow up with two parents here for him. Always." Randall squeezes my hand. "He'll still grow up playing under this tree."

He makes a point but I don't see why we're waiting. "Hm." I feel a little defeated.

"I want to wait so we can plan a proper wedding," Randall says at last, grinning as he changes his line of vision to the swaying branches that click together. "You deserve it all, Liling. I want you to have a great, big, white dress, and we'll have a big cake, a big party, all of it. I don't want to go down to the courthouse to just 'get it done.'"

I'd sort of shelved the idea of a big wedding, or any wedding. "I think it's too late for a white wedding dress."

Now, Randall sits up. "Do you want a white dress?" I shrug, looking away. "Then that's what you'll get. You want a six-tier cake? Done."

"That's way too much cake," I say, now turning so he can't see how silly he is.

"You want a real wedding, I can tell," Randall says, leaning against my shoulder. "So I want to make sure we have time to plan it all."

Only Randall could make delaying a wedding sound like a grand romantic gesture. "So you're not getting cold feet?"

He grins, his breath puffing out in front of us in response. "My feet are actually freezing, but I'll propose to you again right now if it'll make you feel better."

I laugh, pushing him off. I'm cold too, and I'm ready to go find some warmth with the man who is still my fiancé. "Alright, I get it," I say warmly, starting to stand.

He's being playful, grabbing my leg before I can fully get up. "Liling! Gumdrop! Marry me!"

I almost fall right on top of him. "Randall! Let go of me and get off of the ground now, honestly!"

"Say yes!"

"Fine, yes!" I laugh, freeing my ankle.

"Fine, yes." Randall grins, looking up at me. "Gee, I'm going to get that engraved on something. The day Liling said 'fine, yes' for a second time." I roll my eyes at this, my silly Prince Charming.

Whenever I choose to marry Randall, I think ultimately it makes little difference to the scheme of our grand love story, or even to my parents. Even if I had waited, there's a very good chance that my parents never would have accepted Randall. They might have still screamed at me for my choices. I dared to have my own thoughts, my own voice, and take my own actions. Mama and Papa don't like the world Randall and I are making.

Maybe they don't need to be a part of it. This person in front of me is building a world to my exact specifications. He asks for so little in return. Even so, Randall has aspirations of his own. I'll help him with all of that too.

Liling Persch: that's what I'm working toward.

Randall Persch: that's who I'm working for.

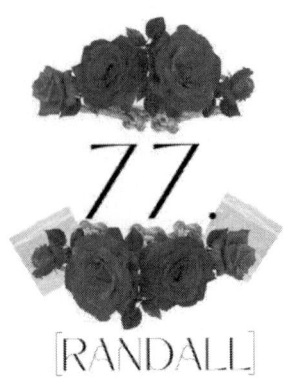

[RANDALL]

I was really close to telling Liling's father to count his fucking days because no one should be able to speak to her the way he did when we told him about the baby. We won't need him.

We waited a week after telling Liling's parents before going to tell my dad. I don't think my dad will be too much of a hassle. He'll probably grumble about how I never think things through but I don't think he's going to kick me out of the family or anything like that.

I'm not too proud to admit my family just barely hovers over the line of white trash. I grew up with my dad after my parents got divorced when I was around twelve. My mom moved to Fort Lauderdale with a boyfriend, then moved to Georgia with a different boyfriend. I think she's still near Savannah, but I don't think she's with the same person she moved there for.

My dad lives in a mobile home that sits on an acre that's out between a cattle farm and some railroad tracks. He loves it out here. I couldn't get this man to live in a residential neighborhood if his life depended on it.

I've got one older brother named Dylan who lives across the street in a new modular home. We get along well enough but

I've felt us growing apart as we get older. Dylan works for the Department of Transportation, working on roads.

"There's always work, it's a guaranteed check." Dylan would argue with me when I said I wanted to go to business school. Dylan is the kind of person that only considers working with your hands real work and everything else is soft pencil-pusher work. He has no idea how dirty I've managed to get my hands in my current line of work.

"I'm not taking any responsibility for anything my dad says," I tell Liling as I drive her to my dad's place.

Liling's got her hand resting on her stomach. We're not going to bother trying to do any sort of reveal, we're just going to show up as is. My dad will know what's going on as soon as Liling steps into the house. "What sort of things are you not taking responsibility for?"

I think about the mystery that is Randall Persch Senior. "He's… you know, he's just…" He's a redneck, that's what he is. "Believes everything he hears unless it's backed by a legitimate data source."

"Hm," Liling says. She's got on her bright red lipstick today, her hair is up in a ponytail with a red scrunchy. "I'm interested to meet the man you're named after."

I laugh. "My older brother won't admit it, but he's pissed about that."

"Don't you normally name the oldest after the father, if you're going to do it?"

"Yes, and there's still time to name our son Randall Persch the third."

Liling is set on Wuhan Persch, first of his name.

The driveway hasn't been plowed so it's good that we're wearing our boots. A train has just passed the house and the ground is still rumbling as we get out of the car. As soon as I'm

443

out of the car, I feel a presence from the other side of the street where my brother lives. Sure enough, I can see Dylan waiting in the window. I flip him off in greeting, knowing he'll be over in the next minute.

"Randall," Liling scolds. I laugh it off, looking forward to seeing my brother. It's sad that Liling doesn't have what I have. My family is far from perfect; we're a bunch of country people that are crazy as hell but we're a good, strong family. We're there for each other.

My dad's never locked the door to his home a day in his life. He sleeps with a rifle next to his bed and would invite the challenge of anyone dumb enough to break in.

Inside is just as I remember it- it smells like cigarettes, it's always sort of stuffy no matter the time of year, and the TV is playing too loudly in the living room.

I help Liling into the house, letting her know she can keep her shoes on. I can tell she's already assessing the place I grew up, noting the grime and the clutter. "Hey, Dad," I call, taking Liling's coat.

My dad's gruff voice sounds from deeper in the house. "Yep, I'm here. Hang on a min'."

Looking at Randall Persch Senior now is a great indicator to what I'm going to look like in nineteen years, if I gain about thirty pounds between now and then and grow an untamed beard. I've grown up my entire life hearing how much I look just like my old man. I'm happy to report that my dad, at his age, still has a full head of hair. The red is starting to get a little sandier as he ages but it's there.

We can hear my dad coming down the hall before he gets here; he's got a real heavy step. My dad darkens the doorway, wearing a red plaid shirt and jeans from when he was ten pounds heavier. My dad's a jolly guy, friendly enough; he just says whatever is on his mind.

As soon as my dad sees Liling, he muses, "Well shit, Randall, what did you do?"

"I'm having a lot of fun at school," I reply, going to give my dad a hug. I can feel Liling's disapproval of my response, making me smile.

"Coulda done all that here for free, son." My dad laughs. "You didn't need to go all that way just to sew your wild oats." I know Liling is mortified.

The women in my hometown are nothing to covet. "Dad, this is Liling. Liling, this is my dad, Randy."

I forgot to warn Liling that my dad's a hugger. He practically scoops up Liling before she can even really say hi. Once he lets her settle back toward me, he says, "Listen, I tried to raise my son with some sense but sometimes he loses it."

I can see Liling trying to calibrate herself to deal with someone like my dad but she's a little more stiff by nature, but she's keeping a smile on her face. I'll jump in for her. "So Dad, there's something I need to tell you."

My dad laughs, putting his hands on his hips. "Gee, I wonder what that is." He starts heading to the small kitchen. "Want a beer, Randall?"

"No, I'm good."

My dad raises a brow to Liling, who quickly shakes her head. "No, thank you."

"Trust me darlin', Randall's mom had a drink or two when she was pregnant with both boys, they turned out fine. Extra toe or two." He laughs. I need to make sure Liling knows I'm not *that* much like my dad when we're on our way back.

Dylan's made it across the street, and he's letting himself in, wearing almost an identical outfit to my dad's but in green.

445

Dylan's a little shorter than I am by an inch or so, but his hair never got any of the red I got from my dad. Dylan's got the same facial features from a pointed nose, small ears, and blue eyes but he's got a harder face from lots of time spent in the sun and lots of cigarettes smoked.

Liling turns to see the new entrant in the room, and Dylan's eyes grow wide. Dylan shakes his head and looks at me. "Randall, you dumbass."

"Ah, shut up," I reply. "Dylan, this is Liling, Liling this is Dylan."

Dylan is a lot more polite when it comes to Liling, and he comes over to give her a lighter hug. "I'm sorry you're stuck with my idiot brother now."

"I'm sorry you had to meet my idiot brother." I shoot back before Liling can answer.

Telling my dad and my brother what I've got coming up is a lot easier conversation than with Liling's parents. I maybe got a four second "Welcome to the real world, being a parent ain't easy" speech.

Liling's a little quiet while me and my family catch up. I don't think she knows how to relate with them. Eventually, after we've talked about Dylan's job, and my dad's job, and the Spartan's football season, my dad tries to get Liling to talk.

"So, Darlin'." Everyone, myself included, seems to love giving Liling a nickname. "Where you from?"

Damnit, Dad.

Liling is still trying to be polite. "I grew up in Dewitt, just twenty minutes from campus."

My dad nods, "Oh, really? What about your parents then?"

"Dad," I say. My dad is one of those types who's wary about too much immigration and its effects on the American

446

unemployment rate. Never mind that Liling's dad is a doctor and I'm pretty sure Liling's dad and my dad wouldn't be in the same prospective talent pool anyways.

"My dad was raised in California," Liling offers graciously. "Mama has lived here her entire life."

I send Dylan a look, begging him to bring up literally any other topic. "So where's all that money coming from, Randall?" my brother asks.

Any topic except for that.

"What do you mean?"

Dylan nods toward Liling. "That big rock on her finger? Damn near blinded me when I walked in this joint."

"I'm a business owner," I say proudly. Even though it's a front for drug laundering, I'm still really proud of it. I'm scoping out buying a seasonal ice-cream place too, but now's not the time to bring that up.

"Business owner?" Dylan asks. "Who the hell would sell you their business? Scratch that- where did you get *that* money to buy it in the first place?"

"Little hard work gets you a long way," my dad offers. My dad never looks at anything too closely unless it's a lotto ticket.

"And I've been saving a lot since I started school."

"It was in need of repairs, a lot of them," Liling jumps in. "The family really wanted to get rid of it. Now, Randall's fixed it up, and it's a respectable little establishment." I know Liling's proud of me, and it really drives me.

Dylan blinks, then looks at me. "She talks real fancy, Randall. Do you even know what she's saying when she speaks to you?"

I'm ready to fire off something mildly suggestive about how well I understand Liling but she knows me so well. She's

447

already sending me murderous threats telepathically, so I decide to say, "It's called an education."

Dylan rolls his eyes and we move on. I thought he was ready to move past it, until he catches me just before Liling and I are ready to leave. Liling waits in the car for me, letting it heat up while I stand on the deck with Dylan. "So tell me," Dylan says, looking at his own house across the street. "Where you're really getting your money from."

I sigh, annoyed. "Why don't you think I can work hard?"

"It's not that, Randall. It's that I saw that ring your girlfriend's wearing from a mile away and I can't even imagine how much that cost." He shakes his head. "I spent almost eight hundred on Judy's ring and it's a quarter of the size of what your girl's got."

"I wanted her to have something nice."

"And you've got a baby on the way, and you're not even worried about how you're going to afford it?"

"I've got a job."

"You own a business."

"Yeah, I own a business."

"Which you bought with what money?" Dylan fusses. "Randall, I know you. You're like me, who's like dad. Shit broke. People like us don't get out of that category unless they're up to some shit."

I see Liling's eyes meet me through the windshield after hearing Dylan raise his voice. "What are you asking?"

Dylan sighs, meeting me with a wary look. "I just want to make sure my idiot little brother isn't getting himself into something he can't get out of."

I calm myself down, jostling Dylan's shoulder. "I appreciate you looking out for me, but I'm fine. I've got a lot of people looking out for me, as it turns out." Big people. Scary people.

"Are you in a gang or something?" *Yes.*

"Of course not."

Dylan's tone lifts in amusement, ready to move on. "You knocking off people at school?" *Yes.*

"Not yet." *This year.*

Shaking his head, Dylan finally says, "It must be quite the motel."

"We've got centralized air now."

"And she must be quite the woman," Dylan sighs.

I grin, looking at my future wife. "She is. She really is."

78.

[RANDALL]

Today is going to be a long, long day. Liling and I are spending our Sunday morning in a large Catholic church with climbing pointed spires and gothic architecture for Rafael Padilla's christening. Afterward, Liling is going to her sister's bridal shower.

This time round, I recognize most of the crowd that have come to celebrate Luis and Blanca's first son. Everyone has come to pay their respects to their family, and as I walk with Liling to find a space to sit, many are even stopping to pay their respects to me. Some people have even started to pick up on the influence that Liling holds and are spending more of their breath trying to stay in her good graces as well.

Liling is officially in "very pregnant" territory. She's huge. In less than two months, we're going to be parents. The thought has me staring at little Rafael from afar, interest renewed in the concept of what a baby really is.

As far as the christening actually goes, I don't think I've been in the religion long enough to understand what's actually happening. There was a lot of prayer, a sermon I didn't understand, and they poured water on a baby and now he won't go to hell. Liling doesn't care for my description of the service.

Afterward, there's a picnic in a nearby park. It's mid-spring now, and we've all been given a perfect day to spend outside. People have brought their families, and I'm surprised to learn that Rogelio is actually a married man with a three year old and a nine month old.

Liling has found herself seated in the shade with Blanca and Carmen, Rogelio's wife. I'm standing by Rogelio, who's manning a charcoal grill.

"All this time, and I didn't even know you had a family," I say, looking at Carmen pull herself up from a table to go chase a toddler on the run.

Rogelio smirks. "Of course, I have a family."

"You've never brought it up," I defend. "And you don't wear a ring."

Rogelio puts a brat on a plate, handing it off to someone. "If something ever goes south with someone and they're looking to hurt me, they see that ring and they know I got someone."

I take a drink from my beer, checking to make sure Liling doesn't need anything. "I don't know who would look at you and want to try something."

Rogelio laughs, prodding the underside of a burger to check its cooking progress. "Yeah? What about you? You enjoying walking on air now, Mr. Inner Circle?"

I actually am. One drug lord says I'm part of the in-crowd, and people really start treating me like it. "Everyone's being nice to me this time, at least."

Rogelio laughs again. "No, shit. Word went around fast after Gael. You got a reputation now."

"A reputation for what?" In all honesty, I only hit the guy once.

"People know if they mess with the Boy Scout, they're going to get whooped." Rogelio puts another brat on a plate. "Don't get drunk on that power."

"You and Diego will keep me humble."

"You know Luis will," Rogelio drawls with a smile.

From across the grass, I pick out Diego looking a little out of place. He's standing by Luis, wearing his oversized coat. I wonder how heavily armed he was at the church. "What about Diego? Does he have a family?"

Rogelio lowers his voice slightly and wipes his brow. "Diego? He's quiet about his life." I just stare back at Rogelio, since it's not much of an answer. It looks like Rogelio is considering how inner circle I really am. "Look by the trash cans, guy in the peach shirt and jeans."

I look for the person Ro is talking about. A little separated from the rest of the party, talking to a small group of people is a person of medium height with shiny black hair in a short ponytail wearing a peach shirt. He's got a thin mustache and a tattoo going up his right arm. I'll add him to the list of people that could probably kill me fairly easily. "Who is that?"

"That's Gabriel," Rogelio says cautiously. "They're quiet about it. Only me and Luis and the wives really know." It's like Rogelio is trying to only give me bits and pieces, hoping I put everything together. "Luis don't really care, but-" Rogelio gestures to the general crowd with his spatula. "Not the most progressive group."

I nod mutely. Diego is the most secretive of the group by far. Diego doesn't seem like the kind of person to hold any relationship. I can't imagine him talking enough to get one. "I'm glad he has someone."

Rogelio lightens up. "Don't get mushy on me, Boy Scout." His smile gets bigger as he sees Luis is on his way over with the star of the show in his arms.

"Hey, Boy Scout!" Luis is wearing a maroon colored polo with a little floral emblem on his chest over cream colored pants. He's got on black shades and a grin. "You ready to join the club in a month?"

Before waiting for an answer, Luis is shoving his baby into my arms. "Don't drop him," Luis orders.

I carefully take Rafael, supporting his head until I transition him over my shoulder. "I've never been so scared in my life." Both men laugh, but I'm now too focused on what I'm holding.

Rafael, as far as babies go, is a clone of Luis. This is a tiny human- so small, so weird. I'm thankful he doesn't cry as soon as I've got him and he seems more confused than anything else.

"I'm excited but I'm worried I'm going to screw this up," I say.

"Don't," Rogelio says. "All you gotta do is be there and be in their corner. Easy as that. And don't give 'em no juice after five o'clock."

"And don't leave the house with any less than three backup outfits," Luis adds, having less experience. Rogelio nods in agreement. Luis is like me, he's always checking on his partner. Blanca, dressed in a yellow dress with tights and a jean jacket, is talking to Liling. From here, I can tell Liling is uncomfortable and hot.

"I think we've got a good thing going here," Luis says to no one in particular. "With our families."

"Life is good," Rogelio agrees.

"Yeah, life is good," Luis repeats, watching me reposition.

453

Looking around, life really is good. It's great. It's not what I thought I'd have when I started school, but my life changed the day I saw Liling. My life changed the day Rogelio pointed a gun at my head.

Looking at the small life in my arms, I can't wait until I'm holding my own son. We're going to have our own house, our own life, everything we could ever want.

LILING

I hate everything about my body right now. I hate how much it aches, I hate how it sweats, smells, and moves. I used to have a nice body, with nice curves and smooth skin. Now the space between my curves is filled with baby fat and my skin is blotchy and oily and dry all at the same time.

I enjoyed my time at the christening; Blanca and Carmen seem more like my sort of people. They're smart, refined, and they're ambitious. They understand *all* aspects of what it takes to rear a successful and healthy family. They feel like someone I could lean on, talk to. It's what I need right now: women. Not Natalia or Ginger, they're still girls.

By the time we drive back from Detroit, I take off my dress to take a nap in one of Randall's t-shirts and get up an hour and a half later to redress, fix my makeup, and drive myself to Lhasa's bridal shower.

Since speaking to my parents in January, I've had minimal contact with them. I haven't seen Papa in months. Mama, I've seen only once. She came to my dorm to tell me Papa just needs time and to make sure I'm drinking water.

Mama's lost some of her strength in my eyes, after this whole ordeal. Mama clearly wants to take over this pregnancy and tell me all the things I should be doing, she can't help herself. She wants to be there, but she won't, because Papa said no.

Because Papa said no.

I will never let a man tell me what to do, especially when it's important. I'm stronger than Mama.

I don't go to church with my family once a month anymore. Lishui, I see regularly, since she's on campus. Lishui keeps me informed on what's going on in the family I don't feel like I'm a part of any longer.

Lhasa has driven up once to see me, shortly after I cemented my place as least favorite daughter and family disappointment. Lhasa is concerned in the most condescending, preachy way she could be. It brought me a little spark of joy to see her eyes change when I informed her Randall and I have a house being built as we speak.

I refuse to be pitied any longer.

The rest of the day will be about Lhasa. Beautiful, perfect Lhasa. I'm a bridesmaid, so my attendance is expected. I'm looking forward to seeing both my sisters, even if I'm going to spend it in the shadows. Plus, I miss my mama.

Lhasa's bridal shower is in the communion hall of our family church. When I pull into a parking spot, I smile a little smile when I see Mama waiting for me at the doors. She's wearing a purple short sleeved shirt and jeans. I'm jittery- knowing what I'm walking into. I'm sure everyone knows I'm pregnant even though I shouldn't be and I'm about to walk in being *very* pregnant. No one could possibly miss me.

Mama starts walking toward me, away from the church. I missed my Mama so much, but I didn't realize it until she's within arm's reach. "Mama! Hi!"

"Liling, hello!" Mama hugs me back, but her voice is gentler than it usually is. She almost lets her eyes pop out of her

456

head when she sees how massive I am. "Liling," she says in a little whisper, putting her hand on my stomach. As if sensing her presence, my son has started moving around inside. Mama smiles warmly, shifting her hand.

"I'm not late, am I?" I ask, taking my present for Lhasa out of the open car door.

Mama shakes her head. "No, no. Not late."

Something is wrong. "Alright, good. It will be good to see everyone."

"Liling." I think I've been uninvited to this bridal shower. "We think… maybe it's best you just see Lhasa later? She can come visit you."

"Later?" I ask, already hearing my own voice become unsteady. "What does that mean, later? This is her bridal shower. I'm a bridesmaid, I should be there."

The look mama gives me says I might not even be a bridesmaid anymore. "Liling." Her voice is between a coo and a scold. "This is best for the family."

"How?"

She's just repeating what Papa's told her. "It's just… not proper." She shakes her head, gesturing to my large stomach. "We need to keep this to the family, until we fix this."

"Am I a secret, Mama?"

She shakes her head profusely. "No! No, it's just-"

"Is this Lhasa's idea or Papa's?" I ask. "This is Lhasa's day."

"Don't be difficult, Liling," Mama dismisses, sounding more like herself.

"Difficult?" I can show her difficult. "Mama, how long is this supposed to last- me not being a part of the family? How long are you going to punish me for Randall?"

It's only when I notice there's a few people hanging around the doors that I suddenly feel sad and tired and embarrassed. "You know what, Mama? Fine." I shove my present into her arms. "I *will* be at the wedding, and I *will* be bringing Randall." I whip my door open.

"Liling," Mama scolds.

I'm not afraid of this woman anymore. I'm not afraid of Papa either. Neither of them have the spine to do half of the things Randall and I have already done for our little family. "Mama," I say through gritted teeth, sitting back down in my car. "You better think long and hard about how you want to act the next time you see me."

Mama's little eyes widen. "What are you talking about?"

"You need to think about whether you *ever* want any access to this child." I point at my stomach. "This will always be your first grandchild. I didn't want to raise him without grandparents."

I think I see just a hint of desperation in Mama's eyes. I love it. I'm controlling things now, even if I'm leaving. "Your father just needs time."

"Does Papa need time? Or do you?" I ask, huffing as I slam my car door. Mama is still standing by the car when I roll my window down and inform her, "We're having a boy, and we're naming him Wuhan."

LILING

Today is the day I've been working toward for years. I just want to get it over with. It's not what I thought my graduation day would be like. I don't even know that I'm happy it's here.

Looking in the mirror, I look at the version of Liling I was never expecting. This Liling is wearing a silken green graduation gown with a matching cap. My hair has been straightened and smooth, my makeup done in a natural color palette. None of the things I'm wearing disguises how heavily pregnant I am, or how much the gown struggles to stretch over my stomach.

I hate thinking about how many people will see me cross the stage like this today. I've given everyone a timeline of exactly when I *wasn't* focused on school.

I did all the things Randall said I would do. I stayed in school, finished my classes, and am graduating with honors. Still, today doesn't feel like a victory. Even if it was, the people who set me on this path, the people I most wanted to see my accomplishments, will not be there.

"I wish you had come just a little bit later," I whisper, petting my stomach. I'm trying to not think regretful thoughts when I think about my pregnancy, but it's hard sometimes. Right now is one of those times.

"What are you telling our son?" Randall calls from the bathroom, where the open door is leaking steam from a recent shower.

I smirk to myself, going to find the white flats I'll be wearing. "What makes you think I'm talking to Wuhan right now?"

"Because you whisper when you're talking to him. Like you're already conspiring."

This makes me chuckle. I like the idea of having that sort of closeness with my future child. I never had that sort of relationship with either of my parents. Hopefully, I can be better. I really need to be better.

**

When I watch Randall cross the stage in his white cap and gown, I can't help but feel so proud of this man. This charming, beautiful man. This man that is all mine. Randall's dad, brother, sister-in-law, and his grandmother have come to watch him walk. Even his mother drove from out of state to watch her son graduate. Randall has warned me that going to dinner with all of them is going to be an absolute circus.

Of course, my name will be called last amongst the business graduates. I am what stands in the way of everybody getting to leave. The ceremony has gone on for hours. Some families, and even some students have snuck out, not wanting to wait for the entire alphabet of graduates to be run through.

As the person before me walks the stage, and I'm at the edge of the parapet, I scan the crowd looking for *my* faces. Randall is there with other students, of course. I can tell he's getting ready to put on a one man show. He knows I'm feeling disheartened today, and he's trying to single-handedly fix it with a smile for me.

Hopefully, I look beyond empty seats and people already milling toward the exit. One person. I have one person out there; Lishui, sitting alone. She waves happily at me, and I flitter my fingers back at her, grateful for my little sister. For as long as I live, I will never forget who was here for me, and who was not.

Mama did not come, and neither did Papa. Lhasa is not here either. My parents aren't here to see me earn this diploma, or to congratulate me on completing this trial.

Liling Zhu.

My name is called, and there's unenthusiastic clapping while Randall drowns all of them out with excessive cheering and hollering. It's enough to pull my face into an embarrassed smile as I make my way toward the dean.

Just a split second after Randall starts his cheerleading act, there's a loud eruption of applause and yawping and pounding of feet. My cheeks warming even more, I try to focus as the dean tiredly shakes my hand with a thin smile. "Congratulations."

We shake hands, a camera, likely from Randall, flashes, and I finish crossing the stage, scanning the crowd to see where my apparent fan club is. Even before I find the group of men in the back of the audience, I know who it is when I hear, "*Ey, Diamante!*" Rolling over the audience.

Luis and Blanca, Rogelio and Carmen, Diego and Gabriel, Carlos, and Jorge are all here. They're all here for me. Randall looks absolutely delighted, and he's ready to meet me with open arms as soon as I descend the stage.

The dean of the business college is making his closing remarks while Randall holds me closely. "You did it, Liling," he whispers in my ear as we're showered with caps that are being thrown in the air, raining back down on us as the room cheers that we are finally done with our degrees.

I'm done with regrets and feeling bad for myself. I'm done missing the people that aren't here. If they don't want a part in my life, then I'm done holding a place for them. All the people here that are *truly* in my corner are here today. Randall. Lishui. Luis and his men.

Today *is* a big day for me. Today marks an accomplishment. It's the end of one era and the beginning of another. Randall tells me that we can hang out degrees above our desks in our shared office. I like the thought; thinking of the house we're building in a quiet forest, nestled under a poplar tree.

Again, I have the feeling. This is love. Right now, the feeling of love is Randall's sweaty hand clasping my own while shimmering white and green gaps rain down on us. It's the sound of Luis and Rogelio hollering behind us, with Lishui's loving presence in the room.

As always, where Randall Persch is, that's where I'm able to feel the warmth of unconditional love.

81.

[RANDALL]

There are a lot of reasons to go to a wedding, but Liling is going out of spite. I'm a little nervous for anyone that dares cross her path today. I'm scared for myself. I'm planning on being on my best behavior all day today. Yes, Liling. No, Liling. Whatever you say, Liling.

Today is a performance piece, and everything I do is being coordinated by her. I love watching her in action. Liling had me go out and buy a new suit, she did my hair for me, and now I'm shining my shoes.

And Liling? I'm sure, somewhere out there, there are people with a fetish for heavily pregnant women... I think I'm in that group when I see Liling ready to go. She's. So. Hot. She's so pretty when she's angry, beautiful when she's cruel.

Liling's got a dark red dress on, made of a shimmery material. It reminds me of what Blanca wore at the party, and I wonder if it's intentional or not. It's more conservative than what Luis' wife wore, but Liling has a beauty that doesn't need any tricks.

I'm going to be on my best behavior, but the idea of punching Liling's father has been on the back burner since we

463

revealed the pregnancy. The wedding is at the church Liling's family has been going to for most of their lives. It's a small, outdated church. There's nothing impressive about it; no grand architecture, no stained windows. It looks like a converted town hall.

Liling is arriving as a guest, not part of the wedding party. We're at about thirty minutes before it starts. Arm in arm, we walk toward the door, heading toward where there are ushers helping to get people seated. I'm relieved Liling's father isn't waiting at the door, ready to intercept.

Within five minutes of being inside, any image Liling's parents might have been trying to preserve is over. Liling's hard to miss. She's said hi to aunts and uncles and cousins. She's introduced me to all of them as her fiancé, proudly.

I couldn't have dreamed about this day even a year ago. I could not have dreamt of Liling happily in my arms, promised to me forever, and carrying my child.

It's when we have less than ten minutes until the wedding and we're seated talking to Liling's great aunt that I get the first glimpse of her father, buzzing around the church. The look that settles over his face when he sees us is nothing short of a death threat, but I invite the challenge. I tap Liling's thigh, alerting her that Mr. Zhu is on his way over.

Mr. Zhu comes over, face set in a hard frown. He discreetly slides next to Liling. "What are you doing here?" He whispers fiercely. He'd better watch his tone.

"It's my sister's wedding," Liling replies coolly, stroking her stomach. I need to find a back room with this woman.

Mr. Zhu checks the room to make sure the conversation is as private as it can be. "I thought your mother talked to you."

"Yes, she did," Liling purred. "I decided not to listen."

"Liling," Mr. Zhu growled. "You are to leave-"

"Hi, Mr. Zhu." I smile, popping my head around Liling. "Nice to see you again." Mr. Zhu looks at me like I'm a flea. I'm ready to be the bad guy here, if only to save Liling the stress of arguing with her father. She doesn't mind letting me take control as long as I go in the direction she wants me to.

"Let me save you some time," I say. "We're going to sit here and enjoy the wedding. We're not going to argue. You're not going to raise your voice at Liling again, or we're going to have a big problem." Liling flicks my leg. The last line might've been too far.

"*You* are not a part of this family," Mr. Zhu hisses, pointing a finger.

"We're about to be in-laws." I smile.

He's such an old, angry man. "You need to leave now."

"Papa-"

"Or what?" If this man thinks because we're in a church I won't beat his ass while his family watches... I lean over Liling. "Tell me what you're going to do about it?" Liling flicks me again, her arm pressing back on mine. I did tell her I was going to be on my best behavior.

Mr. Zhu scoffs. "Do not act as though I should be afraid of you, boy. I fear my God, and my God only." If it weren't Liling's religion, I would have rolled my eyes.

"That's good to know," I say. Liling takes my hand like she knows I'm bordering on lashing out. I'm not going to, though. "The Lord show compassion to those who fear him." I've been reading up, though. Armed and ready. "It's in that verse about how fathers are to nurse their children, isn't it?"

Both Liling and Mr. Zhu are at a loss for words. That's right, I can read. He turns his attention to Liling and gives her a look that says *control him.* The brewing storm is dispersed just before it can really take off. Dressed in a yellow bridesmaid dress,

Lishui skitters up the row and crouches in front of Liling, giving her a hug that looks like it's meant to separate their father from Liling.

"Hi!" Lishui whispers, knowing we've caught the attention of many of the wedding guests.

Liling seems a little overwhelmed now. "Hi, Lish."

"Can you come back in the bridal room?" Lishui whispers. Mr. Zhu's face raises in annoyance. "*Lhasa* wants you."

It doesn't make sense to me either, given what I've heard about the oldest. "Lhasa wants me?"

Lishui nods, already trying to pull her sister. "Come on." Lishui looks at me quickly. "Hi Randall," she whispers.

I have no problems with Liling's younger sister. "Hi Lishui."

"Lishui-" Mr. Zhu's caries the threatened scold of a man that's trying to control his family. I never use that voice.

"Papa, you should get into place," Lishui says, trying to pull Liling up, which takes extra effort given Liling's condition. Liling awkwardly squeezes past her father, leaving me and him in a pew together.

This leaves Mr. Zhu to frown at me longer. I wish I could tell him about the last person that started something with me. Scratch that, Luis can't be used to solve *all* my problems.

"Don't you need to be up there?" I ask Liling's father as a pianist gets into place to start playing music meant to start getting people in their seats.

He's not too happy about it, but I think he's made as much of a scene as he's going to for the minute. "We'll discuss this later, from one man to another."

"We will if you can be respectful," I reply. He scowls, leaving me alone in the pew. I think I'm about to be infamous amongst Liling's family too.

LILING

It's not until I'm in the Sunday school room that's been converted to a bridal suite that I fully believe that my older sister actually wanted to see me. In the small room, all of the chatter immediately ceases. There's two other bridesmaids - Lhasa's friends - Mama, who looks afraid of me, and Lhasa.

Seeing Lhasa in a wedding gown makes me selfishly realize how much I want to see myself in a wedding gown. I want to see Randall waiting for me, telling me he will always be waiting for me. Maybe I'm ok with waiting, if this is what I'm waiting for.

Lhasa, in a beautiful, albeit stiff wedding dress, looks at me in the reflection of a mirror. The dress fabric reaches all the way up her neck, brushing under her chin, long lacy sleeves fully cover her arms in white, glimmering threads.

"Hi, Liling." She turns in her chair, biting her lip. "Can we have the room?" Lhasa says to no one in particular. Lhasa's bridesmaids make a quick exit. Mama seems confused whether this is meant for her too. "Mama, can I just talk to Liling for a minute?"

Mama's little face falls, but Lishui is there to convince her to give us a minute. When it's just the two of us, Lhasa immediately slumps in her dress, letting out a breath. "God, Liling your pregnancy is really inconvenient for me."

"Excuse me?" This is why no one likes Lhasa.

"You were supposed to help me plan all of this," Lhasa says with a softer tone. "It's been a wreck without you." I do like hearing that.

"Papa basically disowned me," I say bitterly.

"I know." Lhasa turns back toward the mirror. "None of us know what to do about that."

"You all did nothing."

Lhasa looks at herself in the mirror again, fixing eyeliner that's bleeding at the corner of her eyes. "What do you want? A rebellion?"

"That's how freedom is won," I say, the silence dragging on. I want to continue to be angry and petty, and point out that nobody, save for Lishui, came to my graduation. I had a cartel cheering me on, but not my own parents.

"I'm about to be free of Papa, what's the point in making him angry now?"

I have so much more than freedom now. I have control. "The point would have been for me to feel like my entire family doesn't hate me for doing something for myself."

I flinch internally, I should not say things my sister can use against me. Lhasa decides to be somewhat gentle. She's very similar to Mama, when she wants to move on. In the mirror, her eyes point to my stomach. "You're huge."

I give her the most condescending of smiles. "It's the price that comes with the blessing of motherhood. You'll understand someday."

Lhasa rolls her eyes. "Is it terrible?" She asks quietly.

"What? Being pregnant?"

"I'm scared of being pregnant," Lhasa confesses, using a tweezer on her right brow. "Is it just awful?"

"Awful…" I repeat wistfully, rolling my fingers over my stomach. "It's… painful and uncomfortable. I'm always tired, I'm always hungry." I have this little feeling, just as my little boy kicks inside of me, that he's listening to me, and what I say is important. "But I've also never been happier. Because of him."

Lhasa lets a rare smile grow. "Mama says you're naming him Wuhan. I love it."

"Mama talks about me?" I peep.

"Mama wants to be excited. She wants to help," Lhasa confides, turning toward me on her stool. "She has a secret stash. Things she's going to give you. She's got a list, this notebook of all the things she's going to tell you once Papa gives her permission."

Once Papa gives her permission.

"Lhasa," I say. "I know I'm not married, but can I give you some relationship advice anyway?"

Lhasa smirks dramatically. "What advice could you give me?"

"Never," I say seriously, brow raised. "Ever, ask a man permission to do anything."

Lhasa laughs at this, swiping her tooth when she sees a lipstick stain in the mirror. "You're supposed to listen to your husband," Lhasa chides.

"Then, it's a good thing I don't have one."

"Liling!" She says with a giggle. "That's the problem."

We both laugh at that. "So I'm guessing you run the show with that boyfriend of yours?"

"Fiancé," I correct with authority. "And yes. And if- what's his name again?"

She's less amused now. "Frank."

469

Not Robert? Still? "Frank, fine. Well, if Frank." I grab her hand, giving her a look known to stop the weak in their tracks. "If Frank *ever* steps out of line, in the way Papa sometimes does, you let me know."

Lhasa stiffens. "Frank is gentler."

"Good," I say releasing her hand. "Because I think I've realized something."

Lhasa stands and straightens her dress. "Yes? What does the ever-wise Liling realize now?"

I check my own complexion in the mirror, loving the darker makeup palette I've elected to wear today. It makes me look something of a sorceress, and I think it's fitting. "*Nothing scares a weak man more than a strong woman.*"

■■

I inspired Lhasa, in some way. Uncaring that I didn't match the rest of her wedding party, she made sure I was up with the rest of the bridesmaids during the wedding. I was in the family pictures, I was in the conversations, and I did not waste a single breath on Papa the entire night.

Randall is too charming, and no one wants to listen to Papa's protest when Randall is just so darn friendly. Everyone. Loves. Randall. He's even won Mama over. Just as Lhasa told me, Mama, now that Papa has resigned himself to the corner, has told me she wants to come deliver clothes and her notes she's written for me. She wants to know if it's too late to have a baby shower.

I do believe I'm back in the family now, via hostile takeover. I genuinely think Papa does not know how to react when someone tells him no.

Who knew overthrowing the head of the family would be so easy? I'm in charge now.

■■

When the festivities are over and I'm in something of a buzz from the thrill of overthrowing a dictator, I decide to play with my little Prince Charming as he drives us away from the church. "Randall?"

"Yeah?" Randall flicks his high beams off as he drives, cracking open the windows as the car starts to get a little too stuffy. Randall runs hot.

"A long time ago, you told me that if I asked for something, you'd make sure it happens," I say in my sweetest, most seductive voice.

Randall thinks I'm going to ask for something serious, so he responds quickly. "What do you need?"

I want to see my future again. "Take me home."

Randall's quiet, thinking. "Home? Isn't that where we're-"

"*Our* home."

I can only see his grin as the streetlights swipe over his face. "It's a little cool, don't you think? And it's dark. There could be animals and-" He stops himself abruptly. "I've got a blanket in my trunk."

Half an hour later, we're laying in the chill of the night, basking in the white light of Randall's headlights under the poplar tree. "It's so quiet out here," Randall whispers. Around us, there's the sound of locusts and frogs and in the distance, something is romping in the trees.

Our arms are intertwined, and Randall's been slowly rubbing my leg, my feet are curling against his ankles. This last month has been terrible. My hormones have been driving me toward nothing but sinful thoughts. Randall moves, even so much as tussles his hair, I'm clenching my thighs. Randall's arm touches me, I need to distance myself. Randall so much as says my name in the right tone, I'm reminding myself that I'm already pregnant.

471

I'm *already* pregnant.

"Randall."

"You really can't use that voice with me right now, Liling." Somehow, he's already at my neck. "I'm a man on the edge."

I'm going to make it very hard for him, then. He needs little encouragement to kiss me back, to let his shirt ride up, to give me more than ten seconds. Good and bad.

83.

[RANDALL]

I can't believe we fucking did that.

I love her so much.

Liling.

84.

[RANDALL]

The shower is running, and I'm just about to get in when Liling pops her head into the bathroom. "Randall?"

She starts going through a blush, like she knows what I'm going to say. "Should I fill the tub up?"

She's not in the mood for it. "Luis is on the phone."

He's at least waited until seven. I thought I was safe this morning. "Fine, hang on a minute," I sigh, shutting the water off while Liling goes to grab the phone.

Once I've wrapped a towel around my waist, I go to the kitchen to where Liling is chatting on the phone. She announces my arrival before handing me the phone. "Hi."

"Persch." Luis has his all-business tone. His unhappy tone. His *I need somebody dead tone.* "Come down to the house. We've got work to do."

When Luis uses the word *we,* he usually means it. When Luis feels the need to step in personally, something's going on. Whatever it is, the whole cartel will know about it in the next day, when Luis makes whatever example he's made known. "What's going on?"

I should know by now that Luis hates questions when he's in a mood. "Damn it, Boy Scout."

"It's a fair question. I like to know what I'm walking into." Luis is cussing me out over the phone but my eyes are drawn to Liling, who's on the other side of the living room. She's standing at a weird angle, slightly bent forward, hands on her hips, looking somewhere between pain and focus on her face.

I interrupt Luis, because he's not really telling me anything of use. "How long do you think this will take?"

"Randall, you know you're the only one stupid enough to argue with me?"

"I'm not arguing, I'm asking questions you're choosing not to answer."

"I'll send Rogelio-" Luis is cussing in Spanish now, so I put the phone on my shoulder. I have this feeling, looking at Liling. "Hey."

It's like Liling notices what she looks like, and straightens herself. She takes a deep breath through her nose, but her face hasn't caught up to her act yet.

It's too early. It's too early. It's too early.

"Get dressed," I tell her. When she raises a brow, inquiring who I think I'm talking to, I add, "Please. We're going to Detroit." At this point, we both essentially work for the Padillas.

"Persch, are you fucking listening to me?" Luis might kill me when I get there.

"Yeah, yeah. I'm coming. Do I need Gordy?" Liling's gone into the bedroom, leaving me alone in the kitchen.

Luis takes a deep breath, sounding staticky over the phone. "I got my own guys. I got weapons. Just get here." Weapons. So it's going to be a day trip.

"We'll be there as soon as we can."

"We? You bringing the diamond? Why?"

I'm keeping my voice low. "Blanca's there, right? I could leave Liling with her?"

Luis growls at me. He hates when I don't answer questions directly. "Yeah, of course Blanca is here."

"I think," I say slowly. "That Liling could be close to labor or something. I don't want to leave her alone for as long as whatever you've got planned but are stubbornly not telling me about. Just in case."

"Why don't you just ask her if she's going into labor, *idiota?*"

"Liling!" I holler. Luis cusses again.

"What?" She hollers back.

"You're not... in labor are you?" We talked about what that looks like already. It's early, but we have a plan. We know we're close enough that we're sort of in that danger zone of when Liling might be ready. Wu is due in June, and we're halfway through May.

Maybe, just maybe, the events that took place last night might have triggered something.

Liling pops back into the living room. She's got on a jean dress over a red t-shirt and white tennis shoes and is pulling her hair up. "Why?" Her face says it all; she's worried too.

The phone is still on my shoulder. "Because you're acting weird. Do we need to go to the hospital?" With Luis' mood, I wouldn't mind an excuse to bypass him today.

"I'm fine."

I don't believe her. "Are you?"

"I'm fine." Alright, now there's two people annoyed with me.

"You ready to go? Luis is about to send a hit out on me."

Liling's grabbing her purse but she's also grabbing the little backpack we've had packed for three weeks. "Just in case." she adds sheepishly.

"Liling's coming," I say into the phone at last.

476

Luis sighs. "Fine, fine. Anything for our little diamond. Just get here, alright?" I've successfully worn him down.

I make my voice as chipper as possible. "Sure, see you in a couple hours, Boss."

85.

[RANDALL]

It takes three bathroom stops and one drive through detour to get to Luis' estate. This time, the security guards know who I am. I have been back to the Padilla estate several times by this point. There's a line of cars parked in the circular drive in front of the house.

Luis' house looked impressive in the winter, but in the spring, this place is something else. The large, burgundy fountain has three tiers of cascading water, with creeping myrtle housed in the center of the fountain, hidden in the shade presented by the upper tier.

The entire lower portion of the massive house is flanked by storied rhododendrons sporting tennis ball-sized purple flowers. The fragrance of the flowers hits me in the face as soon as I step into the balmy day of May, grabbing Liling's pack from the trunk.

Liling has her hand shading her eyes from the sun as she looks at Luis' kingdom. "I want bushes like this too."

I take Liling's free hand. "Then that's what you'll get."

We take what I think is just a quick moment to ourselves when the front door whips open. "Alright, Persch, get your ass in here, already." Luis stands impatiently in the doorway. He's wearing a red polo with a trim of black at the edge of his sleeves and on his collar paired with black pants.

I spread my arms in exasperation. "Why am I the only one getting yelled at today?"

Luis softens with a sarcastic smile. "Because I would never dream of raising my voice to The *Diamante*." He smiles at Liling as we approach the door, holding his hand out to help her up the steps. "*Hola*, Gorgeous. How are you feeling?"

Liling gracefully takes Luis' hand as she's beckoned into the house. "Painfully pregnant." The answer concerns both me and Luis.

Inside the bright house, I'm once again blown away by the opulence of everything here. The tiles of the floor look like they've just been mopped and there's no dust on a single surface of this house.

While we follow Luis to the living room, I spot Gretchen by the door, making sure to greet her in passing. "*Guten Morgen*, Gretchen." She beams at me in response. Gretchen Weiss is definitely down for the Randall Persch charm.

In the living room, where orange couches form a conversation pit, sits Rogelio and six other men I believe I met at least once between the dinner party and the christening. I notice one of the people on the couch is Gabriel. I wonder how Diego keeps this to himself, when he works with his partner in such close quarters. I can't go more than a few minutes without talking about Liling, and if she's in the room, anyone could tell I'm tethered to her.

"Now that everyone is finally here…" Luis mutters, taking a seat on a side of the couch apparently reserved for just Luis. The two people sitting closest to Rogelio get up from their seats, and Rogelio gives us a knowing look. *Inner circle.*

Rogelio leans around me to talk to Liling. "You keeping this one in line?"

"I've given up with that," Liling mutters. I grin at Rogelio when he gives me a look.

"So what's going on?" I ask, noting the small army Luis has assembled here.

The topic instantly sours Luis' face. "One of Ro's guys caught wind of someone else trying to distribute in the same places Gael already has sellers." Gael's lucky to be alive. I wonder how long it took him to lick his wounds.

This is when Blanca, baby in hand, strolls into the room wearing a long, flowing, white dress. Her dark hair is just past her shoulders now, and she's absolutely glowing as she enters. As if she really is the queen, several of the guys stand respectfully, but Blanca's making a beeline for Liling. Luis does something of a quiet scowl at the interruption.

Blanca bursts into the center of the room with no regard for any meeting that Luis might've been trying to have. Like Luis, Blanca is very bold and opinionated, but she inserts her dominance in a much more spirited type of charm. The best way to describe Blanca is that she's like a blast of orange juice with a lot of pulp. She's sweet but can be hard to swallow.

"Ey, closed meeting," Rogelio muses, starting to make a grab for the baby before Blanca dodges him.

"He wants his auntie," Blanca chirps, and Liling has transformed into a new person when she's being handed Rafael. Lately (with the exception of last night), Liling has stated she's 'too tired to smile.' This affliction is gone when she's got a baby in her arms and she's using an octave of voice I've never heard before.

"He's so big!" Liling coos affectionately. Blanca is rapidly firing off baby updates as if they've been best friends for their entire lives. Liling loves having regular access to a phone at my apartment; she'll happily talk with Blanca on the phone for an hour at a time.

At this point, I know Liling, and I know when she's being fake happy and I know when she's genuinely interested. Liling likes Blanca, and I personally think it's just too perfect if she gets along well with Blanca. I definitely think a good 40% of the patience Luis has with me stems from him and Blanca liking Liling.

In the safety of Blanca's turned back, Luis rolls his eyes and stands. "Field trip," Luis announces. Rogelio stands and navigates around Blanca and I get up too.

There's no need to check on Liling if she wants to stay behind because she is completely enamored by little Rafael so I follow Luis, walking next to Ro. The other six men trail behind us while Luis leads.

"Do you know what's going on?" I murmur to Ro.

"You're always last to know, Boy Scout." Rogelio shoulders me playfully before he has another sudden thought. "You been in the basement before?"

"Nope."

"Ah, ok. You're in for a treat, then." We've reached a long set of steps leading downward. Confident we're already following, Luis is halfway down. "But I seen you in action before. You don't seem squeamish."

It's true, I'm not. When I smell the stale stench of sweat and blood in the basement, I'm not even surprised. Business as usual.

"Door." Luis hollers from the bottom. Whoever is in the back of the line shuts the basement door behind them. I wonder what I'm going to do in the future- how I'm going to shield my kids from this. Then again, Liling shares this world too. How do we shield our kids from what we are?

I have to ignore the thought when Luis starts talking again. That, and there's a hostage in the middle of the basement floor. It's a wide open basement layout. There's no rooms, but four thick columns in the center of the room. They don't really look like they're load-bearing, I really think they're just used to secure either a chair or a body to the center of the room.

In this case, it's a thirty-or-so year old guy with brown hair that's plastered to his head from blood and sweat. "This fucker is Benji," Luis starts. Benji has clearly gone through it already.

I'm standing about five feet in front of this stranger. I'm between Luis and Ro, with the others forming a semi-circle around us.

"Last time I left this one, we at least got him to admit he's working for a different distributor." Luis looks directly at me with cold annoyance. "Guess who he works for."
I look at Benji, not sure how I'm supposed to pull a name from unless- I jerk my gaze back to Luis. "No way. "I look down at Benji, who's looking submissively at the floor, trying his best to keep his legs pulled close to him. "You know someone named Toby Larson?"

When Benji doesn't respond, Luis barks, "You can answer him or you can answer Diego."

Benji answers me. "Toby works at the same distributor. He coordinates arriving shipments."

"Good boy," Luis responds with dry pity to the floor.

"When Toby left, I just assumed he couldn't cut it. I assumed this world was just too much for him," I lament. "I never would've guessed he just went to do the same thing for someone else."

"We're going to go get him," Luis vows, hands in his pocket while he surveys Benji on the floor. "Shut down their operation, take what they've got, and clean house."

It's going to be a full day.

"Where's Toby?" I ask no one in particular.

Luis immediately parrots the questions. "Diego, where's Toby?"

From the corner of the room, summoned from the shadows, a demon emerges. Diego's eyes come out of the darkness, and he's wearing a gray apron like he's a butcher, smock covered in blood.

From what I've learned about who does what, Diego is Luis' primary disciplinarian. Carlos reports to Diego and keeps track of anyone who needs to stay in Padilla custody and helps Diego as needed.

Diego has a towel in his hands, wiping between his fingers. "Sterling Heights."

"Got an address?" Luis asks.

Diego nods once, then again in Benji's direction. "Done."

Luis seems skeptical. "We know how we're getting in?" Diego nods. "We know how many to expect inside?" Another nod.

Luis squats down in front of Benji. "Then tell me, Benji, what do we still need you for?"

Reluctant to meet Luis' eyes, his voice is small. "I... there's no reason to kill me."

"Oh," Luis nods in mock understanding. "Is there a reason to keep you alive, then?"

Benji swallows, his fingers are tapping nervously in jittery pats against his arm. "I... I didn't do anything to you specifically. I started selling for someone else because that's who found me and offered it to me."

There it is: my often-absent conscious. Little Benji's right. He, as far as I know, hasn't done anything directly against the Padillas. Benji found himself on the wrong side of a line he didn't draw.

"But what do I need you for?" Luis repeats, testing the resilience of Benji even further.

Benji's gaze sweeps the floor again. "I guess I don't have anything left."

I sneak a look at Rogelio, whose face has the same look it did when we watched Luis make his examples at the dinner party. I think it's an act. Rogelio looks at me, gives me the smallest shakes of the head, like a warning.

"How much do you sell a month?" I ask.

Next to me, Rogelio lets out an annoyed breath. Luis seems surprised but he should be used to me opening my big mouth by now.

Come on, Benji. I'm trying to give you a reason "What, are you that bad at moving product?" I ask when Benji doesn't immediately answer. Honestly, it's hard to be bad at selling coke unless you're stupid. There's a reason it's notorious.

Benji runs his tongue over his lip. "I move about ten thousand dollars a month." Now that's not spectacular, and I could sell circles around him, but it's not nothing. It takes a lot of Benji's to make money, but each one is important.

Now, I look at Luis, quietly asking, "You want another ten thousand a month?" I ask. Luis stares at me blankly, deciding if I'm going too far by suggesting Benji doesn't need to die tonight. "Give him a quota." I look at Benji. "He'll do it."

Luis stands, crossing his arms. "What? Like it's so easy to switch sides?"

"I think we're going to go kill his employer tonight anyway." I shrug. "He'll be in the market for a job."

484

"You know I like to make an example."

I laugh at that. "We all know that, and we'll still do plenty of that tonight. What about an example about how there's only safety in falling in line with the Padilla cartel?" Sure, I'll pump his ego a little bit.

There's silence as everyone considers this. Luis changes his stare over to his number two. Rogelio has his arms crossed too. "It could be a good look either way." Rogelio shrugs. "You either show everyone that there's mercy for those who show loyalty to you, or, if he fucks up, show everyone what happens for those who cross us."

Luis still seems like he'd rather let the blood pour. "Hey." Luis taps Benji's shoeless foot with his own boot. "Benji. What do you want to do?"

This is the most animated Benji's been so far, looking directly at Luis, then at me, then back to Luis. "I'll sell for you," he says with desperation. "I have regulars. And… if you're taking out Albert's gang, I can help find everyone that was selling for him and…" he kneads his hands, which are bound at the wrist, together nervously. "You can try to convert those sellers too."

Now, there's more quiet. It's in Luis' hands now. No matter what he does, there's no more arguing. "You understand what's going to happen if you try to screw me over?" The question sends chills through me. I hope I'm never at the receiving end of that. "If you think Diego was mean today, shit. Diego can keep someone alive for months." Luis drags his index finger across Beji's forehead. "He's got it down to a science; how much blood someone can lose and stay alive."

"You'll kill me," Benji says quietly. "I know, I understand."

"No, I won't kill you. When Diego's done with you," Luis says, turning his attention to me. "He will."

LILING

I've become so good at getting what I want. That's why I'm sitting in the backseat next to Randall while Diego drives us to some warehouse where there's apparently a competing distributor to Luis. Those who stand against Luis stand against myself, I suppose.

When Randall came and found me, playing on the floor with what will only be the world's cutest baby for another month or so (hopefully), he starts piecing together what he and Luis' men are about to do. From the start, it doesn't seem like anyone has a plan other than show up with a large number of firearms and 'clean house.'

Even when Luis comes to ensure everyone knows what they're doing, I'm not convinced. It ends up being something of a presentation, where three cartel leaders are attempting to convince me that they have a plan and nobody is going to get themself killed.

"I'm going with you." It would be a lot stronger of a statement if I was able to stand easily on my own. I am so big right now, and I'm wearing a jean dress, so standing is no easy task.

Rogelio snickers as Randall is helping to haul me to my feet. "Lil, you're over eight months pregnant," he grunts. "You're not going."

His face shrinks a little when I glare at him for attempting to tell me what I can and can't do. "Then why am I here at all?"

"So you have someone with you if you go to early labor!" Randall gestures at Blanca who claps her hands.

"Liling, I need an adult to talk to who isn't-" Blanca looks at Luis' group with distaste. "A man."

I look at Blanca with a hand on my hip. "Do you think their plan sounds like it has any sense to it?"

Blanca shrugs, picking up Rafael as he starts to make a noise between a scream and a grunt. "No."

"*Diamante*," Luis says smoothly. "You act like we're amateurs." He elbows Randall. "I will bring him back to you, ok?"

Rogelio shifts his weight, looking amused by my insistence. Rogelio looks around the room with a furrowed brow. "We've got ten guys who all know what they're doing..." He looks at Randall. "We've got nine guys that know what they're doing." Rogelio grins. "We should be fine."

"And you'll do even better with ten men who *should* be fine when you add one woman who will ensure things will be fine."

Rogelio isn't used to arguing with me. He sheepishly looks at Randall. "Damn," he mutters.

"I know," Randall mutters back.

"You know," Blanca says, sultry grin taking over her face. "You know what's better than one woman?"

Now, Luis doesn't look happy. "No."

"Two!" Blanca chirps. She's a lot faster to get to her feet. "I'm coming too."

"Too?" Luis exclaims. "We're not bringing her either!"

"Gretchen!" Blanca hollers. When Gretchen materializes from the hallway, Blanca hands Rafael off to her. "We're all going out." Blanca tells the house keeper.

Luis immediately takes Rafael back and tries to get Blanca to take him back but she's putting her arms up. "Ah-" She snaps, like scolding a dog. "I'm coming, let me go put pants on."

"*Mi amor,*" Luis groans. "We are not going on a fucking field trip."

"Luis, it's been so long since we've had a date night." Blanca pouts, pulling on his shirt collar while he shifts Rafael in his arms.

"It's not a date night if there's ten other people there," Luis argues.

"I'll close my eyes." Rogelio muses, earning a glare from Luis.

Luis makes a sound similar to what Rafael made on the floora minute ago. "Blanca-"

"I'm coming. So is Liling." Blanca states, and Luis starts arguing, she's looking at me with a grin. "Besides, diamonds are a girl's best friend, yes? We go together."

I beam at Randall in return, who doesn't look like he expected Luis to lose this argument. The entire team has to wait for Blanca to change her clothes, and for Blanca and Luis to make sure Gretchen has what she needs for some impromptu babysitting.

"We're going to need a babysitter, too," I mumble to Randall on the way to the car.

He's clearly not happy with this outcome and just grumbles his agreement. When Blanca comes down the stairs dressed in a black long-sleeved shirt in jeans, Luis pitifully follows her outside.

Rogelio follows, making a whipping sound effect and hand motion. Luis shoots him a death threat. *"Yes, Blanca,"* Rogelio whispers behind Luis' back as we all exit the house.

In our car, Diego drives myself, and Randall. Luis drives Blanca and two of the other men in a not-so-conspicuous blue muscle car. Rogelio drives separately with the remaining men in a black SUV.

I'm sitting comfortably in the passenger seat, turning to see Randall. He's trying his best not to frown. "This is crazy, you know that, right?"

"We're a team," I say, lovingly.

"I know, but I just want to be a team in a scenario where my pregnant fiancé isn't doing cartel missions with me."

He's adorable when he worries. "If you're going to be difficult, I'll talk to Diego," I say, facing forward in the seat again.

I look at Diego, who seems amused. "We'll be fine, won't we Diego?"

Diego's eyes look at me, then flick to Randall in the mirror. "Better in pairs. Fight harder." I'm pleasantly surprised, and Randall looks stunned that I managed to pull anything out of him. I'm happy Diego's answered me, and even happier when he says even more. "Watch." Diego points at the car that Rogelio drives in front of us. "You will see how I fight."

I blink, unsure of what Diego is exactly talking about when he points to the car. *Better in pairs. You will see how I fight.* I'll have to pay *very* close attention to who gets out of Rogelio's car. I like the idea of Diego having someone. Now that I have my own person, I think everyone could benefit from having a partner.

Diego presents as in impenetrable, callous killer. He may be all these things, but there's a lot inside of his armor. There's a lot that he's protecting. I stroke my stomach as Wuhan kicks inside of me. I have a lot that I'm protecting now too. Right now, I'm protecting Wuhan's father.

87.

RANDALL

Sterling Heights isn't far from where Luis lives. That's partially why he's so pissed- he sees the proximity as an insult. We travel in three cars, with our car trailing behind until we arrive. Rogelio's car takes the lead, lane changing until it's in front.

Diego actually drives past the place, letting Rogelio's car go up alone instead of rushing the armed gates with three cars at once. We have information from Benji: a code and legitimate reason that his boss, someone named Albert, should be expecting us. That's option one.

Option two is two just shoot everyone in sight.

Diego sits in park in a nearby street off to the side while we wait. We've got a walkie-talkie and the car phone, waiting for word. Our car will go in second, Luis will go in last.

We get the call twenty minutes later that Rogelio's made it through the gate and that he'll be waiting for the other two cars before rushing in. That's when the madness will start. That's when there will be bullets flying while my fiancé and child are in the room.

When Diego pulls the car in, it's clear that a mix of options one and two were used. It looks like Ro's car made it past

491

the security gate, but something must have tipped them off before they could pull up to what looks like a repurposed school building. I thought we'd be working with a warehouse but this place... there has to be a lot of rooms to cover. A lot of long, concealing hallways.

"Are you sure you don't want to stay in the car?" I plead with Liling one more time as Diego pulls in; he's listening to something on the phone.

"I'm sure," Liling states.

"Lil-"

"If you all go inside, what happens if someone checks the cars?"

Luis has at least got *his* wife to agree to stay at the cars, acting as a watch out with one of the walkie-talkies. "Blanca's packing." Liling doesn't look impressed. "Liling, you can barely walk, you sure as hell can't run." I see her face move. "Please, just stay out here."

She pinches her lips into a frown but sighs her acceptance. "Fine," Liling says, tugging on my collar. "But come back to me. Be smart in there."

"Always."

"I love you," she murmurs. She always says it like she's slightly embarrassed or annoyed, depending on when I choose to say it first, but I know that Liling never says something she doesn't mean.

I smile at her lips before repeating it back to her. "I love you too."

Luis parks his car by the other two, and our three vehicles make an armored wall of sorts. The good news is that a school building isn't as hard to break into as a warehouse might be. The bad news is whoever is inside definitely knows we're here. I wouldn't be surprised if there's cameras and everyone inside is shitting themselves because they know Luis Padilla is here.

In Detroit, everyone from crack addicts to the city council people know who Luis Padilla is. Luis is teaching me that, to stay out of jail, it doesn't always take being on your best behavior. You just have to be discrete and have a shit-ton of money. For as long as the cash hits the right bank accounts, Mo-town will continue to thrive with Luis' support.

The plan is so simple that I understand why Liling has doubts. The plan is to go in and shoot. Find one person to tell us who's in charge. Find who's in charge, shoot that person.

There are three entrances, so we split into three groups. In one group, myself, Rogelio, and two other men. Group two is Luis and two of the men. Lastly, is Diego, Gabriel, and one other men. That leaves one person out with the girls, just in case.

While we're still at the cars, Luis and Rogelio have the trunks open and are rapidly passing out weapons. Pistols, automatic guns, and of course, *la princesa*. As soon as Diego's group is armed, they take off, combing the side of the building and disappearing around it. The shooting starts immediately.

"Shit," Luis mutters, going faster. I barely have time to catch the pistol Luis chucks at me and the magazine that follows it. "Happy early birthday, Boy Scout. *Vamos.*"

I barely have time to inspect what Luis has thrown at me, but it's a custom pistol, mahogany in color, gold interface on the very top. It's engraved with my name and is very heavy for the size.

"Let's see how you use that, let's go," Rogelio says, prodding my shoulder. I follow Rogelio, and the other two men follow behind us. We stop at the doors, where an old *Welcome to Rider Elementary School* hangs from above.

My heart is pounding. I'm on one side of the door, Rogelio on the other. "Ok," Rogelio says softly. He looks at me. "You let me and Ernie go in first. You and Jesus keep an eye on our backs, don't let anyone shoot us, ok?"

I nod, but this is my first raid. I've got a gun, I've shot a person, but I've never done an army-style take over and I'm guessing the army normally doesn't bring their pregnant fiancés.

Rogelio checks the door. It's locked, but there's a lot of give when he pulls. It's an old door and the people inside had counted on the armed gate being the main deterrent.

Rogelio looks like he's about to say something, but from the direction that Luis' group went in there's an outbreak of shooting. At the same time, there's shooting from somewhere inside, and the glass by the doors we're in front of explodes. We all duck and take cover, waiting for the shooting nearest us to cease.

In another moment, there's more commotion from a room far from where we are, accompanied by screaming. Capitalizing on whatever chaos is happening at two other doorways, Rogelio rips the door with shattered glass open like it wasn't locked in the first place.

Ernie and Ro rush through the doorway, automatic weapons lighting the hallway as they take down whoever is waiting inside. My heart is going to explode; there's so much happening. It's hard to keep my eyes focused on the outside while there's so much happening behind me.

Once Rogelio has cleared the inside, we cautiously follow him into the building. Half the lights have been shot out, giving the long abandoned hallways an eerie orange overcast that doesn't light every corner. Rogelio looks around, he's already got sweat rolling down from his forehead, but he looks like he knows exactly what he's doing. I wonder how often Luis has him doing things like this. I wonder how often he'll have me doing things like this.

"See that?" Rogelio points down the hall, where it looks like there's an office with a light on inside. "Let's check it out." He doesn't wait before leading us, and we creep down the hallway, sticking close to the wall.

At the end of the hallway, Rogelio pauses at the corner, peeks his head around only to have shooting immediately break holes into the wall just past his head. The sound of bullets ricocheting against metallic lockers is deafening. "Shit." Rogelio mutters. "Ready, E?" Ernie nods, and the two jump to the open hallway, firing their own weapons while Jesus and I continue to keep watch on the anyone coming from behind.

When the shooting stops again, Rogelio comes back to the corner with Ernie. "Everyone having fun yet?"

"Cake walk," says Jesus.

The office is next, and the door isn't even locked. Rogelio pushes the door open and aims, but there's no one inside. I only catch glimpses of what's happening as Jesus and I cover Ro from behind.

Clutching his long rifle, Rogelio cautiously steps into the office, first swinging the barrel to the right. As he's preparing to check the other angle, from behind the open doorway, a wiry guy launches himself over Rogelio, grappling with Ro until he had his arm squeezes tight over Rogelio's neck.

Rogelio's arms shoot to his own neck, trying to keep the stranger from strangling him completely. Trying to shake the attacker free, Rogelio slams his back into the wall, and the man grunts as he's pounded between the wall and Rogelio's mass. I don't see how that doesn't result in a cracked rib or two.

"Shit," Ernie mutters, jumping to help but stops when the stranger has out his pistol and presses it into Rogelio's head.

"Shit," Jesus repeats, keeping his station at the doorway to keep us from getting swarmed from behind. I don't know what to do now, I need to stay where I'm at to keep anyone else from sneaking up on us.

"Let's have everyone settle down," the stranger says, keeping an arm wrapped tightly around Rogelio's neck while the other points a pistol at Rogelio's head. Ro makes something of a grunt while his wide arms struggle to keep his airway open against the stranger's hold.

"You have three seconds," Ernie warns, keeping his own weapon pointed at the stranger but shooting when he's got Ro like that isn't a good idea and we all know it.

The stranger is minuscule compared to Rogelio but he's got a gun pointed at Ro, so size isn't too much of an advantage. The stranger has a mop of hair that looks like it's dyed black but, his roots are blonde and so are his eyebrows.

"Two," Ernie warns, shifting the way he holds his weapon.

The stranger sneers, knowing the one with the hostage usually calls the shots. "Two seconds or-"

Rogelio flips the stranger clean over his head. With one pull over the arm meant to strangle him, he sends the attacker airbound before slamming him onto the floor in front of him.

Rogelio Esparza is a beast.

Rogelio is back in control now, and he's got his foot pressed over the stranger's throat. Rogelio says something to Ernie, who bends to frisk the man while Rogelio keeps him down, now having a gun pointed at his head.

Ernie finds a wallet and starts going through it, pulling out an ID and pocketing cash. "Brandon Wallace."

"Ok, Brandon," Rogelio says. "My boss is somewhere in here looking for your boss, so know that if you're choosing sides, your safest bet is with me right now." He pushes his boot down further while Brandon claws at Ro's foot. "So why don't you tell us where you're storing your product, and where you're getting it from."

"Fuck you," Brandon curses breathily.

"What?" Rogelio taunts. "You not going to cooperate?"

"All you Padilla pigs are going to be sorry for even trying this."

"Trying?" Rogelio asks, doing a scan of the office. "Look around, we're winning, here." I think it's early to be making that call. "I don't have time to play games with you."

"Might as well shoot me," Brandon says, coughing when Rogelio presses down more.

Rogelio shakes his head. "That'd be too quick." He sighs, scratching his chin. "You're sure you don't want to play nice with me?"

"When pigs fly," Brandon spits.

Rogelio laughs. "Good idea, *cochino.*" Rogelio the beast, Rogelio the tank, bends to pick up Brandon by the collar until he's on his feet again. Rogelio half-drags Brandon to the window that overlooks the hallway, probably used for office staff watching students walk by back when this was a functioning school.

"What're you doing?" Brandon kicks his leg, his heels dragging across the floor as Rogelio tows him behind.

"You said when pigs fly?" Rogelio asks. Before Brandon can say anything in response, Rogelio puts his hands under Brandon's arm and effortlessly punts the man forward like he's throwing a sack of potatoes. Brandon soars straight through the window, colliding through the glass that explodes everywhere.

Jesus and I are supposed to be watching the hallway but nobody can help but marvel. Rogelio just threw a man through a window.

"Hey Persch," Rogelio pants, wiping his forehead. "Go fetch."

88.

[RANDALL]

As it turns out, Brandon, after being thrown through a window, is now unconscious. I go find Brandon on the outside of the window, in the hallway while Jesus covers me. Brandon is surrounded by shards of glass. His face is torn to shreds, he's got glass engorged into various places on his body, and he's about to become one of the cartel's prisoners.

Ernie drags Brandon back toward the door, where he'll be stowed in Rogelio's car and become Diego's problem by the end of the day. Now we're a group of three, and we're going to head toward where there's shooting happening, since we never got an answer out of Brandon. The main goal is to eliminate the Padilla's competition, but if we can get some free product to turn around and sell, that's what we'll go for.

We go through two hallways, clearly going down ground that's already been covered. Passing three bodies and a spare finger, I think it's safe to say this was Diego's hallway.

"None of our guys." Rogelio notes as we pass the dead men. "Looks like they got a good trainer." Rogelio does most of the training.

"You're also the only one that's been a hostage so far today." I add, creeping behind Rogelio's lead.

Ro snorts. "And you see how I handled that shit?"

"He could've given us direction on where we're going." Right now, it looks like we're heading toward what might be the old cafeteria. We're about to clear another corner when there's something of a commotion at the end of the hallway straight down from us and at the same time the room that we're headed to also has gunshots flying from the room.

"Shit," Rogelio mutters, peering around the wall. "Diego's in there." He nods to the cafeteria before looking at Jesus. "You, come with me, let's get in there. Persch, watch the door."

I nod, letting Rogelio and Jesus run past me, bursting into the cafeteria, guns blazing. It's so hard to watch the door when everyone else is dodging bullets.

I'm concealed behind a partial wall when a bullet slices right through it and I hit the floor. It was too close. Way too close. So much happening. There's a colossal *boom* from the hallway to my right, and when I look down in that direction there's a cloud of dust and I think something is on fire now.

Are there explosives in this building? I need to get Rogelio back out here; I'm almost ready to call out to him when I see someone I don't know run out of the smoke cloud.

He's running so fast, headed toward the cafeteria that he misses me crouch down and take cover while he calls, "We got Padilla!"

Fuck.

I jump from where my cover is, watching his eyes get wide. I think by the end of the day we'll be at capacity for prisoners. He doesn't even get his own weapon back out before I've put a bullet in his chest. He's still alive when I leave my post

500

completely, running straight into the clouded hallway he came from.

It was a bad plan. I can't see shit, I can't breathe, and I'm running directly into some sort of fight and I can't tell who's winning. I'm running towards the noise, where it doesn't sound like shooting but it sounds like physical fighting. There's grunting and shuffling and the sound of things hitting the wall.

Running toward the sound, in a room not too far from the east exit of the building, there's a raging fight in what looks like an old classroom. There's five people curb stomping someone into the floor while the person on the floor can do little more than try to protect their head. I'm not even noticed when I peer around the doorframe to assess the situation, to see who is fighting who.

The problem is it isn't a fight, it's a beat down; and it's Luis Padilla who's getting the shit beat out of him.

89.

[RANDALL]

What I'm seeing doesn't make sense. When I fully comprehend what's happening, I'm frozen. This is what being beaten to death looks like. It looks like four against one. It looks like one person, who isn't moving on the ground. It looks like someone being kicked across the floor as their own blood gets smeared from under them.

Where the hell are the people that Luis came in with?

I don't have time for this. Luis doesn't have time for this. I only have one chance to get this right before my element of surprise has been taken.

Pistol in hand, I take aim at one of the four men that are kicking a near motionless Luis across the floor. Point, shoot, he falls directly over Luis who isn't even able to throw the person off of him.

And now I've got three people staring at me, taking their guns back out. Three against one. *Not great odds, there, Randall.*

There's three people in front of me; all of them white, definitely not with our group, all of them look spooked by my sudden appearance, especially after I just killed one of their partners. Now, it's a standoff. And I'm torn between barking at everyone to back up and trying to see if Luis is ok.

502

The person in the middle of the trio that's pointing a gun back at me cautiously starts to speak. "I need-"

I shoot him.

It was an impulse move, but my gun was already raised, finger already on the trigger, and I shot him dead.

"No one moves," I bark, not sure who to point my weapon at next. "I've think we've established that I'm a pretty good shot." Luck.

"Who are you?" The person on my left asks. He's got short brown hair and green eyes with a sporty build.

"Back against the wall," I respond.

"There's two of us, idiot."

I think I'm decent at making deals, and I'm decent at reasoning. "Every single person we've come across so far is dead," I state. "The only person we've spared so far was thrown through a window, so if he wakes up, he might be able to work out some sort of deal. you two have some options here."

There's some movement on the floor and I can't tell if it's Luis or if the person I shot isn't actually dead. When the person on the left starts to notice the movement too, I quickly grab his attention again, because if he decides to try to make sure Luis is finished, I can't get over there fast enough.

"You can back against the wall, put your weapons down, and *maybe* I can convince my boss not to kill you." My boss might be dead, but I don't think they know who they've got on the floor. If they did, they would know that they're only safe from Luis Padilla if he's dead.

"Or you can shoot me." I nod to the floor. "Shoot him. And when my friends get here, they'll shoot you on sight." From the distance, there's more automatic shooting going off before it goes silent again. "How many of your people were ready with a machine gun?" Neither of them answer. "If the answer is no one, then you know that's *my* people."

As if on queue, I hear Rogelio yelling my name from where I left him, his voice bouncing off of the walls of the empty building. We must be close to having the building under control, otherwise he wouldn't risk it. "Boy Scout! Where you at!"

I'm keeping eye contact with the one on the left, with the dirty blonde hair as we keep weapons pointed here. "Over here, Ro," I call. I can see the two are weighing their options. If they've heard rumors about the Padillas, they have to know enough to be afraid.

"The person that's coming won't do anything other than shoot you dead if he gets around the corner and sees you pointing a gun at me."

My heartbeat starts to even out as the two men look like they're coming into the realization I need them to. "Guns on the floor. Against the wall." *I* am in charge right now. People listen to me, or they die. Randall Persch is in charge.

The person with the sportier build backs down first. He looks at the other remaining person with a grumble. "Put it down, Mose. We'll sort this out later."

Mose doesn't look convinced. "Put it down, Mose," I repeat. They put their weapons into the floor slowly, and their hands start to wait as they stand back up. "Back of the room," I remind them. The person on the right has to step over Luis to put himself in the corner of the room, behind an ancient teaching desk that's littered with papers and trash.

As the two men retreat into the corner of the room, I advance into it. The discarded guns quickly become mine, as I hastily make sure they can't be used against me before I'm able to kneel in front of Luis.

504

"Shit," I mutter. "Luis," I whisper. He's alive, but man, he looks like someone that might only be so temporarily. It's hard to lug the person that fell on top of him off with one arm while I keep my arm trained on the other two.

"Luis," I snap again. He groans just a little bit as I continue to pull the other man off of him. Luis' hand starts to lift ever so slowly. I need to get him up, but I don't know how to do that while still guarding myself. Luis is not a small man. He's thin, but his height would make him difficult to try to carry.

I've got half the man dragged off of Luis when Luis groans again and finally takes a state that resembles semi-consciousness. "Shit." It's between a whisper and a grunt but it shows cognitive function and that's what I need.

"That's right," I try to coo in the most condescending voice possible, like maybe I can get Luis annoyed enough to get up try to kick my ass. "It's ok to cry. I'll teach you how to fight so this doesn't happen again."

Luis' purple and yellow face grimaces from the floor. "I'm going to kick your ass in just a minute, Boy Scout."

I laugh softly in relief as I give the person I shot one more tug so that he's mostly off of Luis, only his legs draping over Luis' ankle.

When I finish backing up, there's a familiar cold, metallic prod at the back of my head. This time, I know it isn't Ro pointing a gun at me. "Randall?"

90

LILING

It's taking too long, and there's too much shooting. Blanca and I have been waiting out here alone with one of Luis' men for some time now. I should have gone in with him, because not knowing what's going on is slow and tortuous.

Blanca's getting restless too. "I'm not waiting out here much longer," she touts.

Our assigned bodyguard's name is Juan, and he looks like he's maybe nineteen. Too young to be holding the weapon he's been given. "Please stay out here, Mrs. Padilla." It's more of a plead than an order. Blanca is a force of nature, and I find it inspiring. I'd quite like to have that sort of power. A hurricane, maybe.

Blanca dismissively waves her hand at Juan, her dark eyes trained on the door we're hoping our partners emerge from soon. When we hear another round of gunshots, Blanca clicks her tongue. "You need to distract me," she tells me.

I need a distraction myself. If it weren't for the feeling that Wuhan is trying to actively break out of my body, I might tell her we could go in ourselves. "Tell me about how you met Luis."

Blanca looks at me, her smooth face softening into a wistful smile. She's dreadfully beautiful in the most sinful of ways. "We met in Mexico." She smiles, crossing her arms. "I worked for a tourism company that would try to get travelers in the airports to sign up for excursions, book hotels, just make sure they had somewhere to spend their money, yes?"

"Was Luis vacationing?" I guide.

Blanca shakes her head. "No, but I remember when I first saw him at the airport." Blanca's face lights up in the glow that can only be described as love. "It was just him and Rogelio, but I was caught on Luis as soon as I saw him. I mean, look at my husband, he is beautiful." She clicks her tongue again. "Stunning."

I nod in general agreement. Luis is pretty, in a mean sort of way. Luis has the sort of beauty that appeals to women who want a man that's something of a villain.

"Luis didn't look like a tourist, clearly. He was in Mexico to secure his connections to his supply here, not that I knew any of that at the time."

"It clearly wasn't a dealbreaker," I muse.

Blanca laughs. "So I like the bad guy? So do you."

"Fair enough."

"Anyway," Blanca has relaxed now, ignoring the next round of shooting. "Sometimes the agency tourism I worked for would send us to kiosks at resorts to help their guests book activities. I had a terrible day- just terrible. American tourists?" She shakes her head with a frown. "Awful, just awful."

Blanca's fingers toy with the end of her hair. "So I'm off for the night, getting ready to walk home and there he is- out by the front doors smoking. *My* Luis." She says it with so much protective endearment in her voice.

"Did he notice you?" I ask, letting a warm breeze roll over me as we continue to wait.

"Of course." Blanca smirks, gesturing to herself. I would wager that most men Blanca walks past notice her. "You know, we smoke outside together for a little bit, talking. That was the start, just like that, Liling."

"Just like that," I echo.

"We go out for drinks, then the next night, dinner. The next thing I know, he's coming back from the states every other week just to see me. He brings presents and sweet words and promises- all these promises."

Now, Luis is sounding a lot like Randall. "So you mean to tell me Luis is a romantic?"

"Luis is... he's romantic, and strong, and, God, he is walking sex and I was obsessed with him from the first time I saw him." Blanca closes her eyes in memory. "He helped get me over here, and it's been the two of us fighting for each other ever since. We didn't date long before we got married. We just knew that quickly."

Blanca opens her eyes, a prideful look coming over her. "There isn't anything I wouldn't do for that man, you know? Luis," She points a red fingernail at the building. "*That* is a man. He provides, he protects. He's a father, he's a husband."

I'm meant to be listening about Luis but now I'm thinking about Randall. My Randall. Randall will be all of those things too. With Randall as my partner, there is not a thing I need to truly worry about, so long as he comes through those doors soon.

"You and me? We are the same," Blanca says to me, tapping my arm.

I may have missed something, daydreaming about Randall. "Are we?"

Blanca nods enthusiastically. "We both have good men who do bad things, and do we care?" She shakes her head. "No."

"I wouldn't say that I don't care..." I'm fully aware that I *should* care.

"We don't care," Blanca insists. "You know what I say? We take care of ourselves- fuck everybody else."

"I definitely wouldn't say-"

"Fuck everybody else!" Blanca cheers.

Juan groans from his post. "Mrs. Padilla, we probably shouldn't be yelling-"

She waves her hand again to silence him. "You are like me, strong," Blanca continues, holding her hand into a fist in front of her face. "We are a new age of woman. We don't ask for permission, we don't apologize, and we take orders from no one."

That does sound a bit like me. Maybe that's why I feel at odds with my own religion sometimes. I've never been able to get the submissive woman part down.

At this point, it's a lost cause.

"Perhaps we are the same," I agree, setting my eyes on the door. I know Randall will come back for me. I told him to come back, and Randall always does what I tell him to do.

91.

[RANDALL]

Toby Larson, count your fucking days.

I know the voice as soon as I hear it. Sure, I've got a gun pointed to my head, but Toby likes me. Just about everyone likes me. "Gee, Toby, is that you?"

Luis is a lot more alert now, and slowly starts to stir further. Toby either hasn't noticed Luis yet or hasn't noticed he's still alive. Deftly, I shake my head; *just stay still.* Toby, I know, doesn't need any more reasons to kill Luis Padilla.

Luis, used to always doing whatever he wants, sits up slowly, ignoring my warning. Even covered in blood and bruises, he looks murderous.

"Holy crap." Toby slowly steps around me, walking until he's standing to my right, but he's keeping his eyes over Luis on the floor. "Luis Padilla.

In front of me against the back wall are the two remaining men who were beating Luis. To my right is Toby, and the doorway to the classroom is behind me.

"You don't know how happy this makes me," Toby chortles with a stupid, prideful grin. Toby's got on a white Shania Twain t-shirt that's a size too small for him. He looks just as greasy as I remember, with grubby stubble on his face as an added bonus.

"Toby," I warn. "Don't be fooled into thinking you're safe right now."

Toby's eyes flick to the doorway. "We're evenly matched." We both have guns, we're both pointing them at each other. As if in response, there's more gunfire down the hall.

"I heard you took my place, Randy," Toby continues, his stubby fingers clutching the world's smallest pistol, as if no one trusts this guy with a real gun.

"Well, you left on such short notice," I say, starting to take slow steps until I'm standing in front of Luis. As mean as he is, I like Luis enough to not want to see him hurt any more than he already is.

Toby jerks his gun toward the door and I know Rogelio has arrived, finally. I won't take my eyes off of Toby but I hear Ro cuss under his breath. "Luis-"

"I'm fine," Luis growls, sounding more alert. He's not fine, even if he's awake now.

Toby runs his tongue over his lips, where he's got some sort of blister by his mouth. "Let me finish this, Randall."

Rolling my eyes, I say, "Look around, this is already finished."

"You kill the roach at your feet, I'll get the big one by the door. I can find a spot for you."

"A spot where?" If I talk long enough, maybe the rest of our group will find us.

"Come work for Albert," Toby offers, his face lights up like he's got the deal of a lifetime for me. "He's already left, so you need to think about whether the person you're going to line yourself up with is going to be alive at the end of the day." He sends a pointed look at Luis, who hasn't been able to stand yet.

We have the numbers here, but we also have our most valuable player in a vulnerable state right now. I have no doubt Toby's boss, wherever he's run to, is preparing his own battle team to come take control of the building again. If we take too long here, we'll get swarmed and we'll all die.

"Randall, come on," Toby argues passionately. "You know these people don't really care about you. As soon as you mess up once, just once-" Toby snaps his finger. "You're done. You know Luis is erratic. You think he won't have fun humiliating and killing you as soon as you piss him off?"

Luis is erratic, all right. Being on Luis' side is like being backed by a tiger. You can try your best to train it, but it will always be wild and it will always have an instinct to dismember. I need to ask myself if the person I'm standing in front of, the person who I'm protecting from Toby's bullet, if that person would take a bullet for me.

Toby is taking my silence as an indication that I'm thinking, which he'd be right about. "Make the smart move, Randall. Or at least, what's smart for you right now. Right now, you're trapped in a building that's about to be swamped by our guys, and then what?"

If Albert's side comes, they'll get to Liling first.

"Does Albert have good benefits?" I ask.

Toby grins, his yellowing teeth on display. "Hey, if it was bad, I would've come back."

"And I would've blown you up like a fucking Macy's Thanksgiving parade balloon," Luis says from the floor. I look at him with annoyance because he can't shut up to save his life. I'm not even sure what that means. He can't comprehend not being in control. He's arrogant.

I ignore him completely. "I don't just have myself to take care of."

"What are you doing, Boy Scout?" Rogelio asks cautiously from the doorway.

"Albert can make sure your family is taken care of too," Toby promises.

I have a family to think about now. I can't just align myself with who I make friends with, because I can make friends with anybody. I need to align myself with the strongest side. Safety is hard to find in this world, but making bad bets will put everyone I care about in danger.

"Randall, I like you, I really do," Toby says fondly, using one of his hands to wipe his forehead. He's got unsightly pit stains and a mystery stain on his gut. "But you're wasted here. I mean, look around man, you don't belong with these guys. You don't-hey." Toby stops his speech, looking behind me. "You, Padilla, stay on the ground."

"I'm going to break you open like a piñata." I hear behind me. One of these days, Luis' inability to play any game but his own his going to be his downfall.

That day might even be today.

"I bet you wanna," Toby sneers, pushing his glasses up. "But you're not used to not having the upper hand, are you?"

"Look around," Rogelio says from the doorway. "Does it look like you have the upper hand?" Rogelio and four of his men block the doorway, waiting for a way to get in without Luis getting shot. I'm between Toby and Luis, and two of Albert's guys are unarmed against the wall, looking like they're unsure if they made the right call in surrendering.

Toby's beady eyes look around, judging how he can continue to control this situation. He's never had anything that resembles power before, and he wants to hang onto it.

He's going to need me for that. I'm the closest to Luis.

"I brought you into all of this," Toby reminds me, slowly shifting to his left until he's got his own guys behind him and he's got a better eye on the doorway.

"You want me to be grateful?" I shift as Toby does, making sure I continue to block his view of Luis.

"Well, yeah." Toby laughs. "I want that, and I want you to get everyone else to lower their weapons."

"How are you going to get out of here, Toby?" There's no way to get out of this room without pushing past a group of angry cartel members. Even if they were unarmed, Toby wouldn't make it out alive.

"The two of us could get out of here together, with *him* as collateral." Toby looks behind me, where Rogelio stands. "I bet you'd do a lot to get your boss back."

Luis starts up from the ground again. "Motherfucker, I'd hang you from a tree, but you'd break the fucking branch. I swear I will-"

"Luis, just shut up." There's a stunned silence in the room as the tides turn, and now I'm the one that's going to be giving orders. Not Luis.

I look directly at Toby, not lowering my weapon, but holding it in a less threatening stance in relation to Toby. "Is there really a spot for me?"

This world is so dangerous. Luis is dangerous, he's erratic. For as long as I'm aligned with him, I'm always going to be saddled with a ticking time bomb.

Toby grins like he can't believe his luck, relaxing a little. "You belong with us, Randall. I mean- come on, look around. You're not like them, you're like me." My stomach rolls at the thought. Am I like Toby? Have I always been over my head with the Padillas?

514

"You belong in this world, but you belong with someone who *looks* like us. I can introduce you to Albert and his team. We're a bunch of red-blooded Americans that are going to send each and every one of these pigs back over the border in a body bag."

"And the risk you took when you left," I start softly, thinking not about what's best for me, or who I like more, but about who's most likely to make sure I come back to Liling every night. "Is the risk worth it? Is it really better than this?"

"Everything's better than this, than them." Toby shoots back. "Look at him, Randall. Does he look like the winning side right now?"

For the first time in a while, I take my eyes off of the person pointing a gun at me and at Luis on the floor. He's sitting up now, one leg folded under him. Luis looks like shit. I don't know how he's sitting up at all. He's covered in bruises, his nose has a faucet of drying blood under it, and from how hard he was getting kicked I figure he's got to have some sort of internal damage.

Does he look like the winning side right now?

Still looking at Luis, whose dark eyes are brewing a storm ready to swallow the room, I say, "No, he doesn't." Luis' eyes change from anger to vulnerability and then back to hatred all in one second of staring back at me in disbelief.

I look back at Toby. "How are we getting out of this room?" It might be the most dangerous thing I've ever said.

Victorious, Toby looks between me and Luis. "I don't think any of your friends will let us leave unless they know we're serious. We'll shoot Luis, if we have to." He raises his voice for all the people at the doorway. Diego and Gabriel are here now.

"There's four of us," Toby reminds. "I'll lead the way out, you handle Luis." *Handle Luis.* I better be right about this

515

decision, because if I'm wrong, I've just killed my entire family. I've killed Liling. I've killed Wuhan.

Toby cautiously steps around Luis and myself, turning his back to me and going toward the door. Following his movement, I can now see that everyone we've come with, minus the two or so that are with the cars, are waiting by the doorway, armed and ready. Grave faces wait by the doorway, everyone trying to get me to look at them, and I can't meet any of them in the eye.

It doesn't matter how many of them are here, no one is going to try anything so long as Toby has Luis as a hostage. They don't have a way of getting to Luis and there isn't a way to open fire without catching their leader in the crossfire.

"You can get up now, Luis," Toby says condescendingly. Putting himself right back into the position as my boss, he looks at me to help accomplish this.

"Come on," I mutter nervously to Luis, keeping my own pistol in hand because I know Luis doesn't need a gun to be dangerous. I just have to hope that his injuries will keep him from acting too out of line until we get out of this building, where there's so many people who want to kill me right now. "Did you want to stay on the floor?" I ask testily when Luis is glaring at me instead of rising.

"Boy Scout, I swear I'll-"

I make myself sound bored because sounding as scared as I actually am is going to get me killed. "Yeah, *Padilla,* I know." Luis hates being interrupted, and he knows that his friends all call him by his first name.

Everything's happening too fast. Just another minute later the two men I convinced earlier to put down their guns are now rearmed, I'm apparently sided back with Toby, and he's telling me to 'handle Luis.'

Still drunk on the feeling that someone's actually listening to him, Toby has himself positioned closer to the door but not so close that he's within arm's reach of Rogelio. "Everyone else, weapons down." Toby's not the kind of person that anyone really takes orders from, so no one moves.

Every one of his men, are looking at Luis for direction. Luis always makes the calls. Even now, Luis can claim he's making the calls, but I'm the one who has a gun pressed into his back.

Toby wipes his meaty hands across his head for the fourth time. "Come on Luis, know who's in charge here." I need to hurry this along. I've got Liling outside waiting for me and I need to get her somewhere safe.

After I gently press my own weapon between Luis' shoulder blades, he mutters softly to the room. "Put them down."

No one argues with Luis. With disappointed faces, all of Luis' men put their weapons down. Rogelio is stone-faced, trying to get me to look at him but I can't do it right now.

"One by one, slide what you have across the floor and back away from the doorway, back on the hallway wall so we can get out." Toby's giving instructions, but everyone still waits to move until Luis nods, looking at the floor that's already smeared with his own blood.

Within the next five minutes, Luis' cartel is unarmed and have backed against the walls so we all have an escape route we can take. Feeling more comfortable with the extra space and not having anyone pointing a gun at him, Toby comes back to gloat. He starts by immediately punching Luis across his already bruised face.

Luis takes it easily, but still grunts. "You hit like a little bitch." He spits blood onto Toby's foot. One of Luis' men looks like he's about to storm the room but Rogelio takes his shoulder to stop him.

Toby glares down at his shoes. "Remember when you and all your illegals beat the shit out of me?"

"I dream about it," Luis replies quickly.

"When they were done, you told me I had to pick something," Toby starts. I don't know how this story ends. "You told me I had to pick a body part, and then you flipped a coin to decide whether you'd shoot me there or stab me. Remember that?"

Fuck, Padilla.

"It's my favorite game." Luis' voice doesn't sound like himself. It's tired. It's weak.

"Let's play that game." Toby smiles. "Randall, you have any coins?"

I don't want to play this game, but I've already decided on the role I'm going to play now and it's not where I thought I'd be when I woke up this morning. "Yeah, hang on." Toby takes over with keeping a gun aimed at Luis while I fish out a wallet from my pocket and find a quarter. "Got it."

Toby nods giddily. "Ok, Lulu. You have to pick your part first. I picked my hand, remember?" Toby holds up his left palm that shows a long scar across it. "The coin ruled in favor of the knife, thankfully. The sideshow freak carved me up after that."

"He's even better at it now," Luis promises.

"Pick a body part," Toby encourages. "Unless you're too much of a pussy to play by the rules of your own game."

Nothing riles of Luis more than being called weak, even if he's currently a hostage. "Foot." To me, it doesn't seem like a great call but I don't know what I'd choose if I was forced to play. I guess I'd just have to hope that the coin flips in favor of a stab wound over the gun.

"I guess we have enough people here to carry you out," Toby responds, holding his hand out for the quarter that I found in my wallet. "Heads for a shot to the foot, tails for giving me a chance to use my new hunting dagger."

Toby wipes his palm on his pants before counting "One, two, three-" With Luis' cartel watching in a state of disassociated horror from the hallway, Toby flips the coin into the air. He catches it and slaps it to the back of his left hand, grinning when he reads the results.

"Heads!" Toby croons, holding up the coin for everyone to see. He looks at me now, the person charged with being Luis' handler. "Heads. One shot, to the foot."

Not that there's really any room to turn back now, but once you shoot somebody, you're really telling that person that you're not on their side any longer.

"To the foot," I repeat, pulling my new gun back out.

"Is everyone watching?" Toby hollers, looking happily at everyone cramming as close up as they're allowed.

Everyone's not just watching, they're watching me. They watch me ready my weapon, they watch me pull back the bolt so that it's ready to fire. I take one more deep breath as I raise the gun and take aim. Everyone is watching.

Everyone is watching when I push Luis out of the way and shoot Toby in the foot.

92.

[RANDALL]

Before anyone, myself included, can take stock of what the hell just happened, I do a 180-degree turn and shoot the person directly behind me dead before all hell breaks loose.

Toby is howling and immediately hits the floor, I'm diving for the gun Jeff dropped after I shot him. As soon as I get my hands on the spare, gun I yell, "Luis!" And throw it at him. Luis, about to be tackled by Mose, catches it like a baseball and blasts a bullet straight into Mose's skull when they're within one foot of each other. Fresh blood and brain matter is now splattered over Luis' face as he looks back at me in a stupor.

"Sorry, boss!" I pant to Luis quickly before turning my attention back to the commotion at the doorway.

Diego, Rogelio, Gabriel, and three others have all exploded back into the room and have descended upon the closest enemy like wolves. Now, it's Toby being stomped into the floor, screaming and crying and pleading. Luis, at least, had the pride to be quiet while being beaten to a pulp.

Beating someone within an inch of their life is a four man job, at most, and that leaves Ro and one of his men staring at me with a dangerous look of incredulity while they try to reassess whose side I'm on. With the limited view, there's a major risk that no one saw enough to understand how the chaos broke out.

Ro's man, Miguel, is ready to storm, coming at me like he's intent to pistol whip me before Luis quickly puts his hand up. "He's mine," Luis snaps. The whole room stops.

Luis' voice rings out like thunder over a field, stilling anyone who doesn't want to be struck. Toby is still conscious but he's on the floor in a sweaty, bloody, heaving pile.

I'm cornered as Luis does his best to conceal his limp as he steps up to me, so close I can smell the blood that's drying on his body. I might've shot Toby, but I had to play a game to beat him. Luis doesn't like games all that much.

"You lose your fucking marbles, Boy Scout?" Murder, that's what Luis sounds like when he's angry. When he's covered in pieces of someone else's head, Luis looks like a god of death.

Nervously, I run a tongue over my lips. This feels familiar to when Luis thought I stole money from him. My survival strategy is going to be the same. "Gee, Luis, you're not going to make me apologize like Gael did, are you?"

Luis' bruised, stone face is unamused. "I swear to God, you never answer the fucking question." He shoots his arm forward and I flinch until I realize he's only messing up my hair. "Boy Scout with the switch up, ey?" When he cracks a smile and everyone hears the laughter in his voice, the entire room takes a breath.

"Randall Fucking Persch," Rogelio mutters, tucking his gun away, walking up to Luis with what almost looks like a heavy waterline. Voice still weighed down with worry, Rogelio puts a heavy hand on Luis' shoulder and pulls him slightly. "You ok, brother?"

Luis straightens his face with a nod. "Ah, get off of me." He playfully shrugs Ro off. "I'm still walking, aren't I?"

Intimate moment over, Ro tries to give Luis' face a mischievous caress of the cheek before Luis is deflecting him away again. "What did they do to your pretty face?"

When I laugh, I get Ro's attention and in the next second, the massive man has me in a headlock. "You're really fucking stupid, you know that?"

Hunched over, trying to breathe between Rogelio's tree trunk of an arm, I grunt, "I like to use the word ambitious." And take a deep breath when Rogelio laughs and releases me.

Diego gets Luis' attention, and Luis saunters over to where Toby, the only person left alive from his side of the war, lays on the floor.

Rogelio follows too. "We should get going, in case that Albert guy sends backup to get this place back under control. We take what we can and I can send some guys out later for surveillance.

"Sure," Luis says, standing over Toby. "It's going to take some time to handle this one." He kicks Toby hard in the gut, leaving Toby wheezing.

Toby looks at me when I walk up next to Luis. "Come on, Randall. Don't align themselves with them. You shouldn't be working for their kind- they should be working for *you.*"

I can look the other way for violence, robbery, drug use, kidnapping, and murder, but blatant racism is where I have to draw the line. "You haven't met my fiancé, have you?" I ask.

"Please-" Even I roll my eyes when Toby starts up. He's so weak. I've had my life threatened multiple times today, as has Luis, and no one would ever catch either of us begging.

In fact, Liling loves how I make *others* beg. Loves it.

Luis sighs. "I really don't have time to handle this here. But first, I want to circle back on something you said earlier, Toby."

Toby's already got an eye swollen shut and the other one has a burst vessel, filling the iris with red. Luis crouches down in front of Toby, grabbing the beaten man by the hair and pulling his head off the floor. "You said I needed to know who is in charge." Luis pulls hard and Toby hisses. "Who is in charge, Toby?"

Toby's never been strong. He's never been brave. "You are."

Luis loves pain and humiliation. "Again."

"You are!"

Rogelio steps close to Luis, brushing his shoulder. "Luis, you can explore your humiliation kink later. We need to leave before any one else gets here."

Luis doesn't appreciate the comment but agrees. "Fine." He points at Toby with a circular gesture. "Get some of your boys to drag his ass into one of the cars."

It takes four people to get Toby to the doors, but I'm not one of them, thankfully. As soon as it's been clarified that I'm not an enemy of the cartel, I'm practically running out of the old school. I've left Liling for way too long, and I need to go see the person who all of this is for.

LILING

Even as Blanca and I work to distract ourselves, we're nearly ready to go in ourselves after how long we've been waiting. I don't know if my stomach has been turning from the nerves or the baby, but when Randall finally shows his face, looking relatively unscathed, I thank the Lord as I run to Randall like some love-stricken damsel in a movie.

"I'm alright!" Randall's calling before I've even reached him, seeing the little look of desperation that surfaces. We meet in an embrace one gets when they feared they'd never see their loved one again. I can feel the grit of Randall's face as we kiss and I run my hands over his jaw, his hair, his arms to make sure he's alright.

We're briefly interrupted as Blanca shrieks. I rip myself away from Randall to see what Blanca sees- Luis Padilla covered in blood, bruises and gore. He's clearly concealing a limp and I have no idea how he's walking at all.

"What happened to you?" Blanca screams, launching herself at Luis.

Luis grimaces when he's nearly tackled but he manages to hold Blanca steady against him. "Ran into some trouble. It's alright now, love."

Rogelio, walking closely next to Luis, tries to appease Blanca. "We handled it-"

Blanca cuts off Rogelio by slapping him on the back of his head. "You're supposed to keep an eye on him! How could you let this happen?"

Rogelio ducks away from Blanca as she rants. "Ey! Luis and his big fucking ego probably went off on his own, so he got a big fucking ass whooping."

Luis pushes Rogelio with his elbow. "What, you turning on me when it's convenient for you too?" Luis chides, pushing Rogelio's broad shoulder. "You and Persch, both of you are fired." Luis raises his voice toward the men that are loading a very large hostage into a van. "Which one of you wants a promotion?" A couple of them jeer in response.

I laugh a little, knowing Luis is alright if he's arguing as much as he is and return to *my* man. "How did you get yourself fired during a raid?" I tease, pulling at the neckline of his shirt.

"He acts like he doesn't like me but I'm the first-person people call when there's trouble," Randall says, placing his hands just a little too low on my back before I reposition them as we're in public.

Ro, in passing, bumps into Randall. "What are you talking about, Big Head? You were like the sixth person Luis called and the last one to show up."

"Don't listen to him," Randall mutters, moving to stand behind me so he can watch the rest of the group get ready to leave while he keeps his arms folded over me.

Once he's settled, I happily lean my head back onto Randall's chest. "You're the first person I call."

I flinch a little when Randall nips at my neck and he tightens his arms to keep me there. "I wish we had a tree we could rest under."

"I am over eight months pregnant, you're covered in blood, and we're surrounded by people," I remind him.

He groans in response. "Please don't make us practice abstinence again, that was the most painful experience of my life."

"Shhh," I say quickly, knowing there's far too many people here to be discussing this. That, and my hormones have been raging lately, but have started to quiet as they're replaced by a clenching pain in the lower half my body. It feels like there's a hole somewhere in my body and the rest of my muscles and flesh are constricting themselves to fill it.

Too early, too early. For now, I'm fine, I know it. We're almost through here, and then I can worry about giving birth and becoming a mother. The thought absolutely terrifies me.

Luis and Blanca have stopped arguing, and wait by a large commercial truck, devouring each other in a way that suggest there will be very little space between Rafael and a future sibling. The two stop their wild public display when Diego reluctantly interrupts them to speak with Luis, who listens with Blanca working her lips at her husband's chest.

This reminds me of what Diego said on our way here, about how hard one can fight when they're fighting for their partner. Or at least that's what I gathered he was saying from his three or so words. Evaluating everyone that's come out of the building, watching Luis' men sort corpses from captives, most everyone has at least one minor injury.

Bruises, cuts, and one of Luis' men even has a gunshot wound on his upper arm, although it looks far from fatal. Even Randall, who seems to have fared pretty well, has a small bruise on his neck and has come with his hands stained in someone else's blood.

Everyone looks like they've survived something. Everyone except Gabriel. Gabriel is closing one of the cars after loading up one of the fatalities from the other side. He looks sweaty and tired but it's hard to imagine how he left the school building without so much as a scratch.

My eyes fall onto Diego again. Gabriel must have *quite* the protector.

"Hey," Luis calls, pausing my inquiries. "Everyone hurry up and get over here so we can leave."

"Quickly," Rogelio adds, looking back near the gate again.

Luis, still somehow looking as solid as he always does when covered in bruises, rolls his eyes at the comment but starts making hurrying gestures as we all approach.

All the captives have been loaded into cars, leaving Luis, his men, myself, and Blanca milling around him. "So it didn't go exactly as planned," Luis begins. "But we made out pretty fucking good."

Diego nods, standing next to Luis with his arms crossed. When Luis grins slightly at him, Diego adds, "Real good."

"Real good," Luis repeats happily, getting ready to count on his fingers. "We shut this place down, and we're gonna keep an eye on it until we take out the competition. We got bitches in the car that will tell us where we can find the head of this operation. *And,*" Luis pauses for dramatic effect, nodding at Diego.

Diego, at the base of the truck, hops onto the metal step so he can reach the lever that will open the back up. The back of the truck is opened by raising up against the back wall, revealing whatever Luis is attempting to steal.

It's a commercial transport truck packed at maximum capacity with bricks of cocaine.

There's awed cussing and murmurs as Diego stands proudly next to the haul. "Very good," Diego repeats.

"But we got more," Luis says, and I've just noticed a large leather duffel bag at his feet. "This was clearly their operational building, where they stored product and some of the payments they already got."

There's actually about six bags, and the rest are loaded on the back of the truck. Luis lifts the bag from the ground to the back of the truck for easier access, groaning as he rises.

I'm not too surprised that the bag is full of rolled money. A lot of it. A truckload of cocaine and hundreds of thousands of dollars. Luis takes out three rolls of cash from the first bag. "Ernesto." Ernie comes when called and accepts what I'm assuming is meant to be a bonus for this harrowing day.

As Luis continues to call names, starting with the men I know less of, Rogelio comes to stand besides Randall who still has his arms over me, hands clasped over our child.

"Perk of going on these crazy missions for Luis," Rogelio explains, crossing his arms. "Inner circle usually gets an extra cut, whether we're here for it or not."

"Yeah?" Randall asks, watching Jesus receive several rolls of cash.

"Inner fucking circle, baby," Rogelio adds. When I give Rogelio a look, he smirks, saying, "What? Right, you still pretending to be a good girl, yeah? No swearing?"

"No swearing," I confirm, stroking Randall's hand over my stomach.

"Randall swears," Rogelio points out.

I turn in Randall's arms, giving him a pointed look, which he smiles off. "Not around me, he doesn't."

When Rogelio laughs, Randall adds, "I'm going to have to get to know Carmen better. I need some ammunition against you."

"Nah, my girl's loyal." Rogelio shakes his head with a laugh.

Luis' voice rings out over the crowd. *"Diamante."* My head snaps to Luis in surprise. He looks back, having emptied one of the bags and is waiting for me. "Yes, you. Come on, *Diamante*."

Randall unwraps his arms, kissing my neck first. "Liling Persch does not hesitate, she takes what is hers." I laugh at that, starting to walk away before I really catch what he's said. "What? Too soon?" He laughs.

"I'm still my own person, Randall." I snap with bemused authority. I'll always be my own person, no matter what my name is.

Randall raises his hand in surrender. "Yes, Ms. Zhu."

Meeting Luis at the back of the truck, Luis patiently waits, three rolls of cash in his hand. "I didn't do anything," I say as I approach.

Luis is already shaking his head, holding out the rolls. "Don't act like you don't keep *that* one in line. You help me by keeping that one where he needs to be, keeping him focused on what he needs to be doing. Plus, Blanca loves you." With less patience, he's pushing the three bundles toward me until I accept them.

Thousands. I've just been handed thousands. "Fine," I say, sweetly. "Thank you, Luis."

Luis gives me a smug grin, nodding affectionately. Before I walk away, Luis calls out. "Ah- *Diamante*, wait." I pause. "Show me your hand, let's see it."

I already know he means my left hand, and I hold it out. The ostentatious mound of diamonds sits prettily on my ring finger. "He has good taste."

Luis laughs. "Sure, but it's an engagement ring, right?"
I nod. "Right."

529

"Then don't you let that Randall touch none of this money until he gives you his last name, got it? This is *yours, mi Diamante*." When I laugh, Luis shoots his voice out, mustering his best authoritative voice. "Boy Scout!"

Randall, talking to Rogelio jumps with a start. "What?" He calls back, not sure why Luis has taken a tone.

"You better do right by this woman!" He points a finger at me with gusto.

"I'm trying!"

"You could try harder, now come up here. Rogelio, Diego, you too."

When it's the inner circle's turn to approach Luis, they are not given rolls of cash. They're each given one of the remaining leather bags, overflowing with wads of money.

Rogelio laughs when Randall blanches as he's handed one of the bags that was recovered inside of the school. "This is why everyone wants to be in the circle."

94.

[RANDALL]

After Luis hands me what I think must be at least two hundred thousand dollars in cash, he says he needs to 'have a word' with me, much to Rogelio's disagreement.

"They're going to come finish the job with you, Boss Man," Rogelio calls after us. I leave my loot with Liling.

The two of us wander along the brick walls of the school, walking until the happy chatter of Luis' men fades in with the swishing of the trees in the wind.

I don't know what Luis wants. He's rebuilt some of his stone walls, but I still see a hole in the fortress. "Things got dicey today."

"Dicey," Luis repeats, kicking a rock in front of him. "Real fucking dicey."

"You don't look great," I say, letting Luis give me side eye. "But, as usual, you're coming out of it richer than you went into it."

Luis chuckles at this. "Listen, Persch." I notice the improvement from my usual *Boy Scout*.

"I'm listening," I say when Luis hasn't added anything additional.

"You did good today, ok?"

Even I can tell he wants to say more than that. I had to play a part, I had to be someone who I'm not anymore. I knew what I was doing the entire time; I had confidence I was digging a way out of the trouble that had fallen onto us. For a minute, I think everyone else thought I was digging a grave. "I scared you today."

It feels like a dangerous thing to say, and I flinch when I see Luis pinch his lips into a frown. He pauses, stopping with his hands in his pocket. He's choosing to look up at the setting sun. "You scared the shit out of me today, Boy Scout."

When it comes to Luis' inner circle, all he has is trust. Really, anyone, at any time, could betray Luis. They could sell him out, tell his secrets, kill his friends and family. There's only so much he can do against those threats, and after that, it will come down to trust. For a short time, I've been given that trust, and for a brief moment, Luis thought he'd made a mistake in giving it to me.

"I didn't know what else to do." I really didn't. "I was making things up as I went, banking on the knowledge that Toby is an idiot and desperate for anything that resembles having someone like him. Having someone choose him."

"You know how long it's been since I felt like that?" Luis asks, anger dripping into the sorrowful holes in his voice. "Since I let someone get the best of me- since I let myself get weak?"

I don't like thinking about Luis like that. This is a guy who I definitely look up to. Luis seems to have the whole world spinning on his fingertips. "I don't know anyone that could take on four people alone."

"Rogelio could."

"Rogelio is twice the size of any normal man."

"Diego."

"I don't think he's human." Luis laughs, so I continue. "For what it's worth, I would probably be dead if I was jumped by that many guys."

Luis straightens himself. "No, you got something special about you, Boy Scout. You get yourself out of every problem you ever faced, make a friend with every person you ever met, if you want to."

"If there was a way I could have safely told you what I was trying to do, I would have." This is about vulnerability and betrayal; even if it was a short-lived illusion. There may be a lot of jokes about the inner circle, but to Luis, it means a lot more than who he wants to reward for their hard work.

Luis shakes his head. "You know what?" He looks at me, dark eyes simmering. "I shouldn't have let your little act scare me. I should have known." It doesn't feel like this is my place to speak, and I know Luis hates how I usually don't know when to shut up. "I'm sorry I even let myself be scared when it comes to you, ok? I should have known better."

Luis Padilla just apologized to me.

I know Luis well enough to know he doesn't like to linger. He only likes to take his time when it comes to dealing with his enemies. "Now you know my antics. Now you know that, give me time, and I won't let you down."

Luis turns when we hear some laughter back by where the cars wait. "Stick with me, Boy Scout," Luis says warmly, looking at me directly in the eye with a promise. "You stick with me, and I promise, someday I'll make you a millionaire."

Any promise from Luis is worth its weight in gold.

LILING

Now that Diego's found an entire classroom full of narcotics and loaded it all into one of the vans that have been commandeered, it needs a driver. Somehow, Randall has been charged with driving a stick-shift truck I am positive he does not know how to drive. He claims he can do this, but I have my doubts. Nevertheless, I ride in the passenger seat while Randall drives to one of Luis' storage locations.

The sun has mostly set, and we drive into a pink horizon. Randall's been happily chatting and I've been listening, but I have that feeling again. I'm not saying that driving back eight months pregnant after taking down my fiancé's rival cocaine cartel is the same feeling as when we were on our way to the beach last year, but it's something similar. I love this feeling. It's the feeling that I have someone walking with me, driving with me, standing with me, no matter what. I love Randall.

Luis is driving Blanca home, and Diego will meet them there to deal with Toby and someone else named Brandon. I have no idea where Rogelio has driven off to, but for now it's just myself, Randall, and a lot of cash and cocaine.

It's been a long day, and I'm thinking about poplar trees and cinnamon bark cologne as I drift into a sleep. I've always enjoyed the melodic jostling of a car trip when trying to sleep.

I'm unaware of how close to true sleep I got to when I hear Randall cuss. "Shit."

I can pull myself out of sleep in an instant when it comes to scolding Randall. When I do open my eyes, I'm nearly blinded by flashing red and blue lights. "What-"

"Shit!" Randall says again. "Should I pull over?"

"Of course, you should pull over!"

"We've got a lot of coke here, Liling!"

I shake my head. "If you keep driving, they'll call for more officers and they'll chase you back to the storage lot. Pull over."

Randall frowns deeply, putting on the truck's blinker and pulling the truck over. Now it's time to steady myself. *You're pretty, Liling. Never forget you're pretty.* There's power in pretty, there's a tactic to manipulation. We will be fine because that's the outcome I've decided on.

I will be my most pleasant self, and so will Randall. He's always excelled in social interactions. Randall rolls the window down as we're approached by a short, female officer with her hair tied back in a messy ponytail. I try not to let this bother me, even though I typically do less well with a female audience.

Luckily, there's Randall. "Good evening, Officer," Randall says politely.

She doesn't return the smile. She merely clocks that I'm in the van as well, holding a small flashlight to see into the front of the truck. "License and registration."

Randall stalls, looking at me for approval. I nod at him. "Sure," Randall says cheerily, reaching for his wallet.

"Is that a firearm?"

Randall freezes, I freeze. We both know that Randall is *not* licensed to carry. After today, I will make sure Randall has whatever sort of license he needs. This is my fault, really. Sometimes, if Randall doesn't have me to think for him, he doesn't think at all.

"Yes, it is," Randall says cautiously.

"I'm going to need to see your registration for that too," the officer says, holding her hand out for something Randall doesn't have. She takes a step back, looking at the truck. "What are you transporting?"

"Cleaning supplies," Randall says quickly.

The officer tilts her head in scrutiny. "Cleaning supplies?"

God, Randall. I don't even know how to fix that for him.

She clicks her tongue, quickly putting together pieces of a puzzle that Randall's putting out for her. "I'm going to need you to step out of the vehicle."

Alright, letting Randall be in charge of things was a fun, short lived experiment, but it's clear to see that he's not suited for leadership. Liling the diamond, clocking in. There's a very good chance we both get arrested for possession of illegal substances, unlawful carrying of a deadly weapon, and perhaps, bribery and obstruction of justice.

And that would only be the charges we've occurred in the last half hour.

"Officer," I call from the passenger seat. No sugar in my voice, just the venom of someone ready to strike.

Her badge reads YELLNATS. "You can go ahead and step out as well, ma'am."

"Officer Yellnats." Randall is looking at me like he doesn't know what I'm doing. He should know to trust me by now. Nevertheless, I have her attention. "Let me give you a couple of options for how this can go."

Randall blanches at me. "Liling."

I put my hand on his lap to silence him. From my purse, I pull out two of the rolls of cash that Luis handed me. Officer Yellnats' eyes go wide, and Randall hisses at me, trying to catch my hands. "Liling!"

I swat him away, batting my eyes at the alarmed officer. "This is a bribe," I say bluntly. Randall has all but melted into his seat. "This is option one. Option one is taking this and going on your way."

The officer's mouth has fallen open in disbelief, her hand hovering over her radio. "Ma'am, are you-"

"Bribing an officer? Yes." I do not like repeating myself. "That's option one."

She looks at me like I've lost my mind, but I'm quite certain I know exactly what I'm doing. "Alright, I'm almost afraid to ask what option two is." She's bewildered, covering a hint of amusement in her voice. She's probably only asking about option two so she can have a good story to tell later.

"Option two means you check the back of the truck. If you do that, you'll see that it is stacked full with bricks of cocaine."

Randall's choking over his own tongue. "She's joking, she's joking."

"Randall, shush." I snap waving my hand at him before returning my attention to Officer Yellnats. "You will obviously arrest us both, take possession of the truck and all of its contents. If you do this, there's a very good chance you will be dead next week."

Randall's given up on me, and he's rubbing his forehead. "She's going to get me killed," he mutters.

'Ma'am, are you-"

"Yes, I'm threatening you," I state. "You can arrest us, but that will only send our employer after you." I smile at her. "I think we both know what kind of employer deals with cocaine in the amounts that we have it in."

"Our employers don't care who you are, where you work, or how important you are to your family," I continue, watching her face slowly blank. "They will kill you. And they will make an example of you."

Randall is done with his reboot, and he's smiling charmingly at the officer, his voice still shaken. "Listen, Officer, we don't want to scare you. We just want to make sure you understand the weight of your actions."

"So you're saying…" The officer speaks very slowly. "That if I call this in-"

"You'll die a terrible, brutal death as soon as our employer can bail us out and have us identify you."

Randall holds his hand out to me, taking the rolls. "Or, you can accept this for your troubles, and we'll be on our way."

The officer blinks. "But your truck is full of cocaine?"

"We're helping keep you guys in business." Randall grins.

"Randall," I hiss. I look at the officer. "You don't have to accept this, Officer Yellnats, but you do have to accept the consequences of starting a war with the cartel."

There it is. This is how I'm trying to solve our problems. Bribing a police officer after admitting to carrying cocaine? That's bravery. That's someone not to be messed with. Powerful, that's what I am. Randall sees it, and so does Officer Yellnats.

Officer Yellnats takes the cash from Randall, and we drive off with a fun story of our own to tell.

96

LILING

"I don't even know why I'm surprised anymore," Randall breathes after we've started driving again. "You really can do anything."

The sentiment is sweet, but my nerves are shot now. "Let's get home."

"It's still being built."

"Randall." Pregnancy has taken much of my humor away.

"We're about fifteen minutes out, I think," Randall sighs, putting his hand on my thigh. I feel terrible. Absolutely terrible right now.

"Are you alright?"

"Mm." I'm sweating through my shirt, and the entire lower half of my body is just one massive cramp. "I have a theory based on how I'm feeling right now."

"What's the theory?" Randall asks nervously.

"About Wuhan." I breathe- in through the nose, out through the mouth. "When he's unhappy, the whole world will know it."

"What, are we birthing the antichrist?"

"Maybe."

"Well, then I guess we'll be pretty well off, with our son to take down all of our enemies."

I do like the idea of having a son to teach things to. Yes, my son will be unstoppable with Randall and I at the helm of his life. Just imagining my son doing anything, being anywhere other than inside of my stomach, calms me enough to rationalize my thoughts. Soon, we'll get this truck to the storage lot and we can go home.

We're close to our destination, but the roaring of engines tailing us rips to my little fantasy of what Wuhan will be. Three cars; two SUVs and a yellow charger have raced up to the truck, boxing us in at the sides. The yellow charger speeds again on the road, swerving to a stop in front of us to block our path.

The maneuver is meant to force us into a stop, but the execution was done poorly. Randall cusses and slams on the breaks. He's not able to stop fast enough, and the truck pummels into the muscle car. My head collides into the sun visor which was still down as the world blurs. The seatbelt is the only thing that kept me from flying through the windshield. Something else in the car goes flying past my arm, cutting it as it soars.

"Liling, are you alright?" Randall's unbuckling his seatbelt, trying to grab at me.

"I'm fine, I'm fine." I check my stomach, as if there's some way I would know if little Wuhan was ok with that crash.

Randall looks through the cracked windshield, the smashed charger in front of us now smoking. "What the hell was their plan?"

My head is throbbing from hitting it so hard. I'm hoping I'm not concussed now. "Their plan was to-" I pause, that little thing inside of me that tells me something is not right starts singing to me at the same time the most painful cramp of my life rips through my abdomen.

The vans that flanked us are opening up, letting two men from each car except for the charger, whose drive has his head lulled back into the seat.

"Liling, get down," Randall says, reaching for the lever that uncomfortably whips my seat lower. This is one of the few times I have seen true fear in Randall's eyes. One of the few times he looks at me in a way that says he knows he can't fix what's about to happen. Before I can argue with him, he jumps out of the truck, hoping that if he leaves now, the men that surround the truck won't check the passenger seat.

97.

[RANDALL]

My face hits the road almost as soon as I step out of the truck. I'm wheezing from the following kick to my stomach when I'm told to produce the keys to the truck. I don't know how to stall my way out of this one. Either way, they have to be within seconds of realizing there's someone in the passenger seat.

There's four men, with the driver of the charger likely dead from the stupidest car-chase maneuver possible. After Toby claiming he works with people 'that look like us,' I'm going to assume these four are with his group, coming to reclaim what we took.

"Keys." One of them barks again.

Panting from the gravel, I have this terrible, desperate feeling. "Alright, let me look." I don't even remember turning the truck off. Is it not running because I turned it off or did it stop running when we crashed? I'm disoriented and scared that I can't control these events. These are people that don't want to make friends, these are people that have a boss like Luis.

"He's taking too long." One of them complains over me.

"Fine, whatever. Let's send a message to the Padillas and we'll check the truck."

I know what this means, and I'm out of time - unless I can fight my way out of this, somehow. I may not be big, but I'm armed. Before anyone can haul me up again, I reach to where I have my pistol tucked away only to realize it is no longer where it should be. I'm unarmed, outnumbered, and out of options.

I don't know how to protect Liling.

I'm pulled to my feet, and a person with brown hair that smells like weed checks my pockets. "Randall Persch." He reads, once he's found my wallet. He mutters the name again quietly to himself. "That sounds familiar but-" He inspects me briefly. "You don't look like a Padilla."

"Have you seen what your coworkers look like?" I ask, not sure what I hope to gain from the question.

Brown hair smirks. "Eye for an eye, buddy." He looks at the person standing in front of me, someone with short bleach-blonde hair and brown eyes with dark lines under them. "I heard Luis has a new guy. This could be him; he might know something useful."

The one with the blonde hair is pulling out a cigarette, surveying me. "No, this isn't anyone important." He pulls from the cigarette, giving me a little slap on the cheek. "You were on your way to Luis' storage unit, weren't you?" He grins. "We'll make sure you get there."

Everyone seems to know what this means, and I'm getting hit again. This time, I'm being held up, so every time I'm slugged in the stomach, I'm ready for the next successive hit. I land one good kick to the person in front of me but he quickly retaliates by raising his hits to my jaw. Now, my vision blurs.

I don't know how to protect Liling.

I'm partially hunched as much as I'm allowed when my stomach feels like it's going to collapse in from another hit.

I don't know how to protect Liling.

My head feels like it's full of sand when someone punches near my temple.

I don't know how to protect Liling.

There's a deafening pop and my face is on the ground again and I feel weighed down. I'm so disoriented I don't know what happened, not even registering what took me down or where I'm bleeding from.

It's because I'm not bleeding. I wasn't hit, the person holding me at my left was. He took me down with him. He's been shot, and Liling Zhu is standing across from us, gun in hand.

Liling stands at the end of the truck, legs spread into a ready stance, eyes wide like she can't believe her own actions, but holding the gun like she's ready to do it again.

Liling just killed for me.

I didn't know how to protect Liling, but she knew how to protect me.

"Who the hell was supposed to check the truck?" The blonde hair hollers, outraged.

Liling responds by swinging the pistol in his direction. "Everyone back away from him."

The blonde laughs, taking a step away from me only so he can get closer to her. "Sweetheart-" Liling shoots him. She shot him, the bullet landing somewhere in his calf. He goes down with a scream.

"Bitch," the blonde growls, hunched over and reaching for his own gun just like the remaining two are. Now, there's three guns pointed at Liling. I'm winded on the ground, trying to figure out how to turn this situation around.

Once again, I don't know how to protect Liling.

There's a standoff now. Liling, standing her ground in a denim dress with a red t-shirt under it. She looks so strong. This woman is resilience.

Liling is a diamond.

There's another roar in the direction I had been driving in before I crashed the damn truck, pulling everyone's attention. Six cars are racing toward us, kicking up clouds of dust as they screech to halts, surrounding the entire group. Whatever is about to happen, I have absolutely no control over it. The entire road is blocked now by the new trucks now, and what's pulled up is nothing short of an army.

Three SUVS, and three pickup trucks with men in the back, brandishing automatic weapons like they're coming to take down a resistance. I've never been so glad to see an armed cartel surround us in my life.

In the next moment, Rogelio - God, I love him- is jumping out of the first SUV, and he's yelling at everyone with an authority I'm hearing for the first time now in Luis' absence.

Rogelio is in charge as soon as his feet hit the ground. He clocks Liling with half a second of wonder before starting to give orders. "Any *man* still holding a gun in the next five seconds is going to be dead holding a gun in the next six seconds- five, four-"

Instant surrender. Rogelio Esparza: large and in charge. Now that it's safe to move, I'm crawling out from under the person Liling shot when Rogelio jogs over to me while the rest of our guys try to quickly get the scene under control; taking captives and trying to get vehicles moved in a way that doesn't make it look like a holdup just happened.

"Damn, Boy Scout." Rogelio hauls the corpse off me like it doesn't way more than ten pounds. He's rough in picking me up, dusting off my shoulders. "Tell daddy which one hurt you."

"Go to hell," I grumble on my way up. "And thanks, as usual."

"Why do I feel like you always end up getting your ass knocked down?"

"The first time, I'm pretty sure you're the one who put me there," I point out, thinking about the time when I was doing really dumb things in a bid to get Toby's position.

"You was being stupid." Rogelio grins, slapping me on the back.

I grin too, now moving onto find my savior, my woman, my goddess, my Liling. She's still standing near the truck in stunned solidarity. She's set the gun down on the back step used to climb into the truck, her legs still spread in her fighter's stance.

"Liling," I say, coming toward her with open arms before I stop abruptly in horror.

Liling's looking down at her own body, wet and dripping. Her thighs are wet, the denim of her dress darkened.

Liling's water broke.

Liling is in labor.

I don't know how to protect Liling.

98

LILING

This is my fault. I suspected I was in labor, or was about to be at the beginning of the day. I was measuring the length of my contractions, thinking I had time. By the time Randall came out of the school, I was positive these contractions were too close together to be anything other than active labor. I should have said something then.

But I was scared.

It's like if I admitted I'm in labor then it really, truly, is happening. It means I'm meant to finish this day as a mother if I can survive what is universally accepted as being something dangerous and painful and terrible.

I was scared, and now I've already made my mistake my son's problem.

"It's too early." Randall is holding my hand in the back seat of Rogelio's car while he rips down the road to the nearest hospital. "You're not due for another three weeks."

Mistakes. I've made mistakes, I must have. "Between the stress of everything that's happened today- the school, the car crash," I grunt, squeezing his hand until his fingers turn white. "And... the poplar tree, Randall. We shouldn't have done that."

My family might not be here for the birth of my first child but my self-loathing sure is.

Oh, Mama is supposed to be here. She's over an hour away. We're not even going to the hospital we had planned to deliver at. My baby backpack isn't in this car. In a desperate cry, I close my eyes shut. My face is wet from tears and sweat. I have this gut feeling. "I can't do this," I sob.

"Hey, yes you can, Liling. You can do anything." Randall puts his free hand on the back of my head before wiping my hair back away from my face. "I can't think of one thing that you can't do. I can't think of one thing you failed to do."

"Keep my legs closed." My loathing spits back.

Randall always tries to bring humor during an inappropriate time. "I, personally am really happy about that failure."

I scowl and let go of his hand. "This isn't right, Randall. This is-" The sentence finishes in a grunt as another contraction pulls through me. I'm doubling over as much as I can in the backseat.

"We're less than five out., Rogelio reports, taking a rough turn and honking at someone as he swerves around them.

"We're less than five minutes away," Randall parrots, rubbing my back.

"I need my Mama," I say into my knees. Just being in the vicinity of these men is plummeting my attitude.

"We'll get her here," Randall promises. "How about we focus on all the things that are going well right now?"

There's silence in the car.

"Luis called ahead, now that you're delivering in our territory," Rogelio says. "These people know to take real good care of you."

"See?" Randall continues to rub my back while I breathe into my knees. "That's something!"

I only groan in response, feeling wet and sticky. Rogelio clears his throat, slamming the car into park. "We're here!" He's out of the car in a second, and when I look out the window, someone's coming to address the car that's rolled up to the emergency entrance of the hospital.

It's time. This is it. This is the most important thing I will ever do. I don't even feel that I have much control over the results. I'm already praying, pleading with God to let just one more thing go in my favor. I want to make promises about how good I'm going to be after this but I know not to lie to God.

I've been blessed before. I'm blessed for the opportunities I've had. I'm blessed to be pretty. I'm blessed to have been found by Randall. I'm asking for one more blessing, for now at least.

LILING

This is the most important thing I've ever done.

This is the best thing I've ever done.

This is the most important role I will ever play.

I will do anything for this, for him.

I'll protect him. I'll kill for him. I will do anything, so long as I keep him safe.

He's mine, always.

100.

[RANDALL]

Wuhan Randall Persch was born late into the night on May 26th. He has ten fingers, ten toes, and he is perfect. I know all parents think their kid is perfect, but I'm the only one that's right about it.

I was practically scolded by the doctor for how late I brought Liling in. She really was ready to deliver as soon as we were there. It was a lot of screaming, hand squeezing, and cooing. All of a sudden, we're not expecting anymore.

We're parents.

Wuhan Persch: my son. Our son. You know what? He's a long baby. Doesn't look premature at all; no, this one's fully cooked. Liling's holding him but I've got a hold of his little hand. He's going to do great things with those hands, I can tell. I'm going to teach him so much.

This person, Wuhan, has only been alive for a couple hours and he's already my entire world. Better than that, Liling and I are going to make an entire world for him.

Liling's mother and sisters come as soon as they can, but her father never shows up. The women arrive with bags of presents and clothes, and Liling's mother starts asking rapid-fire questions.

The birth went as well as it could have, even with the extra stress added from the previous day's events. We told the doctor we'd been in a car crash as justification for why we looked the way we did and used it as explanation to our elevated stress that may have caused Liling's early labor. That, and the impromptu outdoor sex.

I sleep in the hospital room in a big green chair while our son sleeps in this plastic box on wheels next to Liling's hospital bed. I'm not sure if either of us slept at the same time. Anytime I heard anything, I was up, looking down at Wuhan. If my son needs me, I want to be there.

The next morning, when Wu stirs without crying, I gently take him out and hold him. My son. We go on a little tour of the hospital room, and I'm whispering anything he might need to know. I show him the window, and the blanket his grandmother left for him. None of it seems to register, but it's important all the same.

"How is he?" Liling's beautiful voice of midnight honey sounds from behind me. When I turn to face her- God, she's just so beautiful.

"He's amazing."

Liling smiles, starting to hold her arms out. "Let me see if he's hungry." Liling, after a staggering fifteen hours of motherhood, already seems to know exactly what she's doing. Liling knows everything.

Lovingly, Liling strokes the little hair Wuhan already has as she nurses him. It's not as dark as Liling's, and I'm hopeful that maybe his hair will look just a little bit like mine. "I can't believe I cried over him when I found out." Her red fingernails lightly trace the side of his face. "That's the only mistake I made. Regret."

"I'd like to think." I recall the avalanche of feelings we went through when we learned we'd be parents. "It's a scary thing to do for the first time. But we've conquered everything else life has thrown at us, why not this?"

"Do you think we'll be any good at this?" Liling asks, not looking like she's legitimately concerned.

"I think we'll be great at this," I say confidently. Liling makes everything a competition and I don't know when to stop. We'll be great parents.

**

Liling will be released from the hospital today. Wuhan is two days old already. I know he's a baby, but I'm already so proud of him.

My dad visited yesterday, and Liling's mother came back too. Today, Rogelio is bringing my car to the hospital so we can take Wuhan home. It isn't surprising that Luis and Diego came with him.

Luis walks in first, with his own son strapped to his chest in a baby wrap, a bouquet of flowers in his free hand, and a diaper bag slung over his shoulder. Only Luis Padilla can look as threatening as he does while wearing a baby. Luis grins when he steps in, quiet and mischievous. "Well look who it is, Boy Scout, a father now, huh?"

"I want my credit in this delivery in the future," Rogelio adds, coming in after Luis. Diego files in as well, only giving me a nod as he enters.

Luis approaches Liling, dropping his voice even further. "Oh, *Diamante*, how are you doing, gorgeous?" He sets the flowers on the table next to the bed.

"Hi, Luis." Liling is beaming. Absolutely beaming. She reaches a hand out to take Rafael's little hand. "Hello, Rafael. This is Wuhan."

"Thank God you didn't name him Nick," Luis jests. "Little man." Luis pats his son's head. "This is going to be your best friend, got it?"

Rogelio nods at me as he fishes through his pocket. "Keys." He hands them off. "There's a car seat in there now. As an experienced parent, I will warn you that car seats are in the top five worst things about being a parent."

"What's in the number one spot of worst things about being a parent?" I ask, taking the keys.

Rogelio's answer is quick. "The kids."

"He says that but have you seen his son?" Luis asks. "He's an exact replica."

"Just like I planned it," Rogelio shoots back. Rogelio's oldest shares both a name and face, and everyone calls him Junior.

This is when the nurse comes in, coming to check on Liling but she gets distracted by Luis. "Sir, are you ok? Do you need a doctor?"

Luis seems put off by the question, forgetting that he was nearly killed a few days ago. "I'm fine, sugar. Thank you." He flashes a smile that the nurse returns. I get how Luis gets so far in life; he knows who to scare and who to finesse. It's how he has all of Detroit eating out of the palm of his hand.

Luis, Diego, and Rogelio visit with us for the next hour. We're both glad to have the company. Liling has spent the time grilling Luis and Rogelio on baby questions, all of which they answer easily. Luis, for as big and tough as he wants to act, takes his role of active father very seriously.

Right now, this is happiness. This life? I couldn't have dreamt of something like this. How could I have known? I'm proud of what I've given myself. A lot of people would be too scared to take the risks I have, but that's why a lot of people will never get to live like I do.

I'm walking Luis, Ro, and Diego to the parking lot. They're helping me lug out bags of presents that have been dropped off at the hospital room over the last two days. Word has gotten out amongst Luis' people that Liling and I have welcomed our first child, and the gifts have caused a safety hazard as they pile up.

It's excruciatingly bright outside as we walk to my car. Rogelio is telling me about how his older son has entered a darting phase when being reprimanded. "You can't tell him shit, he just runs!"

We're almost to the car when I hear someone call for me. "Hey, Randall!" It's my brother, happily jogging up to me. I'm happy to see him, I am. It's just that he was already suspicious about where my money came from and now he's about to meet the source. There's nothing inconspicuous about Luis, Rogelio, and Diego.

All three of my friends tense when they see someone running toward us. Diego goes as far to subtly reach for the zipper of his leather jacket. "Stand down," I mutter. "That's my brother."

"We're your brothers," Luis growls, lowering his hand. Is he packing with his son strapped to him?

Dylan's smile falters when he sees who I'm walking with. Dylan had already make some startling connections and now he's drawing the lines together to make a picture. He especially lingers on Diego.

"What did you tell him?" Luis asks, seeing how Dylan looks at everyone.

I feel that little prick of danger that I get when I stand next to Luis for too long. "I told him to mind his business."

"I hope he has more sense than you," Luis grumbles.

I ignore him, grinning as my brother approaches. "You're late."

"She's early," Dylan shoots back, bag in hand. "Judy couldn't make it, but she'll swing around next time with me, maybe next weekend."

"We'll be around," I say, putting my hands on my belt in the same way my dad tends to stand. There's an awkward pause, with Luis and the gang standing so close that an introduction is inevitable. "So Dylan, this is Luis, Rogelio, and Diego. Guys, this is my brother, Dylan."

Luis doesn't smile, just places a hand over Rafael's stomach as he hangs from his father's chest. Diego, as usual says absolutely nothing, leaving Rogelio to do anything remotely friendly.

"Well, well, well." Rogelio will at least shake Dylan's hand with the least amount of stiffness. "Another Persch, huh?"

Dylan is being a little stiff himself, his imagination definitely getting the best of him. "Hopefully Randall ain't drag the name through the mud too much."

"I'm making it *the* name," I argue. Luis rolls his eyes, which Dylan notices.

"So how, uh, you all meet each other?" My brother and I grew up in a town so remote we could usually count all the minorities we saw in a year on two hands. I'm sure he'd love to know how I ended up with this group.

"We work together," I say quickly.

Dylan eyes Luis. "Do you, now?"

Luis stares at Dylan in the way he does when he's deciding if someone is a problem. "I'm his boss." He nods to Rogelio with a smirk. "This is my assistant vice president."

Dylan looks at me. "I thought you owned a motel."

"He franchised it from me," Luis says it in a way that begs Dylan to keep pushing.

"He leased a family-owned motel?" Rogelio and I exchange glances, knowing that only Luis can control Luis.

Luis smirks until it turns into a laugh. "You really are Boy Scout's brother, aren't you?" He looks at me fondly. "Always with the questions."

We all move out of the way as a car gets ready to pull into the curved drop-off area. Luis frowns at the driver, but turns his attention back toward me. "Blanca will lose her mind if I mess up his sleep schedule." He looks down at Rafael, who is looking around at the world with big, brown eyes. "Let's get all this crap into your car and-"

The car that pulled near us toward the drop off point opens its passenger window, and whoever is inside sticks a gun out the window and starts firing.

RANDALL.

This is my life now. It's dangerous. I'm going to give my kids everything, but if this line of work is how I'm giving it to them, I'm going to have to raise them to be tough. I'm going to have to raise them to be smart.

The day I brought my son home from the hospital, my friend Diego was shot and killed. The Padilla's influence reaches over the entire state and Albert and his men were brought to justice, but there's no power that Luis has that can bring Diego back. He's just gone.

I didn't really have much direction before Liling, but now I know where I'm going. I'll go where she takes me. I didn't have sense of purpose before Liling either. She gives me purpose. She became my purpose as soon as I saw her. Liling doesn't believe in these things, but I knew the moment I saw her that she'd be someone special to me. She is everything to me.

When Liling speaks, I listen. I will desperately hold onto her through all of our family trials, and hold onto the family we're creating.

I know what I want now, I know what I'm working for. I know *who* I'm working for. Now I know what just two people can achieve with love and hard work. I gave her everything, and she's transformed me into something better.

Together, we started an empire. We started a family. I loved Liling on the first day, and I'll love her on the last.

Liling Persch. That's what I'm working for.

LILING

I have it all.

I've always been ambitious, but now I think I have enough. I have more than I ever thought I wanted growing up. I'm somebody important now. I'm somebody's mother, somebody's wife, somebody's boss. I have money, I have status, I have love. I've worked hard for these things, and now I'm reaping the rewards.

Randall Persch: what a man.

I've always lived by these rules I've told myself. While I still believe in them, and I will impart my own beliefs onto my children, for now, I'm changing my little standards.

For now, I've worked hard enough.

For now, there is nothing more that I want.

I deserve respect, and I have it.

When I started college, I was only focused on graduating. I didn't care about finding love. But now, I'm focused on love, and I'm focused on my family. It's a wonderful distraction, a beautiful passage of time.

For now, I am enjoying my new life, my new name, my new career, my new purpose. Right now, my purpose looks like a beautiful red-haired man who carries our son in a little yellow ducky towel cover while walking around the house he built for me. I sit in the sunlight, rocking myself in a chair as I hear Randall's loving voice calm our son into sleep.

He speaks and the sound of His Voice
Is so sweet the birds hush their singing
And the melody that He gave to me
Within my heart is ringing

This is what love feels like. This is what love sounds like; Randall singing to Wuhan with the windows open so that I can hear the swishing of the poplar tree in the wind.

And He walks with me
And He talks with me
And He tells me I am His own
And the joy we share as we tarry there
None other has ever known

Liling Zhu was strong, but Liling Persch is invincible.

THE PERSCH LEGACY LIVES O

Meet the rest of the family.

Read how it will all end.
"Persch Legacy." coming
2024.

Stay connected with the family! Follow
@Evebooktok on tiktok.

ACKNOWLEDGEMENTS

THANK YOU TO THE PEOPLE
WHO READ.

THANK YOU TO THE FRIEND
WHO I SHOWED FIRST.

THANK YOU TO THE PEOPLE
WHO DIDN'T MAKE FUN OF
THIS DREAM.

*If you liked this story, please consider
leaving a review on*

Made in the USA
Monee, IL
19 January 2024